ZERO POINT

ZERO POINT

A PAUL ONDRAGON MYSTERY

ANETTE STROHMEYER

Podium

Translation from German edited by Sarah Rimmington

Cover design by James Iacobelli

ISBN: 978-1-0394-5667-9

Published in 2025 by Podium Publishing
www.podiumentertainment.com

Podium

ZERO POINT

PROLOGUE

July 18, 1899
Colorado Springs
shortly after 11 am

Philemon Ailey stepped off the train, stretched his tormented back, and turned his face toward the clear summer sky. A groan rose from his throat. What a journey! Five days and nights on a bumpy railroad track in a second-class carriage. Two thousand kilometers: uncomfortable seat, uncomfortable seatmates! Religious fanatics on their way West, to Salt Lake City. Not only did his buttocks hurt, his neck did too, from the interminable rocking and jerking of the train. Philemon took out his handkerchief and blew into it gently. His nose was irritated by the sooty smoke of the locomotive; just before Colorado Springs they had passed through several tunnels.

He put the handkerchief away and picked up his suitcase. First of all, he would go to the hotel. He would unpack in peace there, and treat himself to a cold beer in a saloon somewhere, if they even had such a thing in this dump. Philemon's gaze slid over the deserted platform. To the west was a cluster of wooden houses with one of the majestic peaks of the Rocky Mountains rising behind it: the famous Pikes Peak. And to the east was the view of the grander part of Colorado Springs and its Victorian stone houses.

Philemon left the station behind him and walked through a small park toward a construction site that was a hive of activity. He approached one of the workers and asked for directions.

"The Alta Vista Hotel?" the construction worker called out, wiping his brow. "Turn left up there on Cascade; it's only a block away."

"What are you building?" Philemon wanted to know.

"The new Antlers Hotel. The old one burned down last year."

"I see. Thank you." Philemon tipped his hat and walked in the direction described. Cascade Avenue, though broad, was like all the other roads, a dusty track lined with oak trees and apartment houses. It looked as if they had dropped a street from Queens in the middle of the prairie and forgotten all the rest. Curiously, he watched the passersby. A buggy rumbled past.

"Carriage, sir?" the driver called out.

Philemon declined with a wave. He would save his money and walk the short distance on foot.

A few moments later, he was standing in front of the three-story brick facade of the Alta Vista Hotel. In the small and cozily furnished entrance hall, he took off his hat and approached the reception desk.

"Good day. I am Philemon Ailey from New York City."

The gentleman behind the reception desk wore black livery. A non-committal smile appeared under his carefully twirled mustache.

"Ah, we have been expecting you, sir. If you could sign here, please." The concierge handed Philemon a form, which he signed.

"Much obliged to you, Mr. Ailey. Might I ask how much luggage you have with you?"

"Just this suitcase here."

The concierge raised his eyebrows, "Ah, yes, very good. Well then, the bellman will take your luggage up to your room. I wish you a pleasant stay in Colorado Springs!" He gave a bow, a slightly mocking grin on his face.

Irritated, Philemon allowed himself to be escorted to his room. It was on the second floor and had a view of the street. This wasn't exactly "Alta Vista," he thought; on the other side of the building he would have had a fine view of Pikes Peak. What he had heard in New York about the man who was shortly to be his new employer seemed likely to prove true. Cheap rooms for the staff, while the fine gentleman himself resided in the best chambers. But he wasn't going to complain about that just yet. After all, his new employer was preceded by a world-class reputation, and it was an honor to be allowed to work for him.

"What is that suitcase?" Philemon asked the bellboy, pointing to a behemoth of a box standing in the middle of his room.

"Oh, excuse me, sir. This belongs to the guest who stayed here before you. We have orders to send the luggage after him. It seems someone has forgotten to pick it up. I will arrange to have it removed from the room immediately."

"Good." Philemon pressed a few cents into the bellboy's hand and closed the door. After hanging his not particularly extensive wardrobe in the closet and stowing his writing and study instruments in a small leather bag, he lay down to test the bed. The mattress was a little saggy, but he would get a peaceful night's sleep here. Philemon looked at his father's silver pocket watch and sprang lithely out of bed. It was noon, high time he ate something. He freshened up somewhat at the washstand and combed his hair neatly. Then he put on his hat and went downstairs to the lobby, where he asked the concierge to direct him to a good but inexpensive restaurant.

"In that case, I would recommend Benson's next to the Elk Hotel. It's on Pikes Peak Avenue. Just go to the big construction site and turn left. Pikes Peak Avenue is the prettiest street we have here in town."

Well, that's saying something, thought Philemon, who had grown up in the fabulous New York City, whose steely heartbeat beat tirelessly, day *and* night. For him, the tranquility of Colorado Springs was synonymous with deepest provinciality . . . even if the town presented a surprisingly civilized face.

A little song on his lips, he strolled off. The sun warmed his limbs and the fresh mountain air was a boon to his lungs. Slowly, he forgot the stresses of the train ride and a smile flitted across his face—after all, Colorado Springs had already achieved *something*. He felt better. The climate in the spa town at the foot of the Rockies really did seem to be exceptionally conducive to physical well-being.

On Pikes Peak Avenue, Philemon had no trouble finding Benson's and went in. The dining room, which contained about a dozen tables, was flooded with sunlight. The restaurant was busy, but Philemon spotted a free seat at the far end of the counter. He studied the menu, which was covered with greasy fingerprints, and ordered the lamb stew, along with a beer.

"There's no alcohol here, sir! It's prohibited. Mr. Palmer wants a clean and safe city!" said the host. With his thick black beard and his high-collared white shirt, he looked as if he had come straight from the pulpit.

"Who is Mr. Palmer?" asked Philemon.

"The founder of this city and president of the Denver and Rio Grande Railroad Company."

"I see," Philemon replied tersely. The prospect of having to endure several months or even longer here in this joyless place without alcohol was not especially cheering. Not that he drank much in the New York taverns, but what was life without a refreshing beer? "And what can you recommend instead?"

"Root beer, soda water, cola, coffee, or tea."

"I'll have cola, thanks." If there was no beer, he would at least refresh himself another way. He found cola too sweet, but the newfangled drink at least quenched his thirst.

While he waited for his food, he let his eyes wander around the room. The establishment was dingy, with yellowing wood paneling and foxing on the ceiling. The exclusively male lunch guests were eating hastily or talking in hushed voices. Bluish clouds of smoke rose from the tables where some guests had lit a cigar to aid the digestion. At least smoking was permitted.

His lamb stew arrived, and Philemon began to eat. It wasn't too bad. The cola was also pretty cool and tingled pleasantly on his tongue. He let out a satisfied sigh, and the blond guy sitting next to him at the counter turned to him.

"I heard tell earlier that you weren't from around here, sir," he said.

"I'm from New York City," Philemon replied.

"Are you a spa guest?"

"No, I'm going to work here."

"Ah. A new and upstanding citizen of this up-and-coming city!" The fellow leaned forward, allowing Philemon to detect his musty body odor, and whispered conspiratorially, "If you fancy bending an elbow, you'll have to go to Colorado City or Manitou Springs—they have everything a man's heart could desire."

"Hey, Joe!" the host rumbled. "Don't tempt my customers away!"

"But when it's as dry as a fart between a nun's legs, you have to tell the poor people where they can find a little fun!" The blond man laughed loudly and his neighbors joined in. The host grimaced sourly.

"Thank you for the information," Philemon replied, slightly piqued, pulling out his wallet.

"No offense, buddy." The man clapped him on the shoulder. "But that's just the way it is around here. Just by the by, how do you intend to make a living here in Colorado Springs, if you don't mind me asking?"

Philemon had little inclination to answer; the guy was getting on his nerves, but everyone who had overheard the conversation was looking at him expectantly.

"Well, I'm an electrical engineer and I'm going to be working for a Dr. T—"

A distant rumble of thunder wiped the grins off the men's faces. Conversation abruptly ceased and a somber silence descended on the tables. One man cursed quietly, another crossed himself.

"What was that? A thunderstorm?" asked Philemon into the silence. He was surprised, for the sun was still shining in through the greasy windowpanes.

The host shook his head slowly. "That's no storm," he said with a frown. "Look." He turned on the faucet on the wall behind the counter and brown water came gushing out. Philemon didn't know what this meant, and watched as the man held a spoon close to the stream of water. A bluish flash jumped over to the metal with a soft crackle.

Startled, Philemon widened his eyes. "By Saint Joseph . . . what was that?"

There was another thunderclap, and behind the bar the glasses rattled on their shelf.

"This is from those unholy experiments that lunatic is conducting out on the prairie!" the host raged, clenching one hand into a fist. "That lightning maker, who thinks he can play God! Ever since he got here, the world's gone crazy!"

"That's right," the blond man confirmed. "It all started with that fishy laboratory!"

Philemon had a bad feeling about this, but he let the men continue talking.

"Ever since that crazy professor has been doing his dangerous experiments, no one is safe here. Sometimes the horses get electric shocks from the earth and bolt with their carriages; sometimes sparks fly under our feet when we're crossing the street. Children receive shocks when they play with the water in the hydrants: Their hair literally stands on end! Just like you just saw with the faucet. And my brother-in-law says the light stays on all night, even if he turns it off. He can't get a wink of sleep! Not to mention the thundering and hissing that mad doctor causes!"

"Yes, and old Benjamin Foley says he saw strange lights near the laboratory," interjected another man beside the blond one. "Saint Elmo's fire. He says the grass glowed an eerie blue and glowing balls rose up from it. Now he doesn't dare put his goats out to pasture there for fear the spirit will pass to them!"

"That's nothing!" the host said in agitation. "I heard that two weeks ago one of the assistants in the laboratory was struck by lightning and lost his mind on the spot."

"Nonsense! He was grilled like a trout over a fire. Pulverized, he was. He crumbled to dust!"

"Where did you get that from, Joe?" the host asked incredulously.

"Well, old Ben. He saw it for himself!"

Philemon felt unease rumbling in his stomach. The mood of the men was irritable and hostile. So he'd better keep quiet about who he'd be starting work for tomorrow. After all, he knew that the stories that sounded like old wives' tales here could be the grim truth, at least the one about the lightning and Saint Elmo's fire. The one about the grilled man, however, was new to him. A dark foreboding arose in the back of his mind. He had been sent here to replace an assistant who had allegedly had to leave on urgent business. He swallowed. Might the fellow have met a completely different fate?

While the men heatedly discussed the strange happenings in town, Philemon slid a dollar bill across the counter. The host handed him the change and nodded goodbye. His knees weak, Philemon left the restaurant and hailed a hansom cab. He had to pull himself together to avoid stuttering as he told the driver where he wanted to go.

"What? No, I'm not going there! The horse will bolt. I don't want to break my neck. I can take you as far as the edge of town, but no farther!"

Philemon nodded and climbed into the cab. For some unknown reason, he suddenly felt a stifling dread, and he wondered if it had been a good idea to come here.

On the outskirts of the city, the driver let him out and, having been paid, quickly drove his carriage away. Philemon looked after the cloud of dust for a long time, as if not daring to face the inevitable. But finally, he overcame his uncertainty and looked out over the prairie. There he saw a squat, barnlike structure. A row of telegraph poles led up to it, and from the roof, a strange wooden framework with some kind of antenna rose into the sky. It had a sphere at the top.

It struck Philemon that there had been no thunder since he had been dropped off at the edge of town. He mustered all his courage and marched along the row of poles toward the wooden building. A short time later, he was standing in front of the taut barbed wire that divided the laboratory property from the prairie, and now he did hear something coming from the building: a static crackle and hiss. The hairs on his forearms stood up, and after reading the sign on the barbed wire fence, his first impulse was to turn around, get on the train, and go home.

KEEP OUT—GREAT DANGER! was written there in red letters and below: ABANDON ALL HOPE, YE WHO ENTER HERE! That was from Dante's *Divine Comedy*. Part of the inscription on the Gates of Hell!

A tingling sensation like a thousand termites seized Philemon's body and he shivered. It was as if an invisible force was emanating from the wooden building, pulling him irresistibly under its spell. Like a gigantic magnet that drew all iron toward it, holding it in its pulsating grip forever. Philemon had heard much about the strange man who owned this house. He had read all his articles and publications, but now that he was standing here, the rumors were suddenly a great deal more intense than before. It was said that behind this door worked a man possessed, a man who never slept. He was a genius, a supernatural human machine with a brain of cosmic size, a lightning magician, an oblivious maverick with unique and extraordinary abilities.

A man who was not of this world.

All these things went through Philemon's mind as he looked for a gate in the barbed wire fence, but found none. Obviously, visitors were not expected. He climbed quickly over the wire, walked up to the massive wooden door, and raised his arm. After a moment's hesitation, he knocked. Tentatively at first, then more and more forcefully, to pierce the eerie din inside.

Suddenly, the sounds died away and shortly thereafter the door was torn open. Blackness gaped before him. Then, like the moon in the night sky, the pale face of a man appeared in the doorway.

"Who is disturbing me?" he asked gruffly. So tall was he, the crown of his dark head almost touched the door lintel, and Philemon had to crane his neck to look into the deep-set, shining metallic eyes. He tore his hat from his head and bowed hastily.

"Allow me to present myself. Philemon Ailey of New York City, sir!" His heart was pounding in his throat and his hands worked nervously at the brim of his hat. "Are you Dr. Tesla?"

The pale features of his counterpart brightened. The black brows shot up with delight and a gentle smile appeared under the mustache.

"Oh, marvelous! Here he is, our new assistant!" the famous scientist exclaimed, but to Philemon's amazement, he did not extend his gloved hand in greeting, as politeness would have dictated. Instead, he gave a brief nod and said, "Welcome, young man. So please, enter my humble domain."

Philemon tried to smile, but it faded when he saw the bluish flare inside the laboratory. It was followed by a loud bang.

Saint Joseph preserve me, he thought fearfully, and followed Dr. Tesla into the gloomy building.

CHAPTER 1

May 16, 2011
New York City
12:35 pm

Your sister did a swell job!" said Ondragon, thrusting a wad of bills into the hand of the young man in the bellhop uniform. "Tell her I enjoyed working with her."

"Will do, Mr. O." The young man smiled mockingly. "We're happy to help whenever you need us."

Ondragon nodded, but it was clear to him that he would never meet the guy and his sister again. They had done their job and were "used up." He never worked with outsiders more than once. Merely a precaution.

The young man put the money in the inside pocket of his uniform, nodded goodbye, and left the room.

As the door slammed shut, a smile spread across Ondragon's face. How smoothly this job had gone. His clients would be satisfied and the victim ruined.

Man, he loved his job!

He turned and looked at the hotel room. A queen-size bed, a mini-bar, a table, a chair, and a TV on mute. News channel. You had to stay informed, after all. On the screen, a news anchor in an aubergine-colored suit was presenting the latest updates. As Ondragon was admiring her excellent taste in clothes, the image of an elderly gentleman faded in above her right shoulder. Below it was his name.

It was his victim, being taken away in handcuffs.

Ondragon's grin widened. The beauty of this job was that he could watch his successes, live. The scandal had dropped like a bomb! "Top European politician tries to rape maid in New York hotel!" Dream headlines and a dream result. He had used every trick in the book to discredit the guy, just ahead of the elections in his country. *Bam!* and he was out of politics. If the guy had kept a closer eye on his friends and enemies, this wouldn't have happened. But that kind of hubris had always dragged the successful people into the abyss. It was strange that those who frolicked closer to the surface of the shark tank tended to forget at some point that other predators swam there too. And if you put your mind to it, you could always find something that made the other sharks pick up a trail. A tiny little wound was all they needed to give you a mauling! Too bad our gray-haired contender for the Berlusconi award had a penchant for debauched sex parties—not exactly a model hobby. His party guests should be mighty pissed at him. But if Ondragon was honest, this had been a second-rate job too. More of a *standard* problem than a *magnum* one. But no matter, his few coworkers were currently involved in other projects, so he'd had to take on the case as a little refresher, so to speak.

On the TV screen, the newscaster faded out and was followed by a segment about Fukushima. As Ondragon watched the footage of the damaged nuclear reactor, his smile disappeared. The text under the picture read MELTDOWN. *What a damn mess*, he thought, and a spark of worry flared up inside him. He knew people in Tokyo. What would become of them? What would become of the contaminated zone? No one really knew, even now, two months after the nuclear disaster.

He went to turn off the TV, but the next segment caught his attention. He quickly turned up the volume.

". . . the flight recorder was recovered, which undoubtedly belongs to the Air France plane that crashed two years ago. The French Civil Aviation Authority announced today that the data from the black box is readable and experts from the Bureau of Enquiry and Analysis for Civil Aviation Safety are analyzing it. The cause of the crash of the Airbus 330 off the Brazilian coast, which killed two hundred and twenty-eight passengers, is still unclear . . ."

Ondragon stared at the image on the screen. Something about it didn't fit the overall picture, his unerring sense for such things told him. It was one of his tics, to constantly look for flaws in the pattern.

He sat down on the bed and stared at the TV. It was showing the ruptured fuselage of an airplane bearing the letters ANCE, hanging from a salvage ship's crane. Behind it loomed some rusted olive-green debris, also on the deck of the ship. But wasn't there a blob of black on the olive-green surface? Ondragon frowned. And why rusty olive green, when the Air France plane wreckage was painted white?

He had it, the flaw in the pattern! The olive-green parts did not match the Airbus debris. But what had they lost on the ship?

As Ondragon leaned closer to the screen, the image disappeared and the pretty newscaster reappeared.

"And now for the weather," she said with a professional smile.

"What a bummer." Ondragon turned off the TV. He took his iPhone out of his pocket and was about to dial his assistant's number, but the phone started ringing, beating him to it. The number was withheld, which didn't surprise him much, because he often dealt with people who kept their details secret. He did the same himself, after all.

He answered with a brisk "Yes?"

"Good afternoon. Am I speaking to Mr. Ondragon?" The voice on the other end spoke in German and sounded thin and somehow distant, with a faint southern German accent. Ondragon pressed the phone tighter to his ear. "Yes, and who are you?" he answered in German.

"Oh, I beg your pardon. My name is Alexander Kubicki and I work for the Federal Intelligence Service. I'm calling you because it's said in certain circles that you take on very special assignments."

"That's right, but how did you get my number?"

"Well, the thing is, we keep a file on you, and it has your contact information in it."

"A file? About me?" asked Ondragon, disgruntled. His *centrifuge* began to spin, fast. Why did the BND—the German Intelligence Service—have a damn file on him?

"That's right, on you! You are Paul Eckbert Ondragon, aren't you? Son of Siegfried Ondragon, retired ambassador?"

"What do you want?"

There was silence. Ondragon was about to hang up when the man continued speaking.

"We want to engage you."

"German intelligence?" Ondragon let out an amused laugh. "What's it all about?"

"We can only tell you that if you agree to absolute confidentiality."

"Confidentiality is part of my professional ethos. You should really have that in your file!"

The man on the other end seemed unfazed by his sarcasm. "I'll send you a web address right away," he said matter-of-factly. "You will register under the alias 'Sheepdog17' and log in using a password of your own choosing. You will be activated immediately. You need have no concerns—the site is completely secure."

Not from Rudee, Ondragon thought scornfully, and continued listening to the man's instructions.

"On the page you will see a bulletin board with the description of your assignment. Read it carefully and within the next twenty-four hours text *Y* or *N* to the number on the page in the Contact menu. Do you understand so far?"

"But of course!" replied Ondragon in stilted High German. "And what happens if I send an *N*?" He knew already that he probably wouldn't, if only because of the damn file!

"Think carefully. The fee could be extremely interesting to you."

"Oh yeah?"

"Yes indeed," the agent repeated snootily. "Any questions?"

"Why do you want me of all people for this job? Can't your own agents do it?"

The other end fell silent again—or was it hesitation?

"Well, Mr. Ondragon, you have contacts that would take us weeks, if not months, to build. But we don't have that kind of time. We are obliged to take immediate action!"

"And you read all that in my file?"

"That's right."

Ondragon pondered. What else did the Germans know about him and his contacts? He was anything but comfortable at the thought.

"I'll look forward to hearing from you in twenty-four hours, Mr. O!"

Ondragon wanted to reply because the guy was acting very arrogantly, but Kubicki had already hung up. At that moment, his cell phone beeped. It was the text message with the web address. Ondragon typed "www.deutsche-hunderassen.de" into the browser and an innocuous-looking page with pictures of dogs popped up. Despite himself, Ondragon grinned. It was so German! But as he knew from his own experience, cliché still made the best camouflage.

As instructed, he registered on the forum for a login. *At least they've assigned me the name Sheepdog and not Wire-Haired Dachshund or Toy Poodle*, he thought, and clicked on the log in button. After a moment, the unofficial page appeared, and instead of lovely dog snouts, an austere menu was displayed. Ondragon opened the Bulletin Board and quickly found the assignment given to him. He skimmed it, thought about it, and read it again. More thoroughly this time.

Then he looked up.

"Are they kidding me?" he groaned aloud. "What kind of an assignment is that?"

Shaking his head, he stared at his cell phone display. It was a bad joke, after all. The BND wanted to hire him to get a book? A goddamn BOOK? Ondragon exhaled irritably. Him of all people! Wasn't there anything about his phobia in that fucking file? It seemed strange, somehow. Even if Ondragon tried to hide his phobia from the world by all available means, he could not believe the BND was so slipshod in its document management. That would be like the National Security Agency not having an internet connection. Another idea occurred to him. Maybe the file was just a bluff to lure him in.

Well, he thought, *let's assume the worst, let's assume the file exists. What might they offer to actually get me to take the bait?* He clicked the button marked "payment method." A figure in US dollars appeared. Ondragon whistled softly through his teeth. That was a pretty penny. But it wasn't the money that was drawing him in. Nor was it the prospect of a down payment, which certainly had its appeal. No, it was the sentence that was written underneath.

Upon successful and timely completion of the operation, the agent will be given access to the Ondragon/Gemini file.

"The Ondragon/Gemini file?" he repeated thoughtfully. Gemini was from the Latin *geminae* and meant twin. Was it a reference to his twin brother, Per Gustav? Did the BND have information about Per and his death that he did not? It was conceivable. Ondragon's curiosity was piqued, and he felt the *centrifuge* in his head accelerate. He could get Rudee onto it. Maybe the Thai cyber-pirate would find a file with that reference in the BND archives. Or he could just take the assignment. He'd figure out the book thing. After all, he had gone through a grueling course of therapy to address his phobia two years ago.

He closed the website and opened his phone directory. He would check it out and make a decision in twenty-four hours. But before that, he had to book a flight to LA.

CHAPTER 2

May 16, 2011
Fortaleza, Brazil
1:59 pm

I'll look forward to hearing from you in twenty-four hours, Mr. O!"

From his hiding place, Clandestin listened closely to the telephone conversation of the German secret service man. Fortunately, he knew German and could understand what the guy was saying. He saw the agent end the call and dial another number.

"I think he took the bait!" he said quietly, nodding. "Yes. Let's wait and see. Goodbye." The agent hung up, put his cell phone away, and let his eyes roam around the hall.

Quickly, Clandestin pushed himself deeper into the shelter of the wreckage that was stored here in the guarded section of the harbor.

The agent stood there for a while with his hands in his pockets. Then Clandestin heard him give a satisfied grunt and walk toward the exit. A little later, the heavy metal door slammed shut. Relieved, Clandestin exhaled. He was alone and he had the information he needed. German intelligence was chasing the same treasure he was. And if this Mr. O was who Clandestin thought he was, he could sit back from now on and let him do the dirty work. Mr. O would get the treasure and present it to him on a plate. And then he would grab it!

Relishing the thought of his thieving, Clandestin rubbed his hands together. Thanks to this new piece on the chessboard, he would be able to execute his orders cleanly and likely with much less effort than he had thought. He looked around once more and then ducked down, moving in a crouch from one piece of wreckage to the next. The aircraft debris had been neatly sorted. To the left lay the twisted remains of the Air France plane and to the right the olive-colored parts of the other plane the recovery team had fished out of the sea from the same crash site. The reappearance of that plane was as much of a coincidence as the fact that it had been carrying the greatest treasure mankind had ever known.

Clandestin crouched behind a ruptured section of the Air France cabin and looked over at the olive-colored tail, which stood several meters high. It appeared to be intact, except for the fact that it had been completely severed from the fuselage on impact with the water. The force must have been tremendous; the lightweight metal was torn open like paper at the break. Clandestin's gaze slid over the scratched symbol on the outer shell, and a shiver ran through his body—which was half-naked, since he was wearing only swimming shorts. Emblazoned on the tail unit was a weathered German Balkenkreuz, or bar cross, and just behind it another insignia he knew only too well: a black swastika. Clandestin felt remorse for one of the men who had been aboard the plane at the time. He had fallen to his death with the others. A terrible fate that he did not deserve.

Clandestin tore himself away from the sight and crawled on his belly underneath the Air France cabin. An inconspicuous hatch was embedded in the rough concrete floor here—his secret entrance and exit from the hall. He opened the hatch, whose hinges he had oiled beforehand, slipped through the narrow gap, which was only wide enough to take children and very thin people, and lowered himself into the shaft. He then closed the hatch, turned on his small waterproof flashlight, and groped through the low-roofed channel, which reeked of fish and seaweed. But that did not bother Clandestin much; to him, it was the smell of the big, wide world. There were hardly any smells where he came from.

After a few hundred meters, he reached the circular, brightly lit end of the tube. Cautiously, he stuck his head out into the open air, squinting in the sunlight. The channel ended outside the large harbor basin, above which seagulls were circling, screeching. All you had to do was get into the oily water, and a few meters farther on, you could climb up a rusty ladder onto the jetty.

Clandestin soon located his clothes where he had left them among the old nets and oil barrels, and put them on. He was already making mental notes about how to proceed. But before the spectacle, he wanted to treat himself to a refreshing caipirinha in a *boteco* on the boardwalk. After that, he would make inquiries about this Mr. O. It would be a joke if he couldn't find out anything about him.

Concealed by the crooked corrugated iron huts, Clandestin left the area of the port where the hangar with the Air France plane debris was located and a short time later, he eased himself into the busy streets of the Brazilian tourist metropolis.

CHAPTER 3

The second hand on Ondragon's wristwatch jumped to twelve as he opened the door to his office, which was well camouflaged on the top floor of a bank building in West Hollywood.

"Right on time, just like the Swiss railroad," his assistant greeted him. "And congratulations!"

Ondragon paused in irritation, but then he remembered: The chambermaid assignment. "Thank you, Charlize. And sorry, my mind is already on something else."

"A new assignment?"

"Could be. I'm still thinking about it." He set down his briefcase, which was part of his cover as a bank employee, and sat down energetically in the chair at his desk. As usual, Charlize had already booted up the computer and he was able to begin work immediately. He had two and a half hours before the BND's ultimatum expired. He hadn't had the chance to do any research on the flight from New York to LA, and now he had to make up for it. Hastily typing away, he was startled out of his thoughts by the phone ringing.

"Rudee, man, what's up?" he grumbled to the caller. "Why are you only just checking in now?"

"*Koh tot khrap*, Paul. Sorry, I had little police problem in Bangkok," Rudee replied.

Realizing he had been rude to the Thai, Ondragon asked anxiously, "Oh no, is it bad? Do you need any help?"

"Nah, no need. I cleared up." Rudee followed this with an amused giggle, his lighthearted facade revealing the truth behind "cleared up." And in this case, "cleared up" had nothing to do with clearing and everything to do with a septic tank. Anyway. Ondragon had known Rudee for over thirty years. Though small and outwardly reserved, the Thai knew how to keep troublesome blowflies at bay and where to dispose of them if necessary. Whether they wore a police uniform or not.

"What's up? You call ten times?" asked his secret weapon in cyberspace.

Ondragon told his friend about the assignment and the offer from the BND to let him look at his file as part of the fee.

"And you now want me to pay a little visit?"

"Yes, it would be extremely useful to me if you could find the file. And as quickly as possible. Can you do it in two hours?"

Rudee sighed. "No, sir, not feasible. Take me at least a week to do that. Very dangerous job."

Just as Ondragon had feared. Intelligence agency systems were like a virtual high-security wing, and penetrating them was a complicated matter. That kind of thing usually required meticulous preparation and entailed several detours. Ondragon thought for a moment and made a decision.

"Try it anyway, will you?" he said to Rudee. "Doesn't matter if it takes longer. I've *got* to have that file! If only to compare it with what the BND will serve up when the job is done."

"Okay!" Rudee replied, and said goodbye.

Ondragon hung up and only then noticed the full coffee cup in front of him. He took a sip and grimaced. Unfortunately, the coffee was as cold as Ötzi the Iceman's feet.

"You want a fresh one?" asked Charlize, who had been watching his expression from her desk.

"Not right now, thanks."

"Okey-dokey."

Ondragon gave his Japanese-Brazilian assistant an inquiring look. "Oh, Charlize?"

"Yes?" She looked up from her paperwork again.

"Here's the thing: If I take this job, I would need your help. I can't do it without you."

"Count me in!"

"But you don't even know what it is."

"I don't care; the main thing is to get out of here!"

Ondragon looked at his screen, which was showing the map of the deployment site. "It's in Brazil," he said, and all at once he realized who the BND had meant by his "contacts." Charlize.

"I thought so," she replied dryly, stapling two sheets of paper together. "Is this about the Air France plane?"

Ondragon raised his eyebrows in puzzlement. Sometimes she gave him the creeps. It was like she could read his mind. "Have you ever been to Fortaleza?"

"If you mean Fortaleza in the state of Ceará, a former fortress with nearly two and a half million inhabitants and the highest murder rate in Brazil—yep, I've been there. Took a vacation there once." She looked at him with narrowed eyes.

That's her samurai look, Ondragon thought. Was he mistaken or was Charlize slightly irritated today? "Is something wrong?" he asked her, steeling himself. Charlize could be a delicate lotus blossom, but some days she could also be a nasty desert cactus . . . with spikes!

His assistant tilted her head and pursed her lips. Her samurai gaze swiveled up to the ceiling, as if she had to think.

Lotus or cactus? Ondragon wondered.

Suddenly, her face twitched and an index finger shot toward him.

Lotus, cactus?

Lotus, cactus?

"You *bakayaro*, you forgot my birthday! I had even invited you to the party, but the fine gentleman simply did not attend! Do I have to remind you about personal appointments now too? *Kuso!* It's not like I'm your secretary!"

Cactus, then!

Surrendering, Ondragon lowered his head and let the half-Japanese, half-English torrent wash over him. The fact that he had a really good excuse would not interest her. He could have had a meeting with the president or been on a mission in Afghanistan; for Charlize there was no excuse for not showing up at her party. She was stubborn about that kind of thing, and there was only one thing to do: keep his head down and wait for the storm to pass.

"I'm sorry," he finally replied. And he really was. He would have liked to have gone to her party. It had been before he flew to New York for his assignment. But, unfortunately, he had some unexpected visitors that day. In the form of two 9mm projectiles that had smashed through the side window of his car in the evening traffic on La Brea Avenue. No, it hadn't been the Mustang, and, yes, fortunately, the bullets had missed him. Instead, they had hit his company car, an inconspicuous Dodge Magnum. But obviously not inconspicuous enough. In any case, Ondragon could not overlook such a brazen attempt on his life. This was his town and he had to keep it clean! After all, he wanted to be able to jog on the beach or eat at a restaurant in peace and quiet without having to be on the alert the whole time. So he had latched onto the son of a bitch's taillights and followed him. After a nerve-wracking chase down Highway 101 to Thousand Oaks, he had finally caught up with him. It had already been pitch dark when it had come to the showdown, on a narrow road in the mountains—with a precipice on the right and the rock face on the left. Ondragon had rammed the enemy car with all 340 of his horsepower and sent it clean over the edge. In the light of his headlights, he had then watched as the vehicle rolled over several times before exploding at the foot of the cliff with a resounding bang. Whoever that amateur had been, he would never set foot on his turf again, that was for sure! Unfortunately, his Dodge had been badly mangled in the incident and Ondragon had had to take care to remove all trace of it. Afterward, he had not felt like going to Charlize's party. Understandably, he thought.

"I hope you can forgive me one more time?" He looked over at Charlize with a rueful expression. "I'll take you to that new sushi place at LA Live to make up for it. It's gotten good reviews."

His assistant's samurai look became a shade milder. One more thing should do the trick. He stood up and walked over to her desk. "And we'll go on to the lounge at the Ritz Carlton."

"You can forget the restaurant and the bar!" retorted Charlize. "I can think of something much better."

"And that would be?"

"The Mustang—for two weeks!"

Ondragon blinked in surprise. He should have known she wouldn't let him off so lightly.

"Where's your Dodge anyway?" she asked. "I didn't see you coming down Doheny Drive in it today. Do you have a new car?"

Ondragon waved it off. "Oh, I felt like a change." After the cleanup, he had also made the Dodge disappear and promptly treated himself to a new car. Something really low-key this time, almost staid. A silver Audi 4 RS Avant. The thing didn't suit him at all, but if it made him safer on the roads . . .

"Wouldn't you rather drive the Audi?" he offered.

Charlize exhaled dismissively. "Sorry, Boss, but that car would even make my grandma drop off."

"So the Mustang."

"Hai, sō desu."

"Very well. Deal?" He held out his hand to Charlize.

"Deal!" she replied, transforming from cactus back to shyly smiling lotus flower. "So what's with this file from the BND?"

Ondragon sighed. "I'll tell you about it later." He looked at his watch. It was just before ten. Time to text the BND guy. Nervously, he opened the "messages" app on his cell phone. He strongly disliked working for intelligence agencies, and he only did so with extreme caution. But this job had an unusual component that he couldn't get out of his mind: the "Ondragon/Gemini" file. He knew he would do almost anything to get sight of it. Before that, however, he needed to be certain that the file actually existed. He typed a *Y* into the text field and sent it.

He had scarcely finished when the phone rang. He picked up.

"Welcome to Operation Pandora, Mr. Ondragon," Kubicki said, without beating around the bush. "When can you start?"

They're in a real hurry, Ondragon thought, replying "Right away, if you like!"

"Perfect. You need to have a short briefing from our contact in Brazil. His code name is Doberman12. You can use the bulletin board to make the arrangements."

"Oh, I thought you were going to be my contact."

"No, I'm not."

"And how many of your people will be supporting me on the ground?" asked Ondragon.

"Supporting you?" Kubicki let out a dry laugh. "You will work alone, as you always do. Our team will stay in the background and intervene only in case of emergency."

That was interesting. Kubicki hadn't mentioned that before, Ondragon thought. Making no attempt to hide his sarcasm, he answered, "Sure. I guess that's what you'd call conserving resources. But it's up to you. Before I throw my lot in with you, I'd like some proof you're not pulling the wool over my eyes about the 'Gemini' file."

"Your file? Well, I can't show you the document, unfortunately. But I can tell you it says, for example, that your contacts in Brazil come through your assistant, Charlize Tanaka, rather than you. So we are primarily interested in your assistant. Unfortunately, since Ms. Tanaka works exclusively for you, we cannot get around you, Mr. Ondragon.

You will play more of a secondary role in this operation. That of a henchman, if you will. We also know that you have a serious problem with the object to be procured. I'm referring to your book phobia, which you still haven't overcome despite having therapy with a questionable therapist. Congratulations, by the way, on nailing that psychiatry charlatan, even if it was probably by accident. I'm guessing you weren't attending the facility to look at Minnesota bears in the wild." Kubicki laughed softly. His laugh sounded malicious and sly. "Is that enough proof for you, my friend?"

Was it ever! The guy clearly knew *too* much about him! Ondragon bit his lip angrily. His ego was badly dented by the fact that the BND seemed more interested in Charlize than him. But he'd show this guy who he was dealing with. "I hope you don't leave my file lying around for people to read in the bathroom," he said. "To put it plainly, I expect you to keep that confidential."

"Of course!" replied Kubicki. "I know you have a reputation to maintain and so on."

"Well, you don't have to worry about *your* reputation anymore. It's long since ruined!"

"Are you alluding to anything in particular, Mr. Ondragon?"

Amused, Ondragon exhaled. "Do I really have to tell you what the world thinks of German intelligence—"

"Listen," the BND agent cut off this unedifying dispute, "are you with us or not?"

"Of course! After all, you can't do it without me."

"Good, then be at LAX at noon the day after tomorrow. There will be airline tickets waiting for you and your assistant. American Airlines, counter two. Will that allow you enough time to prepare?"

The BND snoot's disparaging tone was starting to get on Ondragon's nerves. It was a pity he would not be meeting him in person in Brazil. He had a great desire to smack him one upside the head, just as a little greeting from his henchman. "One day is more than enough." he replied coolly.

"Fine. You'll discuss all further details with the contact. Good luck!"

"You too, *kusogaki*!" Ondragon saw Charlize look up, startled. He lowered his cell phone. "Too bad, he'd hung up."

His assistant giggled and turned back to the computer. "So do I need to pack my suitcase?" she asked without taking her eyes off the screen.

"You, a suitcase?" quipped Ondragon. Unlike many women, Charlize was known for traveling light.

She threw down her pen and looked at him reproachfully. "What is it? Now are you going to tell me what's going on?"

Ondragon perched on the edge of the desk and began to relay what he had read on the bulletin board about the assignment. "You were right. It is indeed about the Air France plane. Indirectly, at least, because at the site of the wreckage from the Airbus on the seabed, they also found parts of another long-lost plane. A German plane from World War II that apparently crashed in the same place during an escape attempt by high-ranking Nazi officers at the end of the war. The plane itself is of no further interest to German intelligence. But the cockpit is largely undamaged, and they've found a watertight box in there. It's the contents of this box that we're concerned with. They want us to get hold of the thing."

"And what's in it?"

"Not much, but it seems important to the Germans; they're under a lot of time pressure. It apparently contains a gold medal and a logbook."

"A logbook?" asked Charlize, aghast. "A BOOK?! And you accepted the assignment? For some confrontation therapy, huh?" She giggled.

"We're supposed to get them the whole box, thank goodness. I don't have to look inside, do I?" Ondragon gave Charlize an irritated look. She got the message and stopped laughing.

"Right now, the box is in a temporary but highly secure laboratory in Fortaleza," he went on. "They're investigating the sensitive objects found in the Air France plane there. Including the bodies, or rather what's left of them. The Brazilian authorities want to examine the box before they hand it over to Germany. But the BND considers the contents so sensitive that it wants to take possession of the crate immediately. The main issue is what's written in the logbook. Under no circumstances can that be made public."

"I see. And what will my role in this operation be?"

"You're going to infiltrate the lab!"

A broad smile appeared on Charlize's captivating face.

Good, Ondragon thought. She would do it.

CHAPTER 4

May 19, 2011
Fortaleza, Brazil
10:11 pm

Outside the airport building in Fortaleza, they were enveloped in sultry, tropical air.

"Ah, *cheiro da patria*—the scent of home!" purred Charlize, inhaling happily.

Ondragon grinned. His assistant had grown up in Brazil, in São Paulo, to be precise, which was home to the largest Japanese community outside Japan. Her father had come to Brazil from Tokyo with his parents in 1939 and later married a local woman. So Charlize was a *nipo-brasileira*, a Brazilian of Japanese descent. Her real name was actually Sayo-Li, but "Charlize" was easier to pronounce. She had an older brother, Keisuke "Kay" Tanaka.

Ondragon preferred it when his assistant spoke Japanese, because his Portuguese left a lot to be desired. He could understand a few words though.

They hailed a cab, which took them to the Mucuripe district, where their hotels were located. As the lights of the nighttime city passed by the side window, Ondragon thought about how he had met Charlize and how this charming and talented young woman had ended up working for him. Charlize had demonstrated a real talent for disguise even then, and she had actually managed to fool him. Ondragon smiled at the memory. After that, he had no choice but to persuade her to join him as his assistant.

They arrived at the Gran Marquise Hotel on Avenida Beira Mar and Ondragon got out. He took his travel bag out of the trunk, signaled to Charlize that he would call her later, and slammed the door. His assistant was staying at another hotel under a false Brazilian identity. It was necessary for her cover that her lodgings be a little more modest. Besides, it was always good for an operation to have two bases.

Ondragon entered the hotel—a multistory block with a terracotta-tiled facade and mirrored windows that had likely been fashionable in the sixties—through the main entrance. In the sprawling lobby, which had a wall of vast stone mosaics and several seating areas, a piano was tinkling softly. A few patrons were lingering at the bar off to the side, sounding as if they had enjoyed a few caipirinhas. Ondragon scrutinized them and mentally categorized them as well-heeled tourists in search of cheap pleasure. No one who would get in his way.

Having checked in at the front desk and counted all the surveillance cameras on the way to his room on the fourth floor, he was glad to close the door behind him and finally be alone. He set his bag down on the bed, pulled out everything that might suggest he was not a regular hotel guest, and stowed it in the safe. Among the contents were duplicate travel documents for Charlize (who in turn had duplicates for him—just in case), a small but powerful pair of binoculars, a pair of thin leather gloves, pepper spray (which was very useful, even for professionals), his notepad, a handy combination-lock aluminum case containing his compact spy equipment, and a concealed folding knife with a twelve-centimeter blade. For self-defense, of course, since it was unfortunately not possible to get firearms through customs. As with many missions in countries where he did not have a secret weapons store, Ondragon was having to procure heavy ordnance through his contacts and the black market, which required considerably more work in advance. He hoped the BND would at least provide him with a handgun if he couldn't get additional personnel. But if need be, the pepper spray and the knife would do. He had trained in Krav Maga during his time as a mailman at DeForce Deliveries, and he was proficient in the use of blades of all kinds. And in this case, proficient meant deadly.

He entered a four-digit combination to lock the safe and dug out the clothes he would need the next day. Then he took a shower. Having freshened up, he dried himself, set the air conditioner to two, and picked up his phone. Charlize answered after the second ring.

"Have you checked in?" he asked.

"*Hai.* Just got to the room. Looks okay. The view from the window is perfect. You can see the harbor. And looking toward you, the roof of your hotel."

"Good, let's see what we get from the meeting tomorrow."

"All right. Sweet dreams, Boss."

"You too!" Ondragon hung up, went to the hidden bulletin board page on the internet, and left a message there for Doberman12. Then he turned off his cell phone and lay down on the cool sheets.

* * *

The next morning, after a good night's sleep, he was sitting at breakfast by 7:30, waiting for his specially prepared porridge, sipping a triple espresso, and leafing through the scant notes he had made so far. The operation would be supported by the BND, Charlize would act as his proxy, and he would stay hidden and wait. He was unaccustomed to this kind of thing, since he generally always took an active role. But he also knew he could trust Charlize absolutely. They just had to discuss the details with the contact.

His porridge arrived and Ondragon devoured the minimalist meal. He then treated himself to a bowl of fresh fruit and went to a quiet corner of the hotel to open the bulletin board. Sure enough, there was a message from Doberman12:

Meeting point Boteco "Veraneio" at Praia do Meireles opposite Hotel Beira Mar, 12:00 noon. I will find you!

Not until noon, that's good, Ondragon thought; he had plenty of time to run a few more errands and scout out the area. He sent Charlize an email to let her know where to join him in an hour and took a cab to Mercado Central.

Arriving there, he put on his sunglasses and discreetly scanned the surrounding area. He seemed to be alone, but he would have to reconnoiter later to confirm that. First, however, he headed for the modern, crescent-shaped shopping center, which had been erected right next to Fortaleza Cathedral—temples to two different religions.

The four-floor shopping complex was crammed with small stores offering everything that would make package tourists happy. The first thing Ondragon did was buy two city maps, checking continually that he wasn't being followed. There wasn't much going on this early in the morning, and it was easy for him to inspect each individual person. No one looked suspicious. So he continued his shopping spree, buying a few garishly colored T-shirts, a straw cowboy hat, a baseball cap, flip-flops, a small backpack, and beach shorts. Ondragon hated shorts because it was hard to hide weapons under them, but long pants just stood out too much in this vacationers' paradise.

After he had everything he needed for his mission, he went to a men's room and changed. He put the rest of his clothes in his backpack. He examined his outfit in the mirror and put on the embarrassing straw hat. Since he was accustomed to the California sun, he didn't have to worry about his complexion. He looked like he'd been here a few weeks already. Freshly restyled, he left the restroom and went to a café on the lowest level of the mall. He sat down at a table overlooking the large atrium, which was gradually beginning to fill with people.

At 10:30, Charlize appeared with a large number of shopping bags and sat down next to him. Planting a kiss on his cheek, she ordered a *café com leite* from the waiter. They had agreed that their cover when they were on assignment together would be as an engaged couple, though they would go their separate ways in the evening. That was a slight flaw, but it was safer for Charlize's second identity, which she would soon be given by the BND, for her to be in her own apartment.

Ondragon looked surreptitiously at his assistant. She was wearing a floaty green beach dress with a white bikini underneath. Her skin was shining with suntan oil and she was radiating a seductive aroma of beach and sunshine. As ever, Charlize had her disguise well in hand. He grinned to himself and took a sip of his freshly squeezed orange juice.

"Did you get everything?" he asked.

"Of course, honey," she replied in a strong Brazilian accent, which was not her usual habit.

"What about the software?" *Software* was the code word for the contacts they had to make on the ground.

"Already arranged, I took care of everything. Sem's up to speed." She handed him a piece of paper with the email address of someone called Sem written on it. Ondragon knew Charlize had good contacts in the Brazilian underworld, but he didn't know exactly who they were. That had been one of Charlize's conditions when she had originally started working for him. Questions about her past were totally off-limits.

She put a hand on his and purred, "You can count on me, honey!"

Ondragon threw her a warning glance. "Watch you don't overdo it, or your American gringo fiancé will show you what else he likes when he's on vacation. It ain't just a peck on the cheek!"

Charlize gave him a sulky look over her sunglasses. Her coffee arrived, stopping her from going into cactus mode.

"And what's on the agenda today?" she inquired.

"We'll take a cab and do a little exploring between here and the port, where the hangars with the wreckage of the Air France plane and the laboratory are, and then we'll drive through our neighborhood. We'll speak Japanese while we're on the road, so the driver won't know what we're saying. We're meeting the contact at a beach bar at noon. You'll stay close—you're the one being deployed, after all. After that, we'll prepare for the operation."

They finished their drinks, paid, and hailed a cab at the main entrance to the mall. Ondragon was glad of the vehicle's air-conditioning—it was already oppressively hot outside. He was far less enamored of the annoying *forró* blaring from the radio. He asked Charlize to tell the driver to turn the music down, which he reluctantly did. The noise level dropped to a tolerable volume just below that of an aircraft turbine, and Ondragon breathed a sigh of relief. They gave directions to the driver, who was visibly annoyed at the intrusion on his listening pleasure, and they drove off.

The Fortaleza area of the port was ridiculously small and they had soon covered the few streets, which were identified by letters. The actual area with the docks, warehouses, and silos was closed off from the public by a concrete wall with only three entrances. By the main entrance, Ondragon asked the cab driver to slow down a little.

"Pretty run-down," he said in Japanese. "And it doesn't look very heavily guarded."

"*Node sore wa*—That's right," Charlize replied, taking a few covert photos on her smartphone. "They're probably assuming not many journalists are interested in plane debris."

When they reached the west end, Ondragon noticed a pipeline leading over the wall into the harbor area. "This would be a good place to get in at night and smuggle Pandora out. Plus, there's the waterway. Look over there. See that partially collapsed building almost right next to the wall? That'll make a good hiding place. I'll monitor the operation from there."

Charlize nodded.

"All right, let's swing by my hotel now," Ondragon said, directing the cab driver to turn off Vicente de Castro Avenue onto the beach boulevard. "Let's see how long it takes to get there."

A minute later, they passed Charlize's accommodation, which for tactical reasons was only a stone's throw from the harbor. The Porto Joia apartment building was the first in a long line of hotels that stretched for several kilometers along the beach like a mountain range of concrete and glass.

Very unstylish, Ondragon thought, *but typical of this kind of resort*. And not only here, unfortunately, but right along the warm waters of the Atlantic coast. Miami had been similarly disfigured by the construction industry.

Alongside what felt like a hundred tour buses, they jostled their way west on Avenida Beira Mar, with the beach on their right and the high-rise facades on their left. Ondragon counted the hotels. The fourteenth was his, and it was followed by several others. It was a little over a kilometer from his accommodation and Charlize's. A fifteen-minute walk.

They had the cab driver turn into the next street into town and drive around the neighborhood once more. Although it didn't seem as run-down as the poorer neighborhoods to the south, it didn't have any particularly special atmosphere. Shaking his head, Ondragon wondered how anyone could seriously vacation here. In hotels whose best years were long behind them and where drunken tourists consorted with cheap prostitutes. And everywhere nothing but dirt, violence, and misery.

"Grim," he whispered.

"You said it, Boss. It's Rio de Janeiro's ugly sister!"

After another ten minutes, they had seen enough and had the cab driver take them to the Hotel Beira Mar at Praia do Meireles, where they gave him a generous tip; he immediately turned his music back up to its previous volume and sped off. Across from the hotel was a beach park with palm groves, sun loungers, and beach bars, or *botecos*. They found the Veraneio easily, in the shade of rubber trees and with a direct view of the turquoise water.

That's better, Ondragon thought, sitting down at a free table and surveying the surroundings. Doberman12 seemed to have selected the beach bar carefully for their secret meeting. A tall hibiscus hedge shielded the tables from unwanted attention from the street, and the music emanating from the shack speakers was at just the right volume to ensure muted conversations would not be overheard by neighboring tables or directional mics. While Charlize took a little stroll down the beach to scrutinize the people on the sun loungers, Ondragon checked out the guests at the tables. On the far left sat two tanned guys in their mid-twenties, probably Americans. No, wait. One of them was wearing Jack Wolfskin sandals. They had to be German. But would Doberman12 wear that kind of thing? Probably not.

At the next table was a gang of pensioners, three women and three men. Clearly Americans this time, easily recognizable from their bus-driver butts, pudgy arms, and the obligatory enormous glasses. The robust type of pensioner who could only afford the Copacabana's ugly sister, as Charlize had so aptly put it earlier.

At the table next to them, two locals were lounging around in a deliberately cool manner. Casually dressed beach Romeos, sucking on their bottled beers and looking to flirt with white tourists. Their chosen candidates were already seated at the neighboring table. Four blonde and overweight girls in their twenties, with bikinis that were way too tight and cancer-red skin. They were talking so loudly and with such a strong accent that it was clear where they came from. Only the United Kingdom could produce this unspeakable mixture of royal snobbery and the nastiest pub slang. *Hip, hip, hurray—three cheers and more beers for His Majesty!*

Then there were two more guys, each alone at a table.

A young lad, thin and wiry. He was wearing sneakers, a muscle shirt, running glasses, and a white baseball cap on his head. Nationality? Hard to tell. His skin was dark but not black. More likely a southerner, Mexican or Spanish, say. Or a descendant of the white Brazilian upper classes. Ondragon turned to the second guy, who was much more interesting. Dark-haired and slightly stocky, he was sipping his fruit juice, seemingly lost in thought. He was around forty and dressed like a mirror image of Ondragon: T-shirt, shorts, ridiculous hat. He had to be Doberman12! The guy was almost strenuously avoiding looking over at him, pretending to gaze dreamily out onto the beach. But Ondragon noticed that his pupils kept sliding toward the corners of his eyes. Also, the man had made a mistake. He was wearing a clunky Traser military watch, worth at least $800. No tourist would have one of those. Fortaleza was a cheap paradise for vacationers from all over the world, but also for pickpockets and other riffraff, and you were well advised to stick to understated apparel when you were out and about.

Ondragon leaned back nonchalantly and gave Charlize a wave. She minced over in an exaggerated girly manner, sat down next to him, and enthused loudly about the great beach. She was doing a good job. Ondragon smiled at her and put a casual arm around her shoulders. They were engaged, after all, and for a while he even enjoyed being this close to his assistant. What a shame he had to abide by his own first rule: No sex with employees! He gave a restrained sigh and removed his arm again. Then he went over to the bar and got two ice-cold Coronas.

While they waited, they pretended to look at vacation photos on their smartphones. In reality, however, they were checking out the port area again with the help of a maps app. Every building was visible on the amazingly sharp satellite image, and they tried to commit the location to memory. All the while, the guy from the BND stayed exactly where he was. Then it turned twelve o'clock and a shadow fell on their table from behind. Ondragon turned around and was somewhat surprised to see not the guy with the watch, but a petite, white-blonde woman with a ponytail. She was wearing a red bathing suit and had a scarf wrapped around her waist. Her eyes were covered by large, dark glasses.

"I saw her on the beach earlier," Charlize whispered to him in Japanese.

The woman looked down at her, slightly confused, as if she had approached the wrong table.

"Can I help you?" Ondragon asked her in a broad Texas accent.

The woman smiled, flashing white teeth in her freckled face. She looked pretty good. Sexy in an aloof kind of way. Like Claire Danes's twin sister, only with freckles that spilled all over her body, from her face to her shoulders to her arms and legs. As he scrutinized her, Ondragon was glad his eyes were hidden behind his sunglasses.

She looked quickly over her shoulder and then just sat down at the table with them. "I think I'm in the right place," she said in German.

Ondragon raised his eyebrows. "You are . . ."

"Doberman12, that's right." The woman grinned and took off her glasses, revealing a pair of dazzling blue eyes that sent a pleasant shiver through Ondragon. It was news to him that the BND was employing such attractive agents.

"Would you like something to drink? A beer or a caipirinha?" he asked with a gentlemanly smile.

"No thanks, let's get down to business."

"So our contact man is a woman!" said Ondragon.

"Does that bother you?"

"Heavens no!" He raised his hands apologetically. She might look hot but she was cool as a cucumber. What a tantalizing combination.

"My name is Katharina Ritter. I will be running Pandora behind the scenes. I assume this is your assistant?" She cast an appraising glance at Charlize, who was looking around from time to time.

Ondragon realized she did not understand German and introduced the two women to each other. He immediately sensed a slightly aggressive tension building between them. *This is going to be fun*, he thought, but kept his enjoyment to himself.

"By the way, over there at the table is my colleague Mr. Steiner, also known as Setter30," Ms. Ritter now continued in English. "But you'll already have spotted that he's a spy. He's a good distraction, don't you think?" She looked at him challengingly.

Ondragon didn't respond to this little dig. "Nice guard dog you have there. Does he need much exercise?"

"He's pretty low maintenance." The BND agent grinned mischievously, which Ondragon found quite delightful, and he smiled back until Ms. Ritter began rummaging around in her beach bag.

"Since you sent me a photo of your assistant in advance," she said, "the paperwork and schedule for Ms. Tanaka is already done." She pulled a leaflet that looked like it came from one of the local restaurants from her pocket and slid it across the table. Charlize took it and dropped it into her purse.

"The leaflet contains all the identification documents and information about the deployment site," the agent went on. "Everything has been installed for Ms. Tanaka there. Dr. Letícia Matsumoto Souza is expected at her workplace tomorrow. So it would be nice if you could start the operation as soon as possible. We will keep in touch mainly by radio and a small camera during the critical phase. Are your cell phones bug-proof?"

"Yes, but what exactly do you mean by 'everything is installed at the site'?" Ondragon asked, concerned for Charlize's safety.

"The forensic scientist who was supposed to be investigating the contents of Pandora together with his team—you'll find all those details in the memorandum as well—had a little accident yesterday. Unfortunately, he fell and broke his leg. Ten days in hospital. Your assistant will be filling in for him."

Ondragon nodded. So far, so good. He looked at his assistant. Forensic scientist, that could work. Charlize had a few tricks up her sleeve and could even impersonate a circus clown with ease. He saw her nod without mussing a hair. Yes, that was his girl!

"By the way, we have also set up a profile on the bulletin board for your assistant. She can access it under the name Pinscher26." The BND woman couldn't suppress a slight grin, and Ondragon knew he would have to placate Charlize later. The subliminal catfight could not escalate just yet.

"Do you have any other questions, Mr. Ondragon?"

"Don't we get any hardware?"

"Hardware?" The blonde agent frowned.

"Well, toys you can shoot bullets with. You know, like James Bond."

For a moment, she looked uncomprehending. Then the penny dropped. "Don't worry," she replied, smiling openly, "the packages will be delivered to you this evening."

Ondragon finished his beer and scrutinized the agent again. Could he rely on this woman in an emergency? She seemed trustworthy—to the extent any intelligence agent could be said to be trustworthy. Still, it was safer to trust in himself. And his best weapon in the field was Charlize, and she was damned reliable!

"We will be at your disposal tomorrow morning," he confirmed.

"Good, then it's all settled." Agent Ritter rose and slipped a forearm through the loops of her bag. "I wish you every success. Goodbye!" With a provocatively sexy sway of her hips, she strutted away toward the beach. Ondragon noticed Charlize's eyes shooting daggers after her.

"Nice woman," he said jokingly. He wanted to test what happened when he poured a little oil on the flames.

Charlize snorted loudly.

"I don't know what's wrong with you. I thought she was okay."

She turned her head and looked at him sharply. "If by okay you mean fire-breathing dragon, then I agree."

"Now don't be like that."

But Charlize was just hitting her stride. "The Doberman's a blonde! How appropriate! She's an *Onibaba*, and she'd better watch out!"

An old witch? Ondragon began to laugh. He stroked his assistant's heated cheek soothingly. "Calm down, sweetheart, I'm all yours!"

Charlize looked at him, irritated, then her annoyance dissolved into a girlish giggle. "Sorry, Boss. But blondes make me see red!"

"I get it." Ondragon grinned and watched as Setter30 got up from the next table and sauntered away. He wouldn't have heard much of their conversation, as they had been speaking very quietly in Japanese.

A little later, they also left the beach bar and went to the hotel across the street for lunch. After perusing the second-rate menu offered with unpleasant service thrown in for good measure, Charlize left Ondragon at the table and disappeared into the ladies' room, in order to sift through the material from the leaflet. After seven minutes, she was back.

"All good," she said quietly. "The documents look okay. An ID from the São Paulo police, certifying me as an employee of the forensics department there, a driver's license, and a letter of recommendation. Before they realize I'm a fake, I'll have this thing in the bag and be well out of the woods!"

"Good," Ondragon said. "So they can sort the paperwork down at the BND. I'm just wondering why they aren't doing the rest of the job themselves too."

"They may not have anyone who speaks Portuguese and can impersonate a Brazilian police forensic scientist as perfectly as I can." Charlize winked coquettishly, then grew serious again. "The leaflet also included a description of the deployment site and the warehouses. The storeroom with the wreckage is in the building on the western edge of the harbor, very close to the ruined house. The laboratory, which, by the way, is mainly used to examine dead bodies and therefore mostly contains medical equipment, is set up in the hall next door, along with the refrigeration facilities and the tent with the corpses."

"Hmm, bad smells guaranteed!" remarked Ondragon.

"*Hai*, but I'll manage. I already read the memo in the bathroom; you can have it." She pushed the leaflet toward Ondragon.

"Sophisticated, but old-fashioned." He pocketed it. "Does it also self-destruct once you've read it?"

"I guess you'll have to use your good old lighter for that, Boss."

Ondragon called over the waiter and paid the bill. "I think we should go our separate ways for the rest of the day. Pretend you're going to the beach."

Charlize rose, shouldering her purse. "Should I look into Ritter and Steiner?"

"People like that are certain to be working under false identities. Ritter and Steiner will just be aliases like Doberman and Setter, but you can give it a try."

"All right, honey." She leaned down, gave him a kiss on the cheek, and stalked away.

Finally, Ondragon also rose and left the restaurant. He saw Charlize get into a cab outside the main entrance, and set off on foot for his hotel. They would talk on the phone again that evening.

CHAPTER 5

May 20, 2011
Fortaleza, Brazil
2:20 pm

Clandestin stroked his glued-on beard pensively and retreated into the shelter of the concrete pillar by the hotel entrance.

This Ondragon guy was a professional, and crafty. At least it wasn't easy to stay on him, because he was constantly checking whether he was being followed. He had only been able to observe the American—if that was what he was—and his pretty companion from a distance.

In recent days, Clandestin had tried almost in vain to shed more light on the identity of the man the BND had hired. The dubious Mr. O was hidden behind an even more dubious company called Ondragon Consulting, based in Los Angeles. *Smart solutions worldwide*—the slogan was the only thing he had been able to unearth. Nothing else; no phone number, no address or any other contact details.

Was Ondragon Consulting a dummy company? Possibly, but Clandestin guessed it was more a question of insider knowledge. Mr. O was a special kind of consultant, the kind that wasn't squeamish: he could sense it. He hadn't found out much about the man himself either, although the name Ondragon didn't exactly crop up frequently in internet directories—if it was his real name at all! It seemed a little too fanciful to Clandestin. However, he had found a couple of unusual entries for the name. A former German ambassador and a Swedish gold medalist at the 1976 Winter Olympics. Whether these two had anything to do with Mr. O, however, remained an open question. In any case, this Ondragon was by no means an amateur, and he would have to come up with an ingenious plan if he was to catch him off guard. Perhaps the woman, the Asian, would make a good bargaining chip. Her role in the game was not yet clear to him—he would have to work on that. The only thing that was certain was that the lady was not romantically involved with Mr. O, although the two of them wanted people to believe they were together, disguising themselves as a couple. Their displays of affection were too shallow for that. They seemed to know each other very well, but more in a professional context. From his distance, he had unfortunately not been able to overhear any of their conversations, not even the one with the secret service minder in the beach bar.

Clandestin looked thoughtfully after the cab into which the woman had climbed. Since he had known for a long time where they had each alighted, he was able to trail them in a relaxed manner. His motor scooter was much better in this miserable traffic anyway. All he needed was a good plan and the right moment.

He detached himself from the column and stepped out into the bright sunlight. His hands in the pockets of his shorts, he strolled toward the beach, where his scooter was parked.

CHAPTER 6

May 20, 2011
Fortaleza, Brazil
6:11 pm

Sweating from his jog, Ondragon came back to his hotel room and pressed the button on his wristwatch. Twelve minutes for two and a half kilometers out and back. That meant it would take ten minutes to walk the distance one way, at a normal pace. However, it would require caution after sunset. The hotels were unanimous in warning against hanging around the streets after dark. Rival gangs from the favelas—the adjoining poor neighborhoods—made the nighttime unsafe and to take a walk was to risk your life, as was the case almost everywhere in Brazil.

As Ondragon exited the shower, there was a knock on the door. He looked through the peephole and saw a FedEx courier standing in the hallway. The man held a package in his arms and was looking around, bored. Ondragon tucked his knife into the back of the towel he had wrapped around his hips and opened the door.

Ignoring his attire, the courier asked, "Are you Mr. Ondragon?"

Ondragon nodded.

"Would you sign here, please, *seu.*" The guy pointed to a mobile data capture device.

Ondragon signed and accepted the incredibly heavy package with an *"Obrigado!"* He then closed the door, attached the security chain, and went to the bed, where he began by examining the outside of the package. When he couldn't find anything out of the ordinary about the cardboard layer, he tore it open to reveal an aluminum case. Using the code given in the memo, he opened the combination lock and carefully flipped open the lid. Inside the case were some very pleasing things.

With best regards from Q Division, Ondragon thought, setting the things next to one another on the bed: a Glock G19 with spare magazine and a box of ammunition, a surveillance set consisting of several bugs, a tiny clip-on microphone plus receiver unit and a mini camera, a netbook with surf stick, which was undoubtedly already set up for him, and a satellite phone. The lady from the BND probably didn't trust his tap-proof cell phone—well, the thing would be useful in any case. And last but not least, Ondragon found a car key with a photo fob. The two pictures in it were of a dark red, dented Toyota Corolla and a blue Ford van with tinted windows and the name of a local plumbing service printed on its sides. This was presumably the van from which the BND was monitoring the operation. It would be positioned somewhere along the harbor near the main entrance, and they wanted Ondragon to know what it looked like. The key clearly belonged to the Corolla, which was almost certainly already waiting for him in the hotel's underground garage. The jalopy was good camouflage in this run-down town, which Ondragon appreciated, but hopefully it was also reliable. He would park the Corolla halfway to the port, just in case of emergency. Walking was a better way of getting around in these narrow streets. He turned on the netbook and his assumption was confirmed. The profile was tailored to him and the device could be opened with the same password he used for the bulletin board. The desktop contained only a few icons, including for sound and camera monitoring programs and shortcuts to folders with all the relevant information. Ondragon tested the internet connection and logged onto the bulletin board's dog forum.

Doberman12 was asking in English, *Package received?*

Pinscher26 answered, *Y!*

Ondragon likewise typed *Y!*

Shortly afterward, a new instruction from Dobermann12 appeared: *Test equipment at T 700 at deployment site C tomorrow. Site marked on map.*

Ondragon wrote *OK.* Pinscher26 confirmed too.

He logged out, opened the folder labeled MAPS, and found several high-resolution satellite images with all the critical points marked with red letters. The halls, the gates, the location of the parked surveillance car; he even had a small boat at his disposal. It was outside the western breakwater that separated the harbor from the sea. Ondragon turned off the computer. He knew what he had to do. Now to find out if Charlize did too. He dialed her number.

"Yes, Boss?" she answered.

"Just wanted to check you're happy with everything?"

"*Hai*, it's all under control."

"Can you do the whole forensic scientist thing?"

"Now, hold on a minute, Boss! When have I ever blown a cover?"

"I take my question back. You can do it," he replied. Charlize had some knowledge of forensic analysis, after all. It was part of the craft she brought to Ondragon Consulting. However, she specialized in leaving no traces rather than tracking traces down.

"Fortunately, the *Doitsu-jin* gave me the identity of a lab rat. Imagine if they had given me a PhD in German history." She giggled. "It'd be so embarrassing to speak German without knowing a word of it."

"Maybe I should buy you a language vacation sometime," Ondragon joked.

"Oh, yes. I'd love Munich in the fall! I've always wanted to wear a dirndl."

Ondragon snorted. "German culture is more than just dirndls and the Oktoberfest!"

"I know, but you guys are a little stuffy."

"Are you saying I'm stuffy?"

"Well, there's something about you, Boss. But you're nothing compared to the blonde dragoness. She's super annoying!"

"Charlize, focus on your assignment, will you? You can let off steam about Ms. Ritter later."

"Ms. Ritter! The way you say her name. Do you have a thing for her? Miss Doberman is much too skinny for my taste."

Charlize is actually jealous, Ondragon thought, amused. He looked out the window. Outside, the last of the evening glow was giving way to another sultry night. He was kind of flattered by her reaction.

"What is it? You're not saying anything," he heard Charlize ask through the phone.

"Oh, I was just having a romantic daydream."

"Romantic? Surely not about that dried-up hag . . ."

"Oh, my dear Charlize, you know dark-haired girls are my thing."

"*Sō desu ka*—really?" She fell silent, though he would probably never know if it was out of relief or not.

"Okay, I'll see you tomorrow morning at six-thirty," he said, growing serious again. "I'll pick you up on the way to the harbor."

"*Hai.* Good night!"

"Good night, sweetheart!" He hung up.

CHAPTER 7

May 21, 2011
Fortaleza, Brazil
6:00 am

The next morning, Ondragon breakfasted in his room. Since his height of over 1.90 meters alone made it immediately obvious he was a gringo, he left his three-day beard as it was and dressed as shabbily as possible so that he would at least be left alone by the hawkers. A baggy pair of black track pants with holes at the knee, a stained shirt without sleeves, and a dark beanie would have to be enough to turn him into a penniless beach bum who was stuck in Fortaleza. In this disguise, he could make his way through the favelas without setting off alarm bells among the gangs; there was nothing to be gotten from a foreign drunk with no money. He tucked his pistol into the front of his waistband and the spare magazine into his pocket, and taped the knife to his left calf. He stood in front of the mirror, checked his appearance, and pretended to have put away a few bottles of sugar cane liquor. Yes, that was good. With his shoulders slumped and his upper body slightly bent forward, his degree of delirium looked convincing enough to keep him unmolested, and what's more, it concealed his gun.

Ondragon stuffed the netbook, satellite phone, and a few other things into his backpack, slipped into a clean shirt, and pulled the beanie off his head. He wasn't going to put it back on until he was outside. At this early hour, the hotel's usual clientele were lying hungover in their beds, but he had to make sure he could leave the building and return to it later without being mistaken for a homeless person; that would ensure he was catapulted out again in a big arc.

Undisturbed, he reached the underground garage and found the Corolla in a dark corner. He threw the backpack onto the passenger seat and got behind the wheel. The car started smoothly and Ondragon drove off. Outside was the pastel twilight of a cloudy morning. There was hardly any traffic on the streets, so Ondragon reached Charlize's apartment hotel in just a few minutes. He turned around and parked the car at the curb half a kilometer away. Then he took another look around—knowing your surroundings was half the battle. He then retrieved the backpack from the car and set off on foot to Charlize's house. She was waiting for him in the foyer, ready to leave. Ondragon was quite astonished when he saw her and felt embarrassed because he had been intending to check her over. But her outfit reassured him and reminded him once again that Charlize too was a professional.

He approached her, smiling.

"Well?" she asked, a little sharply. "Do you approve?"

"You look like the perfect doctor!" She really did. Charlize was the very image of a forensic scientist. Hair pulled back into a boringly standard hairstyle, black horn-rimmed glasses, subtle makeup, and to tone down the cliché (necessary for the fine art of creating a believable disguise), not a severe pantsuit but a gray sweater and jeans. She also had a cell phone pouch on her belt and a nerdy hands-free clip on her ear of the kind usually only worn by idiots. But it hid the earpiece Charlize would be using to link to radio contact for the operation. Her outfit was topped off by an expression that had been hardened by all the wickedness of the world. And voilà, she was the type of person who was only truly comfortable in her lab among the specimens and stacks of evaluation charts. Rarely conceited, but highly meticulous and particularly fond of technological gimmicks.

Speaking of.

"And where's the camera?" Ondragon asked.

Charlize pointed at her glasses. "The mic is in one of my hair clips. Very clever, considering I'll most likely be wearing scrubs on location. There's no way a camera in my buttonhole or belt buckle would have worked."

Ondragon nodded appreciatively. He had to hand it to the BND, they hadn't only kept records, they'd also thought things through. "Okay," he said, "now you're going to have a cab take you to the main gate of the harbor, but before you go in, light a cigarette and look around a little. You'll see Ritter and Steiner's van then. After the mic and camera test, go inside and register as a new employee at the lab. I'll follow on foot. While you're inside, I'll take up position in the fallen-down house. If necessary, I'll do a lap around the block pretending to just be mooching about. Okay?"

Charlize raised a fist. "*Ganbare masu*—I'll do my best!"

Ondragon also raised a fist and bumped it against his assistant's. "*Ganbare!*"

He waited until Charlize was out the door, then changed his clothes behind a dumpster next to the building outside. A few minutes later, he was staggering toward the harbor in the guise of a beach bum. As he turned onto Avenida Vicente de Castro, he saw Charlize in the distance, standing outside the main gate and smoking. At almost the same moment, Agent Ritter spoke through the little bud in his ear.

"Testing, testing. Position Three, do you read me?" she asked in English.

"Loud and clear," replied Ondragon, then asked, "Position Two, do you read me?"

"Yep!" he heard Charlize say, and grinned. He knew she didn't think much of the conventions of radio communications and he thought Ritter and Steiner would have their work cut out for them with the way his assistant expressed herself. But since most of the communication between Charlize and the Brazilian investigation team would be in Portuguese, there wouldn't be much for them to listen in to anyway; he didn't think the two BND agents were particularly well versed in the language. He himself could understand the gist of it, and he had agreed on some code words with Charlize. "Man, it's hot in here," was one of them and meant "Need help! Now!"

"I'm going in!" Charlize said in his ear. He saw her throw away the cigarette and walk toward the main entrance.

"Position Two entering," Ritter stated.

Ondragon rolled his eyes. He had little desire to hear all the radio chatter. He was much more interested, on the other hand, in the pictures from the camera. So he quickly made his way to his hiding place in the ruined house. He found a good spot by a broken window on the second floor, which even gave him a view of part of the hall where the plane wreckage was being kept.

"Position Two, I can see the grounds. When you take a smoke break, go behind Hall One; there's an *E* on the wall. I'll be able to see you there."

"*Até mais tarde!*" whispered Charlize. See you later.

"Position One here! Always state your position name when you speak, Position Three!" complained Ritter. Why did the Germans always have to be so uber-correct?

"I think with this number of participants, we'll be able to recognize each other's voices," Ondragon put in. "This position nonsense is unnecessary; all it does is waste our time!"

There was an offended silence in his earpiece, then she said, "All right. Carry on!"

Ondragon took the binoculars out of his backpack and placed them on the cracked windowsill. Then he turned on the netbook and opened the link to the camera's live feed. The image took a few seconds to appear. It was black and white and, despite the low output of the camera at this distance, relatively sharp; it was easy to see where Charlize was. She was standing in a small office in front of a desk, behind which was seated a uniformed man talking into a telephone handset. Ondragon couldn't understand a word because the security guard was talking way too fast, but it was probably about Charlize's accreditation.

"Got a visual!" he said into the mic.

"Received!" replied Ritter curtly.

Ondragon watched as the security guy hung up the phone, leaned back, and looked uninterestedly at Charlize. The disguise seemed to be working. A short time later, a man with gray hair and a white coat appeared. He held out his hand to Charlize.

"Dr. Lima," Ondragon heard the man introduce himself. According to the memo, this was the historian and the head of the investigation team. Charlize gave her name and handed him her credentials. Dr. Lima nodded and motioned to her to follow him. Outside, the two of them got into a golf caddy and drove past the stacks of containers and silos to Warehouse 2, entering through a door at the west end. Inside, the light was dim. Ondragon could see that a veritable city of components had been constructed in the hall. At the center was a mobile laboratory on a truck trailer. A huge, light-colored tarpaulin was visible in the background, and through Charlize's mic came an underlying hum. Probably the generators that powered the lab and the cooling units for the tent with the bodies. Ondragon heard Dr. Lima apologize for the smell in the hall, and was glad not to be in Charlize's place right now. In spite of the tent and the refrigeration, the hall would smell horribly of decay.

Charlize was led through an entry gate that opened into the lab and was secured by a magnetic keycard lock. Dr. Lima handed her a gown and ushered her directly into the room, which was located in the trailer and contained all sorts of medical equipment. There was even an X-ray machine.

"That's where the safe with Pandora is," radioed Ritter. Ondragon confirmed that he understood. He saw via Charlize's camera that two other people were already waiting in the container lab. A small middle-aged woman who introduced herself as Marcia Morinho, and a bald man. The woman must be the archaeologist and the guy the graphologist, the one who knew about handwriting. The team to examine the box was thus complete.

Ondragon heard Dr. Lima speaking. "We have waited for you before opening the box, Dr. Souza. As required by protocol. Your predecessor measured and photographed the artifact two days ago. Samples from the outside of the crate have also been taken. So we can now start on the contents."

Charlize let her camera slide over the team members. They all nodded. From their expectant faces, Ondragon concluded that they probably hadn't seen inside the box yet. Once again, he wondered what was so sensitive about it. He looked intently at the image being transmitted by the camera. He saw the group positioning themselves in front of the vault. Charlize stood back, looking over the shoulders of the others. Dr. Lima put on a pair of latex gloves and began to turn the combination lock on the safe.

3-5-9-1-7

Ondragon made a note of the combination, hoping that it was not reset every day. The door of the safe opened to reveal a rectangular object wrapped in transparent plastic film.

"The box has been in the immersed zone for over sixty years," he heard Dr. Lima explain in Portuguese. "It is made of an aluminum-magnesium alloy and has remained watertight over that long time, which is amazing. The crew of the salvage ship forced it open to see what was inside, destroying the lock. According to the captain, however, none of the contents of the box were taken."

All well and good, thought Ondragon impatiently. *But now open the thing already!*

Dr. Lima lifted the box out of the safe and carried it over to the metal table in the middle of the laboratory, which was actually used for examining the bodies. He put the box down on it and began to unwrap it from the foil.

Looks totally unspectacular, Ondragon thought, *a dented aluminum box with two handles on the sides. Nothing more.* The corrosive seawater had given the light metal a dull white crust. The corrosion had been removed from the lid. Probably to examine the engraving that lay beneath it.

"Move in closer," Ondragon said into the mic, and Charlize leaned forward. The engraving was barely legible, but Ondragon could decipher the German words *Luftwaffe* and *Reich*.

"Are you ready for the big reveal?" Dr. Lima now asked.

Man, they aren't the crown jewels! Ondragon thought, and heard Agent Ritter give an impatient sigh. Spellbound, he looked at the screen. Dr. Lima's hands reached for the lid and lifted it slowly. Someone adjusted the lamp above the lab table, bathing the inside of the box in bright light.

Ondragon's throat tightened abruptly and his heart began to race. He heard the awed murmur of the scientists and bit his tongue painfully. Although he had prepared himself mentally for the dreaded object, he could not control his reaction. He realized he was gasping loudly and tried to stop doing that, at least. Ritter and Steiner didn't need to know he was physically freaking out.

Two items lay in the box. A wooden casket with chipped corners and underneath it, a black, almost greasy-looking leather cover. A book, as large and flat as a photo album. The white halogen light brought out all the details. His eyes burning, Ondragon stared at the hated object and felt the familiar disgust rising in his stomach. He swallowed hard to hold it down.

Someone was taking pictures with a flash. A gloved hand took out the wooden box and placed it on the table, then did the same with the book. Again and again, the twitching of the flash caused a harsh white glare in the camera transmission. But the flashes helped Ondragon break free of his paralysis. He rubbed his throat, pushing the nausea down deeper. The only thing he could hear as he struggled with his phobia were the words *ouro* and *diário de bordo*—"gold" and "logbook." His eyes narrowed, he looked at the computer screen. Charlize seemed to sense his anguish, because she kept her gaze mainly on the casket. A hand came into view and opened it. On the tattered velvet pad inside lay a medal about the size of a hand.

Ondragon took a deep breath and tried to focus on the medal. He took a screenshot of the transmission and enlarged the image. The medal showed a beardless man in profile above two crossed oak leaves. With some surprise, he read the inscription above the head: THOMAS ALVA EDISON MDCCCCV.

The text to the left and right of the portrait, which was obviously of Edison, read, AWARDED BY THE AMERICAN INSTITUTE OF ELECTRICAL

ENGINEERS FOR MERITORIOUS ACHIEVEMENTS IN ELECTRICITY. And below that it said, TO NIKOLA TESLA 1917.

"That is the Edison Medal awarded to Nikola Tesla by the AIEE. It weighs six ounces and is made from twenty-four-karat gold," Ritter explained over the radio. She sounded excited.

"Nice investment. But who is Nikola Tesla?" asked Ondragon.

"A major inventor in the early twentieth century."

"German?"

Ritter laughed. "No, Tesla was Serbian and emigrated to America in 1884, where he died in 1943."

"And what is his medal doing in a Wehrmacht plane? What kind of plane is it anyway, and why was it heading to South America?" Ondragon asked, but Ritter simply skipped over his questions and continued her lecture on Nikola Tesla.

"Tesla was a genius. We have him to thank for many things that are still marvels today. He discovered alternating current, for example; the radio and remote control via radio waves were just a few of his countless groundbreaking inventions."

"The radio? I thought that was Marconi," Ondragon interjected.

"Guglielmo Marconi stole the idea from Tesla, but it's a long story; you can read up on it in the encyclopedia tonight."

Encyclopedia? Had he heard a slight chuckle? The woman was laughing at him! Disgruntled, he turned back to the screen. The medal had now been turned over, revealing its reverse side, which showed a naked man with an angel behind him holding a palm frond.

"The electricity genius crowned with glory," Ritter explained.

"Right, great," Ondragon replied. The agent's know-it-all attitude was getting on his nerves. "And what does the medal mean?"

"It means we are on the right track!"

This vague statement was clearly another evasion. The right track? To where and for whom? And what did the medal have to do with it? Ondragon would need to find out more as soon as possible. But for now, he had to be there for Charlize. She was doing a good job of being a forensic scientist. Expertly, she took samples from the surface of the medal and scraped off a few splinters of the metal to test its purity. The first thing the scientists had to do was rule out the possibility of the medal being a fake. Once she had completed these procedures, Charlize panned her camera over to the other object. The book! Ondragon gulped. He wasn't sure he'd get through this. He forced himself to look—at least until he knew what was inside.

At last, one of the scientists opened the greasy cover, which was embossed with a Reich eagle and swastika, revealing a stained fly-leaf. On it was written *Logbook*, and below that a handwritten name, *Oberst Karl Brenner*. Probably the pilot, Ondragon surmised, biting his lower lip. Disgust rose afresh in his throat, higher and higher, like shit up a clogged drainpipe. *Stay with it*, he urged himself. *You can do this!*

Someone turned the page and the first notes appeared, in the form of a table. Before Ondragon could decipher them, however, the transmission suddenly cut out.

"Hey, what's up? I've lost the picture!" he reported to Ritter.

"So have we. Come in, Pinscher26. Do you need help?"

But Charlize went on imperturbably, talking to the scientists on the team. So she was not in difficulty.

"Something must be interfering with the signal. Maybe it's the X-ray machine in the lab. We'll continue monitoring via microphone and try to reestablish visual contact. Over."

For all his curiosity, Ondragon had to admit he was relieved about the loss of the picture. He would get the information about the book from Charlize this evening at the latest. She might also get photos of the records the Brazilian scientists had already made. Much more relaxed now, Ondragon could follow the course of the investigation. Unfortunately, he couldn't understand much of the Portuguese shop talk. He would have to be patient.

When it was finally lunchtime, he heard Charlize say she was going to take a smoke break and shortly afterward she appeared by the big *E* at Hall 2.

"Pinscher26, report!" demanded Ritter over the radio.

"All right, all right!" replied Charlize irritably.

Through his binoculars, Ondragon saw her light a cigarette and take a drag.

"The medal seems to be genuine. At least as far as purity is concerned. The acid tests have confirmed that. Dr. Morinho is currently comparing the medal with old photographs of it. We've also found adhesions that will be examined more closely. The tests will run through overnight. Then we'll know more about its age."

"And the book?"

"It's a Nazi thing. A pilot's logbook in table form. On the first page the entries are neatly noted in the boxes provided, then there are five double pages of handwriting across the table and eight squares with numbers. Might be a code."

"Has it been decrypted?" the BND agent asked jumpily.

"No, not so far."

"And the entries? Has anyone in the group managed to translate them?" Ritter snapped out the questions like lashes from a whip. Ondragon could imagine how pissed off Charlize would be at her commanding tone. Still, he had a certain respect for Ritter's penchant for perfectionism. In that, they were not so dissimilar. And Charlize would get over the fact that another woman knew her job.

"No!" he heard his assistant hiss into the mic.

"Okay, Pinscher26. But remember, delay the translation of the log and destroy the photos before the end of the operation!"

"Yeah, sure. I'm not senile!"

Ondragon heard Charlize swear softly before she said in Japanese, "That old hag is really getting on my nerves!"

"Take it easy. I know what you mean," he replied.

"What are you talking about?" interjected Ritter.

"Pinscher26, get me more information on the plane, you hear? And about anything else you can find. Anything that will give us an advantage over the *Doitsu-jin.*"

"Roger that, Boss!"

"Enough! On this channel, we communicate in English only! If you don't comply, Sheepdog17, I'll cut your voice comms!"

"Sorry, it was pure habit. Won't happen again. What about the camera? Can you get it working again?" he asked, to distract Ritter.

"There's still no signal, unfortunately. But Setter30 is working on it."

"Can you tell me what kind of logbook that is and what you expect to learn from it?" ventured Ondragon tentatively. He was dying to know why the BND was going to such lengths with external service providers like him and Charlize.

At first, all he heard in his earpiece was static, but then came Ritter's calm voice: "We suspect that high-ranking Nazi officers wanted to take the plane to Argentina."

"No shit! And Adolf Hitler was on board?" he joked.

Ritter exhaled irritably. "What is certain is that they were officers. And we hope the log will give us the information we need to confirm who they were. In any case, it wasn't Hitler, that's for sure."

A pity, Ondragon thought. But he was interested not only in who might have been on the plane, but also what. This Edison medal was extremely suspicious. Why was it in the casket? It could have been war booty, of course; that might well have been exchanged for money on arrival. That made a certain amount of sense. But also not, somehow. Ondragon left it there, not wanting to squeeze Ritter any further. She wouldn't tell him anyway—she was too smart for that. He would check her story later against the information from Charlize.

He heard his stomach growl and ate an energy bar. Then he took a few sips from his water bottle and scanned the area with the binoculars. Charlize had returned to the lab, where the tedious documentation of the findings continued. Not much would likely happen in the next few hours. Ondragon put the binoculars aside, turned down the radio transmission, and leaned back against the wall. The really big show wouldn't be for two nights anyway, and until then he could relax his surveillance a little.

He jumped. He had heard a noise. But not over the earpiece—it had come from downstairs, from the house. He quickly flipped the netbook shut and spoke quietly to Ritter. "Something's up here. I'll go check it out!" Then he stood and stole over to the half-collapsed staircase, his gun at the ready. He peered down at the piles of rubble. Dust motes danced silently in the light of the sun's rays that were filtering through the windows; otherwise, he could detect no movement.

If someone was actually creeping around down there, the rubble would be crunching like little alarms under their feet. But he could hear nothing of the sort. Ondragon was about to tuck his pistol into his waistband when he heard it again. A cautious scraping sound. It came from the door to the building, which was hanging from a hinge in its frame.

Holding his breath, he moved down the stairs one by one. He quickly glanced around the room. But he saw nothing. Slowly, he crept toward the door. But with all the junk lying around down here, it was hard to keep quiet, and finally a crunch sounded right under his foot.

Crap! Ondragon thought, dashing through the door with his weapon raised and aiming outside. But his abrupt tactics didn't startle any unwanted visitors. It had probably just been a stray cat, or a seagull; there were hundreds of those flying around. Ondragon put away his gun and returned upstairs, reporting to Ritter that all was well.

Since there was still nothing exciting happening in Charlize's lab, he logged onto the internet via the netbook and typed *Nikola Tesla* into the Google search window. Time to find about this alleged genius.

CHAPTER 8

July 18, 1899
Colorado Springs
noon

Dr. Tesla closed the door behind him and Philemon's eyes slowly adjusted to the darkness inside the barnlike building. Gradually, silhouettes emerged from the blackness. The laboratory was surprisingly sparsely furnished. Along the walls were a variety of measuring instruments and switch relays, from which ran thick wires insulated with cotton cloth and gutta-percha latex, in all directions. On the floor stood a row of oblong accumulator boxes, and directly opposite the door were a number of square containers made of zinc, with wires protruding from their lids. Oil-filled capacitors, Philemon guessed. Next to them were a large metal cabinet fitted with locks and a strange apparatus consisting of dozens of polished spheres mounted in rows.

"My high-power oscillator!" said Dr. Tesla proudly beside him. It was the first time he had spoken since he had admitted Philemon into his realm. The tall master of electricity was simply but elegantly dressed. Black pants, an impeccable white shirt with a starched stand-up collar, and over it a dark vest. His pale face with its prominent mustache hovered above his slender, ascetic figure like the countenance of a ghost.

Philemon nodded devoutly. As a student, he had heard that Dr. Tesla could cause violent earthquakes with just such an oscillator, and that a few years previously he had almost reduced an entire block in Manhattan to rubble. The device had gotten out of control and Tesla had only been able to stop it by destroying it himself—at least that's what the newspapers had said.

"And what is that?" asked Philemon, pointing to a circular lattice paling as tall as a man and made of thick iron wire. It took up almost the entire building.

"Mr. Ailey, this is the centerpiece of my research: the largest coil for generating high-frequency alternating currents that has ever existed. You're familiar with how it works?"

"Yes, of course. This special type of resonant transformer consists of two independent coils of wire," Philemon explained as he admired the huge structure. "An outer primary coil with a large diameter and just a few turns, and an inner, much thinner, cylindrical secondary coil with up to two thousand turns. The resulting high-voltage discharges at the top of the secondary coil in the form of a corona, similar to Saint Elmo's fire."

"Very good, young man. This coil can generate gigantic voltages. It allows me to achieve tens of thousands of horsepower and close to fifty million volts! No one has ever accomplished that before."

Faced with these astronomical figures, Philemon looked at the doctor uneasily.

"Don't be concerned," the latter said calmly. "If you know how to deal with such forces, it is perfectly safe. You must only ensure you work with the greatest of care at all times. I myself have had currents of two and a half million volts flow through my body. I admit it tingled a little, but I was none the worse for it." He spread his arms as if to show that he was still whole.

Of course, Philemon had heard about the inventor's legendary demonstrations, which he only ever presented in New York to a select group of guests. Dr. Tesla extinguished the light in the hall and bravely stood on an electrified plate. According to the reports, his body was immediately enveloped in crackling, phosphorescent flames. From his fingertips, he had reportedly hurled booming thunderbolts over the heads of the terrified spectators like Zeus, the king of the gods himself. Other metallic objects in his vicinity were also said to have emitted sparks and singing noises. Philemon had always wished to see this with his own eyes, and now here he stood before him: the great Nikola Tesla. The electrical wizard! He still could not believe it.

"Forgive my somewhat simpleminded question, Dr. Tesla. But fifty million volts is an unimaginably enormous sum! What are you going to do with such incredible power? What is your plan?"

"That, my dear sir, you will find out soon enough. Come, you can climb over the secondary coil here and examine the interior." Dr. Tesla pointed to a wooden staircase that led over the ring-shaped lattice.

"*This* is the secondary coil?" asked Philemon in amazement. "But it has a diameter of—"

"Of exactly fifteen and a half meters! That's right. And it consists of thirty turns of wire." Dr. Tesla rocked back and forth on his heels in amusement.

Philemon looked around. "And where is the primary coil?"

"Oh, it's hidden under the wooden floor on which the second coil stands. It is a single winding of very thick cable."

"Truly extraordinary!" Philemon replied, and walked toward the staircase, amazed. Ahead of the doctor, he climbed over and reached the interior of the large coil. A collection of various smaller transformers had been set up here, and in the center towered another impressive induction coil, three meters in height, enthroned on a wooden pedestal. Philemon craned his neck, marveling at the crude structure of countless wire coils topped by a bulging hollow ring made of copper. A pipe led from the ring to the ceiling, disappearing through a hole.

"Is that pipe connected to the big antenna that rises to the heavens from the roof outside, Dr. Tesla?"

"You're very observant! With the help of the antenna, we intend to transmit high-frequency currents to distant places."

"Transmit? How?"

"Wirelessly. That is to say, without cables!"

"Without cables?" Philemon was almost speechless. Wireless transmission of energy or messages was prestigious and uncharted territory in science; it was the Klondike gold fields, so to speak, for all researchers in the new field of wave technology, and everyone was trying to get there first. Including, apparently, Dr. Tesla. *That is likely what he needs these gigantic voltages for*, thought Philemon.

"Quite right, Mr. Ailey, my method, which is of course the most promising, will make cables obsolete in the future! One will be able to receive my electricity anywhere in the world. Energy and messages! Spoken text and music. Imagine, one day we may even be able to send images around the globe, arriving with the receiver within seconds!"

Wireless picture messages, Philemon thought, *that is completely crazy!*

"But now meet one of my most trusted employees," Dr. Tesla went on. "This is Mr. Kolman Czito, my mechanic. Like me, he is Serbian and somewhat taciturn. Don't mind him, he is excellent at fixing malfunctions of any kind."

Philemon had not noticed the stocky man's soundless approach. Surprised, he turned and looked at him. The guy was short, appeared to be around forty, and wore a rubber apron and dark oversleeves. He extended a calloused hand and a warm smile appeared beneath his broad mustache.

"Rrrrrillly good to miiit you!" the Serb snarled with a heavy accent. He had a funny gap between his two upper incisors, making him seem especially rude.

Philemon shook his hand. "Likewise. Philemon Ailey."

"Mr. Scherff was kind enough to recommend him to us," Dr. Tesla explained, turning back to Philemon. "My second assistant and engineer, Mr. Fritz Löwenstein, is currently on his way; you will have the honor of meeting him later. He will instruct you as to your work here in the laboratory. And my third adjutant, Mr. Myers, well, he has unfortunately been called away on urgent business, as you may have heard. I hope you will be an exemplary replacement for him in all respects."

"I will do my best, Dr. Tesla!"

"Good, good. I know your qualifications, Mr. Ailey. My accountant, Mr. Scherff, forwarded them to me. You studied electrical engineering at Yale, with Charles Felton Scott among others. He spoke very highly of you in his letter of recommendation."

He did? Dr. Scott praised me? Philemon thought skeptically. He could hardly imagine that, after what had happened at the university. Still, it embarrassed him to hear these words from the mouth of one of the most renowned engineers in the world, and he cleared his throat.

"In any event, I am eager to see how you will fit into the laboratory routine, Mr. Ailey. Let me say one thing before you start: we keep no regular hours here. We work when the time is right. That usually means when the weather is favorable to our experiments. And since the weather does not respect the daily routines we humans have established for ourselves, that frequently means working early in the morning or late at night. So be prepared to be called out by us at any time."

Philemon nodded his head in agreement, wondering what kind of weather the doctor deemed "favorable."

"Good. Then we will now provide you with the equipment that you must always—and I mean *always*—have about you in the laboratory! This is for your safety, Mr. Ailey. After all, I do not wish any harm to befall my assistants." This time, Dr. Tesla did not smile. Instead, he nodded to Mr. Czito, who climbed over the staircase. Philemon and the doctor followed. On the other side, Mr. Czito gave Philemon a package wrapped in brown paper.

"We had the things made especially for you. That is why we asked you to telegraph us your measurements in advance," Tesla said, smoothing his vest with his gloved hands. "Please excuse me now, I must attend to my work. Mr. Czito will take care of you until Mr. Löwenstein returns. Once again, a warm welcome to my humble research station, Mr. Ailey." He gave a curt nod and disappeared into a small room that was separated from the lab by a wooden door.

Philemon was deeply impressed. Not only by the distinguished figure of the inventor, but also by his perfect manners. A true gentleman genius!

"His workroom," Czito said, pointing to the door through which Tesla had disappeared. "If Doctor in there, he wish not to be disturbed."

Philemon nodded and tore open the wrapping paper of the package expectantly. He was a little disappointed to find that it contained primarily pieces of clothing. He took them out one by one. A pair of trousers made of strangely smooth fabric and two white shirts made of the same material.

"Very fine cotton. Antistatic!" Czito remarked.

Philemon put them aside and took out a pair of black shoes. They had soles several centimeters thick.

"Rubber soles made of gutta-percha. You need these to avoid getting a shock from the earth. Me and Doctor wear too." Czito lifted one of his shoes, which actually had raised heels. Philemon had not noticed before because, in spite of them, the Serb was still half a head shorter than he was.

"I see," he replied, becoming uncertain. There seemed to him to be some doubt as to the harmlessness of the experiments in the laboratory. He picked up the next object, which was even more bizarre than the shoe soles. A flexible, bell-shaped shell with four holes. He looked questioningly at Mr. Czito.

"A hood made of rubber. Only for experiments with very strong current," he replied.

Philemon was feeling more and more uneasy. Why had Dr. Tesla said the work was completely safe when he had to dress like a medieval knight going into battle? He reached into the package again and brought out a rubber apron like the one Czito wore, plus oversleeves and gloves.

"And you'll need this." Czito opened a small box. It was filled with earplugs made of absorbent cotton and wax.

"The coils make a lot of noise! Hear it for miles."

"So this is where the thunder I heard from afar came from!"

"That's right. And always remember, young man, most important rule here in the lab: Never wear metal on your body! So no watches, no wedding rings, and no glasses! Also no belt or buttons! Otherwise you'll be grilled!"

Suddenly, Philemon remembered what the men in the restaurant had told him. About the assistant who had been roasted like a trout. But was that really true? And if so, why was Dr. Tesla claiming otherwise? Was he just trying to scare him, or was he—and this caused Philemon even more of a headache—trying to cover up a terrible accident, as the people in the town contended?

He tried to calm himself. Perhaps it was all just idle town gossip. But he was well aware that all gossip, no matter how simple or fantastical, always contained a glimmer of truth. A shiver ran through him and he stroked his forearms uncomfortably. The hair on them was standing up again.

A glimmer of truth—the saying took on a whole new meaning here!

CHAPTER 9

May 21, 2011
Fortaleza, Brazil
5:00 pm

Now, that's interesting!" said Ondragon quietly to himself.

"Excuse me?" came Ritter's voice in his ear.

"Oh, I just took your advice and consulted the internet on Nikola Tesla. The guy had quite a bit going for him." *And that's an understatement*, he thought. How could he not have heard of this man before, when he had so many great inventions to his credit? It couldn't just be down to the lack of interest in physics that had emerged while he was at school.

"So, are you any smarter now?" joked Ritter.

You bet, he thought. The only thing that was not yet clear to him was the connection between Tesla's Edison medal and the Nazi airplane. He would probably have to dig deeper for that. That Nikola Tesla was a genius, however, was undisputed. In the eighty-seven years of his life, he had filed more than seven hundred patents, including such groundbreaking inventions as the three-phase motor, the neon tube light, the remote control, the radio, and even X-rays. But Tesla was also known as the cheated and nearly forgotten genius, and that might have been one of the reasons he was unfamiliar to so much of the general public today. Other scientists and inventors of his time had stolen Tesla's ideas, "developed" them, and taken credit for them. Like the Italian Guglielmo Marconi, who had declared that he had invented the radio in 1901, having based his work on Tesla's patents. It was not until shortly after Tesla's death that the patent for the radio, which had been falsely attributed to Marconi, was revoked by the United States Supreme Court and transferred to Tesla, recognizing him as the sole inventor of wireless telegraphy. As in so many cases, justice had unfortunately been done too late. This was symptomatic of Tesla's entire life, especially his later years. The Serbian inventor had been far ahead of his time and had come up with extraordinarily progressive ideas. This meant he had often been derided as a dreamer and a fantasist. He died in a Manhattan hotel room in 1943, poor and alone.

A tragic end for a man whose inventions were still bringing in billions of dollars today. The most interesting thing about the whole story of this electrical wizard, however, was that shortly after his death, the FBI had searched his private rooms and laboratory and confiscated all documents and equipment. His things were only returned years later. What had the FBI hoped to find in the home of the oddball scientist? And what had they actually found? Even today, a lot of people were asking this question: Tesla researchers, mystics, ufologists, conspiracy theorists, adherents of zero-point energy, even renowned physicists who wanted to use Tesla's work to disprove Einstein's theory of relativity. The genius spirit of Nikola Tesla still seemed to have a magical pull for people. And Ondragon had to admit that now that he had learned more about the man, he felt the same.

"How do you know so much about Tesla anyway?" he asked the agent.

"It's general knowledge!" That was all Ritter said.

Ondragon was silent. Could it be that this was about something completely different than an unsuccessful attempt by one or two Nazi officers to flee to South America? On impulse, he typed *Edison medal* and *Tesla* into the search field. Unfortunately, he did not get many hits. A few pictures of the medal, original photographs of the AIEE certificate that had been presented to Tesla in 1917, and a transcript of his speech at the award ceremony. Nikola Tesla had received the richly endowed award for his early work in the field of multiphase and high-frequency currents. Was that it? Was this whole business only about electricity? High-frequency current? *Probably not*, Ondragon thought, since that was not especially earth-shattering these days. But what was it, then?

"Calling it a day!" Charlize's voice suddenly said. "I'm coming out now. About time; it stinks like a sailor's grave in here!"

"Pinscher26, report to Position One immediately!" ordered Ritter.

"Yeah, yeah, don't stress. I'll let everyone else leave first, then you guys take a nice little drive around the corner and I'll come to you."

" Setter30 will be watching you!"

"I get it," Charlize replied with an ironic undertone. "Man, you guys are paranoid!"

"Surely I can ask for more discipline!" Ritter said, outraged.

"I'll shut up already. See you in a minute. For camouflage, I'll have one more cigarette first."

Ondragon packed his things and made his way unobtrusively to the street corner, which gave him a good view of Charlize and the van. The van had now moved to the next street, so that it could no longer be seen from the gate. Ondragon watched as his assistant stood on the sidewalk, lit a cigarette, and said goodbye to the members of the investigation team. They offered her a ride in their cab, and Charlize politely declined. After the three scientists had finally gone, she flicked the cigarette away and walked in the direction of the van. Steiner followed a few steps behind, as if by chance.

The Germans are really playing it safe, Ondragon thought. What were they so afraid of? That Charlize would pass on secret information to a third party on the short walk from the main entrance to the van? Ridiculous!

Charlize reached the van on the side street and climbed in through the sliding door. Over the radio, Ondragon heard her being questioned by Ritter. In the middle of it, the transmission cut out definitively and he could hear nothing. Ritter had deactivated the microphones; the operation was over for the day.

A little later, Charlize left the van and made a quick call on her cell phone. The van drove away, a cab arrived, and his assistant got in. Ondragon followed on foot, knowing where it was going. Outside Charlize's apartment building, he went to the corner by the garbage cans, took off his mic and cap, and changed from a beach bum back into a tourist. Then he entered the building and went up to the fifth floor.

"Nice view," he said as he stepped out onto the balcony of Charlize's room. Below him, the sea was glowing in the coppery light of the evening sun.

"Oh, man," Charlize sighed behind his back, coming out with two bottles of cold beer. "I'm going to have to take a shower first, to wash off this stench. It's really disgusting!"

Ondragon wrinkled his nose. "*Eau de corpse*—not exactly a turn-on."

Charlize nudged him in the side. "That's not funny. There are the remains of around forty bodies in there. They don't know for sure yet. There's not much left of them after two years in the ocean. Only the ones that were sunk in the mud are . . . brrrr!" Charlize shook herself. "The forensics people are doing DNA comparisons. Must be awful for the relatives to be left with only an arm or a leg to bury."

"At least it's something."

"That's true." She took a long swig from the bottle. "I've got something for you," she said, "that might tell us more about the *Doitsu-jin*'s paranoia. During the afternoon break, I asked Dr. Lima what he thought of the contents of the box. He said it was very revealing and, in connection with the type of aircraft, provided extremely exciting historical context that would be of interest to more than the Germans."

"Historical context?"

"Unfortunately, he couldn't tell me. He said although I had signed the confidentiality agreement, I didn't have the necessary security clearance yet."

"Great! Then we're just as much in the dark now as we were before."

"No, we know a little more. Because I know what type of aircraft it is."

"And?" Ondragon emptied his bottle.

"It's a Junkers 390."

"And what's that supposed to mean to me?"

"You can find that out while I'm in the shower. By the way, did you send the screenshots of the box to the email address I gave you?"

"Sure did."

"Good, then things are going well. By the way, what do you think about the camera suddenly cutting out?" asked Charlize. "Didn't that seem suspicious to you?"

"Yeah, I've been thinking about that too," Ondragon said. "Why did the thing stop working at the very moment I was looking at the entries in the logbook? It makes me think the BND is trying to prevent anyone from seeing any of it."

"Not someone. You! The *Doitsu-jin* want to prevent you from seeing it!"

Ondragon looked questioningly at Charlize.

"Well, they can rest easy with me, I don't understand German," she explained, "but it's different with you. They know that you have a full-blown book phobia, but apparently, they weren't quite so sure. It could have been that you were looking more closely anyway. That's why they turned off the transmission. I bet they did it as a precaution."

"While they went happily on checking it out from the van."

"They sure did."

"Charlize, you're right. The secrecy is suspicious. They don't trust me! But then why did they hire me if they don't think I have the integrity for it?" He looked at his assistant; secretly, he knew. "Do me a favor, Charlize. Before you delete the photos of the investigation from the computer in the lab for them, make copies for me, will you?"

"But we have the original."

Ondragon exhaled in amusement. "I wouldn't even pick that thing up with a pair of pliers! It's still a damn book, remember? Besides, don't think the BND will let us even skim through it for a second. You'll have to hand it over the second the operation is finished."

Charlize put a hand on his arm. "Don't worry, Boss, I'll get you the pictures. Now, you find out all about the Junkers 390. See you in a minute." She set her empty beer bottle on the table and disappeared into the bathroom. Ondragon got the netbook out of his backpack and went to turn it on, but then changed his mind. The computers would no doubt have been configured to track all the actions they performed, including web searches. Charlize's hunch was correct, he was sure of it. The camera failure was no accident. He could not trust Ritter and Steiner.

He logged on to a secure internet connection via his cell phone. There were several entries for JU 390, most of them in German. Now Ondragon understood why Charlize had assigned him the task. She had already checked it out but found she couldn't get anywhere without German. Clever Charlize.

When he was done reading, he pulled out his notepad and entered the facts he had gathered:

<u>Junkers 390—also known as "The Ghost Plane"</u>:
- intended by the Nazis to be a long-range reconnaissance and transport aircraft with a range of up to 8,000 km
- equipped with six propeller engines of 1,750 hp each, maximum speed 450 km/h loaded, 505 km/h empty
- crew 8–10
- max. takeoff weight allegedly 75.5 tons, incl. 8 tons payload (note: i.e. bomb or similar)
- length 32.60 m, span 50.32 m, height 6.89 m
- supposed to be mass produced from 1943, but only two prototypes were built, version I and version II. The Germans themselves set fire to one of them before the end of the war, to prevent it falling into the hands of the Americans. The second machine is thought to have been lost (could be the machine crashed before Brazil).
- <u>Rumor No. 1:</u> the plane flew to New York with a nuclear bomb (with a stop to refuel, South America would also be a possible destination, without a bomb on board, of course)

- <u>Rumor No. 2</u>: version II made a test flight to Japan in March 1945, but there is no confirmation of this, either from the Germans or the Japanese
- <u>Rumor No. 3</u>: a flight of high-ranking Nazi officers with a stopover in the former Spanish Sahara, allegedly with several scientists plus technical equipment on board, including a secret airborne device known as "The Bell." The project was under the direction of one SS-Obergruppenführer Dr. Hans Kammler (but this sits firmly in the category of conspiracy!)

Ondragon entered *The Bell* and *Hans Kammler* into Google and soon found himself deep in the brown swamp of Nazi mysticism. Several pages were devoted to praising the wonder weapons of the Third Reich. Nazi UFO technology, *Reichsflugscheibe*, an antigravity drive, and the *Repulsine* flying saucer. Ridiculous! Ondragon quickly concluded it was a false positive and closed his search. He didn't want to be anywhere near this kind of nonsense. And it could not be assumed the BND was on the trail of such humbug. No, there had to have been something of much greater importance on board the JU 390 than an alleged mysterious UFO.

Charlize came out of the bathroom in a bathrobe with a towel on her head and dropped exhaustedly into the chair across from him.

"So?" she asked, "What's the deal with the plane?"

Ondragon forced his eyes away from the smooth, tanned thighs that were exposed beneath the bathrobe, and quickly told her what he had found out.

Charlize chuckled when he got to the Nazi cliché about secret flying discs. "A wonderful story: SS commander escapes on a ghost plane with a mysterious flying device on board and the plane has been considered lost ever since. It sounds like a script for a Roland Emmerich movie. But who knows, there's always a grain of truth to rumors."

"Please! This clearly belongs in the realm of myths and legends!"

"And how many myths and legends have turned out to be true over the years? All I'll say is Voodoo zombies and the Wendigo! That was some nice alleged nonsense!"

Ondragon raised his hands in surrender. "Okay. I'll admit there are things we can't explain. But UFOs?" He made a dismissive gesture. "They really are bullshit."

"Maybe. I wouldn't be so dogmatic about that. What about the pilot in the flight log, by the way? Is there anything about him?"

Ondragon was grateful not to have to delve deeper into the topic of UFOs and entered the pilot's name into Google. But there were zero hits for *Colonel Karl Brenner* or *JU 390.* "So what do your scientists have to say about the guy?" he asked Charlize.

"Not much. Today was mostly about preserving evidence and taking samples. They'll be verifying the provenance of the text and the authenticity of the handwriting in the next few days."

"Then keep at it and try to shake down Dr. Lima, but do it discreetly."

"Will do. Let's see how much the dragon lady's prepared to tell us. She really put me through the wringer in the van before! Wanted to know everything, every detail of the investigation and what I had found out. The woman's a total control freak!"

"She's professional. And German!"

"You're defending her even though she screwed us with the camera?" Charlize stood up.

"I'm sure she had her reasons. She's probably just following orders. But if it makes you feel any better, I'm not going to take her out."

"How incredibly reassuring!" Charlize began pacing up and down the room. Her bare feet made a soft slapping noise on the tiled floor. Ondragon smiled.

"What are you grinning at, Boss?"

"Oh, nothing. I suggest we go get something to eat now. For the time being, I'll see if I know anyone who can tell us something about the pilot Karl Brenner, and you prepare yourself mentally for your mission tomorrow. Does that sound good to you?"

Charlize hesitated, and Ondragon gave her his irresistible ladykilling look until she began to grin.

"Don't do that, Boss. I'll do anything you say, but please, not that look!" She disappeared into the bathroom and appeared a few minutes later in a dark blue summer dress.

After dinner they parted and Ondragon took a cab to his hotel. He wanted to leave the car at its strategic spot for now. Arriving at his room, he slipped into his bathrobe and ordered himself another nightcap.

While sipping his mai tai in bed, he did a little more internet research on Nikola Tesla. There was a lot of material linking the inventor with

UFOs and secret drive technology. But whether it was hard science or just mystical crankery he could not judge. He closed the connection and dialed a number.

"Hey, Mr. O! It's a long time since I heard from you!" said a sonorous voice.

"Hello, Strangelove. Am I disturbing you?"

"No. You could never disturb me." The young man on the other end chortled. Dr. Strangelove was a brilliant chemist and Ondragon's go-to man for all assignments requiring knowledge of the periodic table.

"Strangelove, do you know anyone who knows about physics?"

"What kind of physics do you mean? There are quite a few disciplines: materials research, quantum physics . . ."

"Someone who's familiar with antigravity propulsion, zero-point energy, or Nazi flying discs."

"So a ufologist."

Ondragon narrowed his eyes at the expression. He hated the term UFO! He waited to see if Strangelove was merely joking but heard no laughter. On the contrary, the chemist seemed to be giving it serious thought.

"Hmm. I know a freak who runs an internet forum on Area 51. It's called 'alienbuster.' He might be able to help. What's it about, exactly? Extraterrestrial or terrestrial flying objects?"

"Extraterrestrial? How should I know?"

"Well, you'll have to come clean if you want him to help you. Don't worry, I won't think you're stupid; you've brought much wackier things to me in the last few years. Compared to those, UFOs are child's play!"

Ondragon struggled with himself. He didn't want to make a fuss, but his knowledge of physics was very limited and he needed someone to advise him. "Very well," he said, "but it's purely speculative so far!"

Now Stangelove chuckled. "That's how it is with UFOs."

Ondragon suppressed the urge to just hang up and took a deep breath. "I need information on how an inventor named Nikola Tesla might be connected to Nazi flying objects."

Strangelove grunted in amusement. "Well, that's truly off the wall. All right, I'll ask the guy. How should he get in touch with you?"

"Is he a straight-up guy?"

"Can a ufologist be straight-up?"

Ondragon saw the nonsense of his question. "Message me if he's willing to talk to me. Then I'll call him."

"Okay, Mr. O. Is there anything else I can do for you? I've got a brand-new invention on the go. It's still in the test phase though. I've developed a special liquid. You drip it into your eyes and then you can see better in the dark! Like a cat. Isn't that sensational?"

"Great . . . I mean, wow! Did you say 'test phase'? I don't think I need anything like that right now, thanks. But let me know when it's out of trials."

"You got it. Goodbye."

Shaking his head, Ondragon hung up. He could not believe that he had just initiated contact with a ufologist. All he was missing was someone who knew about Nazi Germany. His father, he thought, would now be able to provide him with information for sure. Retired Ambassador Siegfried Ondragon had always been good on German history, especially the inglorious chapter of the Nazi era. But he would never ask him for help. He would rip out his tongue and flush it down the toilet first. Ondragon looked at the clock. Unfortunately, it was too late to make another call. He would have to leave that until tomorrow morning. But he could still do a little research on the ufologist. Strangelove had given him the name of his website. He opened www.alienbuster.com and was immediately put off by the garish colors used on the forum, which proclaimed itself "the leading portal on Area 51." He clicked through discussion threads that would awaken deep distrust in any rational person, and wondered how anyone could believe in such nonsense. A little later, he closed the page and took one last look at the bulletin board.

Doberman12 had written: *First day of Operation Pandora satisfactory. Pinscher26 has infiltrated and has done job well according to specifications. Looking forward to more results tomorrow! @ Pinscher26: Remember the PHOTOS!"*

Oh, Charlize would like that, equivocal praise from the dragon lady! But Ondragon would have been surprised if she'd been any more fulsome. He had to admit he admired Ritter's unemotional manner and straightforwardness. She was self-confident and assertive, despite her young age. But in her job, it was never too early to set aside your conscience. Maybe he should get together with her after all, just the two of them. The thought was appealing, but Ondragon immediately dismissed it. Charlize would chop him into little pieces. Worse, she might quit!

And he certainly didn't want to provoke that. Charlize was invaluable to him. She was his fairy godmother, his last-second savior. He could do without the occasional amorous adventures. He returned his attention to the board and read the next entry.

Pinscher26: *Jigoku e ike!!!*

Go to hell! Well, well!

The praise, equivocal or otherwise, seemed to have gone unnoticed by Charlize. That meant he would have to pull out all the stops to keep her happy tomorrow, to prevent the Pinscher from going for the Doberman's throat.

He read the reply from Doberman12: *@ Pinscher26: I assume that your answer was not meant kindly. But don't worry, I don't feel offended. On the contrary, it is quite mutual. Nevertheless, I suggest that we treat this operation with the seriousness it deserves and afterward insult each other to our hearts' content. Good night!*

There could have been no drier way to respond. Ondragon turned off the cell phone and put it on the nightstand. Then he turned out the light.

A little later, he flicked the light back on. He couldn't sleep. All the neurons in his brain were tingling, which was an unmistakable sign that he was dealing with a particularly complicated puzzle here. A top-drawer one! Ondragon looked at the time and jumped out of bed. He would capitalize on the fact that his *centrifuge* was running at full speed. Quickly, he grabbed his notepad and went back to his internet research again. It was actually Charlize's job, but in this assignment everything was different. They had switched roles. Charlize would need her sleep for the operation, and he would take care of the time-consuming search for information.

First, he turned his attention to the only alleged passenger on the Junkers 390: SS-Obergruppenführer Dr. Hans Kammler. Ondragon found some details about him on the net. A German engineer and architect, under the Nazi regime Kammler had quickly risen to the position of Head of the Department for Building and Works, which sounded harmless, but it was under this title that Kammler had committed his worst war crimes. For example, he had supervised the construction of all extermination camps, where he had the gas chambers and crematoria enhanced, since a capacity of 2,650 corpses per day did not seem sufficient to him.

There it is again, Ondragon thought, *that German precision!* One part of him began to feel ashamed; the other, however, remained cold.

But General Hans Kammler was not only responsible for the atrocities in the concentration camps, he also oversaw the construction of underground production facilities for jet aircraft, where tens of thousands of forced laborers lost their lives. His position meant Kammler knew all about the secret projects in which the Reich's best scientists were researching Hitler's "wonder weapons," and he had access to the factory tunnels at all times. This made the magnificent young apotheosis of a Nazi a prime candidate for an escape attempt with secret technology on board, Ondragon realized. One of the underground facilities had been in Silesia, less than 200 kilometers from Prague, where Kammler had been residing at the end of the war. The place was called Ludwigsdorf and had housed a secret research facility. A project known as "The Bell."

Outright nonsense? Or Nazi propaganda kept alive by hard-core devotees of these Nazi myths? The object had, as the name suggested, been a bell-shaped missile that was miraculously able to hover. Two counter-rotating cylinders were said to have created a kind of magnetic propulsion that caused the device to lift effortlessly off the ground. Ondragon found other buzzwords associated with it: antigravity drive, levitation by torsion fields, vortex mechanics, and repulsion forces, all areas of physics he knew absolutely nothing about. It was now urgent that he talk to Strangelove's acquaintance, the ufologist.

But back to Dr. Hans Kammler. It would have been entirely possible for the general to have gotten to Ludwigsdorf from Prague, where the Junkers was standing by with its cargo. Although Kammler's aide-de-camp and his driver claimed the general had committed suicide by swallowing a cyanide capsule in a forest near Prague, his body was never found. A deliberate feint by Kammler to distract attention from his escape?

Ondragon looked up from his notes, thinking. If there was anything at all to this, he would argue for this version, because it fit with the greatest number of the pieces. Moreover, the fact that the US military had searched all over the world for Kammler after the war ended suggested he had survived and possibly escaped. On the other hand, in 1948 the Berlin-Charlottenburg District Court, at the instigation of his widow, had deemed him to have died on May 9, 1945, thus definitively closing the matter.

Ondragon put his notepad aside and picked up the iPhone. He would leave the Kammler piece of the puzzle for today, as there would be plenty of opportunities to talk to the ufologist about it later.

The next corner piece was the FBI. According to the information on the net, the FBI had sequestered all of Tesla's documents and equipment after his death in 1943. If that was true, there had to be a report about it. After all, the Bureau was also an office, and it was at least as conscientious about archiving its case files as the BND.

Ondragon emailed George Hurley, his friend at the FBI. Even though he had a healthy distrust of this quintessentially American organization, he appreciated having someone there who could provide him with information from time to time. Why did the agent do it? Well, Ondragon had known him since he was a student at Harvard and had helped him out of a very precarious situation back then. To this day, George knew he was indebted to Ondragon. And besides, he was actually kind of an old pal, and Ondragon did not have many of those—there was, of course, a reason for that. Friends and family members only made a man in his profession vulnerable to blackmail. So he largely avoided any emotional dependencies on other people. He allowed himself only a few limited exceptions. Charlize was one. Ondragon didn't know what he would do if anyone ever tried to harm her.

This is bad, he rebuked himself. *Very bad! You need to take care to get out of it at the right moment, otherwise it will end badly for you.*

It will anyway, teased a spiteful little voice in his head. *Someone like you will never get a happy ending.*

True again. Unconcerned, he shrugged his shoulders and sent the email to George. Hopefully he would get an answer soon.

CHAPTER 10

July 25, 1899
Colorado Springs
afternoon

Philemon looked up from his maintenance work on the condensers, sweating. Outside, the blazing sun shone down onto the wooden building, making the air inside unbearably close. He would have liked to open the large barn doors on the west side to let in a breath of fresh air, but the dark laboratory remained sealed off from the glare of the outside world. Dr. Tesla did not like prying eyes. Just recently, Mr. Löwenstein had told him, the doctor had had the small windows nailed shut because local children had been peeking in and playing all kinds of pranks on the researchers. Czito had finally chased them away with the warning that if they showed their faces here again, they would get a good beating! *Well, that certainly hadn't helped us get onto better terms with the residents of Colorado Springs*, thought Philemon, who was overhearing more and more malicious talk about the doctor and his henchmen in the eateries and on the streets. Word had now spread that he was working for Dr. Tesla, and the residents were much more distant than before.

He wiped the sweat from his brow and looked over at Mr. Löwenstein, who was bending over next to the oil-filled capacitor boxes, polishing the wires with steel wool. He hardly seemed to notice the heat and the buzzing flies; there was a pensive smile on his face. He was the oldest in this small, strange collection of scientists. Philemon estimated him to be about fifty. A down-to-earth German with blond hair, enormous side whiskers, and Teutonic precision, he was sometimes downright talkative and thus the exact opposite of the small and grumpy Mr. Czito. Fritz Löwenstein had a brilliant analytical ability and, like Dr. Tesla, liked to pore over his notes. But he did not feel the simple task of cleaning the electrodes was beneath him. Philemon got the impression the German engineer regarded all manual work as a salutary counterbalance to his intellectual activities. Exercise and physical training were beneficial for both body and mind, claimed Löwenstein, who was an admirer of Jahn, the German father of gymnastics. "Fresh, pious, cheerful, free!" That was his motto, and he quoted it at least once a day.

Dr. Tesla, however, was quite different; he was invariably of ethereal appearance, fed solely by the energy of his creative spirit, his extraordinary ideas and visions. Tireless and hard on himself in equal measure, he was someone who seemed to float above things. If Tesla represented subtlety and detachment from worldly needs, Fritz Löwenstein epitomized the robust and solid core of the laboratory—the internal power that held everything together. Only the chubby Czito was difficult to classify. He was best described as the laboratory's benevolent soul. Like an old tomcat, he seemed to sense it in his whiskers whenever a problem was brewing, and showed up even before he was called for. He buzzed eagerly around the equipment, fixing any malfunctions with the grandeur of a fat bumblebee, all the while humming Serbian ditties to himself. But when he had nothing to do, he turned back into the lurking cat and melted motionlessly into the background. All you could see was his broad grin floating in the shadows like a crescent moon with a gap in its teeth. Yes, Mr. Czito was the Serbian version of the Cheshire Cat from *Alice's Adventures in Wonderland.*

Philemon turned his head toward the mechanic, of whom not much was visible, though he could be heard quite clearly. The Serb was scrubbing the coils inside the large metal fence, panting like a locomotive.

Dr. Tesla, meanwhile, was crouched in his small chamber, poring over his designs.

"Is the doctor in there day *and* night?" asked Philemon in wonder.

Löwenstein nodded without leaving off his work.

"And when will he come out?"

The German engineer raised his head. "Probably when he has solved his problem. And that can take time. After all, we are proposing to do great things. Things that haven't been done before. And that takes a lot of brain power." He tapped his forehead with an oily finger and grinned from one bushy chop to the other.

"And what exactly will they be, these great things? Wireless telegraphy, perhaps? I mean, do you think it's possible he will actually succeed?"

"Are you having doubts, Phil?"

Philemon felt caught out. Yes, he had doubts and yes, he was afraid. In addition, he found it unbearable that he still did not know which experiments Dr. Tesla was working on here and whether they really were harmless. Nevertheless, all this was overlaid by the secret hope of being able to be part of something truly great. Something that might make history.

"No, I have no doubts!" lied Philemon without looking at Löwenstein.

"That's good, young man. Very good, because we are the doctor's chosen ones, his helping hands." The German straightened up and put a hand on his apron-clad chest. "We see to it that all the apparatus in the laboratory is always in good working order and is ready for use when it is needed. That may seem simple to you, but it is a thoroughly honorable task."

"And why are we here on the prairie and not in Dr. Tesla's laboratory in New York? Wouldn't the city offer a much more suitable environment for the experiments?" The question had been burning in Philemon's mind for some time and he was glad to finally be able to ask it.

"There are several good reasons for this," Löwenstein replied. "For one thing—and this is not entirely irrelevant—Dr. Tesla gets all the electricity we need from the city's power plant, for free. Via the transmission towers, moreover, which are the only means of transmission out here on the prairie. And secondly, the air here on the high plateau is particularly rich in static energy. Colorado Springs is known for its violent thunderstorms and huge lightning discharges. Dr. Tesla needs them to collect his insights. That would not be possible in New York." Löwenstein paused in his work and his gaze slid around the lab. But there was no sign of Tesla, and Czito, still out of sight, was humming his ditties to himself. Then Löwenstein leaned forward, his mouth almost touching Philemon's cheek.

"There's another reason though," he whispered.

Philemon, who had just been musing on why on earth the Lord of Lightning needed more lightning, looked at the engineer in surprise.

"I'll tell you, Phil," said Löwenstein, "but first you have to swear you won't tell anyone. Especially not here in Colorado Springs. People in this town can't handle this kind of thing."

Philemon wondered at the German's sudden confidences, but he raised his hand and said, "I swear!"

Löwenstein's gray eyes rested on him for a while, looking like two cool mountain lakes. Then he lowered his gaze and began speaking in hushed tones. "The real reason for building the laboratory here in this godforsaken area is that Dr. Tesla is afraid someone might sabotage his research."

"Sabotage? Why?"

"You are aware that the doctor's first lab in New York was completely burned out four years ago."

"Of course, the newspapers were full of reports at the time. And you now believe it was sabotage? That would be outrageous!"

"It's just one of many guesses, because no one was in the lab when the fire began. No one saw anything. Besides, we always check all the apparatus and experiment setups before we leave the premises. Even today, I am absolutely certain we didn't miss anything. I myself did the last tour of the lab before turning out the lights. Everything was turned off, no electricity was flowing. That's why I firmly believe, as does the doctor, that someone set the fire deliberately."

"But who, in God's name?"

Löwenstein shrugged. "We'd like to know that too. Whoever it was managed to set Dr. Tesla back years. Valuable designs for unique machines and an entire archive of records were destroyed in the fire. It took a heavy toll on the doctor. As he stood in front of the ruins of his laboratory, he cried. And he cried for mankind, which has been cheated of progress."

Philemon listened with concern. How could there be people who so demonized Dr. Tesla's work that they wanted to destroy it? Did they not see what great miracles this man performed and the generous selflessness with which he bestowed his gifts upon mankind? It was sad, truly sad.

"Maybe it was Mr. Edison or one of his people," Löwenstein continued. "Tesla's accomplishments have always been a thorn in his side. But maybe I do good Thomas an injustice and there is a much higher power behind it. We don't know, unfortunately, and we may never know."

Philemon pressed his lips together. The story had shaken him and made the work out here in the wooden house in the middle of the prairie suddenly appear in a completely different light. The seclusion was intentional, as was the secrecy surrounding the experiments. Gradually, he began to understand.

Meanwhile, Löwenstein had turned his attention back to the capacitor repairs and swathed himself in an uncharacteristic silence. Philemon tried to follow the German's lead, but his attention could no longer focus on such trivial matters as the capacitor. Löwenstein's words reverberated through his head like an ominous echo.

Sabotage . . .

Maybe there is a much higher power behind it . . .

CHAPTER 11

May 22, 2011
Fortaleza, Brazil
7:00 am

Ondragon woke early. He looked at his watch and mentally calculated the time in Germany. Eleven o'clock in the morning. Excellent. He dialed the number and while it rang, tried to recall his best High German.

"Ludewig!"

"Paul here. Good morning, Günther."

"Ah, Paul, to what do I owe the honor? Are you finally showing your face in Hamburg?"

"Not for now, I'm afraid. My assignments . . . you know."

"Yes, yes. But it's still a shame."

"Günther, once again I have a request." Ondragon cleared his throat and was actually somewhat embarrassed that he was constantly having to ask his old friend for help without giving anything in return. He would have to do something about that, he realized. Life was a cycle, after all. Give and take. And it was only those recognizing that fact who were the people not completely alone on the planet.

"Want to know more about Voodoo?" joked Ludewig. "I heard you had a lot of fun in New Orleans!"

"Who told you that?" Ondragon asked sullenly. Günther Ludewig might be a professor at the University of Hamburg, and quite elderly, but he seemed to have eyes and ears all around the globe.

"Oh, my colleague from Atlanta, the one who put you in contact with Madame Tombeau, told me he got in touch with the lady on a matter of science and she told him all about you."

"Hopefully only the good things."

Ludewig laughed. "I don't know what a management consultant like you has to do with zombies, but word is you've become quite good with them."

Good with them? What was that supposed to mean? Ondragon bit his lip grimly. The Voodoo priestess from New Orleans had been a real challenge to him. During his last mysterious case, she had continually tried to convince him of the truth of her gruesome beliefs. Still, he had to admit that they had worked well together, and he would not hesitate to collaborate with her again. Even if he hoped not to have anything more to do with Voodoo any time soon.

"Well, I'm reassured to hear I have recommended myself in such an exemplary manner," he said. "But now to my request. Fortunately, it has nothing to do with archaic cults. It's about the background to something more modern."

"Out with it, then. Let's see if I can help."

Ondragon explained the context to the old anthropologist, mentioning General Kammler, Tesla's Edison medal, and the Junkers 390. He left out the flying saucers; after all, he didn't want to embarrass himself.

When he had finished, Ludewig gave a loud sigh. "That's not my field at all. Although I've been involved in many issues in the course of my life and have touched on the research of others, I really don't have anything to do with the modern era. I'm interested in older matters, you know? Anything that happened over two hundred years ago, none of this new-fangled stuff. Industrial Revolution, hardly. The World Wars, bah! Nazis, even worse! No, no, my boy, it's not for me. I'm sorry."

"Do you happen to have a colleague who might know about it?"

"There are a lot of professors here at the university whose field is specifically National Socialism, of course. There still will be a hundred years hence, I fear. We Germans have got ourselves into quite a mess there! But as to whether anyone can help with your question, I don't know. I'll make inquiries."

"Thanks, Günther. Just let me know if you turn anything up. If not, that's fine too. I can always call my old man."

"Your father?"

Only now did Ondragon realize that he had unintentionally sounded sarcastic. "Sorry. I don't get along with my father very well."

"Isn't he a retired ambassador?"

"He's the one."

"Oh, then he must be an old throwback like me." Ludewig laughed dryly, as if he knew all about the stubborn foibles of old men.

"A throwback?!" retorted Ondragon, unintentionally vehement. "My father is a complete dinosaur with dusty bones and outdated principles! A Neanderthal! An emotional cripple! Oh, forget it! Never mind. Let's change the subject." He stroked his hair absentmindedly. Whenever he talked about his father, he lost his cool somehow. Siegfried Ondragon was a blind spot on his retina; something he didn't want to look at.

"You can talk to me about it anytime you want, my friend."

"I appreciate that, Günther," he replied wearily. He knew the offer was serious. "But it'd take more than a day to cover that quagmire."

"Then maybe some other time. I'll see about finding someone who knows something about your subject, okay?"

"Okay."

"So long, and take care of yourself, Paul."

"I will, thank you." Ondragon hung up and sat dejectedly on the edge of the bed for a time. Why had he lost control just then? Why did Ludewig need to be concerned with the problems he had with his father? Private matters should remain private. He could not let himself believe anyone could actually help him. The only person who could do that was himself. But he didn't want to think about that now.

But one day you will have to deal with it! If only for Per Gustav's sake, or for your mother's. The little voice in his ear was right. Since his brother's death in the library, the relationship between him and his old man had steadily cooled, and had reached absolute zero by the time Ondragon turned eighteen. His family had been living in Japan at the time, the ambassador's sixth posting since little Paul Eckbert had come into the world in Stockholm in 1967. He had mixed memories of Japan. Some were good, like those of the few friends he still had in Tokyo and of his first encounter with martial arts. He smiled at the thought of his *kendo sensei* back then and the countless hard hours of training in the dojo. He had gotten many bruises there, and learned for the first time in his life what it meant to fight. Not only physically, but also mentally. In Japan, he had succeeded in breaking away from the oppressive omnipotence of his father, from the all-controlling superman. And for the first time in his life, he had dared to contradict him.

That was a less pleasant memory. Not the contradicting, which had been a phenomenal feeling, no, everything that followed. When your father withdrew his affection and acted as if you were dead to him. Dead like your twin brother! And all because Ondragon had been tired of living as his father wished him to. He had wanted to go to America to study. But his father had destined him for a university in Germany. He had wanted him to get to know the country of his ancestors. But Ondragon had little desire to do that; he had hardly any connection with Germany. Instead, he had been offered a promising athletic scholarship to Harvard. All he had to do was pass the entrance exam. But his father had forbidden him to go to the United States. Ondragon remembered the day clearly. That had been the moment when his heart had finally frozen over. Without a trace of emotion, he had packed his things and boarded the plane to America. He had never returned to his family. He still felt guilty from time to time for having left his mother with that insensitive bastard, but what could he have done about him, exactly? Nothing! Nevertheless, that event marked his first victory over the great and inimitable Siegfried! He had discovered his father's Achilles' heel and thrust his lance into it!

Ah, crap!

Ondragon rose, pushing away his surging emotions with all his might. To hell with Siegfried the dragon slayer! To hell with all the abilities he might have inherited from this man.

Back to the present!

He needed to focus all his concentration on today's task, on the job he had to do. And maybe in the end he would be granted a glimpse into this mysterious file . . . a glimpse into his past.

CHAPTER 12

July 25, 1899
Colorado Springs
7:00 pm

In the evening, Philemon made his way to the hotel, exhausted. Löwenstein's cautionary words had gradually quieted in his head and were finally drowned out by the growling of his stomach. Philemon painted himself an appetizing picture of what he would have for dinner, and was marching briskly along Pikes Peak Avenue when he was suddenly accosted from the side.

"So, not been struck by lightning yet?" It sounded more like a joke than a serious question.

Philemon turned his head and recognized the blond guy from Benson's. He was wearing a black derby hat and a brown tweed suit that was slightly worn at the elbows, but otherwise fit impeccably. Anyway, the guy seemed much better groomed than when they had first met. Apparently, he was not a simple laborer, as Philemon had hastily assumed. What he had not been mistaken about, however, was the musty sweet smell that still emanated from him.

"No, sir," he replied, stopping, "I've managed to avoid the lightning thus far. And rest assured, our experiments are perfectly safe. It all seems more dangerous than it really is."

"Harmless . . . well, if you say so." The blond man grinned. "Allow me to introduce myself. Joe Herkimer. But feel free to call me Joe." He held out a hand, which Philemon shook as he introduced himself.

"Ah, you're an electrical engineer, aren't you?"

"How do you know?"

"News travels fast around here." Herkimer's grin widened. "Also, that you're living at the Alta Vista Hotel like Dr. Tesla and the other two assistants. Nothing stays secret for long in this hole, you know. There are little birds everywhere, whistling it loudly from the rooftops."

"True enough!" confirmed Philemon. "And what do you do, if you don't mind me asking? I mean, when you're not sitting down to lunch at Benson's?"

The man gave a contagious laugh. "You know, I'm a telegraph operator for the Denver and Rio Grande Railroad Company. So if you ever have an urgent message and the public telegraph office at the post office is busy, feel free to come find me at the depot. I'll take care of it. But now tell me, how are you doing out there in the wasteland? Must be pretty boring working in such seclusion."

Since Philemon had been sworn to absolute silence by Dr. Tesla, he answered as innocuously as he could. "The work is indeed quite tedious, but also exceedingly interesting. I still have a great deal to learn from the doctor."

"From that crazy Dr. Frankenstein with his lightning machines?"

"Dr. Tesla is no Frankenstein; he is an honorable gentleman! A man of the world and a respected engineer. You should give him and his work more respect. If it were not for him, your beautiful Colorado Springs here would be languishing in the Dark Ages! Dr. Tesla brought us electricity, he illuminated the world! It is thanks to him that our homes and streets are lit at night and that the machines in the factories can run. America's economy is thriving, and it's all thanks to him! The doctor is a benefactor, a great humanitarian. You are fortunate he has chosen your little town in which to conduct his extraordinary research!"

"But people here don't see it that way. Just ask around, Phil. Everyone will tell you what they think of your alleged benefactor! He drives away the spa guests with his rumblings and frightens the residents."

"Are you talking about that goatherd's moronic drivel? It's nothing but nonsense!" Philemon had been in Colorado Springs for barely more than a week and had already heard the horror story of the goatherd Benjamin Foley several times. Different variants of it, mark you, which made him doubt the truth of the story.

"Old Ben may be a good-for-nothing sluggard," Herkimer conceded, "but he's not feeble-minded. Go to him, Mr. Ailey, and hear his story. And then reconsider what you think you know about Dr. Tesla. Ben has seen with his own eyes what the doctor gets up to, out there on the prairie at night while everyone else is asleep. He can testify that something inexplicable went on that night. Haven't you wondered what happened to your predecessor?"

"Mr. Myers was called away on urgent business. That's all. The rest is tall tales told by a senile hillbilly!"

"Then why did the good Mr. Myers leave his luggage behind?"

Philemon was puzzled. Was Herkimer talking about the large suitcase that had been in his room when he arrived? The bellboy said that the luggage had come from his predecessor. "As far as I am aware, Mr. Myers intended his luggage to be forwarded to him, presumably because it was too bulky for a quick journey by train. That's quite a commonplace practice, by the way. So it may be that the suitcase sat around the hotel for a day or two before it was sent on the next train."

"But the suitcase has not been sent, it is still here," Herkimer said, regarding him seriously.

"It's still here . . ." Philemon repeated, because he couldn't think of anything better to say. But how did this man know what was going on with the suitcase anyway? He became more suspicious. Sure, the guy had claimed to work as a telegrapher for the railroad company, so of course he would hear over the wires what was being dispatched, but what if he was lying? Philemon stayed alert. "Maybe there were no important things in the suitcase and there was no hurry to send it to him," he replied calmly.

"But the thing is in a storage room upstairs in the east wing of the hotel. Do you think it's customary to store luggage there when it's supposed to be sent on? There have already been three eastbound trains that could have taken the suitcase. But there are no instructions whatsoever concerning it."

The guy and his conspiracy theories were starting to get on Philemon's nerves. He replied, with a hint of irony, "I don't know how these things are handled in Colorado Springs. Frankly, I don't care. I mind my own business, and you'd do well to do the same, Mr. Herkimer. Now, if you don't mind, I'd like to go back to my hotel."

"Have it your way, Phil. I did not intend to affront you in any way. I merely wanted to let you know that sometimes things may not be as they seem. Think about it."

Philemon swallowed another remark. There was no point in arguing with this guy. He didn't have any notion of the magnificence of Nikola Tesla and his marvelous research. "Goodbye, Mr. Herkimer," Philemon said politely, tapping his hat. "I wish you a pleasant evening."

"Believe me, Mr. Ailey, you will change your mind about Dr. Tesla!"

"I hardly think so," Philemon returned.

"Well, so be it. But remember, if you run into any problems, don't lose heart, ask Herkimer!"

Philemon snorted contemptuously as he continued on his way, staring at the road ahead. A little later, he reached the hotel, sweatier than he would have liked because of his rapid pace. In addition to reflecting on Löwenstein's words, he was now also thinking about that confounded suitcase. It was too much of an inconsistency, and Philemon feared it would prey on his mind. Of course, it might be that the suitcase in the storeroom did not belong to Mr. Myers at all, and it was all just a mix-up. Then again, maybe it wasn't. A glance at the name tag would easily resolve the matter. Philemon decided to sneak up to the attic one night and have a look. But now he urgently needed something to eat.

He climbed the stairs to his room, where he quickly attended to his toilet and changed his shirt so as to present a suitably respectable appearance in the hotel's dining room. The Alta Vista accorded the highest importance to correct attire and decorum.

His stomach almost roaring, Philemon entered the salon, which had floor-to-ceiling damask curtains, chandeliers, and ornate furnishings in the Queen Anne style. The furniture conveyed a sense of dignified hospitality, but Philemon preferred a simpler style.

He let the maître d'hôtel escort him, with a professional smile, to his table and took a seat on the chair he pulled out. His back upright, Philemon pushed himself closer to the table, which was adorned with a classic place setting of meticulously aligned silverware, precious lead crystal glasses, and a candelabrum. He unfolded the starched napkin while the maître d' extolled the dishes of the day with nasal affectation. Philemon chose bouillon with vegetables as an appetizer, steamed trout as his entrée, and a carafe of cool mountain spring water—the least expensive items on the menu. Philemon had in fact intended to dine in the cheap eateries in the town in order to save some of his not exactly lavish salary, but he quickly had to revise his plans once his status as assistant to the disagreeable Dr. Tesla had become known. Both Löwenstein and Czito also ate in the hotel for the same reason.

The *commis de rang* brought the carafe of water and poured him a glass. After he left, Philemon looked around surreptitiously and gave an involuntary shudder at the sight of the guests dressed to the nines at the other tables. Overweight matrons in their flowing gowns sat next to pale gentlemen with waxed mustaches and tense jaws. Spa guests. A few years ago, Philemon had spent several months in Davos, Switzerland, and the people there had looked exactly like this. Disgust welled up in him.

Although his parents belonged to the comfortable New York middle class and had schooled him throughout his life in the etiquette that was appropriate to his social rank, he always felt out of place in such establishments. They were the antithesis of his spartan workplace out on the dusty prairie. Philemon loved the simplicity and sober functionality of the laboratory, which spurred him on to creativity he could not have imagined. And on this point he agreed with his mentor: Great ideas could only be born out of loneliness and hardship.

As Philemon was being served his broth, he saw Löwenstein and Czito enter the salon. He beckoned to them and they came over to his table. Once they were seated and had ordered one of that day's menus from the maître d, a cheerful, after-work mood spread through the group. Czito drank freshly prepared lemonade and Löwenstein allowed himself a large gulp of cola.

"Ah, how invigorating! A Coca-Cola at eight keeps you working until eleven! The slogan is actually true!" he joked, thirstily downing the rest of the drink. "I wish we had one of those new Linde refrigerators out in the lab; then we could store the cola right there and drink it cold. I'm afraid this brew is undrinkable when warm." He ordered a second bottle as the entrées arrived. They ate hungrily, for meals were scant in the lab. Nothing could be allowed to distract them from their work, and sometimes all they had were occasional dry rusks and water. It occurred briefly to Philemon that an astonishing person such as the doctor probably lived solely on the energy he extracted from the ether. An exhilarating notion.

"What are you laughing at, Phil?" asked Löwenstein.

"Oh, I just wonder what the doctor lives on. He's been in his chamber for three days, and I haven't seen him eat or drink."

"He's very frugal. But when he eats, he does so in an extremely ritualized setting. He has some unusual habits in that regard, if I may put it that way."

Philemon was curious. He dabbed his mouth and mustache with the napkin and leaned back. "What kind of habits?"

Löwenstein looked at Czito, who nodded imperceptibly. So that was how it was; the Serb called the shots here, albeit silently.

"You must have noticed that the doctor always wears gloves and never shakes hands when he greets people. This is because he is afraid of germs that could be transmitted by contact alone. His constitution is very fragile; although he hardly needs any sleep and can go for days without eating, he has to be careful not to get sick. As a young person he was often ill. He once survived cholera, you know, and he wants to avoid any further serious illness at all costs, since it would weaken him and set his work way back. So not only does he always have a new tablecloth, it is also his habit to polish each piece of cutlery he intends to use with his own hands. To do this, he needs one napkin per course. So if he eats soup, a main course, and a dessert, he needs three spotlessly clean napkins as well as new cutlery. He does the same with the glasses and the china. And he will not have any fruit on the table, because he considers it unclean. His food must always be weighed to the gram. If it is not, he can tell immediately with a single glance and sends the dish back. He even claims to have been at the same body weight for years. Exactly one hundred and forty-one pounds! Isn't that astonishing?"

"Yes, it is," Philemon replied. "Is he also in the habit of dining here at the hotel?"

Löwenstein nodded and jerked his head toward a table that was surrounded by screens. "When he eats, he eats there, isolated from all the other guests."

"But if he's so afraid of germs and disease, why does he not dine in his room?"

Löwenstein shrugged his shoulders. "I don't know. It's an eccentricity of his. Maybe he doesn't want to be completely out of contact with people, and this is his way of compromising. But do you notice anything else about his table?"

Philemon looked over at the screens. "No," he said.

Löwenstein smiled mildly. "There are three screens, and three candlesticks are on the table. Three chairs are around it. The number of napkins must always be divisible by three. And one hundred and forty-one divided by three equals, well? Forty-seven, that's right! A prime number."

"You mean the doctor is obsessed with numbers?"

"With the number three, to be precise," Löwenstein said. "And with prime numbers. But obsessed would be far too discourteous a word for a man of such uniqueness, whose mind is so many spheres above ours that it would take us centuries to access even a fraction of the power of his visions. That is why I am always moderate in the way I speak about him. You should do the same, Phil."

A kindly rebuke, Philemon thought, looking at Löwenstein. The German was right, of course. Different standards applied to Dr. Tesla. And words were far too trivial to describe what he actually was. Terms had yet to be invented that would do justice to the man. "The doctor is certainly extraordinary," he said reverently. "And I consider myself fortunate to be working for him."

"You are at that, my friend. Ah, there he is! He's left his lab!"

Philemon followed Löwenstein's gaze and saw the tall figure of the doctor standing at the salon entrance. The other guests also turned, regarding the late arrival with undisguised curiosity. His hands behind his back, Dr. Tesla waited to be escorted to his table. His face appeared pale, the skin over his cheekbones as translucent as parchment. He looked as if he worked and lived in a cave—a creature who was at home in the twilight.

Dr. Tesla nodded politely to his assistants as the maître d' led him to his table. He took a seat behind the screens. Soon the only thing that was visible to the outside world through the fabric of the screens was his gaunt shadow, and all that could be heard was the quiet clinking of cutlery.

CHAPTER 13

May 22, 2011
Fortaleza, Brazil
3:02 pm

It was already afternoon and Ondragon was once again crouched at his observation post in the dilapidated building in the harbor. His laptop balanced on his knees, he was watching the feed from Charlize's glasses closely. He needed to memorize the route to the lab, the floor plan, and the security measures on the premises to be able to find his way there blind later in the mission. Ritter and Steiner had managed to reestablish the camera connection with the help of an intermediary amplifier that Charlize had taped inconspicuously under a table in the lab.

It's possible the previous day's failure had actually been due to interference, Ondragon thought. Whatever the reason, at least he now had a visual again. As he watched, he could hear Ritter's voice relentlessly passing on instructions to Charlize. The BND agent had seemed oddly nervous that morning, insisting that they needed to conclude the operation quickly. She would really have preferred, Ondragon believed, to have taken the box away last night. He saw Charlize take another discreet look around the entire lab, to enable him to see everything.

"All right, I got it," he whispered into the mic. "Thanks."

Charlize made a hand signal to show that she had understood. Then, wearing lab gloves, she set to work at the microscope on a task assigned to her by Dr. Lima. One by one, she placed glass slides on the microscope stage and wrote something down on a clipboard. Meanwhile, in the background, the other scientists were talking animatedly. Unfortunately, Charlize's mic was too far away for Ondragon to hear much.

"What are they chattering about?" he asked quietly.

Since Charlize could not answer, she wrote something on a small piece of paper and held it in front of the camera. *They're checking the handwriting from the logbook. There are probably two different hands.*

"So what's their conclusion?" Ondragon asked.

"Silence on the channel, please! The tape is running!" Ritter cut in sharply.

Charlize wrote something and held it up.

FUCK U!

"Pinscher26! I ask you to control yourself for just one more day! Is that too much? After that, you can take your charming butt back to your secretary's chair if that's what you prefer!"

Ondragon rolled his eyes. Charlize was overdoing it a bit with the orneriness. "Please do what the Doberman says, will you?"

Tell the Onibaba to stop bossing me around like a serf or I'm out of here, Charlize wrote angrily.

"Please, do it for me," Ondragon whispered, hoping she would listen.

Charlize hesitated. He could feel her wrestling with her pride.

All right, she wrote in reply, and crumpled the piece of paper. Then the picture filled with slides and clipboards again. The murmuring voices in the background continued their debate. Suddenly, there was a crackle on the wire and a second later Ondragon's cell phone rang into the silence.

"Damn, what is that?" asked Ritter.

"My phone, sorry," he apologized "I'm expecting an urgent call." He looked at the display. It was Strangelove. Ondragon got up, put his mic and earpiece aside, and walked to the other end of the room. Then he answered the call.

"My UFO colleague would be delighted to call you," Strangelove said without much preamble. "He thinks your request is extremely interesting and he has quite a bit to say about it!"

"Okay, then give me his number! What's the guy's name anyway?"

Strangelove dictated the name and number of the ufologist and bid him farewell with a jocular "Live long and prosper."

Such a geek!

Ondragon dialed the number. He was slightly displeased. He wasn't really ready to listen to the drivel of a UFO nut, but who else could he talk to about this? He had to bite the bullet.

"Yes?" came a voice after what seemed like an eternity of rings. It sounded squeaky, as if it was breaking.

"Hello, are you *Truthfinder*?" What a dorky name!

"Hey yo, that's me!" the guy replied proudly.

"Strangelove told you about me. I am Mr. O."

"Oh wow! You actually called! I was beginning to think you wouldn't dare!" Truthfinder gave a shrill laugh, his Mickey Mouse voice cracking. There was actually something wrong with this guy. And Ondragon didn't just mean his penchant for UFOs. He wasn't all there.

"Um, may I ask you a question first, Truthfinder?"

"Go for it!"

"How old are you?"

Truthfinder giggled. "Have a guess!"

"To be honest, you sound about fourteen!"

"Bingo!"

"What?" gasped Ondragon, aghast. "Are you kidding me?"

"Nope, why?"

Ondragon bared his teeth. How in the name of Seven of Nine's steely tits was a fourteen-year-old supposed to know about UFOs, let alone have a basic grasp of physics? What on earth had Strangelove been thinking, linking him up with this schoolboy? He went to hang up—the whole thing was getting too dumb for him—when Truthfinder said something that made him pause.

"Repeat that, please," said Ondragon. He wasn't sure he could believe his ears.

"I have a master's degree in elementary particle physics and a PhD in quantum mechanics. Right now, I'm doing research on zero-point energy and proving a connection between seventeenth-century ether theory and Einstein's theory of relativity. The two don't play nicely together, you see. And as far as that chemical tinkerer Strangelove is concerned, I know him from Stanford University's Highly Gifted Fellowship."

"Ah . . . yes. Um . . ." Ondragon was speechless, but soon managed to apologize.

"Yo, no worries, man," Truthfinder forgave him lightly. "You're not the first person to think I'm pulling their leg. As proof of my aptitude, I'll be happy to explain the basics of the Casimir effect on two conducting plates in a vacuum, which can be used to demonstrate zero-point energy experimentally, but so far, unfortunately, only indirectly, if you know what I mean."

"No, no, that won't be necessary. Thank you, I believe you. All right, let's forget my little faux pas of earlier and start over." Ondragon gradually regained his aplomb and quickly filed the misstep in a mental file he spontaneously named "Blunders the size of Lake Superior."

"Fine by me, whatever you like," agreed the mouse-voiced prodigy. "Hey yo, I'm Truthfinder and you're Mr. O. Nice to meet you. And so on, and so forth. Let's keep this short. You had a question: Can Nikola Tesla's research on wave technology be linked to Nazi flying objects? The answer is yes *and* no!"

"What am I supposed to make of that?" Ondragon was irritated.

"That's easy," replied Truthfinder matter-of-factly. "There are people who claim that in 1943, two of Hitler's spies came to New York and paid Tesla a visit. Sounds wacky, I know, but the aim of the spies was to steal the secret notes Tesla kept in a safe in his hotel room. After they left, Tesla was dead. You may know that Tesla was not immediately discovered after his demise; it took *three* days for the maid to find him!"

"No, I didn't know that," Ondragon replied.

"Tesla was a lonely man at that time and it's sad no one was with him at the end. Except for the two spies, if the rumor is to be believed. In any case, the doctor who was summoned certified that he died of natural causes, a heart attack. Well, Tesla was eighty-seven years old, so no one asked any questions. The cavalry only arrived several hours later. The FBI turned his entire hotel room upside down and confiscated everything they could get their hands on. But apparently, two things were missing: a small notebook and Tesla's Edison medal. This eventually led to the rumor that the Nazi spies had taken both objects back to Germany."

"A tall tale, if you ask me. Is there any proof of it?" At the mention of the medal, Ondragon's ears pricked up and his *centrifuge* went into "out-of-control chairoplane" mode.

"No proof, Mr. O. But there are dubious documents, reports of a German-American double agent, which imply there was indeed a Nazi mission to get their hands on Tesla's research. However, there are serious doubts as to the authenticity of the documents. Tesla had claimed in his last years to have come up with some very important inventions, including an extremely dangerous weapon. But he did not intend to use it to destroy the world: he wanted to create lasting peace among the nations. Tesla was a pacifist all his life, you know. So the Nazis may well have considered his research findings of vital importance to the war and—if you believe the double agent's report—taken action to get their hands on the technology."

"What kind of weapon was it?"

"A kind of death ray. In short, a ray gun with unimaginable destructive power. It could have been directed at any number of targets, from towers erected all over the world. Totally rad!"

"Ahem, yes. Were there flying saucers involved? I heard the Nazis were researching a flying object called The Bell."

Truthfinder exhaled in amusement. "The Bell is an old wives' tale. There's not a single piece of proof that it existed. I doubt there was any such research in Nazi Germany. It's post-National Socialist propaganda, or whatever you like to call it. It is true, however, that Tesla did groundbreaking research on radiation and wave technology. Only we still don't know how far he had progressed. Unfortunately, hardly anyone fully understands his work."

"Like with Einstein?"

"Yo, man! That's right. There are only a few guys in the world who can follow his theory of relativity."

"And you're one of them?" Ondragon joked.

Truthfinder fell silent for a moment. Then he said, "I do my best. But sometimes there are people who have a feeling for something that no one will ever understand. Nikola Tesla was just such a genius for me, exactly like Einstein. Which of them was the bigger noise, we will probably never know. Even I don't have the brains for that. But one thing is clear, Tesla was the spirit of modernity born too soon, a visionary. He even predicted the cell phone, in 1907! In his autobiography, he wrote, 'A small handy device with which in the future every person will be able to receive news, sounds, pictures and energy around the globe.' Isn't that cool? Imagine if Tesla were alive today instead of a hundred years ago. Where would his abilities have taken him with the help of modern technology? Where would he have taken *us*?"

Ondragon said nothing; he could not imagine.

"Look! It's too big for the human mind. But back to your question. We just talked about how Tesla's technology could have gotten into the hands of the Nazis. Now we come to the second version of the story, the reason I said no as well as yes at the beginning of our conversation. I personally find this story more believable; it says the maid notified Tesla's nephew before informing the doctor. The three people who hurried over after she told him opened the safe. According to the FBI report, they looked at the contents of the safe in the presence of three hotel employees and only removed a bundle of greeting cards for Tesla's seventy-fifth birthday and a few photographs, as mementos. They claimed to have left the notebook and the Edison medal in the safe, which they locked again. Only when the FBI returned Tesla's possessions to his nephew years later did he open the safe again. The notebook and medal were gone. Of course, the nephew accused the FBI of taking them, but the Bureau denied the accusation. They had returned everything in good order, they said. Most of Tesla's possessions are now in a museum in Belgrade, in a display that the nephew set up to honor his uncle. Where the notebook and the medal are, however, no one knows."

I *know where the medal is*, Ondragon thought. *Should I tell him?* He glanced at his cell phone display. He was still waiting for an answer from his FBI friend. The report of the seizure of Tesla's property interested him more than ever. But George Hurley was saying nothing. So should he bring in Truthfinder? Did he dare? Despite his fears, the boy wonder made a decent impression.

"Can I trust you?" he finally asked.

"To do what?"

"Not to post what I'm about to tell you on your forum, or tell anyone else about it?"

"You have my word, Mr. O. I swear by the Heisenberg uncertainty principle that I'll keep it to myself!"

What that counted for, Ondragon could only guess. It was a risk, but he decided to take it. "I've seen the Edison medal!" he said finally. "I know where it is."

"Rad, man! Really?" exclaimed Truthfinder excitedly. "So which of the two rumors is true?"

"The first one, I'm sorry to say. The one about the Nazi spies."

Silence followed. Then, "Oh, *shit!*"

"But I'll tell you something else, Truthfinder," Ondragon added. "The medal was found in an airplane, a 1943 Junkers 390. The plane crashed into the sea off the coast of Brazil, and parts of it were recovered recently."

There was still silence on the other end. Was Truthfinder shocked or was he just mentally processing the collapse of his favored theory in which the FBI played the bogeyman?

"What do you say to that?" urged Ondragon. The conversation had been going on for quite a while now, and he desperately needed to get back to his post to see what Charlize was doing.

"I don't know, man. Do you happen to know where the notebook is?"

Ondragon hesitated, but then decided to ask a counter question. "Why is the notebook so important? What could be in it?"

"Well, some say it contains Tesla's notes on the death ray, others claim it's his research papers on flying objects with antigravity propulsion." Truthfinder sighed audibly. "Mr. O, is what you're telling me really true? It's not a hoax? The medal was actually in the hands of the Nazis?"

"It's true!" confirmed Ondragon. "I can send you a photo of the medal if you like."

"Fuck! This blows away everything I thought I knew about the mysteries surrounding Tesla! Please don't take offense if I end our conversation at this point, but this unexpected turn of events requires a thorough reassessment of the facts."

"No offense, Truthfinder. You've already helped me more than I could have hoped. And again, I apologize for my initial skepticism."

"You're all right, Mr. O. You can call me again anytime."

"I'll gladly take you up on that, thank you very much," Ondragon said, taking his leave of the strangest person he had ever talked to on the phone. Then he hurried to the laptop and put the earpiece back in his ear.

". . . Damn it, leave me alone, you Xanthippe!" That was Charlize's voice. She sounded very agitated.

"Return to your station immediately, Pinscher26. That's an order!" That was Ritter. "You work for us and are under our orders! Anything else is insubordination and will be punished!"

"Insubordination! My ass! You—"

Suddenly there was silence. Irritated, Ondragon tapped the earpiece. Had someone interrupted the transmission? He glanced at the screen. Uh-oh! The camera image was shaking violently back and forth. He recognized the outer wall of the dilapidated building he was in and saw the door had been kicked in. Then he heard footsteps below. Quickly, he got up and went to the stairs, where his assistant soon appeared at the bottom of the flight. Cursing, she stomped up to him, tore the glasses off, and thrust them into his hand. She then pushed past him like a bulldozer and circled the room furiously.

"That witch! That bitch of an agent!"

"Hey! Cool it, Charlize!" Ondragon shouted at her. "You're going to blow our cover!"

Charlize paused, staring at him. "Are you sticking up for that blonde harpy now?"

"No, of course not! But we need to be civilized about this thing." Ondragon heard more footsteps below and reached for his weapon, though he already suspected who was coming. "I know you don't like Ritter," he whispered to Charlize, "but please don't push it!"

Charlize exhaled loudly, sweeping her samurai look wildly around the room. Then she nodded reluctantly. Not a moment too soon. Ritter appeared on the stairway. She moved toward them with an annoyed expression, Steiner following like a faithful dachshund.

"Damn it, Tanaka, what was all that about?" Ritter grabbed Charlize by the shoulder and spun her around. "Steiner! Frisk!"

The agent obeyed the order and searched Charlize.

"Hey, no groping, you hear me?" nagged Charlize, slapping Steiner's hand away.

"You shut your mouth, Tanaka, and kindly let the search proceed! Meanwhile, I'll have a word with your 'boss'!" Ritter turned her head and stepped close to Ondragon. Her glaring blue eyes met his. She was so close to him that he could count the freckles on her nose, which was quivering with outrage. Halfway composed, he looked back. The proximity of this woman was not at all unpleasant. On the contrary. Her lips reddened with anger, and the myriad of freckles on her face—simply wonderful! He savored the unexpected vision delightedly.

"Your assistant is suspended!" hissed Ritter in harsh German.

"I'm sorry," Ondragon replied politely. "I hereby apologize for Miss Tanaka's inappropriate behavior. She is normally very reliable."

Ritter pursed her lips scornfully. "At home behind her desk, maybe."

"No, she's an excellent employee, especially in the field. I don't know what got into her. But while we're on the subject of mutual accusations: Why did you cut the transmission earlier? How am I supposed to keep in contact with you if you cut the connection during an operation?"

Ritter's eyes flashed blue fire as she replied. "The operation was canceled on my orders because I felt it had been jeopardized by Miss Tanaka's bungling behavior. Besides, I don't like to be insulted. Especially not by an amateur!"

"She's clean!" called Steiner's voice.

Ondragon looked over at him. The expression on Charlize's face would have frightened all the demons of hell.

"Okay," Ritter said to Steiner. "Send Miss Tanaka away!" She turned to Ondragon. "You will not contact your assistant again until the mission is complete! Understood? And I warn you, we will be monitoring both of you. So don't try any tricks!"

"Sure," Ondragon said, thinking, *Crap!* He caught Charlize's burning look and said placatingly, "It's okay, Charlize. You go now. I'll see you at my hotel, when it's all done."

Charlize nodded, smoothed her cheeks as if to calm her anger, and walked down the stairs with her head held high. Ondragon looked after her searchingly. Had she understood his hidden message?

When his assistant had disappeared, he turned his attention back to the agent, who was still standing unapologetically in front of him.

"Satisfied?" he asked.

Ritter stared back fearlessly. Then she nodded, without looking away. Ondragon was impressed. Not many people could handle this kind of staring contest. Ms. Ritter was truly an ice queen. But one who did not keep her emotions in the deep freeze; she released them in a furious blizzard. For once, Ondragon would let her have this victory. She should enjoy it.

Acting casually, he broke eye contact and turned his focus to the moldy wall behind her, asking with false obsequiousness, "What about Pandora? Will the mission continue?"

He noticed Ritter's gaze soften a little, and her voice became warmer. "Are you sure you can do this now that you have to operate alone? We can't take any chances."

"I have everything I need to get you the box. Tonight, Pandora will be yours!"

Ritter relaxed. The blizzard had subsided and the sun reappeared on her face. "That sounds good," she said. "At least Tanaka managed to delete all the images and data on the computer in the lab before she made her inglorious exit. Fortunately, she doesn't seem to have aroused any suspicion among her colleagues in the lab, or we would have had to wrap it up and come up with something new." She gave an ambiguous smile. "The operation will go ahead tonight as discussed. When the contents of the box have been verified, we will contact you regarding the agreed fee. And rest assured, Mr. Ondragon, we will keep our word!"

"All right. Anything else?"

"No, that's it. You can go now and prepare for the assignment." Ritter took a step back, releasing him from her icy aura.

Ondragon resisted the urge to shake off the goose bumps this woman was giving him and walked a little stiff-leggedly over to the netbook. He stowed everything in his backpack and handed Ritter Charlize's camera glasses, which he had been holding in his hands the entire time. With a curt nod, he left the two BND agents and exited the dilapidated building. Once he was out of sight, a satisfied grin spread across his face. Charlize's diversion had worked perfectly.

CHAPTER 14

May 22, 2011
Fortaleza, Brazil
5:34 pm

Clandestin carefully crept after the man named Ondragon. He had just left the dilapidated building and was walking away toward the beach. Clandestin had been watching him all day. It was clear what the guy was up to. He was planning his crime. That was good, because Clandestin was tired of waiting. He saw Mr. Ondragon enter the hotel and followed him. He had now found out more about him. For example, he was not American but German, or half German, and his parents were a retired ambassador and an Olympic champion. How cute! The guy himself was a kind of problem-solver, a presentable gangster who would do anything— only for those who could afford his fee, of course. Because the good Mr. O ranked pretty high on the list of worldwide experts in special affairs. That made him expensive and very dangerous!

Clandestin moved out of the wake of the tall problem-solver and drifted into the lobby of the hotel, his eyes darting to the pretty *nipo-brasileira* sitting in one of the armchairs with her legs crossed, pretending to read a brochure. In truth, she was waiting for her boss.

Clandestin maneuvered himself deftly into the seating area at their backs. He wanted to see what they were doing now. The woman, Charlize Tanaka was her name, had been infiltrated into the laboratory at the harbor by the BND. What had she seen there? Had she been close to it? The treasure? Clandestin felt a pleasureable shiver of anticipation travel through his body. Soon he would have the treasure in his hands, and then it would be up to him to do the second part of his job. He thought of the man who had given him the job and clenched one hand into a fist. He could not fail. That was out of the question!

Clandestin looked around, but the only other people in the lobby were tourists in ridiculous clothes. Those cretins! He hated people who went to another country to do the same things they did at home: eat, drink, fuck! God, what ignoramuses!

He swallowed his blazing hatred and went on observing the lady he was concerned with. Her head was turned toward her boss, who gave her a meaningful look from a distance and then continued toward the elevators. Clandestin took the opportunity to glide past her unnoticed. As he did, he caught the smell of chemicals, perfume, and a hint of decay. Was that what it smelled like where she had come from? In the lab with the treasure?

The woman turned around, as if she had noticed something, but Clandestin had long since disappeared. He stood behind an opaque ornamental shrub and peered over at the elevators. The indicator above the door stopped at four and then moved back down. Mr. Big was now on the floor where his room was. Clandestin heard the woman's cell phone beep and saw her read something on the display. She then put the phone away and continued to wait. It wasn't until ten minutes later that a waiter came over to her and placed a drink on the table in front of her, along with a paper napkin. Clandestin was surprised, since she hadn't ordered anything. Had he lost focus for a moment? But then he understood when he saw the woman pick up the napkin and stare at it just a tiny moment too long before lowering it again. There was a change in her expression. She now looked like someone who knew something, and not like someone who was waiting for something.

The German is cunning, thought Clandestin. He had sent a covert message to his accomplice through the waiter. Whatever was written on the napkin, it had minimally altered her demeanor, though she certainly took pains to hide it. Without tasting the drink, she rose and left the hotel with a confident stride. Clandestin wondered if he should go after her and steal her cell phone. There was still a lot of activity outside on the promenade, and he might well succeed in stealing the device from her without her noticing. Perhaps he would find a clue to the details of Mr. Big's plan. Then he wouldn't have to keep sticking to him like chewing gum in this tedious way. On the other hand, the risk that the woman would become aware of him was too great. So he calmed himself and stayed where he was. He had made meticulous preparations and could let things run their course. When the moment was right, he would intervene and take what was pretty much already his.

He looked again at the guests in the foyer before strolling, as if by chance, to the table where the woman had been sitting. The napkin was still lying there. *It was careless of the lady to leave it behind*, he thought, and slipped it quickly into the pocket of his hoodie. Then he adjusted his tinted glasses and went around a corner, where he read the message.

"Damn it!" he muttered softly, crumpling the napkin in annoyance. The message was written in Japanese! While he knew quite a few languages, Japanese was not one of them. *Merde!*

Clandestin relaxed his posture, put on a carefree expression, and strolled casually out of the hotel. Outside, he crossed the street at a leisurely pace and looked for a spot under the palm trees that would give him a good view of the hotel's main entrance and the exit from the underground parking garage. The car this guy was using was parked at the side of the road some distance away, but you could never tell which way Mr. Big would leave the hotel. He couldn't let him out of his sight for a minute now.

Like a chameleon, Clandestin blended with the strolling crowd of vacationers and calibrated his gaze to pick out tall men. For although Mr. Ondragon had mastered the art of disguise, he could not conceal his height. So Clandestin waited patiently while the shadows of the approaching night grew longer and longer and the colorful lights at the beach bars flickered on like a thousand little eyes, helping him with his work.

CHAPTER 15

May 22, 2011
Fortaleza, Brazil
6:05 pm

Back in his room, Ondragon searched the entire space for bugs. Only then did he dare to take out the chip. Eight gigabytes and not even the size of a contact lens! Charlize had saved all the photos and files from the lab on it before deleting them from the computer. She had then smuggled the chip out of the lab, and Ritter had fallen for her petulant act. The chip had been attached to the inside arm of the camera glasses, and Ondragon had quickly scratched it off and put it into a small pocket in his waistband.

He smiled pensively. There was no one he made a better team with than Charlize.

Soon he had put the chip into an SD adapter and slid it into the camera that was part of his tourist camouflage. Unfortunately, this was currently the only device he could use to get an overview of the photos. He didn't want to use the BND netbook, because it certainly had a mirrored surface that might be seen by someone spying from a distance, if not by Ritter herself.

No matter, the camera would do for now. Ondragon turned it on and clicked through the images. The display was small, but if he used the magnify function, he could at least see the images of the wreckage. The cracked and corroded sections of the Junkers stood out clearly against the "fresh" debris of the Air France plane in the background. All the finds in the hangar had been carefully sorted. Ondragon looked only at the pictures of the JU 390. A chunky cone that had probably been one of the six propeller engines lay on the concrete floor, bent parts of an olive-green wing loomed next to it, and the next photo showed the Junkers' distinctive tail fin. Ondragon made out the vague outline of a swastika on it. Although the deep sea had done its best to destroy the heinous evidence of this machine's origins, it was still there—brutally dragged back into the light from the dark recesses of oblivion.

Ondragon flipped to the next photo, which showed the cockpit and the nose of the Junkers, which was almost intact. He was no expert on airplane crashes, but since the nose and tail were so undamaged, the plane must have hit the sea undercarriage first. It had done a damn belly flop. But why? Had it simply run out of fuel? Ondragon hoped the chip also contained reports of investigations into the cause of the crash. He scrolled through to the photos of the box that had been wedged under the copilot's seat, and reached the moment it had been opened, which he had, after all, witnessed live. He paused. What he really wanted to do was skip over the photos with the logbook, but he got a grip on himself. On a previous occasion, he had missed something crucial because he had not been able to bring himself to look at a photo of a book. Back then he had been mightily annoyed about it. He didn't want that to happen again. So he went to work and clicked on the first photo.

Growing steadily dizzier and with hot waves of disgust in his stomach, he tried to keep his eyes fixed on the *corpus horribilis*. Sweat broke out on his forehead and his focus became narrower and narrower. The dizziness rotated around his field of vision, leaving only the center clear.

Look! Look, damn it, look! It could be important!

But there was nothing there. What could there be? It was a photo of a handwritten chart. Quickly, he jumped back to the shots of the Edison medal, and the gyrating dizziness receded. There was something immensely reassuring about the gleaming gold medal, lying there on the velvet bed in the casket like a precious treasure. Ondragon gradually felt better and finally risked another attempt. As if he were about to make a dive, he took a deep breath and clicked on the photo of the book.

The paper of the page was gray and covered with foxing, and immediately Ondragon thought he could sense the musty smell of old folios in his nose. His disgust flared up again. But he forced himself to keep looking. The writing on the photo was too small to read, so he enlarged the section and saw that the text was written in black ink. *Flight log—Colonel Karl Brenner*, it said. He already knew the name from Charlize's transmission.

Quickly. On to next picture, before . . .

Ondragon choked down his disgust. The noise he made in the process echoed unintentionally loudly through the room. He looked reluctantly at the densely written table, enlarging the image with trembling fingers. The rough fibers of the paper jumped at him as if to attack him, as if they wanted to block his mouth and nose and suffocate him with their papery pulp!

Letting out a cry of disgust, Ondragon threw the camera onto the bed and ran his hands through his hair, digging his fingernails into his scalp. The memory rushed at him. He smelled the books, tasted the paper, felt their weight on his body. He saw his brother lying under the pile of books with his skull crushed, saw his blood running over the carpet, and his mother, her eyes widened in horror, her hands clasped in front of her mouth—the reaction of someone who has just been through something terrible. But suddenly his mother's face changed, as if she were peeling off her skin to reveal a new face underneath! This face suddenly seemed not frightened at all. On the contrary, his mother's gaze was cold and calculating. Ondragon heard her saying callously, "This is our chance, Siegfried!"

Siegfried Ondragon, who also seemed completely unmoved by the scene, turned his head toward her mechanically, like a doll. "Yes, Ava," he replied, "let's do it!"

Then the images blurred and Ondragon couldn't tell whether they were real memories or whether his brain was deceiving him again. Had his parents really reacted so coldly back then? Had his mother really been so indifferent, staring down at his dead brother as if he had never existed? Ondragon could see Per Gustav's smashed head in front of him, lying there buried under the books. The head of a ten-year-old boy who was the spitting image of himself. It seemed to him that he was looking into a mirror, as if he himself were lying there. Suddenly, the head moved and the face turned toward him. A smile spread over the pale lips. But it was not a friendly smile—it was a devilish, bloodred grin. Gripped by horror, Ondragon jumped up and ran to the balcony door. He tore it open and rushed out into the night. Panic-stricken, he sucked the thick tropical air into his lungs but felt no relief; his body needed yet more oxygen. Gasping, he dropped to his knees and closed his eyes.

Concentrate! Breathe in, breathe out. There are no books here! You have enough air! Breathe in, breathe out. Think of the sea out there and the sky. Wide and clear!

Gradually, his asthmatic moans calmed and he was able to breathe again. Covered in sweat, he leaned against the railing and looked out at the sea. It was dark, but it was there. Wide and clear. Per's bloody grin and his mother's cold gaze both blurred into the darkness.

Having regained his composure, Ondragon staggered back into the room and placed the camera in the safe. He hid the tiny chip behind a loose section of wallpaper. If you didn't know where it was, you'd never find it.

Next, he groped his way around the room like an injured bear. He absolutely had to get his head clear, otherwise he would mess up his mission! He began to gather clothes and equipment for the mission that night, setting them out on the bed. When he was done, he sat down at the desk and opened the notepad. He would go over everything one more time before he left. And he was still waiting for a message from Charlize's mysterious contact. He stared at the notes, straining and failing to focus on what was before him. His inability to look at a book, even a photograph of one, caused him to panic. It was devastating! How was he ever going to get over this?

You must force yourself to remember, Paul! Remember what happened back then in your father's library! Only when you remember will you find out what is true and what is not. Find the key and look for the lock it fits. Dare to open the door and see what is behind it. Then one day you will be able to overcome your fear.

Yes, yes, but not today! he argued. *And not tomorrow either! So leave me alone now, let me work!*

He directed his gaze to the map of the lab he had made the day before with Charlize's help, took a pencil, and marked the route he intended to take. If the guards detected him, he would skedaddle in the small boat that was moored out at the jetty.

Ondragon looked impatiently at the clock. It was already after midnight. Charlize's contact was taking his time. Must be his way of showing the gringo that in this town, he was the boss. Ondragon tried not to let it rattle him, pushed back the chair, and did some strength exercises on the cool floor tiles. This awakened his senses and pumped his adrenaline up to the required level. As he completed his forty-eighth mountain climber, there was a knock on the door. Ondragon calmly continued to fifty, rose, and reached for his gun.

"*Sim, por favor?*" he asked through the door, which loosely translated meant, "Yes, please?"

"Your pizza, *seu* Ondragon. Salami and anchovies with special sauce!" he heard a man answer in broken English. That was the agreed password. He opened the door, and after checking the hallway to be sure the guy was alone, let him in. He was indeed carrying a pizza box, which was giving off a seductive aroma. The guy himself was dark-skinned and so short that he could have walked under Ondragon's outstretched arm. He had short, frizzy black hair and dark eyes. He wore a seemingly detached expression and his flattened nose betrayed him as a street fighter. The muscles around his mouth were twitching.

Ondragon frisked the super-duper flyweight for weapons. He was clean. With the barrel of the pistol, he waved the pizza boy over to the table, where he set down the pizza box and grinned slyly.

"Are you Sem?" asked Ondragon.

The Brazilian shook his head. "Nah, man. Sem's the boss, I'm just his messenger, you know, gringo."

Too bad, thought Ondragon. But he had actually been pretty sure the boss of the Fortaleza underworld would not show up in person. He'd do the same. Nevertheless, he had hoped to learn something more about this mysterious Sem.

"Everything okay?" he asked.

"Yessss, man. As discussed. It's all okey-dokey. You can count on Sem all the way, mister! He'll be right there when you need him!"

Well then, Ondragon thought, still skeptical. But if Charlize vouched for the guy, there was little reason to be suspicious. He went over to the nightstand, opened the drawer, and pulled out a wad of dollar bills. "I'll give you the other half after!" he said, thrusting it into the lightweight boxer's hand.

"Sure." The little Brazilian stuffed the money into the pocket of his bomber jacket. Then he raised one hand and made a casual downward motion with two fingers. "See you, man!" He headed for the door. "Oh, and you can eat the pizza, it's good." He winked at him, glanced quickly out the door, and was gone.

Yo, man! Ondragon replied in his head, putting the gun away and opening the box. The pizza looked really appetizing. He tried a slice and then ate another. Then he licked his fingers. He couldn't eat too much, it would only make him sluggish and unfocused. As he was about to close the box, he noticed something under the pizza. He lifted the grease-soaked pie and pulled out a note that had been shrink-wrapped in plastic. *Charlize, you sly fox*, he thought with a grin, reading the Japanese characters.

Don't worry, Boss. Everything is ready. Sem and his people know what they have to do. You can count on him! See you tomorrow. Good luck! C.

Hopefully, Sem is indeed as reliable as Charlize claims he is, Ondragon thought, because otherwise his plan would end up on its ass and he would have to work out how to handle the situation on his own. He glanced at the clock again and decided to get ready for the mission.

CHAPTER 16

May 23, 2011
Fortaleza, Brazil
2:30 am

Clad from head to toe in black, Ondragon stood in a sheltered corner of the harbor, observing the spot where he intended to scale the three-meter wall into the container area. The night was perfect: a nearly full moon sat on the eastern horizon, illuminating the area with a soft light. Every now and then, a cloud slid overhead, briefly plunging everything into deep shadow.

One last time, Ondragon looked from the sky to the pipelines leading over the wall, making sure that there was no one about; finally he spoke quietly into the mic on his collar.

"I'm going in now."

"Roger that," came Ritter's cool voice over the earpiece.

He shimmied up the pipes without any appreciable increase in his pulse and ran, crouching, toward the harbor area. His rubber soles made barely a sound on the metal. Once over the wall, he dropped to all fours and listened from his elevated position into the darkness at his feet. Apparently, the guards considered this spot low-risk; he couldn't hear or see a single person.

Silently, Ondragon lowered himself into the shadows and took cover behind a pumping station. To his right, the ten-story towers of the silos rose like the fingers of a giant, and to his left lurked the inert mass of the oil tanks. There were no guards anywhere to be seen. All he could hear out there in the concrete jungle was the chirping of a few very versatile crickets.

Ondragon turned his gaze ahead to three rusted containers that obscured the view of the hall marked with the capital *E*. As a cloud obscured the moon, he broke cover and ran over to one of the containers. Pressed tightly against the metal, he peered around the corner at Hall 2, where the lab was located. A lone lamp burned above the door, but that was all. He looked over to Hall 1, the one with the wreckage. It was in complete darkness. Either it had no lamp or the lamp was broken. His attention sprang back to Hall 2, because a man in a dark uniform had suddenly appeared there. He walked up to the door and stepped into the cone of light. Ondragon saw that he was carrying a clunky radio and had a pistol at his belt. On his head was a black baseball cap. He paused outside the door and looked around. Ondragon quickly retreated into the shelter of the container and only ventured out again when he heard the clang of the steel door. The guard had disappeared. Presumably, he was now making a circuit of the hall. And he was alone, which surprised Ondragon a little. Didn't security patrol in teams? At least that's what it had said on the duty roster Charlize had taken a secret look at. It listed two people for tonight. *Maybe the other guard is currently in Hall 1, or they are taking turns, which is more likely*, Ondragon thought. Lazy as he believed the gang to be, the men on the night shift surely shared a berth, and when one was done with his rounds, he would wake the other, who would then head off at the next agreed time. It would be good for Ondragon if that was the way it worked. Not so good if it wasn't.

He waited, looking at his watch. The guy had been in there seven minutes. Since the hall wasn't very big and it couldn't be very pleasant in there with all the body parts, the guy would likely not take more time than was necessary over his inspection. And so it proved. The door opened and the guard stepped out. But he didn't go on to the next hall; he stood there and lit a cigarette.

Damn addictive cancer sticks, Ondragon thought, impatiently watching the cigarette glow in the darkness. After two more minutes, the guard finally got comfortable enough to move on. He marched over to Hall 1, and now Ondragon was sure the guy was alone. He tensed his muscles and prepared to sprint. When he heard the squeak of hinges from the door to Hall 1, he began running. It was fifteen steps to the entrance. He reached the door and was surprised to find that it was not locked. Whether the guard had left it open out of thoughtlessness or plain laziness, he didn't care. Quickly, he slipped through. On the other side, he was greeted by impenetrable darkness and . . . something else. A revolting stench. Instinctively, he pressed a hand over his mouth and nose. God, that was disgusting! A nauseating mixture of formaldehyde and sweet rotting flesh. How could Charlize have stood it?

Ondragon felt something crawling over his face and wiped it away jerkily. Humming, it flew off. Only now did he realize that there was another hum in the air other than that of the cooling units. Carefully, he switched on his miniature diode lamp and shone it up into the unfathomable darkness. Of course, the beam didn't quite reach the hall ceiling, but he could still take a guess at the number of swarms of flies massing there, forming a black cloud. He frantically shooed away the individuals that were trying to fly directly into his mouth. It didn't bear thinking about, where the creatures had been!

In order to avoid attracting the next swarm, he quickly ran over to the structures that had been erected in the hall. The container with the lab loomed in the middle of the cluster like a white cube. MEDI-CON was written on one side. Behind the cube, Ondragon could make out the lighter expanse of the protective canvas that had been stretched over the unsavory collection of decomposing body parts. He gulped and soon identified the entrance area to the lab: a porch constructed of thick plastic walls that was hermetically attached to the Medi-Con cube. Quickly, he pulled out Charlize's ID card and swiped it through the slot in the electronic lock. A beep sounded and then there was a hermetic hiss as the door opened. Ondragon stepped through and took an experimental breath through his nose. Relieved, he exhaled again. The stench was much more bearable in here.

After looking around the antechamber, he brought the site plan to mind and purposefully lit his way to the heart of the facility. The lab looked exactly as he had seen it in Charlize's camera transmission. He found the safe easily and entered the combination without further ado. Lo and behold, the lab staff had not changed it. The door swung open silently, revealing the contents.

Pandora!

Ondragon contemplated the bulky box. It would have been so much easier if the BND were only after the contents, he thought, but no, his mission was to get the whole darn thing! At least this way he didn't have to touch the hated object inside. Still, he should make sure it was actually there. He lifted the box out of the safe, set it down on the lab bench, and removed the plastic wrapper. Then he opened the lid and shone a light inside. A violent lurching of his stomach seized him and he knew immediately that the contents were present and correct. He quickly closed the box again and tucked it under his arm. He turned around and froze.

There was a man standing behind him!

A guy from security. But whether it was the same guy he had seen moments before, or a different one, he couldn't tell. Why the hell hadn't he heard him? Had that fucking book distracted him so much?

Ondragon shooed the thought away. He could think about that later—if there was a later. Right now, he had to get this guy off his back. Without moving, he looked quickly at the radio on the man's belt. Had he already sent a radio message to his colleague, or was he as surprised as Ondragon?

The guard barked an order in Portuguese that Ondragon assumed meant something like "Put your hands up!" He looked the guy straight in the face. There was a telltale flare in his eyes.

That told him everything he needed to know.

With an explosive upward movement, Ondragon hurled the box toward him. The guard could not get out of the way in time and the box hit his weapon from below. His hands cannoned upward and a shot rang out.

The loud bang echoed off the walls of the container lab, drilling through Ondragon's eardrums. *Well, that's just great!* he thought with a pained expression, as Ritter's agitated voice came over the radio, trying to penetrate the dull buzzing in his ears. He saw the guard regain his composure, and he lunged again with the box, smashing it squarely into his face. The result was very satisfying; there was a loud crunch. Possibly a tooth, or maybe the guy's nose. He gave a cry of pain and finally dropped the gun. The next blow with the aluminum box knocked him out for good. He slumped silently to the ground. Ondragon made sure he really had knocked the guy out, then took his radio and gun and left the lab. In the hall, the stench of corpses hit him like a blow to the lungs and he held his breath until he reached the door. Cautiously, he stuck his head out. All seemed quiet.

"What's going on? Sheepdog17, report!" Now, finally, he could hear Ritter's words again. The agent even sounded a little worried. But was that because of him or because of the box?

Ondragon looked around. The wall was five hundred steps away. Maybe less. "I've got Pandora and I'm heading to Position One," he said into the mic, but suddenly several shadows loomed out of the darkness in front of him. There were far more guards than had been on the schedule. He quickly changed direction, running toward the jetty.

"Change of plan! They've detected me!" he informed Ritter. "I'm leaving the compound across the water. Rendezvous at Position Two! Copy?"

"Roger that, coming to Position Two! *Over!*" the agent replied tensely.

"Am now at the boat! Next radio contact will be touchdown on shore. *Over and out.*"

Ondragon untied the rope and jumped onto the rickety sloop. He pumped gasoline into the engine and yanked the starter cord. The outboard motor started without a murmur, which kind of amused Ondragon because he had fully expected the antiquated machine to fail. He turned the throttle up and the engine roared loudly over the still surface of the water. Ondragon ducked down deeper in the boat and steered it out to the open sea first. Only a few minutes later did he turn west and head on a parallel course to the beach. To starboard yawned the endless darkness of the ocean, and to port, the lights of the city glittered with a false sense of security.

The guards would certainly have heard the engine and would now know he was escaping by sea. And since he couldn't cross the open ocean in such a small craft, there were only two directions he could go: along the coast to west or southeast. They were bound to try and pursue him on land as well, and they were bound to have called the police and coast guard. So he was left with a tiny little lead and the advantage that they didn't know what he looked like. But unfortunately, he had this stupid box in tow. It would betray him immediately!

Ondragon shone the diode lamp around the inside of the boat and saw something under the thwart. He pulled it out. It was a brand-new duffel bag. The BND must have placed it there for just such an eventually. He gave silent thanks for Ritter's foresight and stuffed the box into the bag, then steered the boat up onto the beach. When it ran crisply aground, he jumped out and, without looking back, left it at the water's edge.

"Ashore!" he whispered into the mic. "Moving westward."

"Roger," Ritter replied curtly, but he could clearly hear the relief in her one word.

Under cover of the palm trees, Ondragon hurried to the promenade and, with the help of the neon hotel signs, got his bearings. He had come out behind the Gran Marquise, but ahead of the Hotel Beira Mar, close to Position 2—a parking lot by the beach for tourists, with several entrances. Ondragon had scouted the location thoroughly beforehand. There were always a few cars parked there at night, which made for good cover, but there was hardly anyone hanging around

He shouldered the bag and marched west in the protection of the palm trees. It was now half past three in the morning and music and drunken laughter were issuing from one or two beach bars. The rest of the shacks lay in deep slumber, their lights extinguished and their windows shuttered. Ondragon skirted the illuminated islands, hoping that not only Ritter and Steiner were on their way to the second rendezvous point, but the other team as well.

CHAPTER 17

May 23, 2011
Fortaleza, Brazil
3:40 am

Ondragon reached the Hotel Beira Mar safely and stopped behind the trunk of a palm tree. The hotel was across the street, its brightly lit entryway deserted. He looked toward the spacious, gloomy parking lot, where a few hunched shadows indicated parked cars. Otherwise, there was no one to be seen. Not a single vehicle drove along the street either, and a lone police siren howled like a wolf in the distance.

Ondragon deliberately let a few more minutes elapse. A car drove past him and shortly after that a couple sauntered along the sidewalk, closely entwined. A short distance from him, they disappeared into the bushes. Ondragon listened tensely, then steadied himself again. There was no need to worry about the couple. The noises in the background made it clear why they were here. They wouldn't hear anything that might happen in the parking lot in the next few moments.

Ondragon looked around one last time. Finally, he ran over to the parking lot, where he hid between two cars to appraise the situation once again.

"Now at Position Two, where are you?" he asked over the radio.

In response, the van's headlights flared briefly about fifty meters away. Ritter and Steiner had parked the BND van in the dark in such a way that it could not be seen from the road, but they could still make a quick getaway.

Ondragon looked at the remaining vehicles in the parking lot. One of them must contain the others.

"I've got Pandora and I'm coming to you now," he said into the mic. He took the box out of the duffel bag, jammed it under his arm, and crept toward the back of the van under cover of the cars. When he was only a few feet away, he heard the sliding door open. A shadow stepped out and looked around. It was Ritter. The agent had hidden her blonde hair under a cap and was wearing dark gear. Behind her, a bluish glow of light seeped from the belly of the van.

"I see you," Ritter whispered in his ear. "I'm coming."

That's good, Ondragon thought, *because that will make it easier*. He quickly glanced over his shoulder. He could see no one who might disturb their little show. Ritter, meanwhile, had stepped into the open space between the cars and stood in front of Ondragon. Despite the darkness, he could see she wore a tense expression. She was on the alert. Would she smell a rat?

"Give me the box!" said Ritter, holding out her hands.

Okay, thought Ondragon, *now it was time*. He held Pandora out to her. Ritter took the box and began to turn back to the van, but Ondragon stopped her.

"Wait, you'd better check the contents. I wouldn't want it said later that I didn't complete the order or that I stole anything!"

Ritter exhaled indignantly, but then complied. "Okay, okay, you're right." She reached out a hand to lift the lid, but suddenly an engine roared behind them and one of the parked cars came racing toward them, its tires squealing.

About time, Ondragon thought, and backed up to give the car a clear path. It approached with its lights flashing. Ondragon registered that Ritter was torn. She wanted to drop the box and reach for her weapon, but she couldn't bring herself to let Pandora go just like that. Instead, Steiner jumped out of the van with his gun drawn and pointed it at the car. He shouted something to Ritter, but the meaning was lost in the noise of the roaring engine.

Irritated, Ondragon looked at the car. Something was wrong with the scene. Why wasn't the car braking? Why was it continuing at the same speed? He began to warn Ritter, but the car was already upon them and hit her with full force. Brakes screeched and the windshield shattered with a loud bang. The agent was thrown through the air along with the box and landed hard on the asphalt several car lengths ahead. Her body rolled over several times and then came to a halt like a mutilated doll. Horrified, Ondragon watched as the car started up again and headed unswervingly for Ritter, as if to complete its malign work.

"No!" Steiner yelled, and fired several shots at the car. The rear window shattered and the car lurched briefly, but it recovered itself and drove on in first gear, screeching. As it passed the motionless agent, the driver's door suddenly opened and a hand shot out. It grabbed the box lying on the road next to Ritter and hurled it into the car. The door closed, and the car skidded around the bend at breakneck speed. Its exhaust spraying sparks, it left the parking lot and disappeared into the night.

Ondragon snapped out of his stupor and hastily fumbled his cell phone out of his pocket. He dialed Charlize's number while Steiner ran over to Ritter and bent over her.

"Shit!" he hissed angrily into the phone when his assistant finally picked up. "What the hell is wrong with you people? I told you not to run her over!"

"We didn't, Boss," Charlize replied in a sober voice. "We're still sitting here in the car!"

CHAPTER 18

May 23, 2011
Fortaleza, Brazil
4:05 am

Clandestin shifted into third gear and sped west along the deserted Avenida Beira Mar. The Corolla was a piece of junk, but that didn't matter; after all, his little surprise had succeeded!

A broad grin spread over his features. The fabulous Mr. O must be pretty surprised right now. Unpleasantly surprised, even! The German had done a good job; she had brought the treasure directly to him. Clandestin had had to do nothing more than reach out and pluck it like a ripe piece of fruit. Well, that's how life went. Sometimes you made a *bonne affaire* and sometimes you were one yourself. Today, at any rate, it was he who had made the good deal. *C'est la vie*, Mr. Ondragon.

Clandestin saw a police car with blue lights coming toward him and slowed down a little so the cops wouldn't notice him. He had already punched out the cracked windshield at the previous junction, and the warm airstream was now blowing into his face. By now, word would have spread about the shooting in the parking lot on the beach, and the break-in at the laboratory would have distracted the attention of the entire Fortaleza police force. Time to get rid of the jalopy.

He turned into a narrow side street and drove deeper into the unlit favela. His senses were crystal clear. He could feel the hard steering wheel in his fingers and the pounding of the engine in his abdomen. The dark power of that monumental moment still flowed through his veins. The moment when he had run over the agent. Clandestin gave an involuntary shudder. It had been a necessary evil, hadn't it? His uncertainty grew. Surely his employer would forgive him?

He glanced at the passenger seat. Yes, he would, when he saw what he brought with him.

The treasure!

Clandestin could hear a soft whisper coming from the box.

Voices from the past. Voices that had been silenced a long time ago. And it was his job to silence them again.

CHAPTER 19

July 30, 1899
Colorado Springs
morning, in the laboratory

I understand you have concerns, Mr. Ailey." Dr. Tesla motioned him into the small chamber and offered him a seat at his work table. Philemon sat down with his hands in his lap.

"Well?" demanded the doctor. "What's on your mind?"

The young assistant lowered his eyes timidly. "The thing is, Dr. Tesla, I do indeed have concerns about certain . . . ideas."

"About Mr. Myers and his whereabouts?"

Philemon suddenly remembered his conversation with Joe Herkimer and the suitcase in the hotel storeroom that allegedly belonged to Myers. He had not yet managed to check Herkimer's claim; he had been too tired after the long days at work. But how did Dr. Tesla know it was bothering him?

"Frederick Myers is a very talented young engineer," Tesla said, as if reading his mind, "Yale graduate, like yourself. He was very familiar with my work and was a great help to us during the few weeks he worked here. Unfortunately, his mother fell seriously ill and he was called back to Boston, so I had to dismiss him from my employ and look for a replacement. That is what brought you here, Mr. Ailey; you came highly recommended. Is there anything to be suspicious about in this?" Tesla looked at him calmly, but Philemon detected a guarded reproach in his gaze nonetheless.

"I beg your pardon," he apologized, "I did not mean to displease you! Nothing could be further from my thoughts!"

Tesla smiled indulgently and his tone softened. "I am going to tell you something, Mr. Ailey. Call it an anecdote or well-intentioned advice. I am a man who has accomplished much, who has been courted and cajoled by industrial tycoons from around world, and who has achieved fame and glory unwittingly, though he has done nothing but follow his innate instincts. I have always undertaken research only for its own sake, never for the sake of money. And I permit myself to number many people among my friends and patrons. However, there are unfortunately also certain people around me who envy my inventions or are even afraid of them. The worst of all, though, are those individuals who consider my theories to be utter nonsense and therefore despise me."

"But, Dr. Tesla, how could anyone attack you and your remarkable work?" interjected Philemon.

The doctor raised one of his gloved hands. "It is not so difficult to understand. After all, I count among my enemies my competitors, renowned scientists who should know better, but who have allowed their scientific spirit to become confused. Remember one thing, Mr. Ailey: The greatest obstacles to new and groundbreaking inventions are envy and prejudice! Prejudice planted deliberately in the minds of experts by those opposed to progress. I frequently encounter such narrow-minded opposition. A few years ago, it caused me to suffer a painful loss, which has shaken me very much, but will by no means dissuade me from my work!"

Philemon knew that the doctor was alluding to the fire in his laboratory. He saw the gaunt man close his eyes and knead the bridge of his nose with his fingertips. A faint sigh escaped his narrow chest, as if he were mourning the time that had been lost not only to him, but to all mankind. After a while, Tesla continued his speech about the fundamental distrust of the unknown.

"In this city too there are persons for whom my research is a thorn in their deluded and petty bourgeois sides, and they would be only too happy to see me pack my things and leave this very day. Even though these individuals would never admit it, they do everything they can to discredit me and my work. The people of Colorado Springs talk a lot and like to talk a lot, as you may have already found, and the information they so glibly and eagerly pass on is not always true. It is due to this circumstance that you, Mr. Löwenstein, Mr. Czito, and I are not well liked in these parts. But I do not intend to allow my work to be influenced by such insignificant trifles. I will continue my experiments until I can say with a clear conscience that I have succeeded. Pay no attention to the gossip on the streets and in the pubs, Mr. Ailey. And if you have any doubts, ask Mr. Löwenstein. You can have confidence in him."

Philemon nodded. "I will. Thank you very much for your advice, Doctor."

Tesla's gaze lit up again. "Splendid; now we can turn to your real question." He straightened up in his chair almost expectantly.

Philemon looked at him, puzzled. He had not asked a question.

The doctor smiled mysteriously. "You want to know what we are researching here, do you not?"

"Yes, naturally."

"Good. The fact is, my young friend, that our planet is filled with electrical vibrations; it is a reservoir of electrical energy, so to speak. I have come to Colorado Springs to prove that the earth can act as a gigantic conductor. If it is as I suspect, in the future we shall be able to send messages simply through the earth—telegraphing without wires, so to speak."

"*Through* the earth?" asked Philemon, confused. "But did you not say at the beginning that you would transmit energy to distant places using the large antenna out on the roof?"

"That is true, but we shall come to the antenna later. There are a variety of ways to transmit energy. First, let's look at the potential of the earth. It is alive, pulsating with tremendous amounts of energy! This is a fact, as I have recently proved. While others still doubt, I am already working to deliver a practicable methodology for my world system! And I am sure I will succeed in this!"

"And what makes you believe the earth is a conductor?" asked Philemon.

Tesla raised both hands like a magician about to reveal his trick. "It was a day I shall never forget. On July 3, almost four weeks ago, I observed a phenomenon—and I think I am the only one who has ever observed it. It occurred during a violent thunderstorm. A new type of recording device I constructed specifically for the purpose indicated slight voltage fluctuations in the earth with each lightning discharge. But as the thunderstorm moved on, rather than weakening as one would have expected, they became stronger, repeating at regular intervals, even when the thunderstorm was already over three hundred kilometers away."

Philemon raised his brows. "And how do you explain that?"

"As impossible as it may seem to you, and as outrageous as the significance of this observation will feel to mankind, it is true: We did observe terrestrial stationary waves on that memorable day!"

"You mean waves . . . *in* the earth?"

"That is right, my young friend. During the lightning discharges, strong electrical impulses were sent through the earth all the way to the antipodes. There on the other side they were reflected, astonishingly like sound waves, and came back with undiminished strength. So the earth responded with an echo in the form of a stationary wave! Isn't that phenomenal?"

Philemon nodded. This time more cautiously.

Tesla's eyes gleamed as he continued. "I was stunned by the discovery at first, but then I performed further experiments and calculations that irrefutably proved my previous hypothesis. It is possible to transmit energy through the globe without any appreciable loss! Just imagine, the stationary wave opens up tremendous possibilities for us." Tesla made an all-encompassing gesture. "We could build hydroelectric plants like the one at Niagara Falls anywhere in the world, regardless of infrastructure. We could even tame Victoria Falls in Africa and send electricity wirelessly to Europe. This would remove our dependence on fuels such as oil and coal, whose reserves are finite and which we should conserve for the benefit of future generations. In addition, we would no longer need transmission cables and thus copper. I tell you, with my world system it will be possible in just a few years to transmit messages and energy over any distance. The export of clean energy will become a main source of income for many countries and man could settle anywhere, even in the desert. All we need to make this a reality is my amplification transmitters. I am thinking of a special kind of tower into which I will integrate my modified coils in an efficient size. We will erect them at specific intervals around the globe and distribute small, handy devices that allow everyone to receive individualized signals! Fast, cheap, and safe! Distance will become meaningless; everyone will be able to communicate with everyone else, without any delay and no matter where they are. The peoples of this earth will be brought together and my invention will enable them to understand one another better. Wars will become senseless and a thing of the past! Man will attain a new level of consciousness."

"That sounds fantastic, Dr. Tesla!" said Philemon enthusiastically.

"Does it not, my young friend? So we are not doing anything illicit here. We are merely creating something new. My laboratory is open to anyone who is interested in my work, but not to those who seek to slander me or even use violence." The doctor leaned back, intertwining his gloved fingers.

Philemon was still enraptured by the vision Tesla had laid out before him. It was revolutionary and promised a bright future in which people would live in peace and have access to unlimited energy at all times. What could mankind accomplish with it? Philemon felt Tesla's spirit touch him and fill him with energy. His gaze wandered from the doctor's pale face to the shelf on the wall, on which stood a long row of black notebooks. Dr. Tesla had set his remarkable thoughts down in them for posterity. A whole world of thoughts, of which Philemon had just been granted a tiny glimpse.

"We can leave the present to those who waver," Tesla said solemnly, "but the future I am working for is mine!" He leaned forward and raised a finger. "In the coming weeks, we have two tasks to accomplish here, Mr. Ailey. First, the construction of a powerful transmitter, precisely tuned to the electrical properties of the earth and other bodies, which will use impulses to tap the vast reservoir of energy within. Second—and now we come to the antenna—we will conduct several experiments in which we will attempt to send energy through the ether via an antenna."

"Through the ether?"

"Yes, because I have discovered that the ether is not liquid but gaseous—this was, incidentally, the significant fact that Dr. Hertz completely disregarded in his experiments with electromagnetic waves. Therefore, I do not recognize his results, which he claims support Maxwell's theory."

"But Heinrich Hertz proved that ether, as postulated by Maxwell, really exists. We know that light, radiant heat, and electrical phenomena are all oscillations in a structureless medium. A medium similar to a fluid, which is unimaginably delicate, but at the same time can be as rigid as the hardest steel. What is wrong with that theory of ether?"

Tesla shook his head. "I have repeated Hertz's experiments with a far more powerful apparatus and have come to a very different conclusion than his, precisely *because* I know that space is filled with a gaseous and not liquid substance in which waves propagate alternately by compression and expansion. I call such waves scalar waves. They are longitudinal waves, similar to sound waves. Hertz, on the other hand, worked mainly with transverse waves. He completely ignored the different nature of scalar waves. I have attended to this error and compensated for it. My results clearly show that ether is gaseous and not liquid, and that it surrounds everything we can and cannot see. Consequently, I will continue to focus my attention more intensively on the study of scalar waves."

Philemon was skeptical but nodded despite that. What Dr. Tesla was saying contradicted all the teachings of the universities. It was obviously the doctor's inclination to take accepted theories apart and turn them upside down. With a tiny flick of his finger, he exploded laws that had been valid for decades and, smiling, put them up for scientific debate. This was a challenge even for the progressive-minded Philemon, and he knew that he too was being tested here. One thing was clear to him from this conversation: Working with Dr. Tesla meant throwing out time-honored tradition and replacing the ordinary with the extraordinary.

"For this second attempt to transmit energy through the air by means of scalar waves," Dr. Tesla continued, unperturbed, "we will use the energy-transmitting properties of certain layers of air in the atmosphere. To do this, we must install terminals at the appropriate height, that is, an antenna on the roof."

"Or on the mountain," Philemon suggested.

"Yes, that is right, I was even thinking of Pikes Peak itself. In the next few days, I shall be drawing up plans for a whole series of experiments to be carried out by you. I am relying entirely on your energetic assistance, as well as that of Löwenstein and Czito. Can I count on you?" Dr. Tesla looked at him penetratingly.

"Of course! I am always at your service!" Philemon said eagerly. Despite his skepticism, he was proud to be allowed to participate in these perhaps revolutionary events.

"Wonderful, my dear fellow. Do you have any more questions?"

Philemon said he did not. He needed to digest what he had heard before his brain was ready for further questions.

"Well, let's get back to work, then, each to his own." Tesla tapped his notebook, which lay in front of him. It bore a gold ring on the cover. Philemon understood the gesture and left the small room.

For a thoughtful moment, he paused outside the closed door, gazing silently into the twilight of the laboratory. Then he joined the other two assistants, who were busy preparing various oscillators for an experiment that was scheduled for later that day.

CHAPTER 20

Once Ondragon and Steiner had called the ambulance for Ritter, they hurriedly fled the parking lot in the BND van. Ondragon had previously advised Charlize to do the same, and she had made a quick getaway with Sem. With all their gear and weapons, even the Fortaleza police wouldn't have had to think for long before immediately linking them to the theft at the lab. And they wanted to avoid that at all costs.

Steiner took them out of danger by means of a few detours, and finally drove to the Joaquim Tavora district, not far from Praia do Meireles. But before Ondragon could ask the grim-faced agent next to him where they were headed, they passed through an unlit gate in a high fence. A multistory building loomed behind it. Was that the German national emblem emblazoned next to the entrance? Alarmed, Ondragon craned his neck to gain a better view. Damn, yes it was! Shit! Now he was actually on the grounds of the Honorary Consulate of Germany. Well, this was going to be fun.

No sooner had they stopped than two consulate employees approached the van and opened the doors. In a friendly tone, they asked Steiner and Ondragon to get out and follow them into the building. There, both men were asked to hand over their weapons and cell phones and were seated in separate rooms.

Sighing, Ondragon sat down at the table, on which stood a bottle of water and a glass. An interrogation room, he thought soberly, pouring himself a glass and drinking. Of course, the BND would want to know every detail of the events of the previous night, and they would likely question Steiner first and then him. So it could be some time before anything happened. He sighed again. If only they had at least left him his cell phone, he could have contacted Charlize and asked her what had gone wrong. Again and again, he went over what had happened in his head, but came to no conclusion. Who the hell had stuck their nose in? Who had run over Ritter so cold-bloodedly? Once again, anger flared in him at the malice of that damned bastard. The guy had been only too happy to kill someone. And that someone could well have been him! And how had the guy gotten wind of what they had planned to do in the parking lot? The only thing that was clear was that he was after the box. That had been obvious. But what did he want with it? Whom was he working for? Was another state power behind the robbery or was it a private action? Far too many unanswered questions buzzed through Ondragon's head. Tired, he rubbed the heel of his hand over his temple and squinted around the windowless room, its cold fluorescent light contrasting with the sweltering heat that prevailed in here. Either there was no air-conditioning, or they had turned it off for psychological reasons. Ondragon felt exhaustion take a powerful hold on his body, and fought it. After all, he didn't know if he was even safe in this place. The building was a representation of the German state and he was officially a German citizen, but it was still unclear whether he was here as a prisoner or as a guest. *Fuck!* He slapped his hand against his head to dispel the fatigue. He was just too limp to work out a solution to all the new puzzles at this moment. And this heat!

Again and again his eyes closed, and again and again he tore them open. As viscous as rubber, the minutes passed, became half an hour and then a whole hour. Impassively, the big clock on the wall ticked away his lifespan. Tick, tock. Tick, tock. *You're getting older and older and older. All right*, Ondragon finally thought to himself. *If I'm going to get older here, I might as well do it in my sleep. Besides, you get through an interrogation a lot better when you're rested.* He crossed his arms over his chest, let his head slump forward, and gave in to his tiredness.

His antennas, alert even in sleep, perceived a change and woke him. Ondragon sat up quickly. He could feel it; it had gotten cooler. Someone had turned on the air-conditioning. He looked at the clock and realized he had slept a full two hours. He shook his head vigorously and exhaled to clear his thoughts. Just then the door opened and a man with metal-rimmed glasses walked in. He looked like someone who never had any fun, was haggard as a scarecrow, and had a grim, pockmarked face. To top off the unsympathetic impression, his straw-like gray hair was an exact replica of Andy Warhol's. When the man began to speak, Ondragon recognized him. He would have known that arrogant, nasal tone anywhere.

"Sorry to keep you waiting so long," the gaunt BND agent apologized. He sounded more laconic than contrite. "I hope it didn't inconvenience you. My name is Alexander Kubicki. We spoke on the phone a few days ago. I hired you, so to speak." He unbuttoned his jacket and sat down at the table across from Ondragon without shaking his hand.

Ignoring the BND officer's lack of good manners and his patronizing attitude, Ondragon reached wordlessly for the water bottle. He drank the contents down in one gulp. Then he slammed the empty plastic container down on the table. "I want my cell phone!" he said gruffly.

Kubicki smiled thinly. "You'll get that when we're done here."

"I see, so that means you're detaining me here."

"It means you are our guest for the time being, until we decide what to do with you."

Ondragon took a deep breath in order to protest, but Kubicki beat him to it. "Don't give me any of that 'I'm a free citizen and I have rights' crap! It won't do you any good. Here you are a German under German jurisdiction. So the sooner you think about what you are saying and cooperate with us, the sooner you will be allowed to leave this building!"

Well, that's clear, Ondragon thought. He was stuck here. So much for his German passport. Another fine mess. Maybe he should make an official application for American citizenship soon after all.

Unwilling to chat with Mr. Important under these circumstances, he simply folded his arms and looked indifferently past the man at the clock. Another lifetime passed.

Kubicki smiled sedately, as if he knew what was going on in his interlocutor's mind. He leaned forward and began speaking in a sickeningly confidential tone: "Might it help if I told you that I am the head of Operation Pandora and can refuse to let you see your file?"

Ondragon knew this BND beanpole was merely trying to provoke him and remained calm, even though it was difficult. "My mission was a success," he said coldly. "Pandora was in the hands of your agent. The fact that she was attacked and the box was snatched from her is not my fault. We agreed that I would be able to inspect my file, and if you refuse me this now, it is a breach of contract!"

"Of an oral contract, mind," Kubicki countered with a confident look on his face.

Ondragon lowered his voice. "Are you always so reckless with your contractors? I'd be careful if I were you, or word will get out, and then no one will lift a finger to help you." He knew, of course, that all intelligence services, regardless of nationality, were dependent on outside help. And if their sources dried up, they were out on a limb.

"You let us worry about that, Mr. O," Kubicki replied indifferently. "All I want to know from you is, who interfered with the handover? And where is Pandora now?"

"How should I know?"

"Maybe because you organized this stunt?"

Ondragon remained silent and stony-faced. Could it be that the BND knew of his plans for the handover, or was Kubicki just guessing? Ondragon was familiar with these kinds of interrogation methods and was on guard. Without answering, he waited.

"The perpetrator fled in the car we provided to you. That leads us to believe you were involved."

"I had parked the car on the street. Anyone could have stolen it."

"That's true, but how did this guy know the handoff at Position One wasn't going to work because you got busted too early? And how did he get to Position Two so quickly?"

I'd like to know that too, Ondragon thought, and said, "Maybe he was watching us. Weren't you supposed to be monitoring us continually? Didn't you notice anyone?" Question ping-pong was still the best defense.

Kubicki remained silent.

So it had all been for show. Scarecrow had merely been bluffing. No one from the BND had been tracking them round the clock, so no one had any proof that he had made alternative plans. It had already been clear to him on the flight to Brazil that there might be something fishy about the whole thing. That the BND might not keep its word after the job was done. As was apparently the case now. That was why he had wanted to get a little reassurance with the help of Charlize and the sinister Sem, a little hostage he would have released after the exchange—his file for Pandora. But someone had gotten in his way and now they were in a fix.

"We didn't notice anyone," Kubicki now said, with feigned authority. "Incidentally, I would be very interested to know where your assistant is right now."

So they hadn't picked up Charlize. Good, Ondragon thought, looking thirstily at the empty bottle. He doubted, however, that they would bring him more water. He shrugged his shoulders indifferently. "Since you refuse to give me my cell phone, I can't find out where she is either. Presumably she has seen how you're treating me and has gone AWOL. Or maybe she's already on a plane back home. Who knows." He hoped Charlize was safe. If only he could talk to her on the phone. Maybe she had seen something or even knew who the stranger was. But as it was, he was completely in the dark. It was a poker game played blindfolded.

Kubicki looked at him appraisingly. "Mr. Ondragon, your lack of cooperation disappoints me. I had expected more professionalism from you of all people." He shook his head. "Besides, a female agent was seriously injured during the operation. Doesn't that concern you at all?"

Ah, now he was trying the pity ploy and appealing to his conscience. But he was talking to a brick wall there. Nevertheless, Ondragon was relieved to hear Ritter had survived the attack. After all, he had nothing against her personally, only the agency she worked for.

"How is she?" he inquired.

"Ms. Ritter has a basal skull fracture, multiple rib fractures, and a contusion of the right thigh. She is in an induced coma in the intensive care unit at Fortaleza Medical School. Doctors say they don't yet know if she'll pull through, let alone when she'll be responsive. We'll have to wait and see."

Ondragon nodded. So Ritter could not tell them anything about the incident. All they had left was Steiner. "Could be the leak came from your side," he said pointedly. "Pandora must be worth a pretty penny, might easily make you want to shift your allegiance."

"Do you think one of my agents would let themselves be run over just to avoid suspicion?"

Ondragon shrugged again. "I've seen it before."

"I have complete confidence in Ritter and Steiner!"

"If that's the case, then you'd better think hard about who the great unknown might be." Ondragon realized he had a problem. They both had a problem. He was being denied access to his file, and Kubicki had to find a way to explain to his superior why Pandora had fallen into enemy hands. Too bad he hadn't heard back from Rudee about the Gemini file. If the Thai managed to hack into the electronic version of the document, he wouldn't have to rely on Kubicki's goodwill and could send the BND packing. But as it was, he had to negotiate with them. Grimly, he bit his tongue. He detested situations where he was forced to compromise. But he simply had to have this file. Had to see what the BND knew about him and maybe about his brother. There was no way around it! Ondragon leaned forward. At least he had one trump card. The photos from the lab that the BND didn't have the faintest clue about. Sure, maybe they had the recordings of the camera transmission, which might only have failed for him that day. But maybe they had also neglected to record what went down, and now their asses were on the line because they were heading for a fiasco.

"Mr. Kubicki," he said, "I am right in thinking you are empty-handed now that you have lost the box and its contents. I mean, there were photos of the logbook and the medal. Too bad my assistant deleted them from the lab's computer on the instructions of your colleague." He saw Kubicki's lips narrow even more. So he had hit a nerve. The BND had nothing, absolutely nothing, and was now under massive pressure. "They're running out of time. Every hour this guy is out there running around with that box gives him more insight into the secret of Pandora. Or maybe he's already sold it to someone, his client perhaps, while we're sitting here having a nice chat. Yet it was a secret you believed needed special protection, which your operation was aiming to keep from falling into the wrong hands." Ondragon leaned his head to one side and adopted a sympathetic tone. "Well, I can see the predicament you're in. Your phone will likely ring in a moment and your supervisor will ask how the hell you lost control of Pandora. He wants results, not new problems! Like all bosses in the world—always impatient and always with one finger on the trigger. But I feel for you and I'll make you a deal that might allow you to hold on to your job." He paused artificially, savoring the tension in Kubicki. Then he pointed to the empty water bottle. "But first I'd like something to drink!"

The BND senior officer stared at him, motionless. Ondragon could almost hear his thoughts rattling around. Kubicki blinked and a resigned smile appeared on his gaunt face. "But of course, Mr. Ondragon." He rose and left the room. He was likely not only fetching water, but also making a phone call or two, just to cover himself. *It was pathetic, not being able to make your own decisions*, Ondragon thought, and he was glad he was his own boss. He couldn't help but think of Roderick DeForce, his former boss at DeForce Deliveries. He owed a lot to him. Rod had been a swell supervisor, tough as nails but fair, and a benevolent mentor. Still, Ondragon was highly appreciative of the fact that he was now accountable to no one. Unlike Kubicki, who must be kowtowing to his boss right now. Schadenfreude tingled in his belly as he imagined the conversation.

The door opened and Ondragon unobtrusively wiped the grin off his face. Grimly, he accepted the water bottle Kubicki offered him. It was chilled and he poured himself a drink. *There you go*, he thought, and took a few sips with satisfaction. As he did so, he regarded Kubicki over the rim of the glass. Mr. Important was standing next to the table, looking contrite.

Ondragon emptied the glass in a leisurely fashion and placed it on the table. "So, and now to business! But please do sit down. It's so uncomfortable otherwise." He pointed to the chair and Kubicki actually did as he was told. The reprimand from his boss had likely had a lasting effect on the order processing center in the agent's brain.

As Kubicki sat, the spirit seemed to return to his scarecrow body. His gaze fixed on Ondragon and his jaw muscles twitched. "If you have information of any kind about Pandora, we would be pleased if you would share it with us. State your terms."

Yes! thought Ondragon. It had worked. He sat back and adopted a serene expression. "My terms have just changed!"

"I thought they might have," Kubicki replied cynically. He wasn't stupid either.

"I want to see the file. But this time right away!" demanded Ondragon. "Plus double the fee, and I want you to tell me what's so important about this box! In return, I'll get Pandora back for you."

"And how are you going to do that?"

"That is my business. My methods are no concern of yours. But may I remind you that you hired me because I am the best there is." Ondragon spread both hands. "It's my job to solve problems like this. So it's lucky for you that I'm available right now." He grinned cheekily, knowing that this would only drive Kubicki even crazier.

But the BND agent gave nothing away. He merely folded his arms over his chest. "Unfortunately, we can't help with the file. It's in the Berlin-Lichterfelde branch office. We can talk about everything else."

"Then have the file emailed to you over an encrypted line."

"It has never been digitized."

"Are you saying it only exists as a paper document?"

Kubicki nodded.

"Then copy it and send it by fax."

Kubicki shook his head.

Ondragon began to seethe inwardly. What were they playing at? Yes, no, maybe, or what? "If you care about Pandora, then get me the file. I don't care how!"

"I'm not authorized to do that."

"Are you kidding me? Call your boss and get it approved!"

Kubicki shook his head again. "Unfortunately, that won't work."

Ondragon stared at the BND officer. "File—or I won't do any more for you!" he growled. Slowly, he realized why Rudee hadn't got back to him. If the file only existed in paper form, he would have a long search for it in the BND's digital archive.

Kubicki adopted a grieved expression. "Mr. Ondragon, I promise you will be given access to the Gemini document when the mission is complete and Pandora is back in our hands."

"*You* promise?" exclaimed Ondragon contemptuously. "When you were going to prevent me from seeing it a moment ago?"

Kubicki raised a hand. "I'm sorry if you got the wrong impression. I apologize. And I assure you this right has been granted by the highest authority. But not until we have Pandora back!"

Shit, Ondragon thought, *the guy was tough*. He knew how to play poker. He would probably have to be satisfied with the rest. Briefly, he weighed the risks. Charlize would now say he was obsessed with the file and he should just ditch it before he got himself exploited by anyone else, but there was more at stake than the stupid file. Of course he was dying to know what was in it, but there was still this mystery about Pandora. And that appealed to him almost as much as the fucking file. It was a top-shelf puzzle, a gem you didn't come across every day. It was just crying out for him to solve it. Him and no one else!

"Okay," he relented, "I'll take your word for it, and I hope you don't make promises lightly, because I can be very vindictive." He shot a sharp look across the table to emphasize that he always made good on his threats.

Kubicki understood his silent message. For a brief moment, the two men appraised each other. Two old hands who were in the same line of work and knew how to read between the lines. Then the BND agent folded his hands on the tabletop and began to explain the operation.

"Pandora is not just a name, it is a symbol of something that can change the whole world once it is opened."

"Pandora's Box."

"That's right." Kubicki lowered his eyes. "The reason this box is so important to us is that it may contain the clue to something that has been considered lost for over sixty years and could possibly have a major impact on all of our lives on this planet."

Ondragon had forebodings—after all he knew what was in the box: a logbook and Nikola Tesla's Edison medal. He remained silent and let the BND agent go on. Kubicki continued. He spoke of the Junkers 390, the alleged escape of General Hans Kammler in May 1945, and the plane's secret cargo. All of which Ondragon had already gathered himself or learned from Truthfinder, but which also revealed that Kubicki was reasonably serious about being honest. He also mentioned the two theories, and the whereabouts of the medal and Tesla's notebook: the one with the Nazi spies and the FBI.

"Now that the box has been found, it should be possible to prove that the FBI was not involved at the time," Kubicki said thoughtfully. "The notebook was long gone when the Bureau searched Tesla's premises after his death. Presumably, therefore, the first theory is correct and the Nazis did indeed send spies to Tesla in 1943. However, whether they also killed him"—he raised his shoulders—"we can only speculate. As far as the cargo of the JU 390 is concerned, we know from analyzing the data from the operation to recover the Air France plane that the cargo hold was in all probability empty. In the warehouse at the port, there are parts of the wrecked Junkers, but no cargo. Of course, it could be that it was carried on the current over the years and deposited somewhere else on the seabed, but we suspect that the crew, in order to save fuel, unloaded their freight somewhere else before they crossed the Atlantic. From the logbook we found, we hoped to shed light on where this happened. It's our job to secure what could be sensitive technology before someone else does."

"Sensitive technology you're going to do *what* with?"

"There are many conjectures about what the cargo might have been. The most popular is certainly that it was the fabled flying object known as 'The Bell,' which the Nazis, under the direction of Hans Kammler, are said to have been researching at the end of the war. Well, that's one possibility, albeit an unlikely one. Another is that it was the death ray invented by Tesla. This mysterious, all-important weapon that would give whoever possesses it power over all the peoples of the earth."

"But haven't we had weapons like that for a long time?" asked Ondragon. "After all, isn't a death ray completely antiquated today? I mean, we have laser beams, the atomic bomb, and intelligent, self-guiding weapons systems that could pulverize entire cities if just one person pressed the button. What use is that kind of death ray to us?"

"Tesla's high-energy particle weapon was unlike any technology we know of in terms of annihilation. Throughout his life, the great inventor was engaged in the study of waves. Sound waves, light waves, electromagnetic waves, scalar waves, or dark cosmic rays, as he called them— these are previously unproven, invisible particles that fill our space and have tremendous destructive power, if only we knew how to accelerate and direct them. Tesla supposedly figured this out and developed an all-destroying, perfect weapon." Kubicki's voice had become almost sad. "If this weapon falls into the wrong hands, then God help us."

Well, if the BND was the right hand there, Ondragon thought. Everyone was always claiming they were right and all the others were wrong. But basically, they were all the same. They were all only after the one advantage that would give them power over the entire world. The neverending struggle between nations, and once again Paul Eckbert Ondragon was in the middle of it. Great! But he too, after all, was only an opportunist who was thinking of his own interests. He wanted something and would do almost anything to get it.

"Is the death ray something like the laser cannons in *Star Wars*?" he asked. He knew the question must sound foolish, but he liked to think in terms of visual metaphors.

Kubicki nodded. "Yes, you could think of it like that. Have you ever heard of the Tunguska event?"

Ondragon shook his head.

"Well, it's an unexplained explosion that devastated an area the size of greater Los Angeles in 1908 around the Tunguska River in Siberia. But no crater or anything like it was ever found, only fallen trees and charred earth."

"And you think now that it was Tesla testing his death ray?" Ondragon laughed.

"Yes, we do. At least that's what people claimed at the time. Today, some scientists believe it was a meteorite that exploded a few kilometers above Tunguska before striking the earth."

"But then wouldn't there be small impact craters from fragments nearby?"

"Yes, that's right. But there aren't. It's thought that the meteorite, or rather a comet fragment made of ice and methane, exploded above the earth's surface and vaporized completely."

That sounded strange, Ondragon had to admit. He was a skeptic and had to see things to believe them. He was therefore inclined to consider the death ray unlikely, because if the Nazis had had it, they would have used it, and it was easy to imagine what the world would have looked like then. The Robert Harris novel *Fatherland* would be a bedtime story by comparison. The thing with the UFOs and The Bell, on the other hand, was outrageous. He simply could not believe the Nazis had built such flying objects. The technology would have come to light after the war. Sure, there were certain theories that the US military had brought German scientists and their know-how to America in secret after the end of the war. But where were the flying saucers today, where were the legendary propulsion technologies? All still classified? No way. Sooner or later, even the Americans would have wanted to brag that they had developed the only true propulsion system or the all-destroying weapon. And NASA wouldn't still be blasting rockets into orbit with millions of tons of fuel on board if they had long since uncovered the secret of antigravity. Ondragon leaned forward and looked at Kubicki.

"And what do you think was in the Junkers?" he asked in a low voice.

The BND senior officer took off his glasses and wiped his eyes. If he wanted Ondragon to continue working for them, he would now have to come up with a plausible and more detailed explanation. Kubicki seemed to know that. He replaced his glasses and looked at Ondragon as openly as was possible for an intelligence officer.

"In 1901, Nikola Tesla filed a patent application for 'Apparatus for the Use of Radiant Energy' with the US Patent Office, but then withdrew it. No one knows why. The apparatus could supposedly collect dark cosmic rays from the so-called ether. We believe it was a device that collected free energy from the environment and converted it into electricity. Tesla was firmly convinced of the existence of ether at that time. Today, the theory is outdated and the concept of the vacuum has replaced the idea of ether. Today, the concept of free energy tends to be put forward by parascience and is generally considered chicanery. Modern physics calls it zero-point energy, or the over-unity effect. There are conflicting opinions about this as well."

Zero-point energy. Ondragon had heard the term before, from Truth-finder. Wasn't that even his research field? But what was this zero-point energy actually? He could still just about imagine what ether was all about. But free energy? Man! His ignorance in this area was troublesome. Like trying to dance on raw eggs.

"And what can this supposed device of Tesla's do?" he wanted to know.

"An apparatus that captures zero-point or free space energy," Kubicki explained, "would be able to generate energy for free—clean and unlimited."

"So a perpetual motion machine?"

"No. We're not looking for a damned perpetual motion machine. Tesla's device—if it exists—is much more incredible. Because not only does it run on its own and without any energy input whatsoever, it also produces surplus energy! Do you know what that means? Our energy problems would be over!"

CHAPTER 21

August 2, 1899
Colorado Springs
evening

The sun was setting over the crest of the Rocky Mountains, bathing the plain in orange light. Everything was ready—the equipment had been calibrated and the assistants were full of energy. Dressed in their rubber aprons, they waited for Dr. Tesla to come out of his chamber and give the signal for the experiment to start. Philemon was squatting on a wooden stool out on the prairie, gazing at the laboratory building and enjoying the cooler air. His task had been to stick several rows of light bulbs into the ground a hundred yards away. Two hundred of them, to be exact. Now he was waiting for the great miracle that Dr. Tesla had announced, but which he doubted would come about. He knew the doctor was capable of transmitting energy wirelessly over short distances; Czito had demonstrated this in the laboratory beforehand, to check that the oscillators were functioning. Philemon had marveled when the light bulb in Czito's hand had begun to glow as if from nowhere, and the grinning Serb could roam with it at will within a certain radius. But to try the same thing now over a hundred meters using the earth as a conductor . . . it was completely crazy, no matter what the doctor claimed.

The sun was sinking behind the jagged ridges, and purple shadows were settling over the vast open space. Philemon went to take a look at his pocket watch, but realized he had left it at the hotel. After all, you were not allowed to wear anything metallic during the experiments. And so he waited until the last streak of violet in the firmament had turned completely to black and the prairie had become as dark as pitch. Crickets chirped and a coyote called in the distance. Into this subdued symphony of nature broke a loud crackle, so abruptly that Philemon winced. He was about to head back to the laboratory, when at that very moment the light bulbs at his feet began to glow. All two hundred of them!

With shock and excitement, he jumped up from the stool and ran through the rows of lamps that stuck out of the dry prairie grass as if strung on a garland. Some of them were flickering slightly.

"It works!" cried Philemon, raising both arms. "It actually works! It's a miracle!" But just as suddenly as the lights had come on, they went out again, and Philemon was in darkness. The crickets continued to chirp and he heard the *yip-yip* of the coyotes echoing down to him. It was all as if nothing had happened. Philemon lowered his arms and tried to peer through the darkness to make out what was going on in the lab, but there was absolute silence. Then the light in the building was switched on and Löwenstein and Tesla looked out the door.

"Did you see it?" shouted Philemon, pointing to the light bulbs.

"Yes, marvelous, wasn't it?" Tesla exclaimed in reply. "Wait, we'll repeat the experiment right away with a higher voltage, and the lamps should shine even brighter."

And they did. When the bulbs began to glow again, Philemon was blinded by their brightness and had to shield his eyes with one hand. He heard some of the bulbs burn out with a soft *clink*, but the others continued to shine with undiminished power. Enchanted by the sight, Philemon walked through the rows of bulbs, his arms outstretched. They turned night into day and attracted quite a few moths, which danced above the magic light as if drunk. Philemon tilted his head back and looked up at the sky. The first stars shone back at him, as if reflecting the lights at his feet. He took a deep breath and closed his eyes. Through the soles of his shoes, despite the rubber, he thought he could feel the energy pulsing through the earth in a quiet but powerful beat. Yes, he was in the right place! And yes, he was ready to believe in things he had previously thought impossible. Because *he* was here. Nikola Tesla. A god in human form. Prometheus, who brought fire to mankind!

When he opened his eyes, the golden glow of the lights had gone and the prairie was in complete darkness. The static crackling of the apparatus in the laboratory had also stopped. Philemon turned around. Löwenstein and Tesla had disappeared. What was going on? Was the experiment concluded? Full of happiness, he walked toward the building. He felt refreshed, as if his senses had been heightened by the energy that had flowed into his limbs through the earth. Philemon heard the grass rustling under his shoes and the cracking of the wooden building as its walls slowly released the heat of the day. Almost floating, he moved toward the dimly lit doorway. The few streetlights of Colorado Springs glittered in the distance; they were also a legacy of Nikola Tesla. *Ungrateful people*, Philemon thought. *After all, it had been the doctor who had brought them out of the darkness of the Stone Age into the enlightened century.*

Another crackling sound came from inside the lab and the light in the door went out. *Hey, what was the point of leaving him here in the dark?* Philemon wondered. He walked faster.

But it was no longer remotely dark, he soon realized, looking around in amazement. A bluish glowing mist was flowing around the contours of the laboratory building, seemingly originating from the antenna on the roof. Like burning alcohol, the glow flowed over the wooden walls into the grass, where it spread farther and soon reached Philemon's feet. Fearfully, he backed away from the ghostly apparition. It could not be fire, for he did not smell burning. But what was it, then?

He looked at the building. The loud crackling inside had become a rhythmic banging. It sounded as if a troupe of electric goblins was dancing.

Bang! Bang! Bang!

Again and again, small flashes of lightning discharged and flared brightly in the doorway. Philemon glanced over his shoulder. The light bulbs on the prairie floor were glowing dimly. What the hell were the others doing there in the lab? And why hadn't they told him?

Suddenly, Philemon saw hundreds of points of light rising from the greenish shimmering grass. Like overgrown fireflies, they flew up before him into the cool night sky. Were they will-o'-the-wisps?

Cautiously, Philemon reached out a hand to the fairy-tale apparition. But when his fingers brushed one of the points of light, there was a tiny discharge and the glow went out. Something small floated to the ground. Philemon bent down and picked it up. It was a dead moth with stiff wings. Curious, he touched the next glowing spot in front of his nose. It also went out and fell to the ground. Again, it was a moth. Could it be that what he thought were will-o'-the-wisps were just statically charged moths, compelled by the invisible force of electromagnetic waves to buzz helplessly in circles?

Philemon let go of the unfortunate little insects and made his way to the building. He wanted to know what was going on inside. When he reached the door, the banging stopped and he saw only absolute darkness.

"Hello in there? Are you all right?"

He heard a wheezing and then Löwenstein answered. "Yes, everything is fine. We merely had some problems with the center coil. It wasn't responding the way we wanted it to. What did you see outside, Phil? Were the lights still on?"

"Yes, at first, then they just flickered. But instead, I saw something else. An electric glow like Saint Elmo's fire. The whole building was enveloped in it." Philemon entered the laboratory, which was still dark. Suddenly, a low hum sounded and the ceiling lights came on. Philemon caught sight of Dr. Tesla and the two other men inside the large coil paling. They were looking thoughtfully at the medium-size transformer on the wooden frame. A pungent smell of metal hung in the air and bluish smoke was rising from the copper ring at the top.

"Did it burn through?" asked Philemon, climbing the stairs to the inside of the enclosure.

"Yes, the voltage was probably too high after all," Löwenstein replied. "It arced right at the windings and the wires melted through. We'll have to repair the coil." He seemed disappointed and ran a hand over his sweaty forehead.

"I'll get right on it," Czito grumbled sullenly.

"Now, now, gentlemen. Why so downhearted?" interjected Tesla almost gleefully. He stepped over to his assistants and smiled happily. "We do have something to celebrate. Our experiment has succeeded. Across the board! We have sent energy through the earth over a distance of one hundred meters and made two hundred light bulbs glow. A huge success, on the basis of which I can assure you that we will see much greater successes. We will soon be able to illuminate thousands of bulbs on the summit of Pikes Peak! You will see, it will be a fantastic spectacle that will convince even the last doubters of the value of our work here."

Philemon looked at each face in turn. Tesla seemed euphoric, Czito and Löwenstein, on the other hand, depressed. Why were they so unenthused by the doctor's success? Had they expected something different?

"So," Tesla broke the silence, "since I have no further need of you tonight, Mr. Ailey, I relieve you of your duties and order you to take an extended night's rest and recuperation until noon tomorrow. I do not want you to rejoin us here until after lunch. Rested and in good spirits! Mr. Löwenstein and Mr. Czito will stay and try to repair the coil. And I shall make haste to record our findings while they are still fresh in my mind. Such a significant moment should not be allowed to pass without the proper recognition. I wish you a pleasant night's rest, Mr. Ailey."

Philemon wanted to offer to stay and help with the repairs, but the doctor turned away and climbed over the paling. The conversation was over. Thoughtfully, Philemon watched him go. It was strange, but it almost seemed as if they did not want him to be present while they went about their work. He felt a hand on his shoulder. It was Löwenstein.

"No offense, kid. That's just the way he is. You go on back to the hotel. You're lucky. I envy you the sleep." The German gave him a friendly wink.

Philemon nodded. He said goodbye and stepped into the darkness outside the laboratory. He looked pensively up into the starry sky and heard the door being locked behind him. A short time later, strange hissing sounds came through the wooden wall. He was sure of it! They were keeping secrets from him. Philemon felt the bite of mortification in his chest. Was he not reliable enough? Had his diligence in recent days not proved his devotion to the doctor? Apparently not. Tesla had said there were no secrets here and that anyone could come to his laboratory and have a look. So why had he been shown the door? It didn't fit.

The elation of the previous moment faded, and with it the joy of the observations during the experiment: the glow of the two hundred light bulbs on the prairie floor, the illuminated moths spinning through the night, and the phosphorescent glow that had enveloped the entire laboratory building. All these wonderful images could not mask the bitter disappointment that gripped him at that moment.

Philemon sighed and, his head drooping, marched off across the dark prairie.

CHAPTER 22

May 23, 2011
Fortaleza, Brazil
2:23 pm

A driver from the Honorary Consulate took Ondragon to the hotel. On the way there, he looked out the window, lost in thought. The conversation with Kubicki had been strange, and it was still sinking in. Could there be such a thing as a pimped version of a perpetual motion machine, if the utopian apparatus itself did not exist? It sounded completely implausible. And if Nikola Tesla had held the solution to all of mankind's energy problems back then, why wasn't the world a different place by now? No one would want to buy overpriced gas or oil today if they could get energy for free. But maybe there was actually something to it. If so, it would be no wonder that people other than the Germans were hot on the heels of the technology; it threatened the power structures of politics, industry, and business that had been established for decades. Putting an apparatus for generating free energy out there would bring an end to all energy corporations!

I have to make an urgent phone call, he thought. *But not until I get to the hotel.*

The car reached the Gran Marquise and Ondragon got out. He went to his room and checked to see if anyone had been there during his absence. His bug detector showed nothing, but the map of Fortaleza on the nightstand was not quite in the same position. So the BND or someone else must have searched his room. He quickly went to the spot on the wall where he had hidden the chip behind the wallpaper. It was still there. Relieved, he took it and then turned on his cell phone, hoping the BND technicians had had a tough time trying to crack it. He dialed Charlize's number and waited, tapping his finger tensely on the nightstand. The fatigue he had felt at the Honorary Consulate was gone, and the *centrifuge* was running at full speed.

"Hi, Boss! Did they finally let you out?" his assistant answered. She sounded breathless, as if she had run to the phone.

"Yes," he replied curtly. "Where are you? Is everything all right?"

"*Hai*, I'm with Sem; we just had a little discussion about the deal because the situation has changed. But good to hear from you, so you can sort it out with Sem in person right away. Plus, we have a possible lead on the guy who stole the box!"

"Excellent! Where can we meet?"

"I'll send you an address right away. Go there and wait to be picked up."

"Okay, see you then! Oh, and, Charlize . . .?"

"Yes?"

"Compile a list of the largest energy and oil companies in the world and their shareholders. That would be great."

"Will be done. But why energy companies?"

"Just a hunch. I'll explain later." He hung up, packed up all his things, and left the room. Down at the front desk, he checked out and looked up the address Charlize had sent him. It was a bar on Praia do Futuro, the beach on the east side of town.

Out on the street, Ondragon hailed a cab and instructed the driver to take several detours on the way. While they were en route, he scanned his overflowing inbox for important messages. He skipped over the piles of customer inquiries and the interim reports on assignments progress from his employees Dietmar and Achille. Sadly, there was nothing from Rudee, but he did find an email from his friend at the FBI, which he opened immediately. George Hurley wrote:

Hi, Paul,

Are you now caught up with the conspiracy theorists dealing with this topic? It's old hat. Nothing but a modern-day myth that has even made it into our top ten. You can read about it here: https://archives.fbi.gov/archives/ news/stories/2008/july/myths_072408. The complete file was published a few years ago under the Freedom of Information Act, on the "FBI Records—The Vault" site, which we created. It's 290 pages long. I hope you enjoy reading it! It's quite a jumble of documents: letters, reports, memos, notes, and so on. Everything is Ondragon-friendly, by the way, if you want to know that in advance, hehehe.

You can find the file at the link: http://vault.fbi.gov/nikola-tesla. The blacked-out passages are not relevant. They're mainly the names of agents, informants, or other persons who did not want to be named in public. From page 5 onward you will find the reports of the events after Tesla's death, about the search of his apartment and the confiscation of his possessions. I want to emphasize that, contrary to popular belief, nothing was retained or taken by the FBI during the raid. The idea that the FBI found secret records about superweapons or UFOs at Tesla's place is complete nonsense. Fairy tales that have mushroomed on the dung of some incorrigible conspiracy theorists.

Tesla's belongings were confiscated back then because of fears that records of potential weapons technology might fall into the hands of enemy nations. After all, Tesla's nephew was first on the scene after his death. He was a member of the diplomatic corps of Yugoslavia, a country that then sympathized with the Soviets. In 1943, World War II was still in full swing, and the US needed to prevent technologies that might be critical for the war—however hypothetical they might have been—from falling into the hands of spies. They were forced to investigate.

Of course, these circumstances only fueled the myth surrounding Nikola Tesla. It's not surprising, as the man was already a kind of electrical engineering pop star during his lifetime. He had many contacts in the high society of New York and a talent for grand gestures. It is understandable that he fired the imagination of many of his contemporaries.

The fact is, Nikola Tesla was an extraordinary man and inventor, but he suffered from delusions at the end of his life, in which he claimed to be communicating with aliens and to be in possession of a death ray and other hair-raising gadgets. In old age, many an outstanding mind has become whimsical. Sorry, Paul, but that's all there is to say about it.

Tesla's lost miracle machines remain a legend, a topic that obsesses a few tireless do-gooders who fill whole forums on the net with it, but any serious scientist would wave it aside when mentioned.

But if there's any more you want to know, just get in touch. Stay clean! And give my regards to your charming assistant.

Best regards from Washington,
George

There was little in the message that was new to Ondragon, but George's slightly ironic tone made it clear what he thought of the matter. It was obvious that the FBI no longer attached any priority to Tesla and his inventions.

Ondragon opened the two links George had sent him: the top ten

FBI myths and the Tesla file in "The Vault." He read the first few pages, which were indeed difficult to decipher because the copies were abysmal and some of the people responsible for them had covered them in messy scribbles. After all, the reports of interviews with witnesses about Tesla's death confirmed not only what George had written, but also what Ondragon had learned from Truthfinder. The opening of Tesla's safe had been witnessed by six people: the nephew, the science journalist, a lab assistant, and three hotel employees. The FBI and the ufologist agreed on that. According to the FBI report, in the end the nephew was the only one who claimed the notebook had been there *before* it was confiscated. However, neither Tesla's assistant nor the science journalist nor the three hotel employees confirmed that. The picture slowly fell into place for Ondragon. With the additional knowledge that Tesla's Edison medal had been in the German Junkers, it was clear to him that the FBI most likely had nothing to do with the book's disappearance. Everything pointed toward the Nazi spies theory, as adventurous as it sounded.

Be that as it may, he thought tensely, at least it was clear from the "Tesla" file that the case had been closed by the Bureau and styled as an amusing anecdote. As far as George Hurley was concerned, Ondragon could rely on him to tell the truth. Only what about Pandora? Did the FBI know about the BND operation? While Ondragon didn't believe that whoever had run Ritter down was working with the FBI, he couldn't be sure. Unfortunately, he would not be allowed to talk about it with George. Pandora had to remain secret for the time being.

The cab stopped at the corner ahead of the address Charlize had given him. Before Ondragon got out, he wrote a short email to Rudee, telling him to stop searching for the Gemini file and that he needed a double encryption key. A few minutes later, as he stood at the roadside looking around, his cell phone beeped. Quickly, Ondragon opened Rudee's answer:

Sawadee khrap, Paul, you got it, stop search. Code can be found in the attachment.

See ya, Rudee.

Excellent, Ondragon thought, and closed his fingers around the phone. Now all he needed was a clean computer.

On the way to the bar, he kept checking he wasn't being tailed. The coast was clear. Finally, he stopped in front of the *boteco* and opened the map. He pretended to look for a street, and while he waited for someone to identify themself, he let his mind wander. If the FBI wasn't behind the attack on Ritter, who was? CIA, NSA, the Russians, the Chinese, the Arabs? Anyone could have an interest in Pandora. In reality, the technology race had long been the new Cold War. Industrial espionage was far more important today than it had been thirty years ago. In the struggle for supremacy in world markets, the expertise of Western companies was in demand, much more than the strategy of some calcified Soviet leader. Today, capitalism ruled, no matter what guise it was hidden behind. It was all about money and the distribution of wealth, of which of course everyone wanted a piece, and about controlling the masses, i.e., the little people. More and more emerging nations were elbowing their way into the upper echelon of industrialized nations, turning from Third World countries into emerging economies, with the West crawling up their asses. The tiger economies and BRIC states were choking the world market with cheap goods. The new instrument for maintaining power in the globalized society was no longer the universally feared nuclear bombs; no, it was something much less remarkable. It was what drove all the wheels of this shitty world. The thing for which all humans hungered. Plain and simple—consumption!

Ondragon felt a tentative brush against his sleeve. He looked to the side and saw a child holding out a hand expectantly. He took a ten-real bill from his pocket and gave it to the boy, but he continued to tug at his sleeve.

"What? Wasn't that enough?" he snapped at him. But then he understood. He quickly folded up the map, shouldered his travel bag, and allowed the kid to pull him across the street.

On the other side, the child let go of him. "*Vem comigo*—come with me!" he said, and then disappeared into the narrow alleys of the favela. Cursing softly, Ondragon struggled to follow him through the confusing maze. He had never set foot in such a slum before, and now he knew why. The favela looked like a city that had been dropped on the earth from a great height. All around him stood houses that looked as if they had been thrown away, surrounded by mountains of trash and junk. It was anarchy. The domain of the drug gangs. The air had a dangerously high lead content. Average life expectancy: twenty-five years. All the favelas were divided among the drug lords, who ruled their sectors with the high-handedness of little would-be dictators. And the Brazilian state? It looked the other way. Vigilante justice was the order of the day. Including the infamous *microonda*—the microwave—method, where the victim was put in a tower of car tires, doused with gasoline, and burned alive. Welcome to hell! With the small difference that in the biblical hell there was only one devil.

The boy set a crazy pace and Ondragon had trouble following him. Every time he disappeared around a corner, Ondragon was overcome by the slight panic that he would never find his way out of this maze of alleyways. But the boy always waited for him, jumping impatiently from one foot to the other, as if he had to go urgently. Once he saw the gringo was following him, he quickly ran on. The little one likely had only the one speed on his speedometer.

While Ondragon plunged after the boy through the alleys, he noticed he was getting curious looks everywhere. Except that hardly any residents were on the streets in the fading heat of the day. All the eyes of the favela peered out from the shelter of the dark window cavities, gaping at him as if he were fair game. They were probably already placing bets on how long such a conspicuous white man would last here before being hit by a bullet. Involuntarily, Ondragon ducked his head, hoping Sem's people were already watching and would intervene if anyone approached him with ill intent. Otherwise, all he had left was the Glock from the BND. Fifteen rounds. Not much in a place where even children carried guns.

The little boy ran and ran without the slightest sign of exhaustion. His bare feet made hardly a sound on the dusty ground, so weightlessly did he fly along. Ondragon felt the travel bag on his back slowly getting heavier; sweat was streaming from all his pores. His shirt was completely soaked and was sticking to his skin. The bare brick walls of the buildings around him were baking in the shimmering heat. And the deeper they went into the favela, the more oppressive and malodorous the air became.

After what felt like half an eternity, they reached their destination: a house that looked like the architectural dream of a cubist artist who had sniffed too much glue. Cube-shaped units had been added everywhere to a central, pyramid-like base building and then painted in different colors, depending on what had just fallen off the back of the truck. Pink, light blue, green! Actually, the colors might have looked cheerful, if there hadn't been graffiti all over the walls. *CA*—these initials, Ondragon knew, revealed that behind these walls was the headquarters of the local drug gang. A hornets' nest it was better not to kick.

He stopped and scanned the surroundings. Not a soul was to be seen; it seemed as if he had crossed some invisible boundary. Deadly still, the humid air hovered over the cube pyramid, which stretched into the sky like an angry fist through the tangle of power cables.

The boy urged him on and eventually brought him to an entrance. Behind it, a staircase led upward. The little boy pointed to it and said, "*Vai lá pra cima*—up there." Then he disappeared like a weasel that feared being glimpsed by an eagle.

His hand on the pistol, Ondragon climbed the stairs. At the top, a dark corridor opened up, with a single door at the end. It was made of rusting steel and the obligatory *CA* was emblazoned on it in royal blue paint, like an ominous calling card.

What was waiting for him behind the door?

Charlize, hopefully. Ondragon had little desire to face the Fortaleza drug lord without her support. He stepped up to the door and banged his fist against it. The blows echoed hollowly through the building. A moment later, he heard a bolt being pushed back, and the door opened with a squeak. It was even darker inside than in the hallway. Ondragon noticed shadows in the room, hesitated, and then entered. The door closed noisily behind him and at the same moment he felt the barrel of a gun at his head. He dropped his bag and raised his hands placatingly. Someone patted him down, reached for the pistol in his waistband, and took it from him.

"*Eu me chamo Ondragon. Você é o Sem?*" he asked, hoping the guy understood his poor Portuguese.

"But of course! *Boa tarde, senhor Ondragon!*" he heard a voice reply; it seemed somehow familiar. A light was turned on, and the shadows in the room transformed. There were five men. One by one, Ondragon scanned their faces. There were two black guys who looked like they had stepped out of a rap video: tattoos on their upper arms, thick gold chains around their necks, low-slung, baggy pants, and blue scarves on their heads—bandanas. They both held newer AK models and did not give the impression they would hesitate to use them. In the background, a third, youngish fellow was leaning against a desk, quietly smoking a cigarette. Ondragon could only make out the guy holding the gun to his head from the corner of his eye. A sinewy Rastafarian with a puffy face and a wild beard. The fifth guy was standing right in front of him. It was the small boxer who had brought the pizza to his hotel. His shrewd, black eyes were checking Ondragon out from head to toe.

"Where is Charlize Tanaka?" asked Ondragon.

"You mean, *a filha do sombra*." A grin appeared on the face of the mini-gangster.

Ondragon frowned. Daughter of the Shadow? He had guessed Charlize had good contacts with the Brazilian mafia, but the fact that they had given her a name like that impressed him. He nodded.

The little boxer guy called something over his shoulder and a door opened in the far corner of the room. Someone came out.

"Oi, Paulinho!" greeted Charlize nonchalantly, coming up to him. "Sorry for all the sneaking around, but the guys here are very cautious types."

Ondragon looked at her admiringly. His petite little lotus blossom was wearing a turquoise-blue Carmen blouse and a white miniskirt. Her black hair fell loosely over her shoulders and various gold bangles jingled at her wrist. She looked like a graceful Japanese dragon in a crowd of dirty street dogs. His gaze wandered over to the pizza delivery boy, who was still grinning broadly under his flat nose.

"So which one of you is Sem?" he wanted to know. Now that he knew Charlize was with him, he felt much safer.

"You're standing in front of him!" said Charlize.

"What, that tiny guy?" Ondragon exclaimed. Inwardly, however, he immediately cursed himself for it. "I'm sorry, but when we first met, you told me you weren't Sem."

"Well, you fell for it, man!" Sem, the feared drug lord of Fortaleza, gestured with his hand and the Rastafarian lowered his gun.

"Sem is the head of CA, the Comando Azul," Charlize explained, "an offshoot of the Primeiro Comando da Capital from São Paulo, also known as the PCC."

Aha, so that's the way the wind is blowing, Ondragon thought. Charlize had grown up in São Paulo, and somehow she must have found her way into Brazil's largest criminal organization. He resolved to grill her a little later. Just a teensy bit of research that might help him uncover something about her past. It wasn't that he distrusted her, she had simply piqued his curiosity.

"Let's make ourselves comfortable," Sem offered kindly. He seemed to have overlooked the previous insult. "I think we have a lot to talk about."

He was right; there was a lot they needed to discuss. And they had no time to lose. The clock was ticking. With each passing minute, Pandora was moving farther and farther out of reach.

They sat down in a corner of the sofa and one of the rappers brought them cold beers, which Ondragon gratefully accepted. He quickly drank a few sips, put the can down, and looked at the little gangster boss again. Although he doubtless had a lot of lives on his conscience, Ondragon did not presume to judge him. His philosophy was that everyone was free to pursue their trade, as long as they did not get in anyone else's way. His, for instance! He quite liked the cool rapper demeanor the guy adopted. At least he was not quick-tempered, and he seemed to have a gift for sizing up a situation correctly and reacting appropriately. He had understood that in his position as king over a small but fragile kingdom, he had to keep a cool head. Good man!

"I suggest we start with the things that are most urgent," Ondragon said.

"And for you, those would be?" inquired Sem.

"The first thing I'd like to do is send data to someone, and I'd need a computer for that." Ondragon glanced briefly at the desk, which stood across from the sofa corner and was crammed with computers. A stark contrast to the dirt and squalor outside the door. "Then we can discuss our deal and try to catch the son of a bitch who got in our way. *Está bem?*"

"Yeah, man, you got it. You can use that laptop over there." Sem pointed to a brand-new MacBook. Then he sat back and talked to Charlize in Portuguese. Too fast for Ondragon to understand, unfortunately. Charlize replied, giggling, and gave him an amused look. Grimly, Ondragon looked at the two of them. Were they making fun of him?

"I was just telling Sem you can be a little too German sometimes." Charlize smiled. "I mean, your quirk of always categorizing things. Not, of course, the method you then use to get down to business. That's usually more cowboy American."

"I see," Ondragon replied, moderately enthusiastically. He grabbed the proffered laptop, activated a special virus scanner program over the internet, and then turned back to Charlize. "I have the data from the lab here," he said in Japanese, because that way he could be sure Sem and his people wouldn't understand. "I'm going to send it to Truthfinder, the young physicist I told you about. It's reinsurance. Rudee will also get a package to put in his safe. After that, I want you to edit the photos from the log so I can read the entries. Preferably print them out, along with the list of power companies."

"Can you even trust this Truthfinder?" inquired Charlize.

"I think so. If Strangelove recommended him to me, he'll be reliable."

"Okay, whatever you say."

The virus scanner had completed its checks and the computer was ninety-eight percent clean. Ondragon took his cell phone and sent Rudee's encryption code to the laptop via Bluetooth. He then downloaded the data from the chip to the computer, ran the coding over it, and compressed the file. He opened his email account and sent the encrypted package to Rudee and Truthfinder. Of course, Truthfinder would look at the photos and possibly read the logbook entries, but Ondragon was counting on that; his gut told him he would still need the help of the young physics genius.

After sending the email, he deleted everything from the laptop again and erased all traces from the memory with a few clicks. He left only the images from the logbook on the desktop. He handed the device to Charlize. "So now it's your turn. Please hurry up. Because I have a new deal with the BND and time is running out. If I can get them Pandora, they'll double the fee!"

Charlize looked at him skeptically, but set to work. Ondragon watched briefly as her slender fingers scurried across the keyboard. When he finally turned his gaze back to Sem, he detected a certain distrust in the latter's eyes. "Sorry, but that was confidential," he apologized.

The little drug lord waved it off with apparent approval.

"Good; now let's get to our deal," Ondragon explained. "Sem, you and your people were contracted to deliver the box to me. Unfortunately, for reasons best known to us, things went awry. I realize that you also took a risk in order to complete the job for me, even if you were unsuccessful. Of course, I will pay you your fee in full, but I have another proposal to make. If you help me catch the bastard who interfered, I'll add the same amount again on top! Well, what do you think of that?" The offer was only fair. Ondragon was aware that he was depending on Sem, because he himself didn't have the slightest clue as to who the guy was. Certainly, he had an idea who might be behind it, at least as a client, but he was keeping that to himself for the time being.

Sem stroked his goatee and pursed his lips as if he was weighing the offer, but then something strange happened. Just for a split second, Sem's black pupils flitted over to Charlize and back again. It was only a very slight flicker, a barely perceptible movement. But Ondragon registered it, and got the impression that the big boss of Comando Azul was seeking the approval of the *nipo-brasileira*. Slightly puzzled, he wondered who was king and who was subject here, but pretended not to have noticed.

The little Brazilian stretched out an arm and drove it through the air in a rapper-like fashion. "Okey-dokey, Mr. Ondragon, I'm in!"

Excellent, Ondragon thought silently, while Charlize clicked her tongue next to him in apparent approval.

"Almost done," she then said, tapping the "return" button with her index finger. "Sending the data to the printer."

In the background, the printer went to work, and Ondragon watched Charlize delete the files from the computer as he had done with the others. She then closed the machine and placed it on the coffee table. "There. Now I'm all ears!"

For a moment, Ondragon glared at her. His diligent assistant was more cunning than he had thought. "Daughter of the Shadow"—who was this Shadow, he wondered?

"Great," he said in response, leaning forward. "Finally, we can move on to the operational part. Out with the info, then! What did you find out about the guy who now has the box?"

CHAPTER 23

August 2, 1899
Colorado Springs
the same night

Philemon walked quickly through the darkened streets. Disappointment still gnawed at his self-esteem; the others had excluded him, and he wondered what they were doing in the lab right now. He should have stayed and listened. Dejectedly, he sank his head between his shoulders and quickened his step. At this late hour, Colorado Springs was deserted, and it felt eerie to be out alone. Every now and then, Philemon thought he heard the sound of footsteps behind him and turned around, but of course there was no one there. It was likely only his tense nerves playing tricks on him.

Suddenly, a figure appeared in front of him as if by magic. Startled, Philemon jumped back and raised both fists. He was ready to defend himself. In New York, a situation like this on the street at night was never good news, and he was always prepared for a confrontation with street thieves. At the university, he had participated in the weekly boxing training and had even held his own against older students.

He stared challengingly at the guy, whose mustachioed face was hidden in the shadow of a peaked cap.

"Well, who else is out at the witching hour?" the figure asked.

"Who wants to know?" Philemon threw back belligerently.

"Me!" the man said importantly, raising his head so that the glow from the nearest streetlight fell on his face. On his cap flashed the brass badge of the local police station.

Philemon put his fists down and relaxed a little. "Sorry, I didn't recognize you, sir," he quickly apologized to the constable. But why had the guy jumped out at him so abruptly?

The constable lifted his flabby chin and gawked at Philemon overtly. "Well, well, and perhaps you will answer my question now? Who are you and what are you doing here?"

Philemon explained the reason for his being out so late. In the process, he was overcome by the vague suspicion that he was not being delayed in order to determine what he was doing here or who he was. The man seemed to know exactly who he was dealing with. The disgust in his gaze was unmistakable.

"Mr. Ailey, well, well. And you're working out there in the lab with the lunatic doctor."

Philemon started to say something in Dr. Tesla's defense, but then didn't. He was tired and he didn't want to get into trouble with the local lawman. "Yes, I am," he replied instead.

The constable pushed out his belly and hooked his thumbs into his belt, raising his shoulders like a bull about to charge. He growled something Philemon did not understand.

"Excuse me?"

"We don't want you here!" the guy repeated. "You, and this doctor and his experiments! It is not good, what you are doing here. You are disturbing the peace of our town. I'll give you some advice: Pack your things and get out of here as fast as you can. Before something happens to you!"

"What could possibly happen to me?" asked Philemon lightly.

The constable's bushy mustache inflated as he exhaled indignantly. "Are you that simpleminded, or are you trying to take me for a fool, my friend?"

Philemon looked at him in confusion.

"I don't know what that madman of a scientist told you, but one thing is certain: A man was grilled out there. *Pow!* Struck by lightning. *Bang!* Gone, he was! A pile of ashes."

Philemon's throat tightened. Unconsciously, he ran his finger down and around his collar. Why the hell were people here so obsessed with this story about the lightning strike? And why did Tesla and Löwenstein tell a completely different version of it? Who was he to believe? The respected scientist or the townspeople, who had no idea of the great things that were happening on their doorstep?

"I can assure you," Philemon tried to explain to the constable, "that there is nothing unusual or dangerous going on in the laboratory. We are conducting serious scientific experiments. Come and see for yourself. Why don't you stop by and take a look? We are working with high-frequency currents and electromagnetic oscillations, simply put, with electricity—this is progress, not witchcraft!"

The constable snorted. "But there is a witness to the incident! So don't talk such nonsense. Safe? It's nothing of the sort!"

"Witness? Don't make me laugh! You call a boozy old goatherd a witness? Not exactly credible, if you ask me."

"You have no idea," the constable hissed.

"No, obviously I have no actual idea of the astounding bigotry that reigns in this town. You should rejoice that Dr. Tesla has chosen this insignificant place as the site of his great research. Who outside of this one-horse town is aware of its existence? It is only because a railroad magnate holds all the land here, and has created his own little empire, that Colorado Springs exists at all. But believe me, if the doctor's experiments succeed, this little backwater will be world famous!" He took a deep breath. He was tired of the malicious gossip against Tesla.

The constable remained silent, his expression grim. "You're going to get a shock," he said, and then moved aside reluctantly.

At last, he lets me go, Philemon thought, taking his leave with a curt gesture. His own expression grim, he marched past the fellow, only slowing his pace when he turned onto Cascade Avenue. Relieved, he let his shoulders sag. It was truly unbelievable how stubborn the people here were!

He reached the hotel just a few minutes later and crossed the foyer, greeting the startled and blinking night porter. Then he climbed the stairs to the second floor and went to his room by the dim light of the frosted-glass lamps in the corridor. He already had the key in his hand when suddenly the image of the suitcase flickered through his consciousness . . . together with a small spark of suspicion that had taken root in him against his will.

Now would be a good time to check on the case, he thought. *I could check whether Herkimer is right and there really is something to the general Colorado Springs conspiracy theory.*

Philemon put the key back in his vest pocket and looked around. Behind the doors, all was quiet. And Tesla and the other two were still in the lab, so no one would notice a thing. He sensed certain qualms within himself. If he actually gave his suspicions rein, wasn't he betraying his mentor's trust? Tesla had sworn him that morning to always turn to him with any doubts. But the doctor didn't seem to have been completely honest with him either, else why would he have sent him away so readily earlier?

I'll do it now, thought Philemon, *it's the only way I can finally be certain.*

Quietly, he crept back to the stairs. He looked up. The light in the stairwell flickered, went out, and glowed again. Probably because of the fluctuating voltage produced by the Colorado Springs power plant. Not for nothing did Tesla convert the electricity supplied to his laboratory out there to a steady current before using it for his experiments.

The laboratory out there . . .

Philemon shivered involuntarily. Perhaps the flickering was also due to the fact that they were carrying out new experiments there—without him!

Thrusting his chin forward resolutely, he climbed one flight of stairs after the next. When he reached the third and final floor, he paused and looked down the corridor. It looked exactly like the one on the second floor, but with one small difference. These were the more expensive suites with the better views. Among them was Tesla's room, number 303—divisible by three, of course. Philemon smiled softly as he walked past it. He followed his hunch and headed for the door at the far end of the corridor. It bore no tag with a number. Carefully, he checked to see if the knob would turn. Against his expectations, the door swung open and Philemon stared indecisively into the darkness.

Was he even allowed to enter the room? What if he was caught?

But it was surely just a storage room, and if the hotel didn't want guests to go in, it would surely be locked. Hoping to find a light switch somewhere, Philemon finally entered and felt cautiously along the wall. But there was no switch. Perplexed, he looked around the dark room, but could only make out formless shapes. Then he noticed a cord dangling from the ceiling right in front of his nose. He grabbed it and pulled. With a soft *click*, a bare light bulb came on. Quickly, Philemon closed the door, turned, and looked at the items stored in the chamber. Against the walls were shelves of fresh bedding, extra pillows, and blankets. Soap and tin canisters of lye were stored on another shelf. There was a faint smell of wax and cleaning products. In the center of the room was piled all sorts of furniture, some of which was covered with sheets. In one corner was a table. Plates and empty cups had been placed on the white tablecloth. Apparently, the maids spent their breaks here.

Philemon took off his hat and ran a hand over the top of his head. He could not see a suitcase anywhere. Perhaps it had already been returned to Mr. Myers. So it had all been a false alarm and Mr. Herkimer's mysterious hints had been merely a ploy to make himself seem important. Philemon was annoyed at having listened to the gossip. He reached for the cord and was about to turn off the light when his eyes fell on the table again. Something about it bothered him. Why was there an obviously expensive tablecloth covering such a simple table where the maids drank their tea? And why did it reach all the way to the floor?

Philemon let go of the string and went over to the table. He put one hand on the white linen and stroked it reverently, then rapped on the top. It sounded hollow. This was not a table. Philemon moved the dishes to the floor and lifted the cloth. He was not surprised to reveal a large trunk with metal fastenings. Philemon recognized it. It was the exact piece of luggage that had been in his room. It was the kind of case that was used for overseas travel.

He dropped the cloth, crouched down, and looked for a name tag. He found a small leather pouch attached to one of the two leather straps. He flipped open the pouch. It contained a slip of paper with an address. Philemon read it and felt his heartbeat accelerate instantly.

Mr. Frederick Myers, 114 Beacon Street, Beacon Hill, Boston, Massachusetts.

The trunk did in fact belong to Myers! He ran nervous fingers over the two locks. They would not open. As if in the grip of a fever, Philemon pulled out his jackknife, which he had brought with him from Switzerland, and fiddled with the heavy latches. One by one, he managed to snap them open with his thumbs. The hinges squeaked softly as he finally lifted the lid.

He found a pile of clothes and two pairs of shoes thrown messily into the suitcase, as if the person had been in a hurry. This fitted what he had heard about Myers's departure. His mother had been seriously ill, so he might be forgiven a hasty departure and a sloppily packed suitcase. Cautiously, Philemon dug through to the bottom. Myers clearly had a more extensive wardrobe than Philemon had ever owned. The case itself also looked expensive. What kind of family did the missing assistant actually come from? At least it was clear that he was at home in Boston, and judging from his luggage, belonged to a very wealthy family. *Well, that wasn't a crime in and of itself,* Philemon thought, smelling one of the shirts. It was worn, but otherwise gave off no unusual odor. He dropped it back into the trunk and felt in the side pockets for anything unusual. His fingers unearthed some toiletries: a comb, a pair of scissors, a tin of pomade, a mustache trainer, and shaving cream. Nothing he didn't travel with himself, but then he came across something in the next compartment: a leather portfolio. He pulled it out, opened it, and flipped through the empty pages. A new fountain pen was stuck in the loop in the middle. Otherwise, there was nothing special about the portfolio. Or was there? Philemon paused. One of the final pages had been torn out. But where was it? And what had been written on it?

He put the portfolio back in the case and rummaged again. But there was no loose note among the clothes. Philemon sighed and paused, disappointed. As he did so, his eyes fell on a seam in the fabric that lined the case. One thread was hanging loosely. He pulled at it and found that the seam was open at that point. He put his fingers through and felt behind the fabric. Indeed, there was something there! Quickly, he pulled his hand out again and looked at a piece of paper. It was the missing page from the portfolio—it bore the same torn-off edge. Excitedly, he unfolded the paper and looked at the sketch on it, puzzled. It must have been of a technical apparatus; at least, it showed a complicated circuit with a handwritten calculation next to it. Philemon recognized the variables W, Q, and U, which stood for work, heat, and internal energy. A thermodynamic equation? But there were also the symbols for electric field strength, magnetic field strength, and flux density from Maxwell's equation, E, D, H, and B, each with a right-pointing arrow above them. Philemon tried to make sense of the scrawl. It seemed that Myers or someone else was trying to connect and reconcile several different laws of physics. After the result of the calculation, several exclamation marks had been punched into the paper.

Philemon pursed his lips, perplexed. It was impossible for him to quickly comprehend what this value meant, especially since it was not marked with any unit. He put the paper in his vest pocket. He would find out later. For now, he should be sure to get out of here. He shut the case again and clicked the locks into place, feeling some disappointment as he did so. He hadn't discovered a thing about Myers's whereabouts. But then, what had he expected? Charred pieces of clothing? Or better yet, the body of Mr. Myers?

You are a fool, Philemon Ailey, he scolded himself. *You should not have listened to idle talk, but to the doctor!* He rose and carefully spread the tablecloth over the case again. He also replaced the plates and cups as he had found them, and reached for the string. Taking one last look at the scene, he turned out the light.

As quietly as he had come, he crept downstairs to his room and hurriedly went to bed. It was already after three o'clock in the morning and he was dog-tired, but his distrust blazed more strongly than ever. It shone like a warning beacon in the expanse of his conscience. Restlessly, Philemon tossed back and forth. All he wanted was to have no more doubts. He wanted to trust Tesla. Wanted to believe what he had said. However, he feared he would not achieve that simply by forgetting and repressing. He knew he would have to find out more about the "incident" before he could finally put his suspicions to rest. And had he not been released from work tomorrow morning? If he slept until nine, he would still have plenty of time to go in search of the alleged witness and interrogate him properly. It would be extraordinary if he did not expose the old goatherd as a liar!

CHAPTER 24

May 23, 2011
Fortaleza, Brazil
7:07 pm

Outside, it was now dark. Another tropical night flowed over the city like thick syrup, and the favela slowly came to life. Ondragon could hear the sounds of voices and footsteps through the open window. He squatted on a sagging bed and stared at a flickering television. Both were in a small apartment located on one of the upper floors of the pyramid. A faint smell of mold hung in the air. Its source was the wet room, or rather, the breeding ground for novel, algal-fungal symbioses, which looked like it might once have been a bathroom. The toilet had been replaced by two buckets, one holding water, the other . . . well, better not to talk about it. Otherwise, the place was reasonably clean. Sem had given him the quarters to use for as long as they were looking for the unknown man in Fortaleza. Ondragon had stayed in worse places and was glad of the temporary safety, because the whole city was in an uproar due to the burglary in the laboratory at the harbor. Thorough searches were happening everywhere in an attempt to find the perpetrators.

Two photos appeared on the TV screen. One was from Charlize's accreditation card. "Dr. Letícia Matsumoto Souza" was being suggested as a potential accomplice because she had not returned to her workplace since the night of the robbery. The other image showed the shadowy figure of Ondragon himself. It had been taken by a surveillance camera that neither Charlize nor he had noticed. Fortunately, both photos were plenty blurry. The news did not mention what had been stolen from the lab, but there was talk of a possible operation by a foreign gang. It was still unclear whether the shooting in a parking lot at Praia do Meireles was connected with the theft, they said.

Ondragon, who knew for sure that it was, lowered the sound and looked down at the bed, where the pictures of the logbook lay. He rubbed his fingertips together in anticipation. In a moment, he would unravel the mystery of Pandora, but first he had to sort through his thoughts—or, as Charlize had put it so well earlier, give in to his German sense of order. He pulled out his notepad and wrote down what he had learned so far from Sem about the great unknown.

Sem's people had trailed the old Toyota after the crime and found it before the police, in a quiet side street of the favela. The front and rear windows were broken, and the car was empty. But a favela wouldn't be a favela if a resident or two hadn't seen something. In the favelas, as a Brazilian saying went, the walls had eyes!

So Sem had asked around and lo and behold, it had emerged that the guy had fled through the neighborhood. Like a glowing trail, his path stretched through the labyrinth to a secret corner of an abandoned factory building. He had hidden out under a pile of torn plastic sheeting. Unfortunately, he was already gone again, and some of the items he left behind suggested he had vacated his hiding place hastily. He must have been in the building at least a week, Ondragon estimated from the scraps of trash Sem had collected and brought with him. Smart boy. But that also meant Mr. Unknown had been there before he and Charlize had come to Fortaleza. Had the guy known about Pandora and been awaiting their arrival? Or had he been running his own operation and just happened to get in their way?

Ondragon once again went through the stuff Sem had brought from the hiding place. It was mostly food wrappers and soda cans. But there were also a few helpful clues that enabled Ondragon to make an initial assessment of the stranger. First, there was not a single usable fingerprint on the trash. This was unusual and could mean they were dealing with a professional. Second, among the packaging remains was a yellow candy tin containing Cachou-Lajaunie pastilles. The licorice-flavored lozenges were only available in France, Ondragon had discovered, and they could well indicate that the tall stranger came from France, or at least had recently been there. Moreover, the plane that had crashed off the coast of Brazil was an Air France plane. So who would have been the first to get wind of the wreckage of the Nazi plane than someone who was in constant contact with the recovery operation? Ondragon guessed he was either a member of the BEA—the French air accident investigation agency headquartered in Paris—or one of the sailors who had opened the crate. The French could well be aware of the legend of the Junkers 390 and the disappearance of Hans Kammler along with his mysterious Nazi technology. And their interest in it would be as great as that of any other country. Perhaps said BEA employee had blurted something out and thus—intentionally or not—triggered some chain of events.

Ondragon wrote *FRANCE* in his notepad and circled the word several times. It was a first, lukewarm trail.

But there had been something else that had downright alarmed him: a matchbook labeled GRAN MARQUISE. His hotel! So the guy had been close by and had been watching him! Ondragon rummaged in his memory, but it contained no suspicious face he might have encountered at the hotel. Obviously, the guy had been very clever and hadn't caught his eye, although he always checked his surroundings thoroughly. A shiver ran down the back of his neck like icy water. He had to be dealing with one of his own kind, someone who knew what he was doing. A secret service agent, or worse, a mercenary like him?!

He flipped to the next page and entered the description of the stranger, given by the inhabitants of the favela, on a fresh sheet. The information was a little confusing, since it did not 100 percent fit with his France theory. The guy was not very old, around thirty, and quite small—scrawny but in good shape. He was unusually lithe as he scurried through the dark alleys. Like a lizard—that's what two of the reports said. His clothing was inconspicuous and consisted of a T-shirt, shorts, and leather sandals. Several favela residents thought they had seen a silver ring on his left arm. A bizarre, wide thing, "like a metal cuff." Whatever that meant. But that wasn't what was bothering Ondragon. It was the color of the man's skin. The inhabitants had taken him for one of their own. A mulatto with light brown skin and short, frizzy, black hair.

Ondragon added *BRAZIL* to his list. Was the unknown man a mulatto with French and Brazilian roots? It was possible; like the United States, Brazil was a country of immigrants. Indigenous Brazilians made up little more than one percent of the population. Someone of mixed heritage would, of course, be perfect for such an operation. Inconspicuous and polyglot.

Ondragon turned to the last piece of the mosaic. It was a drawing. The bracelet had not been the only unusual thing about the fellow, nor was the box he had carried effortlessly on his shoulder. Someone had noticed a tattoo on his neck and actually tried to draw it. It was a kind of cross made of many small strokes.

Ondragon looked at it for a long time but had no idea what it could mean, except that the symbol in the center was distantly reminiscent of the German Wehrmacht's bar cross. But what could the unknown person—a black man, moreover—have to do with the Nazis?

He took his cell phone and looked through the most common cross symbols on the internet. But he quickly found that none resembled the tattoo cross. He wrote *WHY?* under his notes and wondered what the man's purpose could have been. Who might be his client? This brought him to the hunch that had occurred to him when Kubicki had told him about the perpetual motion machine. He picked up the list Charlize had compiled. It set out all the sectors that had anything to do with electricity, nuclear power, gas, or oil. Free energy—corporations like this could only want to prevent it. What if one of them had hired someone to find and destroy the perpetual motion machine? He read the names on the list and raised his eyebrows in surprise. No less than four of the ten largest corporations were based in France! It was quite possible they had their fingers in the pie. Only which one of them was it? Or was it all of them together? Ondragon ruminated, but couldn't come up with a solution and finally closed his notebook. He looked at the copies of the logbook lying next to him on the bed. Perhaps he would learn more about the background of the unknown man if he knew what was in the book.

He touched the paper expectantly. He had saved the best for last. Would the secret reveal itself right away, or did it hold a few challenging twists and turns? Ondragon felt his pulse quicken. This was what he lived for. This was his religion! The restrained whisper of unsolved mysteries.

Suddenly, there was a knock on the door, first once, then three times, and finally once again. That was the sign he had agreed on with Charlize. Ondragon got up and let his assistant in. She had quarters elsewhere in the pyramid, and presumably her abode was a little more luxurious, since Milady was apparently among the crème de la crème of the local mafia. Somewhat ruefully, he offered her the bed, the only place to sit.

To his great delight, Charlize had brought cold beer and a bag of fragrant churrascos. Ondragon pounced hungrily on the grilled meat skewers in hot sauce.

"Hmm, that was good!" he sighed a little later, wiping his fingers. Then he finally picked up the copies of the logbook. "And now let's see what's been down at the bottom of the sea for so long!"

"*Hai*, Boss!" Charlize said, giving a small nod.

Ondragon frowned. So she'd stopped playing the mafia chick? Now she was the ever-ready assistant? He eyed her. Was she just acting the part of eager employee, or did she actually enjoy working for him? At any rate, he had never noticed her being unhappy or feeling as if he was beneath her dignity. Over the years, Charlize had become the secret heart of Ondragon Consulting, and he couldn't imagine doing his job without her. So he smothered his creeping sense of distrust with a good dose of optimism and moved a little closer to Charlize. The scent of her shampoo drifted into his nose and he wondered where she had found the shower he so desperately wanted. He'd been awake for thirty-six hours and must stink like a polecat. Fortunately, Charlize, with her Japanese reserve, gave no indication that she'd noticed.

He looked at the first sheet, took a deep breath, and concentrated on the author's handwriting. It was razor-sharp, and Charlize's editing made it stand out, black against the white background. There was nothing left of the formerly fibrous texture of the logbook pages. Nothing to remind him of a book.

Charlize tilted her head to one side as Ondragon began translating each section into English. On each page was a preprinted table with headings. Ondragon had seen something like this before, during his flight training. The pilot had to enter various details before and after each flight, much like a logbook for a company car. The first two pages had been filled in by the pilot as required.

Aircraft type: JU 390 - V II. Registration: RC-DA. Pilot: Colonel K. Brenner. Purpose of the flight: transfer of aircraft for the Führer's flying squadron. Cargo: none. Departure: Prague/Bohemia. Destination: Rerik/ Baltic Sea.

According to this, a flight from Rerik to Bardufoss, in Norway, had been registered on March 28, 1945, and two days later one from Bardufoss to Tokyo via the island of Paramushiru.

"Tokyo?" Charlize exclaimed in amazement.

"Yes, I had thought that was a rumor until now, but this flight seems to have been completed successfully. Really remarkable for the technology of the time," Ondragon replied, and went on reading the table.

The Junkers 390 had flown from Tokyo back to Bardufoss shortly afterward and then on to Ludwigsdorf in Silesia, on May 2, 1945.

"Bingo!" said Ondragon, jabbing his finger at the entry. "There it is."

On May 10, 1945, the pilot had recorded a flight from Ludwigsdorf to Spanish Sahara. The names of the passengers were given as: General H. Kammler, Dr. F. Eschenberg, Dr. W. Kahn, Dr. X. Schuch, and Dr. A. Schwarz. Cargo: unknown. The last entry was dated May 11. Passengers: General H. Kammler, Dr. X. Schuch. Cargo: none.

"Wow!" Charlize murmured eventually, impressed, while Ondragon quickly flipped through his notes to what he had written about the Junkers 390. If the entries in the flight log were genuine, and he had no doubt that they were, then General Hans Kammler's escape was not a figment of some Nazi mystics' imagination. It had really happened! Moreover, the flight path and landing in Spanish Sahara fit with Ondragon's previous research on the internet. Unfortunately, the flight log gave no reason for the landing in the West African state, which had been a neutral zone around 1945. It was striking, though, that by the final entry, only two of the original five passengers were still on board. General Kammler and a certain Dr. X. Schuch. This could only mean that the cargo and three of the passengers had been left behind in Spanish Sahara. After that, the entries in the table broke off, presumably because of the crash. But who were the doctors listed as passengers? Scientists or medics? Ondragon guessed they were scientists because of the Bell project associated with this flight. Unfortunately, there was not one mention of the cargo. The pilot was silent on that point.

He took the third sheet from the flight book and saw that someone had written over the next pages without any regard for the preprinted lines.

"But the pilot didn't write this," he noted, "the handwriting is clearly different." He ran his index finger over the words, as if that would tell him who had written them. The script was hasty, almost horizontal, as if the author had been pressed for time. And as Ondragon began to read, he knew why:

May 12, 1945, 1 am—The pilot has allowed me to use his flight log. Admire Colonel Karl Brenner for his tenacity at the controls. Speaking little. General Kammler has retreated to the rear of the empty cargo hold. What he is doing there? I don't know.

We don't have much time left. The tank is almost empty and only four of the six engines are still running. The coast of Brazil is a long way off. Not looking good. I write these lines to put what has happened into perspective. Maybe one day someone will read this note and free me from my oppressive sense of guilt.

Addendum of May 10, 1945—Our escape began in Ludwigsdorf/Silesia on a course to North Africa. Crossed the Mediterranean during the night, then Algeria. Below us only desert. Our destination: Spanish Sahara. There in no-man's-land was a research station we had set up. Tried to make radio contact, unfortunately without success. Thought we could hide there.

Addendum of May 11, 1945—Landed in the early morning on flat piece of desert. Near a mountain range. Found station in chaos. Workshops, radio station, laboratories—all destroyed and all scientists gone!

Whether it was a raid by a desert tribe or the allied forces, we could not determine. General Kammler seemed furious. It was clear to everyone that we could not stay. But where could we go? Someone suggested Uruguay or Argentina. Asked the pilot to calculate whether enough fuel remained for such a crossing. A little later we knew we would not make it to South America. Schwarz was very agitated about this. I couldn't blame him, as I felt a similar despair in myself. None of us wanted to stay here in the desert and die. Discussed it. General Kammler made suggestion that seemed hopeful. Now blame myself terribly for not realizing what this man was up to.

Kammler decided to unload plane. Without cargo, it would weigh less and also consume less fuel. The pilot also confirmed this was our only chance. We agreed to Kammler's plan. We brought all the crates to the station. Felt like the safest place for the valuable material for a time. At least here the fruits of our research would not fall into the wrong hands so quickly and could not cause any damage. Nobody except us and the missing scientists knows about this station in the African wasteland. When Kammler explained it was his intention to return here and recover the precious equipment, we were glad to hear it. That way, our research would not have been in vain.

Once machine was empty, Kammler urged that we leave. Went to board the Junkers, but Kammler drew his gun and forced Kahn, Schwarz, and Eschenberg to stay outside. Three men fewer saved even more fuel! He let me on board. Why? I didn't know, but I got on without looking back, just left my colleagues behind.

Of course they fought back, but Kammler shot Eschenberg in the leg as a warning. They stopped and Kammler closed the door. We took off as the sun was setting. Can still see the three we left behind, crouched in the sand below, watching us go. Was relieved, I have to admit. Reassured myself that I was just a scientist and not a warrior. Had no choice but to bend to the will of the general. Fortunately, there was an oasis down there and I hoped the others would be able to make their way there.

1:30 am—The Atlantic Ocean below us. Pilot has just shut down two more engines. Have to save fuel. Will that help? I'm skeptical and don't want to get my hopes up.

I now know why Kammler took me with him. I am the only one of our research group who had read and understood Nikola Tesla's notes. The diary of the great inventor was unique. A blessing for the German people. We're so close to realizing Tesla's dream, to find the Holy Grail of science! But Tesla book has disappeared without trace. Have the contents stored in my memory though. Could reanimate all devices again, power of my mind. Kammler knows that. We worked together on Tesla's diary two years ago. So no charity on Kammler's part taking me along—pure calculation. He wants to at least save the knowledge, even if he had to leave the expensive equipment behind. Kammler is a very ambitious and prudent man, he knows he needs something that will secure his future in a foreign country. He wants to capitalize on my knowledge. If only I'd had the courage to stay with the others in the desert. It would have been my duty to stand by them, my brothers in spirit. But the wheel of the sower can be turned back only with difficulty. My knowledge will perish with me. I am inconsolable. An infinitely valuable treasure will be lost forever. Imagining that one day a brave explorer will comb through the desert and come across what we have left there. I wish this for the good of the German people, no, for the good of the whole world! And I hope that fate will bring it about.

2 o'clock—Both engines are still running. But fuel gauge needle at zero! Preparing to land on water. I can't swim, grew up in the mountains. My fate is sealed. I will feel the cold water of the Atlantic Ocean in my lungs, just as the unfortunates on the Titanic once did.

Heard a gunshot in the back of the hold. No one needs to look to see what happened. We know. Kammler has stolen away! That cowardly traitor!

Waiting for the two engines to fail. Pilot and I are silent. Each caught up in our own thoughts.

Gliding. Don't know if we can get close enough to shore. What will it be like to be eaten by fish? To disappear without trace in the tides of the ocean?

Airplane groaning beneath. Will make a good coffin. Must now put the flight log in waterproof box. May God grant that posterity know something of our fate. May the finder use it wisely.

Signed Dr. rer. nat. Xavier Johann Schuch

Ondragon thought it a very moving account of the dramatic conclusion of an escape attempt. He didn't even want to imagine what the last minutes on board the Junkers must have been like before she hit the water and took her occupants down with her . . . what a crushing moment. And yet this Dr. Schuch had been disciplined, held it all together. Until the last moment. Unfortunately, there was no mention in the text of the kind of equipment they had left behind, nor of where exactly they had left it. At an oasis near a mountain range somewhere in Spanish Sahara. That was all. But there must have been several dozen oases in the area mentioned. Why hadn't Dr. Schuch left any more specific clues, if he so much wanted the "treasure" to be found someday? Was it, after all, too secret? Too dangerous? After all, Schuch also spoke of the wrong hands and the damage it could cause. Was it Tesla's infamous ray gun? Or was it the bell-shaped flying object with an antigravity drive? Ondragon bit his lower lip, thinking. And what could Schuch have meant by the "Holy Grail of science"? The perpetual motion machine? Tesla's notebook? But where was the book now, if it had been lost to the German scientists back then?

With a vague feeling of disappointment, Ondragon released his maltreated lower lip. The stuff was somewhere in the middle of the desert. It would entail the familiar search for a needle in a haystack if he got involved. And the Sahara, of all places! Not exactly the friendliest and most accessible place on this planet. Perhaps the good Dr. Schuch was right in his assumption: Tesla's legacy was lost forever. Buried under the hot sands of North Africa.

Ondragon picked up the final sheet and was surprised to see that it contained only numbers.

"We discovered this on the back page of the logbook," Charlize explained. "It's almost certainly Dr. Schuch's handwriting."

"So he did add something after all. What could this represent?" Ondragon looked at the numbers, which were arranged in eight squares of equal size, in two rows of four, one above the other. He shrugged his shoulders.

"Maybe they're cargo listings . . . or coordinates," Charlize said.

"Hmm, wait a minute. We can figure out quickly if they're the latter." Ondragon entered one of the columns into a geoconverter on the internet. "No. Not coordinates. The numbers must mean something else. Would have been too easy."

Charlize ran a finger over the rows. "Could also be a code," she murmured thoughtfully.

CHAPTER 25

August 3, 1899
Colorado Springs
morning

The next morning, Philemon quickly took his breakfast in the dining room: coffee and sweet rolls. There was no sign of Dr. Tesla or the other two. Either they were sleeping or they were already back at work in the laboratory. Philemon felt a twinge in his chest. It still bothered him that he had been excluded.

But that didn't change his plan, he thought grimly, and if it went well, he would have done his bit to save Dr. Tesla's honor and prove his loyalty. The doctor would recognize this with satisfaction and hopefully not send him away next time.

But you know you are deceiving yourself, an inner voice warned as he drained his coffee cup. *You are not doing this merely because you want to clear Dr. Tesla's reputation, but because you are driven by mistrust. You have deep doubts as to the doctor's sincerity and are merely afraid your great idol might be tainted. What if you find out that there actually is something rotten about the whole thing?*

Philemon grimaced unwillingly and choked down the coffee. There would be plenty of time for ifs and buts later. He dabbed his mouth with the napkin and got up from the table. He picked up his hat, left the hotel, and stepped out onto the sunlit street. There was nothing to remind him of the eerie march of the previous night and the threatening words of the constable. Philemon walked resolutely to Benson's Restaurant. There he would ask for directions to old Foley.

When he stepped through the door into the taproom, all the faces turned to him. About a dozen men stared at him, some hostile, others curious. Philemon clenched his jaw and did not betray how uncomfortable he was with the situation. His head held high, he walked over to the counter, where the host scowled at him.

"What are you doing in here?" he asked.

Well, thought Philemon, *what had become of the hospitality of the first day? How easily one fell out of favor in this place.* He drew himself up and adopted a nonchalant expression, "If you could tell me where I might find Benjamin Foley, I'll be gone in a jiffy and I'll never darken your door again." He added a smug smile, hoping he looked confident. In reality, he didn't feel that way at all.

The host propped himself on the stained counter with both hands and leaned forward. The muscles on his hairy forearms stood out clearly. Philemon felt the oppressive gazes of the two men on either side of him and grew hot under his jacket. He tried to breathe calmly.

The host ground his powerful lower jaw, and eventually turned and spat a long brown stream of chewing tobacco behind the counter. He then wiped his beard, in which a few strands of the nauseating secretion had caught. "Foley," he said in a dark voice. "Oho. What does he want there, the big-city whippersnapper?"

Philemon ignored the insult and waited.

The host exchanged a glance with the men, who nodded barely perceptibly. "Go east on Pikes Peak Avenue to El Paso Street," he said, "then turn right, go to the end and out into the prairie a few hundred more yards. There you'll find a wash, a dried-up riverbed. Follow the goat smell; you can't miss old Foley's cabin. But watch your elegant city shoes, it's dusty out there." The host grinned insolently.

"The prairie is not for swells like you. Take good care of yourself!" one of the men added, baring his yellow teeth.

"My thanks, gentlemen," Philemon replied, unimpressed, doffing his hat briefly. "I bid you good day." He left the eatery and quickly trudged east. As he followed the directions, his anger at the men dissipated. They didn't know any better, after all. He turned onto El Paso Street. It was lined with large wooden houses overshadowed by tall trees: well-kept Victorian-style estates. How on earth did people get the idea to settle here in Colorado Springs, of all places? A dusty plain in the middle of nowhere! And on top of that, in a smug town without any real hint of cordiality! Philemon shook his head uncomprehendingly.

After a while, the rows of houses began to thin out and the road became a path. The houses were less splendid and by the next bend Philemon was standing in the middle of the prairie, which was shimmering with heat. No more shady trees grew here, only shaggy desert mugwort and withered sweetgrass. He marched out onto the plain under the blazing sun. The trail wound south between some rock formations and impenetrable brush. Several times a roadrunner or a startled flock of California quail crossed his path.

As advertised, he soon came across the wash. Under his jacket, his shirt was now soaked in sweat. He gazed with burning eyes at the dried-up watercourse, which consisted of smooth white pebbles that indicated a torrent regularly flowed through here during the rainy season. Philemon made a left turn and marched farther along the edge of the wash, keeping his face into the wind. And indeed, the unmistakable smell of goats soon met his nostrils—the cabin could not be far away. He rounded another rock and saw the crooked structure in front of him. It crouched in the shade of several mesquite trees whose branches had been removed from below, down to a clear line. Goats really did mow down everything that got in their way!

Philemon stopped and glanced back. There was hardly anything to be seen of Colorado Springs. Only the church steeple rose into the sky against the pale gray silhouette of the mountains. He turned back to look at the wooden, sun-bleached cabin. A whiff of the old days wafted around it—a pitiful remnant of the Wild West, that fabulous era of pioneers and covered wagons. Philemon had never traveled farther west than Chicago, where, in 1893, as a recent high school graduate, he had marveled at the wonders of the World's Columbian Exhibition. The electricity had been supplied by Nikola Tesla himself, after he had won the battle with Thomas Edison over the alternating current he had generated. But Chicago, and New York too, were progressive, up-and-coming metropolises compared with Colorado Springs, which seemed so ridiculously insignificant that one almost felt sorry for it.

Determinedly, Philemon made his way to the hut. After all, he needed to verify something with its occupant. When he arrived at the dwelling, he looked around. There was nobody to be seen; all he could hear was the bleating of the goats.

"Hello?" he called out, to be on the safe side: He had little desire to get a load of buckshot embedded in his hide. "Hello, Mr. Foley! Are you there?"

No answer. Philemon stepped into the shadow of the dilapidated porch. Close up, the shack looked even more dilapidated. So this was life west of the Mississippi as a respected citizen of an important health resort! Far enough from high society, but still close enough to be a source of gossip. Philemon raised a hand and pounded vigorously on the closed door. Silence.

He hesitated indecisively. Should he open the door and look? Or search for the goats? Perhaps the herder was with them. He let out another call into the shimmering heat of the morning. Farther back on the plain, the yellowish column of a whirlwind danced in the dusty air. Philemon squinted into the sun. Then he turned, and jumped. Behind him stood a ragged fellow with a matted beard and floppy hat. His huge paws were clutching a shotgun.

"What the hell are you doing here?" he snapped.

"Are you Mr. Foley?" asked Philemon fearfully, quickly raising both hands.

"Yes, by my father's balls, that bastard! And who are you?" The old man's face was almost completely concealed by a greasy layer of dust and sweat. For all that, his blue eyes shone all the more clearly. They flitted warily over the uninvited guest.

"'Fine swell you are, ain't you?" he growled finally. "Not from 'round here."

Philemon cleared his throat, introduced himself, and explained his business: "I'm from New York, and I work out in the lab with D—"

"What, in that haunted house? Get the hell out of here! I don't want anything to do with it! Go on, git out of here!" The barrel of the shotgun twitched.

Philemon pressed his lips together. He should have known the guy would not blurt everything out so lightly. Especially not to a stranger. It occurred to him that this was the reason the men at Benson's had grinned so maliciously. But he wasn't going to give up that easily. He pulled his hat off his head and made another attempt. "Mr. Foley, I didn't come here to scare you. On the contrary, you're right. From your point of view, there are strange things going on in that laboratory. But it's nothing that can't be explained in simple terms. Please put the gun down and let's talk like gentlemen. I believe you saw something strange, and maybe I can help clear up the mystery."

The old man did not move. His suspicious gaze continued to flicker over Philemon.

"Please. Mr. Foley. Your account of what happened that night is important to me."

"And you're not going to make fun of me like the other idiots in town?"

"No, absolutely not."

The old goatherd seemed to reflect. Then he lowered his gun and limped toward Philemon. "All right, I wouldn't say no to a little company anyway." He pointed to a rickety rocking chair and bench that stood on the porch. Philemon thanked him politely and sat down carefully on the bench.

"Do you want water? I have a well," Foley asked.

Philemon considered whether to risk an upset stomach from unclean water, and then nodded. His throat was dusty from his march and some refreshment couldn't hurt. At that, the old man disappeared around the house and came back a little later with a battered tin can. He poured clear water into two enamel cups and handed one of them to Philemon, who wiped the rim clean with his sleeve and took a sip. The water was cool and tasted fresh. Thirstily, he emptied the cup and placed it beside him on the bench. Old Foley, meanwhile, had sat down in the rocking chair and was filling a pipe. He lit it with a match. Bluish smoke rose and wafted out into the parched landscape. He took a few leisurely sips from his cup.

"So you're from the big city to the east. Nice and green there, huh?" he asked, blinking dreamily at the smoke from the pipe. The tobacco smelled awful.

"Yes," Philemon replied.

"Rains a lot."

"You could say that."

"Well, well . . ."

That seemed to be one of the standard phrases here in Colorado Springs. "Well, well" meant something like, "That may be, but I don't care." Philemon shifted his weight on the bench, wondering when the old man would finally open up. He wiped the sweat impatiently from his brow and watched Foley smoking quietly. He had to be back in town in an hour, to get something to eat and then get to the lab.

He was so deep in his thoughts that he did not notice old Foley suddenly turn his head and give him a penetrating look. "What do you want me to tell you, stranger? How a man was struck by lightning that ill-fated night, or that men have been walking around outside the laboratory calling for him, night after night ever since?"

Surprised, Philemon looked into the bright blue eyes. "Calling his name? Who?"

"Well, the crazy doctor and the other two, the blond one and the little fat one. Almost every evening after sunset they walk around the building calling the guy. Always at the same time. I hear them; I graze my goats thereabouts."

Philemon thought about it. He had never heard Tesla or the others calling anyone. On the other hand, he had not often been there after sunset. "And what do they call?" he inquired.

"The man's name. Frederick, always Frederick!"

Frederick Myers, Philemon thought agitatedly. *Something had happened to him after all!* "Tell me more!"

The old man regarded him quietly for a while and then gazed out at the prairie. "All right, but only if you don't laugh at me. I'm tired of being mocked. Because I'm not stupid, I know what they're saying about me behind my back. But I saw what I saw, and it wasn't my imagination, as people in the village would have me believe. It happened as true as I'm sitting here!"

If he only knew it, his story was the *gossip in Colorado Springs*, Philemon thought, and quickly gave the goatherd his word of honor.

"Very well, my boy. I'll tell you the story." Foley set his pipe aside and folded his hands in his lap. "It was over a month ago. There had been a downpour a few days before, and I had turned my goats out on the prairie to feast on the fresh green grass. That evening, I set out to bring them back in. I followed their tracks, passing the laboratory as usual. I have often heard strange noises coming from inside, but that evening it was silent. I went farther into the prairie, found my animals, and called them to me so we could make our way back. It was dark by then, but I know the plains like the back of my hand. As we passed the building, I got such a strange feeling. A tingling sensation, like all over my body, you know what I mean?"

Philemon nodded and Foley shook himself as if reliving the horrors of the night. "It was a premonition, most certainly! The animals too were more restless than usual. They wanted to move on quickly. I followed them so they wouldn't run off in all directions. But then a rumble began to come from the laboratory. At first it was only a low hum that grew higher and higher. Lightning flickered through the cracks in the boards and suddenly there was a loud bang! After that, all of a sudden, it was dark again, but the terrible rumbling went on. Never in my life have I been so frightened, believe me!" Foley paused to catch his breath.

Philemon noticed that the old man's hands were trembling. He looked deeply troubled.

In a hoarse voice, he continued. "There was banging and crackling. It sounded as if a thunderstorm was raging inside the house. I could hear the crashes echoing off the distant mountains, a rolling, ominous sound. But what happened next literally made my hair stand on end. At first, I thought my eyes were playing tricks on me. The house started to glow! Don't think I'm stupid, it did. First just the tower on the roof, then the whole building. Little balls of light rose from the grass and flew all around me. Saint Elmo's fire! Will-o'-the-wisps from the underworld!" Foley crossed himself, although it was obvious he did not often attend the Colorado Springs church.

Philemon smiled to himself. Thus far, the old man had seen nothing more than he himself had seen. And it was also clear that Foley might well think it was an evil spirit. But how could he make such an uneducated man understand that what he had seen had nothing whatever to do with ghosts or will-o'-the-wisps, but was simply physics?

"Do not fear," he said instead, "these phenomena are completely harmless. Think of it rather as a spectacle of nature, a display of elemental forces."

Foley stared at him in irritation. "It was Saint Elmo's fire!" he insisted. "And you won't make me believe it was anything else. It was a sign, to warn me and others of what's going on in the laboratory! I tell you, it's the devil's work. It ain't never done no good to meddle with the forces of nature!"

The old boy was right about that. Nobody knew what would come from pumping millions of volts through the earth, Philemon thought, let alone what effects it would have on living beings. It certainly hadn't done the electrified moths any good. Which brought them back to the question of what had happened to Frederick Myers.

"Now, what about this man who was struck by lightning?" he inquired.

Foley looked at him. There was an unfathomable fear in his eyes. But was it only the fear of memory or the fear of calling evil by its name? The old goatherd wanted to say something, but he was shaken by a coughing fit. When he had regained his composure, he spat noisily out onto the veranda and then continued in a low voice, "Well, I saw the light of the Saint Elmo's fire. It was hovering all around me. Then suddenly a scream rang out."

"A scream?"

Foley nodded. "And it was filled with mortal fear."

"Mortal fear? Are you sure?"

"Yes, I am! I shed my blood in the Civil War with the damn Confederates. I know exactly what that sounds like, young man!"

Philemon raised a hand. He understood. "And what happened after that? After the scream?"

"Then there was a loud bang, and suddenly everything in the building went dark! The glow and the rumble stopped . . . and so did the screaming. All at once, everything fell silent! As if someone's throat had been cut!"

Philemon felt the hair on his forearms stand on end. If he had been thinking calmly about the whole thing a moment ago, he now felt a dull horror creeping through his mind. He suspected that old Foley was about to say something that would shake the very foundations of his thinking. That this time he would be the one to doubt reality. Like a little child, he held his breath, unconsciously digging his fingers into the fabric of his pants.

"I didn't know what to do," Foley continued, croaking. "Run away or see if they needed my help in there. I took a few steps toward the building, up to the barbed wire fence, and listened. I could hear muffled voices. They were talking frantically to each other—"

"Could you hear what they were saying?" interrupted Philemon breathlessly.

"Hmm . . . yeah. Something like 'For God's sake!' and 'Frederick's disappeared.' Until one of the men said he must have been struck by lightning. At that, the other got nervous and shouted loudly that they'd better get help, but a third voice intervened. 'No!' it said, 'we mustn't be too hasty, or we'll put the whole experiment at risk!'" The old man nodded, lost in thought, as if he were checking the accuracy of his information. "That's how it was. That's what the voices said."

"Frederick has disappeared? Didn't you say he burned to death?"

"I don't know that for sure! I can only tell you about what I heard. Do you think I'm making it up?" replied Foley irritably.

"No, no," Philemon relented. "But then why do you claim that the man was burned to ashes? You couldn't have seen that at all, if the whole thing took place in the laboratory."

"I didn't see it, I smelled it!" the old man said testily.

"Smelled it?"

"Yes, it was a smell. A terrible smell indeed! Breathed from the mouth of hell!"

Philemon frowned.

"There's no call to give me that dumb look, my boy, it was the stench of hell, the same as I smelled in the war! It stank of gunpowder, hot metal, and burning flesh!"

An unwelcome memory stirred in Philemon, and he quickly pushed it back into the dark abyss it had come from. He did not wish to think about what had happened at the university.

"Yes, burning flesh!" Foley confirmed. "And one thing is certain: That night a man was roasted there. Whether it was a lightning bolt or the thing they call electricity, I don't give a damn! But the experiments they're doing there are dangerous, I'm sure of it. They should shut down that workshop from hell and send everyone who works there packing! And now leave my land right now! It was a mistake telling you all this. You're one of those." Foley seized his shotgun and pointed it at his visitor.

Philemon jumped to his feet. "What do you mean, I'm one of those?"

"One of those snoopers who loiter 'round town and ask people questions! The Pinkertons!"

"Pinkertons?"

Instead of answering, Foley fired a shot from the gun without warning. Shocked, Philemon pressed both hands to his belly, searching for a hole, the report still ringing in his ears. But Foley had fired into the air: All his limbs were intact.

"Are you mad?" Philemon shrieked, appalled.

"If anyone 'round here is mad, it's that crazy doctor out there!" growled Foley, raising the shotgun anew.

"You damned oddball!" shouted Philemon. He turned on his heel and fled out into the prairie. Only once he was out of sight of the hut did he slow his pace. Panting, he returned to the town.

CHAPTER 26

May 23, 2011
Fortaleza, Brazil
9:30 pm

It's definitely a code," Charlize said again. "Look, this might be a way to decode it." She tapped her pen on a sheet of the notebook, on which she had written a numbered alphabet.

"1 equals A and 2 equals B?" asked Ondragon skeptically. "I think a scientist of Dr. Schuch's caliber might have had more up his sleeve!" He yawned, putting a hand over his mouth. The initial excitement over the contents of the flight log had faded and he felt only fatigue. They would not get any closer to the mystery today.

"No offense, Charlize, but I really need to hit the hay. You keep on tinkering with it, if it makes you happy. Also, that weird cross tattoo. Pick me up at eight?"

"*Hai. Oyasumi nasai*, Boss."

"Same to you. Sleep tight." Another yawn squeezed at his jaws and he just managed to see Charlize out and bolt the door behind her before it burst out loudly. His gun at the ready under his pillow, he was soon asleep.

There was a melody running through his dream. A dream in which his mother stood in the library with an impassive expression and kept saying, "This is our chance, Siegfried. This is our chance!" But what kind of damn chance did she mean? And where the hell was that music coming from? A realization gnawed doggedly at his subconscious.

Soon afterward, Ondragon came wide awake. He reached for his cell phone, which was singing loudly, *"I know there's something going on!"* His longstanding ringtone by the singer Frida. He blinked tiredly at the number; it was a Hamburg area code. Quickly, he answered.

"Hello, Paul!" said Günther Ludewig. "What's the matter? You sound as if you're still asleep! Oh darn!" Ondragon heard the professor smack himself in the head. "My mistake! I forgot it was still night over there with you. Sorry. Do you want me to call later?"

"It's okay, Günther, I'm awake now. What is it?" Ondragon sat up. The sheet was soaked in sweat. More than ever, he longed for a cold shower. He reached out to turn on the decrepit ceiling fan. As the mild air current cooled his skin, he sighed softly.

Ludewig cleared his throat. "It's about your question. I found someone who might be able to answer it. A historian of science. He deals mainly with the natural sciences during the Renaissance, but his hobby is science myths. So he knows quite a bit about the research that was done during the Nazi era. I will give you his number and email address. He is Polish and has a chair at the Technical University of Krakow, but he speaks excellent German. His name is Professor Szymon Krupa."

Ondragon took down the details. "Excellent. I'll give him a call as soon as I've caught up on my sleep."

"You do that. And sorry again to bother you."

"No problem, anyone can call me anytime, even if they sometimes catch me when I've powered down. 'If you've got problems, to end them all, anytime, you better call Paul!' At least that's my unofficial business slogan." Ondragon chortled gleefully. "Thank you very much for your efforts, Günther. I owe you one."

"No, no, not for that. Go back to sleep!"

Smiling, Ondragon hung up. It felt good to have friends like Ludewig. He must be sure to take good care of them. He would be a pretty toothless dragon without them. A glance at the clock told him it was close to five. Two more hours of sleep. He left the fan running and lay back on the pillow.

Once again, he entered the elusive realm of dreams and was standing next to his mother. She looked as if she had been waiting for him and gave him a kind smile, but it seemed false somehow. She said, "My boy, we must make sacrifices. All of us!"

Ondragon looked at her with the wide eyes of an uncomprehending child. Fearfully, he took her hand, as he had always done when a vague feeling of fear took hold of him. Sacrifices? Why? What did his mother mean?

Ava Birgitta Ondragon—or rather, the young version of her from the seventies—leaned down toward him. Her red lips were pressed together in a hard line. "Do you know what a secret is, Paul?" she asked in a dark voice.

Ondragon's tongue stuck to the roof of his mouth. He did not dare answer. All he could manage was a timid nod.

"Well, *this* is a secret!" Her finger pointed to the pile of books under which Per lay. His brother had turned his face toward him and was grinning his bloody grin.

"This is something no one can ever know about!" his mother exhorted him. "Do you understand that, Paul? Never! So forget what you saw. Forget it! Forever!"

Ondragon nodded again. He knew what a secret was. But he didn't know it could feel so evil. His eyes jumped from his brother's grin to his mother's red-painted mouth. Both of them were moving their lips, but the sound seemed out of sync. Their words were delayed before they reached him.

"No one can ever know about this!" they both said. "NEVER!"

Little Paul jerked his hands upward and pressed them over his ears. The sinister red lips continued to move and he closed his eyes so he didn't have to look at them. But the words continued to cut deep into his consciousness.

"I know there's something going on!"

Irritated, he opened his eyes . . .

. . . and found himself on the bed in the dark room. Above him the fan was sputtering and next to him on the sheet the indignant voice of Anni-Frid Lyngstad sang from his cell phone: *"I know there's something going on!"* How right she was!

Annoyed, he hit the iPhone and ignored the call. What a soothing silence!

Groaning, he rubbed his eyes. Oh, man, did he have a nightmare that night? It was six in the morning! He picked up the device and glanced at the display. When his sleep-drunk brain registered who had called, he hastily pressed the "call-back" button.

"Mr. O, thanks for calling back! I . . ." The boy who called himself Truthfinder choked on his excitement and coughed dryly. "Phew, sorry. I meant to say that I got your email and kept the data safe, as you asked. But man, I was curious and looked at the pictures. I don't even know what to say—that's totally gross!" The childish voice on the other end went up an octave. The young physics genius was like a pot of milk that was boiling over. Patiently, Ondragon waited for the torrent of words to subside.

"This flight log, is it real? If so, then—holy shit, dude—the theory with the Nazi spies who stole from Tesla and murdered him is really true. Although I would have preferred the other version with the FBI, honestly. And the escape of General Kammler in the Junkers 390 is awesome! I mean, it actually happened. Wow! I think I have some serious apologies to make to some of my forum visitors. Mr. O, I'm still blown away by it. It's like speed, only better! Also, this report from the scientist, this Dr. Schuch. He's really crazy!" Truthfinder exhaled loudly and took a deep breath.

This was Ondragon's cue. "Glad you read the report, Truthfinder," he said kindly.

"I shouldn't have, oops, shit, I know. I'm really sorry. What are you going to do with me now?" The last question sounded almost fearful.

"Don't worry, I'm not angry with you. If I'm honest, I expected you to. But how come you understood the text so quickly? Do you speak German?"

"No, I don't know German, but I have some high-quality translation software. I was able to fix the few discrepancies. Together with the photos of the Junkers wreckage and the contents of the box, there can no longer be any doubt about the truth of the Nazi theory." Truthfinder now sounded more like the young scientist extraordinaire again, rather than a freaked-out teenager. But it was nice to hear that his youthful mind was not yet completely buried under the mountain of accumulated expertise.

Ondragon smiled. The boy was really great. He would have to thank Strangelove for the contact.

"The report from Dr. Schuch," Truthfinder continued, "is a revelation! We now know that there is something hidden in the Sahara that must have been precious enough to take with them on their breakneck escape. In other words, a real, genuine treasure! The Holy Grail of science! At least that's what Schuch calls it. But what might it have been? He doesn't say a word about that."

"That's right. But it must have been something extraordinary. Maybe the number squares will tell us more about it when we decode them."

"Hey yo, Mr. O! I took a closer look at those. I'm sure it's a code. Unfortunately, I haven't cracked it yet. I'm running the numbers through a program right now, although I don't think we'll be able to do much with modern technology. Dr. Schuch was in a dire situation. He certainly didn't have a calculator with him and had to resort to a manual procedure. However, a number of well-known ciphers can be used for this purpose. For example, the Cesar cipher, the ROT13 encryption, or the Polybus square. The keyword could consist of letters and numbers. I've already tried Schuch, Xavier, Tesla, Bell, Junkers, Sahara, and Fatherland, combined with the dates from the logbook, but nothing! Do you have any ideas? Because to keep trying to solve it on the off chance would take forever. There are a gazillion possibilities!"

Ondragon thought about it. Truthfinder had already named all the words that would have immediately occurred to him. "Are you sure it's a code?" he asked again.

"A hundred percent! It can't be anything else. Schuch wanted to leave something to the world, a clue. But he didn't want to do it openly. Seemingly, he was too afraid that the treasure would fall into the wrong hands." Truthfinder gave a short laugh. "Kind of ironic that a Nazi scientist, of all people, would write something like that."

Nazi. That word rang a bell with Ondragon. "Was Dr. Schuch even a Nazi? In the Third Reich, scientists were forced to do research for Hitler. Especially at the end of the war."

"Yes, that's right. A number of brilliant scientists were conscripted into Hitler's war machine. Viktor Schauberger, for example; his research field was also vortex technology, and his Repulsine, an apparatus that supposedly overcame gravity by free levitation, is now considered by some experts to be one of the first free-energy converters. But there is disagreement about how the Repulsine worked, much as there is over Tesla's research on the subject. But that is only in passing. In Dr. Schuch's case, it could be that he was a conscript, but I have never heard of him or of the three other men mentioned in the flight log. Schuch mentions in his report that he worked with Kammler on Tesla's notebook in 1943. That must have been right after Tesla's death and the theft of the book. But whether Schuch participated in the investigation voluntarily, or was forced to, we will be hard pressed to find out. Although at the end of his report, he has the welfare of the German people very much at heart."

"I may have someone who can help us with that," Ondragon revealed. "I'll give you . . . um, I'll let you know as soon as I have something."

"Good. Then all that remains is for us to find the key word for the number squares. The fact that Dr. Schuch chose the shape of the square could also be a clue. I'd best try the Polybus square right away. All I need is a code word for that. Hmm . . ."

"Maybe the password is hidden in Schuch's report," Ondragon said. "There are some strange passages in it, after all. Why don't you try these: *Tesla's Dream*, *Holy Grail*, and *Sower*."

"What does *sower* mean?"

"It's someone who sows the seed in a field. Dr. Schuch writes: 'But the wheel of the sower can be turned back only with difficulty.' That sounds very unusual. I have never heard the phrase before. Off the top of my head, I can only think of the wheel of time or the wheel of fate."

"Okay, I'll try."

"Oh, and there's something else I can't figure out. It's a picture of a cross. It's a tattoo and it might be important. I'll send it to you. Maybe you'll be able to find out something about it."

"Sure thing, Mr. O."

Ondragon briefly considered asking Truthfinder about zero-point energy and the possible existence of a perpetual motion machine, but he let it go. It was too early in the morning for a physics lesson. He postponed it until later, just as he had always postponed his physics homework at school. That famous time known as "never."

The dream about his mother prodded unpleasantly at his memory. "NEVER!" she had said with eerie insistence, and Ondragon wondered if that meant something, or if it was just nighttime nonsense concocted by his brain.

Do you know what a secret is, Paul?

"Hey, Mr. O, is everything okay?" asked Truthfinder's voice on the other end of the phone.

"Uh, yeah." Ondragon shooed away the image of his mother's red lips and asked in a carefree tone, "Why?"

"You just mumbled something to yourself. It sounded like *blood sacrifice*. I don't know German, but that's what it sounded like, at least. What does it mean?"

"Oh, nothing," Ondragon had to work hard to hide his astonishment. "I was just thinking out loud. Nothing in particular. Okay, you'll get back to me if you find out anything new about the code?"

"Yo!"

"Great, talk to you later." Ondragon quickly hung up and stared into the pale dawn light seeping through the threadbare curtains. The red lips were still moving. *"Blood sacrifice!"* they whispered.

At eight o'clock, Charlize came to the door as arranged. Ondragon had given himself a makeshift wash with the stale water from the bucket and put on a lesser-used shirt from his bag. His whole body felt like it was itching. Not to mention the smell. Even the strongest deodorant could not cover it up. If he didn't get a shower soon, he would go insane. On top of that, a murderous hunger was churning in the pit of his stomach. He had long since digested the churrascos from the night before, and the assembled union of his organs that were responsible for nutrition was screaming for more.

"So, did you find out anything about the code or the cross?" he asked without much hope.

"Unfortunately not, Boss. Are you coming?"

Ondragon suppressed the urge to scratch his armpit and followed Charlize at an appropriate distance through the squalid corridors. The air was stuffy and had barely cooled overnight. A fresh layer of sweat quickly settled on his skin. Ondragon dropped back even farther.

Charlize reached the door with the large *CA* sign and turned around. "What's wrong? Why so slow today?"

"Too hot. Too unshowered. Too hungry. Take your pick."

She looked at him compassionately. Then that other, harder expression entered her eyes. The samurai look. No, this one was more like the mafia-bitch-drug-gangster look! She turned back to the door and knocked vigorously.

A little later, as they sat on the sofa next to Sem and ate *esfirra*, a kind of mini pizza with minced meat, for breakfast, he felt much better. At least the werewolf-like stomach growl that had prevented him from thinking was gone. The shower would certainly be organized during the day, when he broke into Charlize's quarters!

Sem had news for them. He had not given up and had continued to question the eyes of the favela. And indeed, someone had observed their stranger fleeing from his hiding place in the dilapidated factory: a short, slender man with a box on his shoulder. He had left the favela yesterday morning shortly after sunrise and headed toward Praia do Meireles. A crowd of children had followed him for fun. They had watched him make several calls on a cell phone and change his clothes at a beach hut. Afterward, he apparently looked like a fine gentleman. He had hidden the change of clothes in the box, which he had then taken to a hotel.

"And which hotel was that?" asked Ondragon.

"The Gran Marquise," Sem replied.

Puzzled, Ondragon raised his brows. "Is he still there?"

Sem raised his shoulders. "I don't know. The kids stopped watching him after he went into the hotel."

Ondragon noticed that Charlize had stopped sipping her coffee. "I don't get it!" she said aloud. "Why is this guy walking around with such a flashy box and risking being seen? And why is he staying at a hotel when he was previously staying under a tarp? And at the hotel you were in, of all places, Boss?"

"Maybe he thinks that's the last place we're likely to look for him," Ondragon said. "But I wonder why he hasn't left town with his precious loot long ago. At least he seems to still have the box and he hasn't flogged it off. I find that extremely strange though. Who might his client be? Don't they want the box?"

"Maybe the guy is just trying to set a false trail and lead us astray," Charlize suggested.

"But maybe he's going to hand over the box soon. In the hotel!"

"Could be." Charlize set her cup down on the coffee table, where the remnants of various joints were still giving off their specific aroma. Ondragon wondered yet again how these potheads managed to maintain a tightly organized drug trade when they were constantly taking excursions to the "highlands" themselves. He looked around the room. The faces of Sem's goons were shuttered. They didn't give anything away. And Sem, the boss? He looked like the ruler of the jungle, sitting there with his legs akimbo on the sofa. Animal strength and a nimble mind. He certainly didn't take a crumb of the stuff he got hold of for people. And one thing was clear: If he ever did, it would be a death sentence, because the hyenas were just waiting for the lion to show weakness. The eyes of the favela were everywhere.

"Hmm, but something's still not right," Ondragon finally said thoughtfully. "With a target as in-demand as Pandora, the client would have been there long ago, eager for a quick handover. He would never let so much time pass and risk Pandora slipping from his clutches again."

Charlize nodded and Sem listened with a neutral expression. They were talking in English and he seemed to be able to follow them.

"Could he be working alone and waiting for something other than the drop?" asked Charlize.

Ondragon considered it—not for the first time. "I'm not sure, but this delay thing could point to that. It seems pretty unprofessional to me."

"Maybe that's what it's supposed to look like," Charlize said. "Apparently, the guy had a change of clothes with him. That looks to me as if he's well-prepared. And even if he's working alone, he must have an informant who briefed him on the box in the lab, even if he's planning to auction it off to the highest bidder. That's what I would do if I were him, anyway. That would bring in the most profit."

"But why do that here in the city? The area is much too hot. Not only are we after him and the box, the police are too," Ondragon pointed out.

"But he doesn't know about Sem!" Charlize looked at him meaningfully and Ondragon looked over to the little drug lord who had spread his arms comfortably along the back of the sofa.

"If he's actually working alone," Charlize continued, thinking aloud, "there's no way he could have been keeping tabs on both of us at once. And I'm pretty sure I wasn't being followed. I was very careful."

I thought so too, Ondragon thought, but kept his uncertainty to himself. He didn't want to get into an argument with Charlize about being careful. Besides, there was little point in speculating about whether the guy was an amateur or a professional. He had the box and they had to do something about it. Time was running out. "We'll split up," he said, slapping his thighs with both hands. His jeans stuck to them like a second skin, much too tight. The climate in the room was like an equatorial sauna . . . with a hashish infusion. "I'm going to take care of some organizational matters and you, Charlize, are going to slip into one of your disguises and keep an eye on the guy at the hotel. He'd recognize me in a heartbeat." *And smell me*, he thought, disgruntled. He then turned to the mini Snoop Dogg with the boxer's nose. "And you, Sem, continue to keep your eyes on the favela. Deal?"

Sem took his arms off the back of the couch and bent his upper body forward. As he did so, the tattoos on his dark skin came to life. One of them was a grinning skull with a hole in its forehead. Beneath it was tattooed a tally mark. A very long tally.

"Deal, Mr. O," he said. His voice sounded rough, and Ondragon got his first inkling that this fellow was not to be trifled with. He was glad to have him on his side, at least for the moment. He rose and checked the magazine of his pistol. More as a sign that he was master of his craft than a real check. But he felt he had to stake out his territory in front of this little man, who was really a giant. He didn't want the guy to think he could even begin to have a go at Charlize.

Meanwhile, his assistant rummaged through her travel bag, putting together a camouflage outfit. Ondragon saw a black frizzy wig (her traveling fiffi, as she called it), a pink push-up bra, two silicone butt pads, and a leopard-print dress. He stifled a smile; he loved this outfit. Although Charlize had unmistakably Asian features, with her bronze complexion and Foxy Brown outfit, she could pass for a light-complected, sexy African American. She could even talk like one. "Hey baby, wassup?"

Good, he thought, *the show could begin.* He pulled out his cell phone and pointed at it. Sem understood the gesture and pointed to one of the doors at the back of his headquarters. Ondragon left the room, closed the door behind him, and leaned against what had once been the kitchen sink and now presumably served as a meth lab. Ignoring the acrid smell of cat piss, he dialed the first number.

CHAPTER 27

August 19, 1899
Colorado Springs
early in the morning

More than two weeks had passed since Philemon had talked to crazyman Foley. Two weeks in which he had not found a minute to follow up on the clues from the old crank, because he had been so preoccupied with the work in the laboratory. He had not been able to unravel the case or the strange calculation on the note, and certainly not what these supposed Pinkerton detectives were all about. He slaved alongside Löwenstein and Czito from morning till night and fell into his bed dead tired every evening, not even able to blink an eye. He was always glad to make his way home with his eyes still open and to have a little dinner just before going to bed, without nodding off at the table in the dining room, to the indignation of the other guests—if anyone was still present at that late hour, for Philemon usually returned to the hotel well after sunset.

Dr. Tesla didn't come to the Alta Vista at all now. He spent almost every night in his little chamber in the lab. Philemon wondered if he ever slept.

The longer Philemon worked with the eccentric inventor, the more supernatural he seemed. Tesla made gigantic efforts and achieved unimaginable feats with his brain, which had unprecedented capacity. The uncanny thing was that you could not see any sign of privation in him. At all hours of the day, Dr. Tesla was either poring over his notebooks with pen in hand or over the intricacies of an apparatus with a wrench. And when he wasn't keeping quietly to himself, in his ocean of thoughts, he was whirling around the laboratory with ecstatic elegance, exuding a drive that was simply infectious. But Dr. Tesla alone was able to march to the beat of his own drum, which kept as furious a tempo as the heartbeat of a small bird you might hold in your hands. It was as if his brain was fed with the millions of volts he chased through the coils every day, discharging them in popping lightning bolts as his extraordinarily tough body cast twitching shadows on the walls in the bluish, flickering light.

Philemon yawned behind his hand as he trudged to the lab at dawn. It was gloriously quiet in the streets, and there was a wonderful peace out on the prairie too. For now. Because soon the next experiment would begin and all creatures in the immediate vicinity of the building would be startled and driven away.

Philemon turned his head as he walked and gazed at Pikes Peak in the distance, its gray mass as still and motionless as the withered grass on the prairie. Over the past few days, they had erected an antenna and a terminal up there. It had been hellishly rough going, despite the propitious circumstance that they had been able to transport the material up to the summit comfortably by the Manitou & Pikes Peak rack-and-pinion railroad. A wonderful achievement of modern technology that had saved them an agonizing ride on a mule, but which, to Tesla's chagrin, was still operated by antiquated steam locomotives. The doctor hated the smoke that constantly wafted around one's nose during the ride and clouded the view to boot. In his opinion, it would be easy to set up an electric mountain railroad on the line. He was even inclined to submit a proposal to the town's elder, William J. Palmer, in return for his kind hospitality, so to speak. Whether the doctor meant this ironically, however, Philemon had not been able to determine. Nevertheless, the climb up the crumbling limestone cliff and the erection of the antenna, including the towering terminal, had been dangerous. But the effort had been worth it, and when they had returned to Manitou Springs after three days of work at low-oxygen altitude, they had seized the opportunity to toast the success of their experiment, naturally in a saloon licensed to serve alcohol. They'd eaten heartily and had railed against the dry kegs in Colorado Springs. Even Dr. Tesla had taken several glasses of whiskey, proclaiming in a buoyant mood that alcohol was an indispensable stimulant for body, mind, and spirit. Chewing gum or drinking tea was far more dangerous, he said, than enjoying a whiskey now and then!

Philemon looked ahead once more, along the dusty path. It was useless to try to see the antenna or the terminal at an altitude of 4,300 meters from a distance of 16 kilometers. Nevertheless, it was now up there: one of the first receiving stations for the wireless transmission of energy, constructed according to the plans of Nikola Tesla.

He reached the locked laboratory building. No one seemed to be there. The only strange thing was that the padlock was hanging open in the door latch. So someone was already here. Philemon opened the door and called a cheerful "Good morning!" into the silent building.

When no one answered, he entered, his brow furrowed. He closed the door behind him and groped through the lab in the dark until he reached the door to Tesla's small study. He knocked, but nothing moved.

"Hello, Dr. Tesla? Are you there?"

Still no answer. Strange, why was the lock open and no one in the building? A sudden thought flashed through his mind. What if someone had broken into the lab? Had those Pinkertons been here? Had the notorious detectives come to Colorado Springs to steal the doctor's ideas? He quickly flipped on the light switch and the room was bathed in yellowish light. He went to the apparatuses and examined them one by one. None were missing or damaged. Everything seemed to be in order. Philemon hurried into Dr. Tesla's chamber and looked around. The small room looked as it always did. On the wall shelf the row of notebooks stood undisturbed and on the table lay papers and drawing materials, carefully arranged. Even the notebook with the gold ring on the cover was still there. Philemon picked it up reverently and felt the smooth leather. Finally, he opened it and read some of the lines, which were written in razor-sharp handwriting.

All my studies on the wireless transmission of energy have shown that it is very feasible. And even more than that! Impossible things will become possible if I succeed in establishing my world system. I will be the pioneer of a new age. An age without borders. The secret lies solely in the nature of the ether. With this knowledge, I will succeed in sending signals around the globe and transcending time and space.

He continued to turn the pages. The book seemed more like a personal diary than records of experiments. Philemon came across a beautifully executed drawing of a structure. It was a tower and obviously a development of the two terminals, one of which they had erected on Pikes Peak. But unlike the tube-shaped terminals, the tower was octagonal and tapered toward the top. At the pinnacle sat a massive, mushroom-shaped dome surrounded by a corona of rays. Between the rays and the dome, a strange word nestled in the curve. *Worldwireless.*

This was Tesla's World System, Philemon thought, reading the name written under the drawing. *Stanford White, NY—architect.* And he could not help but marvel at the scale of the structure.

Fifty-six meters high and twenty meters wide for the copper torus! By Saint Joseph, that was enormous! He turned the pages curiously and found a place where the lost assistant was mentioned.

June 25, 1899—Röhnfeldt experiment, experimental phase I. Frederick Myers is a daring man. Not only did he have a brilliant idea, but he put himself forward for the experiment with the enthusiasm I anticipated. And it is with great pride that I can report that he was the first person to participate in a transmission of etheric solute matter in the form of electrical energy.

Philemon frowned. Etheric solute matter? Röhnfeldt experiment? He had never heard Tesla and the others speak about that. What was it? He read on.

I was beside myself with joy, and my assistants shared this euphoria. The experiment had succeeded and I was sure that we were now only one tiny step away from our great goal. But then an unforeseen incident set us back and put an abrupt end to our hopes. Although I had personally calibrated all the apparatus for Test Phase II and optimized the transmission frequencies, something went wrong, much to my chagrin. Frederick Myers was in the terminal when we raised the voltage to thirty million volts, but then there was a short circuit and the power supply collapsed. We rushed to the terminal and looked, but Myers was . . .

"It makes for impressive reading, does it not?"

Philemon closed the book in shock. He wheeled around. Behind him stood an upright, gaunt figure with the glowing eyes of Mephistopheles.

"Dr. Tesla! I . . . uh, beg your pardon. The lock on the entrance to the lab was open, but no one was here. I . . . thought someone had broken in and stolen something." Philemon felt himself blushing at this flimsy explanation. Frightened, he gasped for air but could hardly get anything through his throat, he was held so captive by the doctor's hermetic gaze. Tesla's face looked as forbidding and motionless as that of a man who had been sorely disappointed. Philemon had never felt so small and shabby, and he cowered involuntarily. But the expected deadly lightning strike from Tesla's eyes failed to materialize; instead, his pale features turned abruptly mild. He approached Philemon with his hand raised.

"This," he said, pointing to the notebook Philemon still held in his trembling hands, "is my legacy! In this book I have immortalized all my thoughts about my greatest invention. It is more valuable than all the other records put together, and I always carry it with me."

Philemon wanted to say something in reply, but the doctor would not let him get a word in edgewise. "I was already here when you came, my friend, and I watched you."

Philemon swallowed. His throat had turned into the thin neck of an hourglass, through which only one grain at a time could trickle. Grain by grain—too little air for a grown man. Panicked, he struggled for composure, but secretly he knew it was over. The doctor would fire him and send him home. He had missed his chance. Tears of shame welled up in his eyes.

"I am truly sorry!" he said chokingly. "Of course, I shall pack my things and leave immediately."

Tesla turned his gaze to the notebook and then back to Philemon. "You will not! After all, I need you here!"

Astonished, Philemon looked up. "But I entered your study and read your notes without permission. That was . . ."

". . . most unseemly, indeed! But it also shows your extraordinary interest in my work. Incidentally, I have noticed the unselfish and uncomplaining dedication with which you have carried out your duties over the past few weeks. I know you are an inquisitive and intelligent young man, Mr. Ailey. Much more intelligent than Löwenstein or Czito—without wishing to offend either of my assistants. But you have that certain something it takes to become a true researcher. Grit, perseverance, and flash. And I am strongly appreciative when someone is diligent and sincere. There are not many men who follow me without reservations. My friends Löwenstein and Czito are such rarities, and I hope you are too, Mr. Ailey."

"Of course. So I can stay?" asked Philemon anxiously. His heart beat violently in his chest. Tesla's unexpected praise was making him jittery.

"You may do much more than that, my friend. I'm going to let you be the first senior assistant on the experiment today."

"Senior assistant?"

"Quite so. In point of fact, I had intended that the good and reliable Löwenstein would do it, as always, but I have come to the conclusion that I owe you something for your loyalty."

Philemon bit his lip, infinite gratitude flowing through him. "You owe me nothing, Doctor. On the contrary, I am deeply indebted to you for your patience and forbearance with an overly clumsy student like me. And I am honored to be permitted to perform the experiment for you today." He handed Tesla the book with a slight bow.

The doctor accepted it wordlessly, stroked it devoutly, and signaled to Philemon that he might leave. With a pounding heart, the young electrical engineer left the chamber and entered the laboratory, where he leaned happily against the wall. At last, he would be promoted from mere lab apprentice to the rank of full-fledged assistant. At last, he would be accepted into the circle of Tesla's closest confidants. He heard Löwenstein and Czito enter the building. The two men were laughing about something and hung their hats on the hooks next to the door. They greeted Philemon cheerily and together the three of them set about preparing the experiment.

CHAPTER 28

August 19, 1899
Colorado Springs
noon

Shortly before noon, everything was ready. Working together, they had moved the second terminal—a copper tube taller than a man, and with a dome-shaped roof—outside, and set it on a flat section of the prairie. The tube was wrapped with an insulated wire, the end of which was anchored in the ground. The intention was to pass energy through it, over the ground, and into the coil, and transmit it from there to the terminal on Pikes Peak. The frequencies arriving at the peak would be recorded by a small measuring device, to be analyzed later. At this terminal, a light bulb attached to the tube would indicate whether the current was flowing as planned.

Excitedly, Philemon stood next to the small copper tower and looked over at the laboratory building. He was wearing his rubber apron and the shoes with the insulating soles, on which he was bobbing back and forth impatiently. He was the senior assistant and would prove that he had what it took.

Czito had been assigned to the main circuit breaker for this experiment, and Löwenstein was supervising the coils inside the building. Whether the two of them were resentful of his role in this assignment, Philemon could not say. He stopped bobbing abruptly when Dr. Tesla appeared in the doorway of the laboratory and peered out at him with an expectant smile. As always, the experiment would begin at his signal.

Then the doctor raised a hand, and Philemon knew that the voltage was rising to unbearable levels, not only with him but in the large coil in the laboratory. The hum of the transformers grew louder and louder as they produced higher and higher voltages.

Then it was time. Tesla's hand dropped and Czito flipped the switch. There was a pop and the buzzing became so strong that Philemon could feel it in his stomach, even at this distance. He raised his pen and began writing notes on a clipboard. He wanted to record his observations as precisely as possible so that the others would be impressed later. He heard exclamations of excitement from the others and noticed that the lamp on the tube next to him had begun to glow. His pen flew across the paper, documenting every detail.

The experiment was working. Like the experiment with the two hundred light bulbs, energy was being transmitted through the ground. But would they also succeed in sending it through the air, or rather, through the ether, to the terminal on Pikes Peak? What would the readings be?

Philemon noticed the tube next to him begin to crackle. Small spark discharges formed on the dome roof. They looked like electric fingers groping around in the statically charged air. As a precaution, Philemon took a few steps back to avoid being hit by them. At the same time, his pen continued unswervingly, noting every phenomenon, no matter how small. All at once, a lightning bolt several meters long detached itself from the dome and struck the prairie with a loud crash. Startled, Philemon ducked his head and squinted over to where a tuft of grass had caught fire. The bang was still ringing in his ears, but he could hear Tesla yelling at him to keep a greater distance. Philemon ignored the warning and stepped boldly up to the terminal, where a new bolt of lightning of incredible length was already flickering on the dome. With a sudden shower of sparks, the hum of the transformers ceased and the lightning sensor on the dome collapsed soundlessly. A low hissing sound emanated from the tube, as if hot air was escaping from somewhere, smelling of ozone and heated metal. There was a clearly palpable residue of static energy in the atmosphere. Philemon looked over to the laboratory. Dr. Tesla was walking toward him with long strides. He seemed happy and almost tipsy with enthusiasm.

"Isn't that fantastic?" he said when he got to him. "I'm sure the gauge on Pikes Peak will have recorded fluctuations!"

"I hope so, I cannot wait to see the results."

"Czito will go up with you in the morning. Right now, though, let's repeat the experiment once more."

Philemon looked questioningly at the doctor.

"We still need observations from inside the tube," Tesla explained.

"From the . . . inside?"

Tesla nodded. "It is essential for us to know what is going on in there during the transmission. Would you do us the honor of recording these observations?"

"You mean you want me to go in there while the experiment is going on?" asked Philemon, aghast.

"That's right. But if you don't want to, then you're welcome to take Löwenstein's place and he'll get into the terminal. It wouldn't be his first time."

The handwritten lines from Tesla's diary appeared in Philemon's mind's eye. *Myers was in the terminal when we raised the voltage to thirty million volts, but then there was a short circuit . . .*

"And what happens if there's a short?"

"It can't hurt you out here. We've also set up a second circuit and a spare capacitor for just such cases."

Philemon was still not convinced. "What about the lightning bolts on the dome?"

"They will only appear on the outside. Inside, everything will be quiet. The tube is a Faraday cage, after all."

Philemon was torn. He had terrible misgivings about going into the tube after all he had heard about Myers, but on the other hand he didn't want to look like a quitter in front of the others, now that he had been given the job of first assistant. The thoughts flashed through his head like glittering lightning bolts. He didn't know what precisely had happened to Myers or if it had even happened in the tube. And that might not have had anything to do with his disappearance. Philemon took a deep breath. There was only one way to find out. "All right," he agreed without further ado, "I'll go in. But only if you promise no ill will come to me."

Tesla regarded him seriously. "Nothing will happen to you, I can vouch for that. All you have to do is put on the rest of your protective clothing and make sure you don't touch the walls of the tube, and you'll come through the spectacle safe and sound. You'll see, apart from an invigorating tingling sensation, you won't feel a thing, I bet. I'd do it myself, I'm so eager for the experience, but as the father of the idea, it's my duty to supervise the experiment." The doctor hooked his thumbs into the pockets of his vest and cast a pensive glance into the distance. "I hope that I will soon be granted the privilege of going into the terminal myself. In any case, I'm very anxious to hear your report, Mr. Ailey."

Philemon straightened up and resolutely pulled the rubber hood over his head. He adjusted it so that only his mouth, nose, and eyes protruded, and slipped on his gloves. Then he signaled to Tesla that he was ready, and the doctor opened the waist-high door in the tube. Philemon bent down, crawled inside, and stood up again. He watched Tesla close the door and was instantly enveloped in oppressive darkness. Only through the slit in the door was there enough light for him to just make out his hand. But that wasn't enough for writing, he realized uneasily, and looked around. Finally, he discovered the light bulb above his head. Ah, so they had thought of that after all. The lamp would light up when the current began to flow through the earth. For Philemon, a sign that the experiment had started. Tensely he waited.

"Are you ready, Mr. Ailey?" he soon heard Dr. Tesla call from a distance.

"I am! Fresh, pious, cheerful, free," he shouted back, quoting good old Fritz Löwenstein. As he did so, his voice echoed dully off the curved walls of the tube. In the silence that followed, sweat broke out under his hood. *Damn*, Philemon thought, scraping the pencil across the rubber skin to stop the itching. *Get a grip!*

The next moment, his entire body was shaking. It felt as if his skin was shrinking. The lamp above his head blinded him brightly, and a high-pitched whirring sound entered his ears. Philemon tried to ignore the all-pervasive noise and remembered his job as a recorder.

Persistent goose bumps, he wrote. *Tension of the skin, especially on the head. Increased salivation and vertigo. Uncontrolled trembling of the muscles. First in the legs and then in the arms. Pressure on the ears.*

He paused because he was barely able to hold the pen. What was happening? Were these the effects of electricity on his body? Suddenly, a jolt went through the floor and a biting cold penetrated him. The air inside the tube cooled abruptly, and without him being able to do anything about it, Philemon's teeth began to chatter. He saw his breath condensing and went to make a note of this phenomenon, but the pen fell from his stiffened hand. He fell to his knees, unconsciously peering through the slit in the door. Startled, he remained in a crouch, staring at the gap. Was he mistaken? Had the millions of volts coursing through the floor clouded his brain? He approached the rift. In an instant, it grew warmer again and the pressure on his ears eased. The lamp above his head went out, and through the slit he could make out the dry grass of the prairie and Dr. Tesla's shoes! With a jerk, the door was opened and fresh air crowded in.

"Mr. Ailey? Are you there? Is everything all right?" Was that a slight note of concern he could hear in the doctor's voice?

Philemon didn't care. He just wanted to get out of the narrow tube. His legs wobbling, he crawled out into the open, pulled the rubber hood off his head, and took several deep breaths. Feeling the afternoon sun on the top of his head and the wind on his face, he gradually calmed down and smiled tentatively at the doctor. Tesla gave him what seemed like a knowing look.

In the evening, Philemon walked contentedly back to the city, alone once again. But he didn't care this time. He was filled with pride that he had accepted today's challenge and mastered it with flying colors, and was now looking forward to a hearty dinner. Today he wanted to treat himself to something as a reward for his courage. Perhaps a nice steak. Yes, that was good, a juicy piece of meat would bring his strength back. Even though he was in the best of moods, he was aware of the strain his body had been subjected to during the experiment. He still thought he could feel the weakness that had invaded his whole being in the tube, and the strange coldness. But he also remembered the enthusiastic pats on the back from Czito and Löwenstein when he had returned to the lab, grinning from ear to ear. The brotherhood of the two assistants and the appreciative look from Tesla had made him immediately forget the horrors of the tube.

Philemon kicked a pebble off the path and strolled through the streets of Colorado Springs with his hands in his pockets. Attentively, he watched the people going about the business of the evening in front of the restaurants and the other venues. They didn't seem to notice him at all. He felt all the more like a silent observer. If people knew what they were doing out on the prairie! If they knew that they were creating the future there. But they didn't! Fortunately, because perhaps they would become fearful and anxious, as he had done in the tube. Philemon continued on his way with a pleasant shudder and soon reached the hotel. In the dining room, he ordered the most colossal steak the hotel kitchen had to offer and devoured it hungrily.

An hour later, exhausted, he lay on his bed looking up at the ceiling, still very excited by the day's events. Finally, he took his father's pocket watch from the nightstand and was about to rewind it for the next day, when he noticed the date. Strange, today was only the nineteenth of August and not the twentieth already. He shook the watch and held it to his ear. It ticked quietly but steadily. Must be a defect in the date display.

Philemon set the date back to the nineteenth and wound the watch. He would see if it was wrong again tomorrow. He put it back on the night-stand and rested his head on the pillow. With his hands folded on his stomach, he pondered once again what he had seen through the slit in the door during the experiment. It must have been imagination or the effect of the high-current frequencies on body and mind. There was no other way to explain why he had believed himself to be standing in the tube on the drafty summit of Pikes Peak . . .

CHAPTER 29

May 24, 2011
Fortaleza, Brazil
9:17 am

Hello, Professor Krupa? This is Paul Ondragon. I got your number from Professor Ludewig in Hamburg. He said you might be able to help me."

"Ah, Mr. *On Drrrrágon*! Good day to you."

Ondragon had expected a heavy Eastern European accent, but the professor spoke flawless German. He was probably of German descent or had studied in Germany. But he had mispronounced Ondragon's name, with emphasis on the *A* and an exaggerated rolled *R*, which made him sound more like a flying beast. No matter, he had better things to do right now than correct this. He explained his purpose, revealing only as much as he considered appropriate. Of course, he wrapped everything up in his socially acceptable management consultant mantle, because Günther Ludewig had no idea about his real job, and accordingly neither did Professor Krupa. Ondragon explained to the Pole that he was investigating a tricky insurance case from the end of World War II.

Krupa seemed to take the bait. "That's a good one," he said. "Nazi secret technology is my private hobby horse."

Outstanding! thought Ondragon. He pulled out his notepad and put it on the sink in the filthy drug kitchen.

"In my spare time, I have researched all the underground production sites of the Third Reich," Krupa meanwhile explained. "The mine and the Gross-Rosen concentration camp in Ludwigsdorf, Silesia, will likely be of interest to you. It's thought to have been a test site for The Bell. You know what that is?"

"A flying object with gravitational propulsion?"

Krupa laughed softly. "That's what they say, at least. I have discovered that there was indeed a research project with that name. I can prove this from dispatches sent to Reichsmarschall Göring by a certain General Hans Kammler. Kammler is said to have escaped toward the end of the war in an airplane with a secret cargo on board that is said to have come from the Bell project. Have you heard of the Junkers 390, the so-called ghost plane?"

"Yes, I'm aware of it."

"Good, then I don't need to tell you that the plane has been considered lost since then, and with it the cargo."

"No, but what do you think of the Bell project? What was it?" Ondragon urged the Pole.

"Well, it wasn't a flying object with an antigravity drive, if that's what you mean. Also, the polygonal structure of concrete columns, which is still standing on a dilapidated site near Ludwigsdorf, was certainly not a UFO launchpad; rather, it was the foundations for a larger construction that came to a halt or was torn down in a hurry."

"Perhaps the foundations for a superweapon. Some kind of death ray, like Nikola Tesla's?" Ondragon dared to ask.

"What does Nikola Tesla have to do with your insurance case?" Krupa asked. Was the Pole getting suspicious after all?

Ondragon groped quickly for an excuse, then said, "The scientist on behalf of whose granddaughter I'm investigating the case is supposed to have worked on the Bell project. And I'd be really interested to know what it was all about. That would be a great help in my research."

"Hmm," Krupa replied absently, and Ondragon feared that he had lost him as a source of information. But the Pole finally went on easily with his explanations. He gave the impression of actually being quite happy to be able to share his knowledge with someone.

"Well, the Bell project is actually connected with Nikola Tesla," he said, "but not through UFOs, as most people believe. By chance, I discovered something in the research papers of a German physicist at the time. His area of expertise was high-frequency technology—incidentally, this also gives more weight to the ray gun theory than to the mysterious flying object. In any case, my find quite surprisingly established a connection between The Bell and Tesla. In the documents was a handwritten file number, which read: NT1943NY. For me, this quite clearly stands for 'Nikola Tesla 1943 New York!' There is a rumor, you know. It says that two German spies killed Tesla in New York and stole his notebook, which allegedly contained plans for a secret miracle machine."

"What kind of machine?"

"I'm afraid I don't know, because I've never been able to locate the file in the memo. Which is a real shame."

"And what else was in the physicist's papers?" Ondragon wanted to know.

"Nothing special. Most of them were technical papers and calculations, but they had nothing to do with the secret research in Ludwigsdorf. But I did find something else: a telegram. At least I think it is. It is an almost illegible piece of paper. The recipient is General Kammler and the station from which the telegram was sent is New Jersey. The sender is unfortunately indecipherable, but the text can be read. It is quite short: 'Have Pandora—tomorrow contact with U-boat—meeting in a week in L —Heil Hitler.'"

Pandora! Ondragon thought, stunned. Was this possible? Could there be such a crazy coincidence? Or had the BND known about this document and named the current operation in parallel? Scratching his head pensively, he asked, "So the telegram was sent by the spies?"

"I assume so," Krupa replied. "Pandora certainly meant Tesla's notebook, and the *L* stands for Ludwigsdorf. I tell you, the book was the basis for the Bell project!"

There seems to be no doubt about that, Ondragon thought. Krupa had dug deeper into this matter than anyone. There was no reason not to believe him. Hastily, he noted down the information while the professor chatted blithely on.

"A year ago, I went public with my theory about the ray gun on the relevant internet forums. I wanted to consult with other myth hunters about it, but particularly militant supporters of the Nazi UFO theory put me down mercilessly for it. After that, I withdrew from the net and continued my research in private."

"Was the name-calling on alienbuster, by any chance?"

"Exactly! How do you know?"

"I read the thread, before it was deleted." That was an outright lie, but Ondragon was determined to keep the Pole sweet. At least now he knew it had been Krupa whom Truthfinder had meant when he said he needed to apologize to some of the forum members.

"I have one more question," he finally asked. "Will you tell me the name of the physicist in whose papers you found the file number?"

"Of course. But he was pretty much unknown. His name was Schwarz. Dr. Albrecht Schwarz."

Ondragon almost dropped his pen. Dr. Schwarz? He had been one of the passengers on the Junkers 390. One of the ones who had been left behind in the desert. "Then perhaps you also know the names Schuch, Kahn, and Eschenberg?"

"Yes," Krupa replied, "they're on the list too."

"What list?"

"A directory listing all the scientists who were based at the research facility in Ludwigsdorf. I found the list in an archive in Berlin. But where—?"

"You have been a great help, Professor Krupa. Unfortunately, I have to go to an urgent appointment now. Thank you very much."

"You're welcome," the Pole said irritably. "But—"

"I'll be in touch if I need to know anything else about the case. Goodbye!" Ondragon quickly hung up before Krupa could ask any more awkward questions. He looked at his notes. Whew, that had been immensely informative! Half of his pad was filled with Krupa's fascinating information. Normally, he avoided asking others for help, especially strangers. They almost always wanted him to owe them a favor, and he hated to get tangled up with reciprocal arrangements. For this damned case alone, he was already hung about with as many favors as the threads of a spider whose web he had gotten caught in. They all led to names that echoed reprovingly through the empty refrigerator compartment of his conscience.

Charlize! Sem! Ludewig! Strangelove! Truthfinder! Krupa! Yes, even Kubicki!

All these people would one day demand something in return for their services. Sure, he could fob some of them off with money or counter-information. But what about his few friends? He owed them. Things that were normal in relationships between friends, but that he would never be able to repay. Real friendships were dangerous. Dangerous for him . . . and for his friends. Ondragon felt the thought threatening to constrict him, and fought it. He had to be even more careful in the future not to deviate from his maxims. Not a single millimeter. He would not allow a normal, middle-class life to catch up with him, with friends and regular work.

Regularity, uniformity, consistency, all that was synonymous with stagnation . . . death!

On impulse, Ondragon dropped the pen into the dirty sink and wiped his hands on his T-shirt. He had more important things to do than think about his life. He had obtained valuable information and now he wanted to focus on what lay ahead for him and Charlize. The recovery of Pandora!

Two hours later, he was sitting in his beach boy disguise under the palm trees at Praia do Meireles, watching the main entrance of the Gran Marquise Hotel. He was enveloped in an olfactory haze made up of the scents "sumo wrestler's armpit" and "construction worker at the jackhammer in forty-degree heat"!

Charlize had now discovered which room their Mr. Unknown had been staying in. And thanks to her cleavage, which she had held under the nose of the unsuspecting boy in reception, she now also knew the individual's name: Chester William Black. Ondragon wasn't assuming the name was real, but cover names often bore some relation to someone's real identity. Many who operated in the demimonde, as he did, were vain and used an alias with a deliberate reference that they thought was sophisticated and bombproof. He had made the same mistake himself when he had started out. His first false passport bore the American name Peter Drake. It was busted immediately, of course, and Ondragon had had to establish a new identity. Today he had complete sets of forged papers for the names Jerry McCoy, Bernd Fuchs, and Asbjörn Bengtson. All of them innocuous and with a certain natural authenticity. The only passport that always caused customs officers to frown was his real one with the name Paul Eckbert Ondragon.

Chester William Black sounded too trivial and much too English. Precisely because of this, Ondragon suspected, it might conceal a French background. In his head he translated the surname into other languages: *Noir*, *Negro*, *Black*, *Nero*, *Czarny*, *Cherno*. Well, maybe that was the name of their stranger.

There was a lot of activity on the street. Cars and buses were pushing past him in a single line of metal, and tourists from all over the world were bustling along the boardwalk. The sun was hidden behind a thin veil of clouds, keeping the temperature bearable. Seemingly relaxed, Ondragon listened to the muted bossa nova emanating from the speakers of the busy beach bar and took a sip of his beer, which had long since warmed up and was serving more as camouflage than refreshment. His bare feet were stuck in the warm sand, right next to his flip-flops and the backpack in which his pistol was hidden.

He waited for the stranger to leave the hotel so he could go after him. But he just wouldn't show. Charlize, aka "Cherry Jones," was posted in the lobby and kept in contact with him via the BND radio equipment.

Ondragon put the beer bottle down on the table and scanned his surroundings, noticing a guy strolling past him for the second time. He was young and wore beach clothes, yet he seemed so conspicuously inconspicuous that Ondragon became suspicious. He was probably a junior spy for the BND, because the intelligence agency also wanted to stay on top of this operation. The guy disappeared down the street and Ondragon continued to watch the hotel entrance.

After an hour, he changed location, slightly annoyed. It was like they had been bewitched. Mr. Chester William Black remained out of sight. Charlize was also sighing impatiently into her mic more frequently.

"I can't sit around here much longer or it'll be too noticeable," she said quietly.

"Roger that," Ondragon whispered. "Position roulette in twenty minutes."

"Okay."

Then she was quiet again, except for the sighing.

Ondragon strolled along the boardwalk and stopped by a street performer who was juggling burning torches. While watching the performance, he kept an unobtrusive eye on who was leaving the hotel. Hopefully, they wouldn't have to hang around until tonight, he thought irritably. As the juggler extinguished each torch individually with his mouth, the earpiece in his ear suddenly came to life.

"There he is! The guy is coming out of the elevator and heading for the exit!" said Charlize. "He's wearing dark pants, a white shirt, and the silver bangle on his left arm. You'll recognize him right away! I can also see the tattoo. It's on the left side of his neck. Under his ear."

"Got him!" replied Ondragon, looking at the guy more closely; now that he was seeing him for the first time, he seemed somehow unimpressive. His skin was coffee brown, like that of every other Brazilian on the street. He might actually be a local. Only the bracelet marked him out. Very wide and polished to a shine. Way too flashy. Why was he wearing it? Was it his trademark or the sign of some affiliation? Like the tattoo? Ondragon watched as the guy stopped in front of the hotel and looked around. As he did so, he sniffed the air like a dog. Ondragon quickly ducked into the cluster of people that had formed around the juggler. When he looked back toward the hotel entrance, the guy had started walking and was strolling toward the harbor.

"I'm going to glue myself to his heels," he told Charlize into the mic. "And you get into his room. He doesn't have the box with him, so it must still be in the hotel."

"Maybe he only has the book and the medal with him."

"Could be, but then I'll take both off him! The bastard has it coming!" Determinedly, Ondragon set off in pursuit. The guy was indeed weaving through the crowd strangely smoothly, just as the favela dwellers had described. It was as if a man had been crossed with a lizard. Uncanny! Unfortunately, the crowd on the sidewalk gradually thinned out and it became increasingly difficult to find cover. It was afternoon, and people were now lying on the beach, full of lunch, frying in the sun. Ondragon had to be careful as all hell not to be spotted, because the guy kept looking around. For this reason, he dropped back even farther, so that he almost risked losing him. As he did so, he heard Charlize in his ear.

"Going up," she said, and the *pling* of the elevator sounded in the background. "In the hallway. No one here."

"Be careful, Charlize!"

"I will." There was a crackling on the line, probably because he was slowly moving out of transmission range.

"Hurry, Charlize! This guy is still moving, but I don't know what he's up to."

"Right outside the door." There was a clack as she inserted the swipe card into the slot. "And in! The master key was a good idea."

"All right, search the room. Where's the box?" Ondragon almost faltered as the guy turned around and looked right at him. Quickly, he lowered his head and pretended to be busy with his smartphone. The straw hat covered his face.

What kind of beginner's crap is this? he thought angrily. Looking at your cell phone or even pretending to make a call was one of the biggest mistakes you could make during a tail. For someone who was familiar with the practices of the intelligence services, this was tantamount to unmasking. As a tail, you might as well shout, "Hello, here I am!" He had often observed this kind of amateurism on recordings from surveillance cameras around the globe. Most recently in the Mossad operation in Dubai, when they had treated Hamas extremist Mahmoud al-Mabhouh to a most unnatural demise. Ondragon pulled himself together. He was a professional, after all!

He squinted out of one eye at the guy and waited, but his mistake seemed to have gone unnoticed. Mr. Black just kept on walking and turned into a side street. Ondragon hurried to follow. Corners were always a tricky business. He himself liked to use them on reconnaissance, to check if anyone was following him. That's why he also pretended to cross the street first, glancing randomly down the street. Where was the son of a bitch? Ah, there! He was walking faster now, and suddenly disappeared into a hotel in the second row. Was he planning to hand over Pandora there? If so, Ondragon had to stop him at all costs and grab it while the guy was still alone!

"Charlize, what's going on?" he asked into the mic, walking over to the hotel entrance. "Do you have the box?"

"Yes, Boss!" There was a crackle and Charlize's voice cut out for a moment. ". . . it's in the closet. Not a very good hiding place, if you ask me. But I have to admit, the thing is hard to hide. There's nothing else in the room, not a single clue to the guy's identity. It looks like he wasn't here at all. The bed is untouched."

"Open the box! I almost have him. If the two things aren't in the box, I'll grab him. But first I need to know."

"Sure!"

Ondragon entered the hotel Mr. Black had gone into and looked around cautiously. The lobby was quite small. He was bound to attract attention now!

"Damn it, Charlize! What's taking so long?"

"The box is empty!"

"And the safe?"

"Empty too!"

"Fuck!" Now it would get complicated, he thought, and slid his hand into the backpack, where it covertly gripped the pistol.

"But there's something else in the box," Charlize said in his ear.

"What?"

"Clothes. Different things. I guess that's what the guy was wearing." A prolonged hiss drowned out her words. ". . . a piece of paper in his pants pocket. There's a phone number on it. 0033 and then 1-7776969!"

"A Paris number. All right, if you don't think you've missed anything, then tuck the box under your arm and get out of there!"

"Yes, Boss. See you in a minute!" He heard his assistant gasp. It sounded surprised.

"Charlize?"

No answer.

"Charlize, come in!"

Still silence at the other end. Had the connection cut out completely? Just a moment ago, it had been fine. Ondragon scanned the lobby frantically while a moped rattled past noisily on the street outside. In the small room there was a counter, a receptionist looking at him questioningly, chairs, and the corridor to the elevators, but no Mr. Black. Shit!

He went up to the lady behind the counter and asked if she had seen the guest who had just come in. She shook her head, and suddenly Ondragon had the uneasy feeling something had gone terribly wrong. Wordlessly, he turned on his heel and ran back to the Gran Marquise.

CHAPTER 30

May 24, 2011
Fortaleza, Brazil
2:20 p.m.

It had worked, the trap had snapped shut! The beautiful *nipo-brasileira* lay motionless behind the door. Slightly out of breath, Clandestin entered his room and looked down at the woman. Her eyes stared into space. He quickly donned rubber gloves and put a finger to her warm neck. Her pulse was slow but regular. Good. He reached for the box lying next to the woman, set it on the bed, and opened it. *She had been the perfect bait*, he thought as he pulled out the clothes and looked for the note with the phone number. It was gone. Carefully, he patted the woman down and found the note in her sequined purse, which also contained another surprise. Whistling softly, he pulled out a switchblade and snapped it open. Mademoiselle knew how to defend herself. He tossed the knife into the trash can and took the note. Tearing it into small shreds, he flushed it down the toilet. Then he took a small atomizer out of his pocket and sprayed all the clothes, the handbag, and the box. He had known that the woman would search these items, and he had spiked everything with TTX. Tetrodotoxin was a very effective contact poison and had many uses. This weak dosage took effect within a few minutes and immobilized the person completely. With full consciousness, mind you! The special spray he had used would neutralize the poison and he could now safely leave the things here in the hotel.

He looked thoughtfully at the woman's even face, her dark, expressionless eyes. What was she thinking now? There was a slight smile on her red-painted lips. She looked as if she were lying in a meadow, dreaming with her eyes open. He brushed the wig off her head and freed her wonderfully straight hair from the hairnet. Then he began to tie her up.

It was their own fault that he had to respond in this way. They had backed him into a corner! That was why he had set this trap for the woman. She had blown the cover of his hiding place in the favela, however she had found out about it. She had likely had help from the little

Brazilian she had contacted before. And now she was lying here. Bound and gagged. And he needed to decide what to do with her.

"Do you want me to kill you?" he asked, looking her straight in the eye.

The woman remained motionless. Naturally. Though she certainly understood him. "Or would you like me to have a little fun with you?" With a look of pleasure, he let his hand slide down into her cleavage and placed it on one of her breasts.

"*Mon Dieu*, even a *faux* one! Why is everything always false?" Disappointed, he pulled the push-up insert out of her bra. "It suits your character, *chérie*. But you're lucky I have more pressing things to do right now. Keeping your overly solicitous partner at bay, for example! He should show up here soon." Clandestin jumped up and pulled a small pistol from a holster on his calf. "I'll send him over the Jordan River with this if he gets too close!" He looked at his cell phone. Seven more hours and he could finally leave this damn country!

Less than three minutes later, there was a pounding on the door.

Voilà. The dance around the golden calf could begin.

CHAPTER 31

May 24, 2011
Fortaleza, Brazil
2:47 pm

Charlize! Open up!" Ondragon pounded on the door again.

"I'm afraid your charming partner can't open the door!" He suddenly heard a male voice say from inside the room. He put his hand in his backpack and pointed the gun in it at the door. He could just pull the trigger and shoot through the cheap veneer. But maybe the guy wasn't even standing behind the door, or worse, he was hurting Charlize.

"Where is she? What did you do with her, you asshole?" he shouted.

"Don't worry, she's here with me. She's fine, but unfortunately she can't speak—a little precaution. After all, I don't want her to yell the hotel down. And the same goes for you. Get away from the door and don't make such a racket! We all want to be reasonable, don't we? Go down to the lobby or onto the fire stairs for all I care, but go! Otherwise, your little birdie here will never chirp again. Call me on my cell phone. Here's my number."

A note was slipped under the door. Ondragon picked it up, took one last look at the door, and hurried to the fire stairs. In the neon light of the stairwell, he hastily dialed the number and after the third ring, the call was answered.

"*Bonjour et allô*, Mr. O! Oh, how beautifully it rhymes."

"How do you know who I am?"

"Oh, it doesn't matter. Let's say I know how to get information. Let's talk about your partner instead." There was a rustling on the other end, as if the guy was shifting the phone from one hand to the other. "She's lying here in front of me, all nicely tied up. She's a real beauty. I could hardly contain myself."

"You fucking—"

"Now, now, now, who's getting abusive?" The stranger made a snorting sound. "I advise you to listen carefully to what I am about to tell you, after which you can end the conversation and use whatever foul language you like. When you have calmed yourself, you may call me again and agree to my offer. *Compris?*"

Was this guy taking the piss? He spoke like an affected French etiquette teacher. But that was the cue, Ondragon thought, secretly pleased that he had guessed correctly. Mr. Black was not English. Judging by his accent, he was French, or at least a native French speaker.

"What kind of offer is that?" he asked.

"Well, it's quite simple. So simple that even you will understand it, Mr. O!"

Ondragon clenched his teeth. He would have loved to storm the room, free Charlize from the hands of this bastard, and smash his skull in. But he wouldn't get far with that kind of cowboy approach this time. "If you hurt my partner, I will kill you!"

"*Naturellement!* That is perfectly clear to me. I would do the same in your place. The good thing is, I don't mean her any harm. At least not as long as you do what I ask."

"And that would be?"

"Get out of here and stay away from me!" The guy's amused tone was gone. His voice was pure ice. "Otherwise, your partner will suffer the same fate as the woman from the secret service! Let me go my way in peace and nothing will happen to her."

"You ran over the agent in cold blood!"

"Tell me you'd have done anything different in my place!"

Ondragon was silent.

"See! That's what I thought. And what do you think of my offer now?"

Ondragon weighed his options, but kept coming to the one conclusion that he had no other choice. Even if he asked Sem and his gang for help, it would be next to impossible to get to Charlize without putting her in danger. He closed his eyes and rubbed his temples. This was it. The situation he had never wanted to get into! He was being forced into a decision, with someone he cared about being used as leverage. What would Charlize say in this situation? *"Don't mind me, shoot the fucker!"* Yes, that's about how she would phrase it, and she would absolutely mean it. She would sacrifice herself for him. That's how she was, his little samurai. But he wouldn't abandon her. Never! He would rather let this guy blackmail him. He opened his eyes and lifted the phone to his ear. "Okay. I'll leave you alone. But only on condition that you tell me how long this is going to go on. When are you going to release my partner?"

"You're too impatient." The guy sighed as if he was dealing with an unreasonable child. "All right, she'll go free at midnight. Is that enough for you?"

"Where? Will she be here at the hotel?"

"You'll find out!"

Ondragon's hand clenched around the phone. "Good, then I'll be going now, Mr. Black. Or should I rather call you *Monsieur Noire?*" It was an attempt, a tiny straw he was grasping at.

"Do what you can't help doing, Mr. O! The main thing is to stay out of my way. *Goodbye!*" The stranger hung up.

Had there been a slight hesitation? Or had he only wanted to read that into it? Ondragon angrily rejected the call and would have preferred to throw the cell phone at the wall. But he needed the device to call Sem and the BND. He didn't want the Germans to interfere and put Charlize in danger. He put his head back and stared at the ceiling. How humiliating to have to admit to Kubicki that he had fallen into the unknown man's trap and had maneuvered himself into a hopeless fucking situation!

Hour after hour passed and nothing happened outside the hotel. Ondragon sat at his old table in the beach bar and stared irritably at the glass facade of the Gran Marquise. The sun had set and the promenade was busier again. An incessant stream of tourists strolled throughout the sultry evening. The young BND informer was back too. Since Ondragon's call, the German secret service knew what was going on and was staying in the background. To his astonishment, Kubicki had not laughed at him at all, but had pointed out to him with insistent seriousness that, no matter what happened, he had to fulfil his agreement and get hold of Pandora. And not only if he wanted to have a look at the file. That fucking file! It was to blame for everything! Charlize had been right. He should have left that thing alone! Now it was too late to listen to her, and there was nothing he could do but wait. At least Sem had arrived as backup and was watching the hotel just a few feet away from him while his men guarded the back exit. He was not going to let the same thing happen again. The stranger had managed to trick him. Presumably, when he had chased him earlier, he had only pretended to go into the small hotel in the side street and had then driven back to the Gran Marquise on a moped, where he had lured Charlize into his trap. Sem had been very concerned that the Daughter of the Shadow was in the hands of that goddamn son of a bitch, and Ondragon wondered again what position Charlize held in the complex web of the Brazilian mafia. Should he ask Sem? He turned his head but could not make out the little Brazilian in the night shadows under the palm trees.

His cell phone buzzed. It was a text message from Kubicki. Agent Ritter had woken up from her coma. That was good news, at least. Suddenly, he remembered what Charlize had said to him before she'd been blindsided by that son of a bitch. She had found a phone number. A number in Paris. What was it again? He tried to remember the sequence. It had been simple, really. Something with three sevens and . . . yes, two times sixty-nine. Ondragon dialed the number but didn't take his eyes off the hotel for a second.

"Groupe Hexagone, you are speaking with Madame Deniel. What can I do for you?"

Groupe Hexagone! He had heard that somewhere before. "Ah, excuse me, Madame Deniel," he replied quickly in French, "which department am I connected to?"

"*Recherche et développement*, monsieur. To whom am I speaking, please?"

Ondragon hung up. Now he knew what Groupe Hexagone was. It was one of the companies on Charlize's list. A French energy company, mostly owned by the state and the third largest energy producer in the world! Was the unknown person working for this company? More precisely, for someone in the research and development department? Had the guy actually made a mistake and inadvertently revealed his employer by giving them his phone number? If so, that was extremely unprofessional and changed the way he looked at things. Ondragon recalled the endless catalog of Tesla's research areas and patents. The man had experimented with electricity, improving or even reinventing the technology of the time. He had given the world alternating current and with it the possibility of transporting this kind of energy over hundreds of kilometers. He had built the first large hydroelectric power plant at Niagara Falls and spent his life working on the generation of clean energy. Hydropower, wind power, and solar energy. Even then, Tesla had been aware that fossil fuel resources were not infinite. He wanted something different for people, a clean environment and peace. And energy for free! It was like the scales were falling from Ondragon's eyes. What if there was no mysterious flying object or superweapon hidden out there in the

African desert, but actually the key to a world without energy problems? Kubicki's pimped perpetual motion machine! Then it would be obvious why Groupe Hexagone was after this secret! They didn't want to bring the world relief from rising electricity prices—quite the opposite. They wanted to prevent people from becoming energy independent. In the hands of such an unscrupulous energy company, Tesla's legacy would be lost. For Ondragon, it was now clear what he had to do. Not just for the BND or for himself or the stupid file. He had to do it for everyone. For all humanity!

Damn it! That's how far it had gone, that he should even be thinking that way! This thing with Charlize had clearly made him sentimental. He mentally erased the point about humanity and then focused his attention fully on the hotel again. Still four and a half hours until midnight!

CHAPTER 32

May 24, 2011
Fortaleza, Brazil
11:20 pm

The phone rang just as Ondragon had stopped expecting it to. And the sudden adrenaline rush made his fingers tremble so much that it almost fell out of his hand. He jumped up and answered the call. "Yes?"

"So, Mr. O!" said the guy on the other end. Unfortunately, he seemed to have a penchant for poetry. "I'm leaving the hotel now, along with your lovely assistant. She's awake again, by the way, and has something to say to you." Ondragon heard the phone being passed over, and a moment later he heard Charlize's agitated voice. Relief washed briefly over the biting sharpness of his worries.

"Boss? You hear me? Just kill this asshole. Don't think about me, okay? When he comes out of the hotel, shoot the bastard! I'll—"

Obviously, it wasn't what the guy wanted to hear; he snatched the phone from Charlize and continued speaking. "So you see, she's alive and well. If you want her to continue to be, then stay where you are. Got it?"

Hatred roiled in Ondragon. How he would love to do what Charlize had asked him to do! But he couldn't. He felt the whole weight of this shitty case on his shoulders. It would be his fault if anything happened to her, his fault alone. He would never forgive himself for that. For the first time in a very, very long time, he decided to do something for someone else.

He lowered his voice and replied, "All right, I'll let you go."

"And call off your guard dogs. If even one of them comes within a hundred paces of me, your assistant dies! Do you understand?"

"Clearly and distinctly, *Monsieur Noire!*"

"Stop fucking calling me that!"

"But that's your name, isn't it?"

"No, you're wrong!"

I don't think so, thought Ondragon. *That's your name, friend, or you wouldn't be so upset. I'm going to find out who you are and who you work for and track you to the ends of the earth. You don't blackmail Paul Eckbert Ondragon! That was a mistake. A huge mistake!*

"I'll be outside in a moment," he heard the stranger say. "Your assistant will be with me. So don't try anything stupid!" The conversation ended.

Ondragon turned his head and spotted the guy at the hotel entrance. He wore a baseball cap pulled low on his face and was holding Charlize in front of him. She was staggering and appeared drunk. Ondragon couldn't see the box anywhere. The guy had probably left it in the room and pocketed the book and the medal. He was likely carrying both on his body, because he didn't have a bag either.

Ondragon took a picture of the guy on his iPhone before he got into a cab with Charlize. A short time later, it drove off. Ondragon ran to the street and was about to hail a cab as well, when suddenly a black car pulled up next to him. Agent Steiner opened the door and said, "Quick, come on!"

Him again! Ondragon thought sullenly, but he did as he was told and jumped into the passenger seat. Steiner took up the chase at an appropriate distance.

"Be careful he doesn't spot us!" Ondragon warned him, staring anxiously at the road. "Where on earth is he going? To the airport?"

"Could be, the airport is to the south." Steiner stepped on the gas as the cab turned south at an intersection and disappeared from their field of vision. But moments later, they saw the white car ahead of them driving along the largely empty Avenida Desembargador Moreira. The lack of traffic made pursuit easy, but it also meant the bastard was more likely to spot them. They had to make sure they put a few cars between them and him. Steiner seemed to have had the same thought and pulled in behind a red VW. The cab stayed on the avenue that led directly to the airport. So the guy wasn't going to hand over the contents of the box here in Fortaleza after all; he was going to head out by plane instead.

Steiner picked up a radio and informed a colleague that the target was headed to the airport.

Now you're falling into a trap, my friend, Ondragon thought, rubbing his hands together. *We'll catch you at passport control at the latest!* But his anticipation turned abruptly to confusion when the cab turned left a few moments later and continued east.

Not the airport after all? Or was that just a diversion?

After nine blocks, the cab made another left turn onto the wide Via Expressa Parangaba. Was the guy going back to the hotel? Darn, what was he up to?

It didn't dawn on Ondragon until he recognized the area they were passing through, and he slapped his forehead in frustration. Why hadn't he considered this possibility sooner?

"Shit!" he gasped. Steiner cursed too. Apparently, the BND agent had also realized where they were. He spoke rapidly into the radio and stepped on the gas. The car lurched forward, throwing Ondragon back into the seat. The engine howled, almost like the car that had run over Agent Ritter, and then came to a stop, its tires screeching. Ondragon jumped out of the car and ran toward the large barred gate that was on the point of closing. Defying the loud protests of the guard outside, he slipped through the narrowing gap, drew his pistol, and ran out into the darkening area. Steiner and the guard were close on his heels. He could hear the agent panting and the security guard's frantic shouts behind him.

The bright floodlight of a crane pointed him in the right direction. He saw the stranger's cab stop at the quay and the guy get out with Charlize. Ahead of him, a narrow gangway led to an opening in a rusty hull. The guy entered the gangway, but then turned to face them. He clutched Charlize and raised a pistol above his head. He fired once into the air and then pressed the barrel to Charlize's temple. The bang echoed off the steel of the ship several times and faded over the expanse of dark sea. Instantly, Ondragon stopped. Behind him, Steiner and the guard also stopped.

"Nobody move! Or else the mademoiselle will be fish food!" the guy shouted to them, walking slowly backward up the gangway, the gun pointed unerringly at Charlize's head. Waiting for him at the other end was the dark opening in the hull; an anxious-looking sailor stuck his head out. He disappeared when the stranger shouted something over his shoulder. Ondragon saw bluish smoke billowing from the oil tanker's funnel and that they had long since hauled in the lines. The ship would cast off as soon as the guy was aboard, and then Pandora and Charlize would be out of his reach. He bit his lips. How could he free Charlize?

The guy reached the opening. Suddenly, Ondragon heard his assistant yell out. "Shoot him already, Boss! What are you waiting for?!" She seemed dazed, but started to struggle with the guy.

"No!" roared Ondragon, wringing both hands. "Don't do it, Charlize!"

But it was too late. A second shot rang out, more muffled than the previous one, and Charlize slumped down onto the gangway. At the same instant the guy dove through the opening, and the door closed behind him with a loud screech. A ship's horn sounded and the tanker cast off sluggishly, like an iceberg. Slowly, the rusty hull disappeared from the cone of light and slipped out into the night. Only the navigation lights indicated where it was.

Ondragon didn't care; he rushed up the rickety gangway and knelt beside Charlize. Blood had soaked through the front of her dress.

"Oh no!" His hands rushing over her, he scanned her body for the wound and found a bullet hole above her right hip. He pressed his hand to it and looked around wildly for Steiner. He came running up the gangway, followed by the agitated guard.

"Call for help, damn it! And fast!"

Steiner raised the radio to his mouth. But Ondragon didn't hear what he said; he had bent over Charlize's pale face and was holding her gently in his arms. The bloodstain on her dress grew inexorably larger.

"Please don't," he whispered. "Please, stay with me. Do you hear me? I need you, Charlize, honey!"

CHAPTER 33

May 25, 2011
Atlantic Ocean
2:45 am

Clandestin tossed and turned restlessly in his bunk. He had a cabin to himself—his employer had organized it that way. But it had been close. He almost didn't make it onto the ship. It was good that his ruse with the assistant had succeeded. This Mr. Ondragon had been damn hard on his heels. Much too hard! Besides, the guy had worked out his name. *Monsieur Noire.* That had been close.

Merde! Clandestin slammed his fist against the wall of the cabin. Mr. Big was smarter than he had assumed, and he was overcome by the feeling that he was far from rid of the stubborn German and his secret service entourage. He was probably after him all the more determinedly now because the attack on his assistant had made things personal. His employer would not be very happy about that either, although they had left him no other option. Despite this thought, Clandestin felt reasonably safe. He knew that his pursuers would never find out where he was headed. That was his trump card. Yaqub would understand why he had acted as he did.

To calm himself, Clandestin tried to focus on the odors in the cabin. It smelled like heavy oil, rust, and old men's sweat, but it also included the much more delicate nuances of sea salt, seaweed, and the ingredients of the ship's paint. Clandestin thought of Yaqub. His mentor and master. Back then, Yaqub had been the one who was always on the road. Today, he himself traveled around the world. It was a strange feeling after spending so many years in seclusion. The world was frighteningly large, but also full of wonders. Nevertheless, Clandestin always looked forward to coming home again—to his little chamber, far from the hustle and bustle.

He felt his heartbeat gradually decelerate in time with the dull throb of the ship's drive shaft. And soon it was beating so slowly that he lulled himself to sleep.

But a little later, Clandestin started up again and groped for the treasure. Relieved, he let his head fall back onto the musty pillow. The treasure was still there, nestled in the belly bandage against his skin. He would not let it out of his sight until it reached Yaqub, he had sworn by his blood. And he kept his oaths. That's why he was Yaqub's best man.

The Guardian of the Holy Grail.

CHAPTER 34

May 25, 2011
Fortaleza, Brazil
3:10 am

The oil tanker with the unknown man on board had long been in international waters when Ondragon squatted down in front of a frosted glass door marked ENTRADA PROIBIDA in the Fortaleza hospital. Sitting across from him was Kubicki, wearing an impeccable gray suit and tie and drinking coffee from a paper cup. The neon light in the hallway was reflected in his round glasses, making him look pale and tired.

Ondragon looked at the clock, as he had done a minute before. And the minute before that. When would they finally hear anything? He jumped up impatiently from his seat and walked down the hall. His face expressionless, Kubicki sipped his coffee. They hadn't heard about Charlize since she had been admitted to the hospital half an eternity ago. She had lost a lot of blood and the doctors had been trying to stabilize her. If Ondragon had been religious, he would have sent a silent prayer up to heaven right now, but unfortunately, he didn't believe in God, only in chance and the present moment and the vigor of his own actions. What would he do if Charlize died?

Suddenly, footsteps sounded in the hallway and Ondragon wheeled around expectantly. But it was only Agent Steiner, who had also gone to get a coffee. He slumped weakly into a chair next to Kubicki.

Ondragon turned away from the two agents and trudged farther down the corridor. He heard a soft beep from somewhere and saw Kubicki looking at his cell phone. The BND man got up and went outside before any of the hospital staff could give him a dirty look. After quite a while—the hand of the clock had moved forward to 3:40 am—Kubicki returned. His expression had brightened considerably and he beckoned to Ondragon and Steiner.

"I just got word that the satellite link is up. We have the tanker in our sights, with infrared and radar so we can also observe nighttime activity, if there is any. Right now, everything seems quiet on board."

Most people thought it was impossible to track a moving object the size of a vehicle or a human being via satellite. This was true if the tracking was being done with orbital satellites that circled the earth and did not return to the same spot for ninety minutes. However, combining several geostationary satellites, the US military and a few other organizations had achieved a stable and permanent live transmission of images with a resolution of up to ten centimeters! Enough to identify a license plate or a face. So perfect surveillance from space was no longer just the wet dream of the world's intelligence agencies; it had long been a reality.

"Is there any more information on the ship?" inquired Ondragon.

"The ship is called *Tethys II* and sails under the Moroccan flag. An oil tanker with a capacity of one hundred and fifty thousand tons gross. It brought oil to Brazil a few days ago and is now returning empty. Its destination is its home port of Casablanca."

Ondragon listened. His colleague Achille Mercier was stationed in Morocco. He could inform him today and order him to Casablanca to prepare for the tanker's arrival, and then book a ticket there himself. "How long will it take the tanker to make the crossing?"

Kubicki seemed to calculate the distance in his head. "At an average speed of fifteen knots, that's twenty-eight kilometers per hour, it'll take about . . . eight days."

"That's a hell of a long time," Ondragon muttered to himself. "I wonder why the guy is doing this? Why has he taken a ship?"

"Well, I guess he knew he couldn't get through the airport controls, so he chose the sea route. It's not quite as stupid as it seems at first glance, because as long as the ship is in international waters, there's nothing we can do. It's as simple as that."

"Then the guy must have been planning this for a long time. It's not that easy to book passage on an oil tanker," Steiner interjected.

Kubicki nodded. "I agree."

"Where could he be going?" Ondragon already had an idea, but of course he could not reveal to the BND agents that he had read the Junkers' log. "What other destinations are on that route?"

"The Cape Verde Islands and the Canary Islands," Kubicki said.

"Hmm." Ondragon pondered. "Could this guy get off the ship by boat or helicopter?"

"Yes, of course, but we would pick up on that through satellite surveillance. An alarm system informs us of any movement on board or near the ship. I have arranged for a German Navy helicopter to be on standby in the Canary Islands. The islands belong to the EU and therefore we can operate there without having to submit time-consuming applications to the Spanish state. With Morocco it is different; there we have to operate covertly. Unfortunately, the same applies to Brazilian coastal waters. In the absence of an international arrest warrant, the Brazilian authorities turned us down and gave the tanker free passage. However, if it gets too close to the Canary Islands, we can strike."

Ondragon doubted the unknown man would make that mistake, but you never knew. In any case, it was good that they had air support to fall back on. As for his own options, he kept them close to his chest, because he wanted to operate in Africa on his terms and not depend on the help of others. That had caused him enough trouble already. He had already worked out the plan in his head and now all he had to do was implement it. Ondragon fumbled in his pocket for his cell phone. It was high time he made a call.

Suddenly, the door behind them opened and a pale-faced man in a white coat appeared. Ondragon rushed up to him and asked, "How is she?"

The young doctor raised both hands. "She's fine so far. Don't be concerned. We were able to stop the bleeding and take care of the wound," he explained in heavily accented English. "She will now go to the intensive care unit, where she will stay for observation for the next few days."

"Can I see her?" Ondragon heard himself ask, feeling like he was in a cheap TV show about doctors.

The medic shook his head. "Come back tomorrow morning. You can see her then. Meanwhile, please be patient."

"We should go now," Kubicki said in a calm voice, and Ondragon allowed the BND officer to escort him out of the hospital. It had gotten a little cooler outside and he took a deep breath.

"Where will you go?" asked Kubicki. "To the favela?"

Ondragon looked at him, surprised. But then he relaxed again. What had he imagined? That the BND didn't know where he had spent last night? He needed to stop underestimating Kubicki and his people. "I've got some business to take care of," he said, glancing down the dark street. There was hardly a vehicle on the road. Where would he get a cab now?

"Would you mind dropping me off?" he asked wanly. Now that he knew Charlize was out of mortal danger, his remaining energy was evaporating and his ability to concentrate was shrinking to that of a housefly.

Kubicki nodded and Steiner led Ondragon to the car they had used to get to the hospital. A short while later, the car stopped at the edge of the favela and Ondragon got out. Like the shadow of a tired ghost, he groped his way through the dark maze, following not his sense of direction but an elaborate system of markings on the walls of the buildings that Charlize had shown him. Several times he looked around, thinking he had heard a noise. But he was alone. At least he seemed to be. He knew the eyes of the favela never closed.

CHAPTER 35

August 21, 1899
Colorado Springs
morning

When Philemon woke up, he was dizzy and it took him quite a while before he felt able to stand up. Boiling hot, he remembered that Czito was due to go with him to Pikes Peak today, to secure the records of yesterday's experiment. He looked at his pocket watch and was startled. It was already after nine! Darn it, way too late! Czito had said eight o'clock. Hastily, Philemon gathered his clothes and got dressed.

After his morning toilet, he hurried to Czito's room and knocked. Inside it was dead silent. Had the Serb left without him? Why hadn't he woken him? Philemon was annoyed. He would have loved to be there when the records were analyzed. He turned away from the door to his room and, without taking breakfast, made his way to the laboratory.

In the morning bustle on the unavoidable Pikes Peak Avenue, he encountered Joe Herkimer. Philemon quickly looked at the ground, but the chatty telegraph operator noticed him and approached.

"Good morning, Mr. Ailey! How are you?"

Philemon mumbled an answer and made to go on his way, but Herkimer fell into step beside him and offered him a cigar. Philemon thanked him but declined, and Herkimer lit one as he walked. He tossed the match away and took a few pleasurable drags on it until it was burning properly. Sweet, tart tobacco smoke wafted around Philemon and he moved half an arm's length away from the intrusive telegraphist.

"I haven't seen you in a while, Phil; you're pretty busy out there." Herkimer grinned at him.

"Well, we're not here to enjoy ourselves!" countered Philemon. "Scientific experiments are hard work."

"What exactly are these experiments? I'd be interested to know."

"I'm not allowed to talk about that."

"Secret?"

"Not exactly, the doctor just doesn't want to sow more suspicion. And even if I were to explain it to you, you wouldn't understand it. This is applied physics." Philemon hoped to scare Herkimer away with his snide tone, but the blond man remained stubbornly at his side.

Silently, they crossed El Paso Street and approached the edge of town, where the golden-brown strip of prairie shimmered in the morning sun.

"I have something to tell you," Herkimer said when they had passed the last houses and reached the parched plain. "It concerns a certain detective agency."

"The Pinkertons?" asked Philemon in amazement, stopping.

"Exactly." Herkimer gazed pensively at the smoldering tip of his shriveled cigar. Then he threw the stub to the ground and stamped it out. Dust settled on the toe of his shoe. "If you're interested in what I have to say," he said almost conspiratorially, "come to the back of China Jim's store on East Pikes Peak Avenue at nine tonight. You pass it every morning."

"You mean, the store with the Chinese trinkets that always has the scent of perfume wafting out of it?"

"That's the one. Say to the man at the entrance: 'The dreaming Buddha looks through the gate of eternity.' Then they will let you in."

"What is located there?"

"You'll find out. Well, see you soon," Herkimer winked at him and walked back at a leisurely pace toward the city. Perplexed, Philemon looked after him. What a strange fellow.

When he arrived at the lab shortly thereafter, it was bustling with activity. Löwenstein and Tesla were busy renewing the contacts on the batteries and had rolled up their shirtsleeves to their elbows, Tesla still wearing his gloves. Czito was nowhere to be seen, and Philemon suspected, not without some disappointment, that the Serb was at that moment scrambling around on Pikes Peak.

"Ah, there you are, Mr. Ailey!" exclaimed Tesla, noticing him. "I hope you have had a good rest."

Philemon, who thought this was a veiled rebuke, scratched his head in embarrassment and joined the two sweating men. It was punishment enough that he couldn't be where Czito was, and he hoped Dr. Tesla wouldn't add to it. "I apologize for my tardiness, Doctor," he said somewhat meekly. "I promise you it won't happen again. Tell me where I can be of assistance, and I'll get right to work!"

"What won't happen again?" asked Tesla casually, pulling a corroded wire from the battery and examining it.

Irritated, Philemon looked at him. "Well, I won't be late."

Tesla raised his head and looked at him. "Oh, that's what you mean. That's all right. After all, you had a busy day yesterday. That's why I had instructed Czito to let you sleep. You've earned a little rest."

"But I would have loved to have gone up Pikes Peak."

Tesla let out an amused laugh. "For that you would indeed have needed to rise earlier."

Philemon still didn't quite understand. He wanted to say something in reply, but at that moment Czito walked in the door. Puzzled, Philemon looked at the Serb. How could he be back so soon?

"Did you fly up to Pikes Peak?" he asked jokingly, hurrying toward the cheerfully whistling Czito. "What do the records say? May I see them?"

Czito looked from him to Tesla, astonished. "But we analyzed the records yesterday, didn't we?"

The expectant smile fell off Philemon's face. He stared at Czito, stunned. "Yesterday?" he heard himself say. "But how can that be? It was yesterday we did the experiment, was it not?"

The Serb's face was expressionless. In his stead, Löwenstein replied, "You slept all day yesterday, Mr. Ailey!" The German engineer stepped over to him and wiped his oil-smeared hands on a rag. Dr. Tesla too had stopped obsessing about the battery and was looking over at them.

"Slept all day?" repeated Philemon.

"Yes, you did," Löwenstein confirmed. "Mr. Czito tried to wake you, in vain. You must have been so exhausted from the experiment that your body took a whole day off." He twisted his mouth into an encouraging smile. "Don't worry, it's happened to me too. It is the effects of high-current frequencies on the human organism."

Philemon still stared around, dumbfounded. "And what day is this, then, if I may ask?"

"The twenty-first of August," Löwenstein said.

"Ah, I see." Philemon wondered what his pocket watch might show. Unfortunately, it was lying in the hotel room as he had been instructed. "Slept a whole day away," he muttered thoughtfully, "unbelievable."

"I think this phenomenon is easily explained," Tesla replied, joining them. "Gentlemen, do you remember my sleeping apparatus?"

"Oh, yes," Czito grumbled sorrowfully.

"You bet!" said Löwenstein. "Just stay away from me with that devil's device, Doctor!"

"Now, now, this is a truly useful invention of mine," Tesla explained, addressing Philemon. "It's a small, very functional device that you hold to your head for just a minute. After that, you fall into a deep sleep, from which you awaken about half an hour later and can go back to work alert and refreshed. I like to use it in my lab in New York, whenever my concentration wanes. My two subjects here have also tested the apparatus, but apparently have not found it particularly refreshing."

Czito and Löwenstein scowled at Tesla, who stood with his arms behind his back and smiled unconcernedly.

"Now, what about the Pikes Peak records?" Philemon asked.

"Oh, that!" said Tesla. "Well, unfortunately, the meter didn't record anything."

"Nothing?"

"I'm afraid so."

Philemon bit his lips. What had he expected? A brilliant breakthrough they could have used to impress the people of Colorado Springs? *Yes, something like that*, he thought dejectedly. He looked at the others. It didn't seem to bother them that the experiment had been unsuccessful. They were always so enthusiastic about their work and so downhearted when an experiment didn't work. Had the experiment perhaps yielded something after all? Something he was not allowed to know about?

"I think we'd better get back to work now," Löwenstein said into the uncomfortable silence, and the other two nodded. Silently, they went back to their maintenance tasks.

Philemon looked after them suspiciously. What were the three men not telling him? What secret did they share?

"Come, Mr. Ailey," called Löwenstein, beckoning him over. "We need your help!"

Late in the afternoon, Dr. Tesla sent all three assistants away. He did not want to be disturbed until the morning, he announced, locking the door of the laboratory building from the inside.

Together with Löwenstein and Czito, Philemon made his way into town. The two older men were in good spirits because of the unexpectedly early end to the day, and discussed where they could best spend it. The choice fell on the Kensington Gardens, a large spa hotel with many guests, among whom the Tesla assistants could mingle unnoticed without being antagonized by the city's residents.

"What I'm looking forward to is a nice piece of apple pie with whipped cream and a hot chocolate to go with it! Wonderful! You can't get any other stimulants in this backwater to transport you to seventh heaven. What about you, Phil? Are you coming?" asked Löwenstein.

"No offense," Philemon apologized, "but I'd better get right back to the hotel. I still feel a bit limp." In fact, he still hadn't quite come to terms with his coma-like twenty-four-hour sleep and wished to keep to himself for a while.

Löwenstein nodded in understanding. They parted on Pikes Peak Avenue and Philemon hurried straight to the Alta Vista. In his room, he took off his hat and jacket and went to the nightstand, where his pocket watch lay. The date it showed was the twentieth of August. Frowning, Philemon picked it up. If he had set it back to the nineteenth the night before last and skipped a whole day through sleeping, surely it should now read the twenty-first. Strange.

He pulled out the winder and turned the date display forward until it was correct. Then he put the watch down, went over to the closet, and opened both doors. With practiced movements he unhooked the few hangers holding his clothes and lifted out the bar. It was hollow and inside it were some rolled-up sheets of paper. Ever since Philemon had heard about the Pinkertons, he had wanted to take precautions to ensure that no one read his private notes. He pulled the papers from the rack, sat on the bed, and unrolled them. After finding Myers's suitcase in the storage closet, he had begun to write down his thoughts. There were three pages on which he had recorded in close handwriting what he had been able to find out so far about Myers, including Benjamin Foley's account of his disappearance. But right inside the roll was the piece of paper he had found in Myers's suitcase. He pulled it from among the others and looked once more at the puzzling calculation and the sketch beside it. It showed two boxes, one square and one oblong. Both were connected by a cable, or whatever the line meant. In the square box was a coil-shaped structure, perhaps a transformer, and in the oblong one a series of numbered circles. Both boxes were also filled with countless small dots. What were they supposed to represent? Sand? Air? The cable between the boxes had a circle in the middle. It was decorated with lines like a clock face. Was that a clock? Or a measuring device? Philemon looked more closely, but still had no idea what this device might be. Nor did he know how big the boxes were, for there were no measurements. Maybe it was a design for one of those portable receiving devices that Dr. Tesla talked about all the time in connection with his world system.

His lips pursed, Philemon directed his gaze to the circuit drawn next to it. It showed several coils connected in parallel in what looked like sealed tubes, and a square with a diagonal cross in it. Oddly enough, this circuit completely lacked a power source. He didn't even need to do the math; without magnitude or units, he couldn't do the slightest thing with the numbers. The only thing he could glean from them was that Myers had tried to add more parameters to a thermodynamic equation. But did the many exclamation points after the result really suggest that Myers thought he had succeeded? And could the thick plus sign in front of it represent a supposed surplus of energy? Philemon shook his head. That would be thoroughly foolish, because the first guiding principle of thermodynamics was Helmholtz's law of the conservation of energy, with which every first-year physics student was familiar. It stated that in a closed system, energy could be neither destroyed nor generated. At most, it could be transformed from one form to another, for example from liquid to gas. The total energy in the system, however, remained constant at all times. Whatever Myers had calculated, he had been vastly mistaken. To believe one could create energy from nothing was as stupid as to believe in the existence of a perpetual motion machine!

Philemon exhaled disdainfully, put the paper aside, and dug a pencil from the drawer of his bedside table. He noted tersely what he had experienced two days ago during the experiment in the copper tube and that he distrusted Tesla's statements that nothing had come from the experiment. Then he rolled up the papers again and hid them in the bar, which he hung back in the closet. Next, he freshened up and went down to the dining room, where he ate dinner, deep in thought.

CHAPTER 36

Ondragon awoke in a strange room. He sat up quickly and looked around. The place was surprisingly clean; even the bathroom seemed to be usable. In one corner, he saw Charlize's travel bag and concluded that he was in the quarters Sem had given her in the pyramid.

Suddenly, there was a knock at the door. Alarmed, Ondragon reached for his gun. "Who is it?"

"Diego from the Comando Azul! Sem sent me!"

Ondragon let the guy in. It was one of Sem's gorilla rappers, only today he wasn't carrying a brand-new AK, he had his bag. The uninvited guest looked at him and grinned. "Hey, man, you've looked better too."

"Very funny!" retorted Ondragon. "What do you want?"

"Here are your things." The gorilla stretched out his arm and dropped the bag at his feet. "Besides, Sem is expecting you; he wants to know what's going on."

"What time is it?"

"After ten already!"

"Fine, but first I'm going to take a shower. And if you're going to hurry me unnecessarily, forget it! I'll take that shower, even if the world outside is coming to an end!" Ondragon pulled out his cell phone and called the hospital; after all, he wanted to give Sem the latest update. According to the doctor on duty, Charlize's condition had improved and she was even conscious. Relieved, Ondragon ended the call and began to undress, while the gorilla continued to stare at him. "May I ask for a little privacy? You don't have to play nanny here. I'm a grown man and I can find my own way to Sem. Go tell your boss I'll be with him in a minute."

With an unwilling grunt, the guy turned around and disappeared through the door.

Not twenty minutes later, Ondragon, freshly showered and in reasonably clean clothes, was standing in front of the diminutive drug lord, wanting nothing so much as a strong coffee. Sem sat on the sofa with a worried expression on his face, listening to his report of the events of the previous night. He seemed relieved when Ondragon told him that although Charlize was still in the hospital, she was doing better.

"Bem," he said simply when Ondragon had finished.

Bem? Good? Nothing else? That can't be it, Ondragon thought. Admit it, you were scared shitless! That's what I saw in your eyes. Scared for the *a filha do sombra!*

"Who is Charlize Tanaka?" he asked abruptly.

Sem regarded him for a long time. An unusually long time. Then a smirk began to spread over his face under his flat nose. "She's been working for you for seven years and you don't know who she is?"

Embarrassed, Ondragon stared at the stained wall behind the mini-gangster. He swallowed and just barely managed to keep himself from blushing. "Fuck it, no. Now come on, out with it!"

"Man, that's funny!" Amused, Sem looked around at his gorillas.

Ondragon was getting tired of constantly taking a beating. He bent down and reached for his luggage. "Ooookay, if everyone here just wants to laugh at me, I'll be on my way. Thanks for your help, Sem. You'll find the money for the job in the fridge of the room I first stayed in. *Tchau!"* He was about to turn and open the door when Sem jumped up and blocked his way, all five feet of him. The top of his head was level with Ondragon's sternum, and his black eyes shone like polished onyx.

"Your assistant, Mr. O, is the daughter of a very influential man here in Brazil," he said forcefully. "We call him the Shadow. Not only because he wishes to remain hidden, but because he is actually a shadow! A man without a face, but with a thousand eyes and ears!"

"Ah, and that is why you tremble before him so?"

Sem's smile disappeared as if he had turned it off. *"O sombra* is different from us. We're just small fry. So are the leaders of the other *comandos."*

"But how can one man strike fear into all the *comandos* in the country? And a Japanese man, an immigrant at that!"

"Because he is a man without limits," Sem hissed softly, as if afraid of being heard by *O sombra.* "He can be where he wants and go where he wants. He *is* everywhere! Don't take this lightly, Mr. O. He has long known what happened here, and he will be very displeased about it. Take care! If you fall out of favor with *O sombra,* his daughter won't be able to help you either."

Ondragon did not let on that this worried him. A lot, in fact. Not only because he had been targeted by one of the most powerful men in Brazil, but also because Charlize had not thought it necessary to warn him. She had only told him that her father had come to Brazil as a child and had had a normal career as an employee of a large company. He couldn't have known that this company was known as the *yakuza*, or *mafia*! And even less that Charlize's father was the I'll-kick-the-shit-out-of-your-butt boss of the Brazilian underworld! Fuck! Ondragon grew hot with discomfort. He hated being hoodwinked. And what's more, by people he trusted. He had known from the beginning that Charlize had a secret, and he had promised her not to meddle with it. But the fact that it was so powerful both surprised and offended him in equal measure. All at once, he felt Charlize had taken advantage of him. He felt like she was double-crossing him behind his back. Why did she pretend to be his hardworking employee when she was the future queen of an underworld empire? Why was she with him in America? Had she been spying on him? For seven fucking years? He needed to clear this up before he could trust her again. He needed to know which side she was on. Shot or not, he was going to confront her about it!

Without saying another word, he left the Comando Azul headquarters and trudged angrily through the alleys of the favela to the main street. There he hailed a cab and rode to the hospital.

Without looking at the surveillance cameras, he entered the hospital a short time later and took the elevator to the floor where the intensive care unit was located. At the counter, he registered as a visitor and took a seat on the chairs in the waiting area. When he was called, he rose and was handed protective clothing by a nurse. He put it all on and was about to put the face mask on when the automatic doors to the intensive care unit swung open and a man accompanied by two others came marching out at a brisk pace. They all wore face masks and gowns over their street clothes. Obviously, they were visitors as well. Ondragon paid them no further attention, but then sensed the man in the middle staring at him. He looked back, but the guy had turned around and was walking away, flanked by the other two. Ondragon watched them thoughtfully. There was something strange about them. He saw the three men, their backs to him, discard their scrubs and hoods and toss them into a laundry container. Without looking back, they left the unit. As the double doors closed behind them, Ondragon quickly tied on his face mask and followed the nurse through the ward. He felt queasy; even though he had only seen the three men from behind, they had clearly been Japanese!

He entered Charlize's room expecting the worst. It was sparsely furnished. A closet, a table, a chair, a bed, nothing else. Around the bed was an armada of medical apparatus that looked like the bridge of the Starship *Enterprise*. The curtains at the window were drawn and the lights of the devices were flashing in all sorts of colors. A steady sine wave was displayed on a small monitor: Charlize's heartbeat.

His assistant was lying on her back, and in the light of the neon lamp over her head, her face looked greenish. She had pulled the sheet up to her chin and her eyes were closed. Ondragon could see that her long black eyelashes were trembling slightly.

"Only for a moment," the nurse admonished, then left him alone with his assistant.

Had the three Japanese been here before him? Or had they been visiting someone else? *Of course they had been here*, Ondragon thought with some certainty. *Where else!?* He pulled up a chair and sat down beside the bed. With mixed emotions, he looked at Charlize. Then he reached out a hand and gently stroked the back of her hand, from which protruded an IV tube.

Instantly, Charlize's eyelids flew open. She pulled herself up from the bed and glared at him, startled. So her reflexes were still working. But then pain seemed to overtake her and she slumped back onto the pillow.

"Oh, it's you," she sighed softly, raising a hand to her forehead. A thin film of sweat shone on it.

Who else could it be, Ondragon thought. *O sombra?* He put his hand in his lap and asked, "How do you feel?"

Charlize groaned. "How anyone would feel with a hole in their stomach: kind of leaky." She grinned. "Hurts like a bitch, but I'd rather take as few painkillers as possible. I need a clear head. Anyway, the doctor says I'll be fine. Probably no permanent damage. I was lucky. The bullet went through smoothly above the hip bone and didn't hit any organs. That's funny, isn't it? Like the son of a bitch knew exactly where to shoot. By the way, did you get him?"

"No, he escaped with Pandora onto the ship. It's going to Morocco."

"Morocco?" repeated Charlize. "What's he going to do there?"

"Don't know yet." That was only half the truth. Ondragon wrestled with himself. Should he speak to Charlize here and now about her father? What if she freaked out? Or even quit?

Well, he had to take the risk. In any case, he couldn't work with her if the trust was gone.

Charlize was cunning, even in this state, and had noticed his preoccupied expression. She raised her head and propped herself up on one elbow, her face contorting in pain. "What's the matter, Boss? I can tell you have something on your mind!"

Ondragon lowered his head and played with his switched-off cell phone. "I found out something, from Sem, and it makes me, how shall I say? Shy."

Charlize tilted her head to one side, but said nothing.

"It's about you and your father. *O sombra!*"

For a moment, Charlize looked at him and dangerously deep lines formed above her nose, but then her pretty face lit up and she let out a bright giggle that immediately turned into a moan. "Fucking pain! Can't even laugh!" she cursed, wiping tears from her eyes. She looked at him again. "Well, that took a while!" she finally said, amused.

Irritated, Ondragon raised his brows.

"Well, it took you a whole seven years to ask me about it, Boss!"

"You told me not to!" he protested. "That was your condition!"

"And you actually stuck to it? That's kind of sweet. Must have really been torture though, you of all people, not knowing the secret." She giggled and moaned again. With one hand pressed to her stomach, she continued. "But it shows me how much you care about me. And that makes me happy." She reached out and placed her hand on his.

Angrily, he pulled away. Now he felt even more offended.

"What? Just as you tested me the first few months when I started with you, I wanted to do the same with you. That's perfectly legitimate, isn't it? Besides, it's not my fault it took you so long."

"I just stick to agreements!" he grumbled.

"So do I!"

Ondragon scowled and jutted out his chin. That was true. Charlize had always kept her word. "But damn it, why didn't you tell me about this before we came to Brazil? That would have been very helpful."

She shrugged her shoulders. "I thought you knew long ago, and I assumed that was the only reason you were taking me along in the first place."

Ondragon sighed, "I didn't know shit about this until two hours ago."

"I'm sorry about that. But is it such a big problem? I mean, it doesn't matter who my father is. I do my job well and I want to continue to work for you, if I may." She looked at him, seeking his agreement.

He looked her straight in the eye. He had two choices now. The first was to fire her and turn his back on her, and the second was to give her a chance to rebuild the trust. But to do that, he needed to know why she wanted to work for him so badly. "Why don't you just stay here in Brazil? You'll be treated like a princess here. You could have it all. Wealth, power, a life of luxury! Why do you want to do the dirty work for me of all people and put yourself in danger unnecessarily? You see what comes of it." He pointed to her belly.

Charlize hesitated. "If I tell you, you'll laugh at me."

"No, I promise you I won't."

"All right. I'm with you because"—she sighed—"because daddy's little girl got tired of being daddy's little girl. I wanted to stand on my own two feet. Have a life of my own. Can you understand that?" Charlize rolled her eyes. "Of course you can. After all, I know the story of you and your father! Besides, I love the thrill. What I need is danger and not an overprotective father who keeps an eye on me all the time. All this mafia princess crap pisses me off! For real!"

Contrary to his promise, Ondragon burst out laughing. He quickly pressed a hand over his mouth. "I'm sorry," he said.

Charlize's eyes were sending out glittering death rays. "If I wasn't tied to this fucking bed, I'd kick your ass right now, Boss!"

"That's all right. Feel free to do it later." He bit his lip, relieved to have his old Charlize back. "I'm very glad you're okay, honey. Really."

"I like you too, Boss, I really do!"

Their eyes met. Heat shot through Ondragon's veins and he blushed. Man, she always managed to embarrass him!

"Are you going to Morocco?" Charlize asked after a while. She had lain back on her pillow and was breathing more shallowly now. Probably because of the pain.

"Yes, I'll get in contact with Achille," replied Ondragon.

"What a shame I can't come with you."

"I'll keep you posted." He pointed to her phone, which was on the nightstand. "I'd stay here with you, but this thing is far from over."

"I know."

"I left your bag at the front desk. When you get back on your feet, fly back to LA and hold down the fort there. I'll notify Lupita Lopez, and she'll take care of you." Ondragon didn't make his Mexican maid available to just anyone, but in this case he could make an exception.

His assistant nodded. "Will you do me a favor, Boss?"

"Of course!"

"Kick that fucking bastard's ass! I'm all Old Testament on that one. An eye for an eye, a bullet for a bullet! I want you to punch at least one hole in his stomach in retaliation! If not several! I would do it myself, but as you can see . . ." She raised both hands and dropped them again.

Ondragon smiled. He got up from the chair and stroked her cheek paternally. "Keep your chin up."

"Hai." She winked at him. "And don't you let those BND guys walk all over you."

"Sure won't." He waved at her again and then left the room. Outside the door, he looked around. There was no one to be seen in the ward. His gown flowing, he walked down the hallway, reading the labels on the doors. When he found the name he was looking for, he slipped into the darkened room.

She was lying on the bed. The spaceship consoles around her were blinking and beeping like Charlize's. But the woman under the sheets looked even more translucent than his assistant, who was already bursting with life again. Her freckles looked like dark swarms of flies that had settled on her pale skin, and her chin looked more pointed than usual. A thick bandage covered her blonde hair and one eye. Her left leg hung, tightly bandaged, from a strap over the bed. Agent Ritter was a frightening sight. She appeared to be asleep, and Ondragon approached her quietly. He did not want to wake her.

He looked down at her for a while. Then he heard the door open behind him. He turned around and came face-to-face with Steiner and Kubicki.

"What are you doing here?" growled Steiner, pushing past him and taking up position next to the bed with his arms folded. "You have no business here!"

"I know, I just wanted to see how she was doing," Ondragon explained calmly.

"Badly! So now you know!" Steiner barked.

Ondragon looked at the agent piercingly. Was he jealous? Did he feel possessive toward the young agent? If so, Ondragon couldn't care less. "Can I talk to you for a moment?" he asked, addressing Kubicki. "In private?"

The older BND agent nodded and followed him out of the room. Outside in the corridor, they moved to a corner where they could talk undisturbed.

"I will fly to Morocco today and complete my mission," Ondragon began. "And you will get Pandora. I promise you that!"

"What are you going to do?"

Ondragon smiled wearily. "I'm not going to tell you."

Kubicki nodded. "I wouldn't have expected anything else of you. How do we stay in touch?"

Ondragon pointed to his cell phone.

The BND agent remained impassive. "By the way, there are two things that might interest you. First, we have recovered the box from the hotel room. As expected, it's empty. But then we found something else: an airline ticket torn into miniscule pieces in a trash can in the lobby. We put it back together. Air France from Paris to Fortaleza in the name of Chester William Black. The very name our stranger rented the room under. Does that mean anything to you? Because our database has nothing on him."

"I'm afraid not," Ondragon lied. "Paris, you say?" He mused. While that matched the Groupe Hexagone phone number, it was only a lukewarm lead. He didn't believe the unknown man was headed for Paris but kept that assumption to himself, as well as the fact that a new player had entered the game, in the form of an energy company. Secret knowledge was his capital in this game where Pandora's box was the jackpot.

He nodded and raised two fingers to his forehead in farewell. "I'll be in touch if I need air support. Oh, and you'll find your radio equipment downstairs in locker number forty-four. I'll see you around."

"Most definitely," Kubicki said dryly, looking after him.

Outside the intensive care unit, Ondragon peeled himself out of his sterile clothes and tossed them into the dumpster, just as the sinister Japanese men had done before him. At least now he knew his hunch had been right. One of the three men had been Charlize's father, *O sombra!*

He took the elevator downstairs, where he grabbed his bag from another locker before leaving the hospital in a good mood. On the street, he hailed a cab and had the driver take him to the airport. It was time to switch continents!

CHAPTER 37

August 21, 1899
Colorado Springs
evening

Around a quarter to nine, Philemon left the hotel and marched in the gathering dusk to Pikes Peak Avenue. Only a few spa guests were still strolling along the street, and a carriage rolled past in the direction of the railroad depot. Behind the elongated building, the black cloud of a waiting locomotive billowed out, darkening the sky even more. At nine o'clock, the last train from Colorado Springs departed, and as its whistle rose into the cool evening air, Philemon knew he had reached the store with the goods from the Far East in good time.

He looked surreptitiously up at the facade. Above the store entrance, a red dragon writhed on a sign. It hovered over a row of Chinese characters and the words *James Bo Fun Da — Chinagoods*. The store window was brightly decorated and a sign reading CLOSED hung on the door. Below it was emblazoned a saying, translated into English. BEWARE OF MEN WHOSE BELLIES DON'T SHAKE WHEN THEY LAUGH!

Amused, Philemon grinned. What did this Chinese wisdom mean? That an honest man laughed with his whole body and not only with his lips? He looked around. No one seemed to be paying him any attention, and he seized the opportunity to slip through the gateway into the dark courtyard. Beyond it, the only light came from a twinkling red lantern hanging over the back entrance to the store. Philemon went over to the door and knocked. A Chinese man opened. Was that China Jim?

"The dreaming Buddha looks through the gate of eternity." Philemon recited the saying, and the man let him enter without a word, walking ahead of him down an equally dim corridor to a staircase leading to the basement. A pervasively sweet smell hung in the air. Philemon descended the steps curiously, brushed aside a heavy red curtain at the bottom, and marveled as he looked into the large room beyond it. Everywhere, low couches were hidden behind curtains and screens, with people lying on them, mostly on their sides and with their eyes closed. They had long filigree pipes in their mouths or in their flaccid hands. A handful of Chinese men moved from couch to couch, checking on the sleeping people. Thin threads of smoke rose from the pipes, gathering into a reddish mist between the purple lanterns hanging from the ceiling.

Philemon knew what this was but felt as if he had entered a netherworld.

"You can buy pleasant dreams here," murmured a voice beside his ear. "Do you want one too?"

Philemon turned his head. Next to him stood Joe Herkimer, grinning at him with a glazed expression. He was wearing only his shirt and pants and looked slightly deranged. Philemon wondered if he had already had his dream for the day.

"No, thank you," he declined.

"Well, maybe later." Herkimer shrugged. "You know, this is the only pleasure left in Colorado Springs. That old bastard Palmer has already banned alcohol and whores, after all."

"Then it won't be long before he shuts this establishment down too," Philemon said. He followed the telegraph operator across the dim room to a flat table where they sat down on large cushions.

Herkimer shook his head. "I hardly think so. Good Mister Palmer has a little vice he keeps secret from the Methodist snipe who calls herself his wife."

"Buddha's dreams?"

Herkimer slapped his thigh with a laugh. "That's right—you are a poet, my dear Phil! Buddha's dreams! Once a week, when Madame Palmer is at the St. George Ladies Club, Mr. Palmer comes here and smokes his pipe."

Philemon was not particularly surprised by this. Hypocrisy reigned everywhere in the world. So why not here as well?

"And what did you want to discuss with me that was so important?" he asked without beating about the bush. He had no intention of staying in this smoking den any longer than was necessary. His eyes were already beginning to burn from the billowing clouds of opium.

"Now, now, don't be in such a hurry. First, let's have a nice drink together and toast our friendship!" Herkimer whipped out a hip flask and poured a clear liquid into two small glasses. "Vodka! The purest witch's brew! There are two Poles in Manitou Springs who distill the liquor in their backyard. It's made from potatoes, they say, but tastes at least as good as bourbon." Herkimer raised his glass. "Come on, what is it? Or are you another one of those ossified guys from the Anti-Saloon League?"

Philemon shook his head, pulled himself together, and toasted with Herkimer. He downed his glass in a single gulp and gasped. The stuff burned like hell in the throat, but was in no way inferior to a decent whiskey. Philemon shook himself and felt the liquid warm its way into his stomach. Ah, how good that felt after all these weeks of abstinence! Secretly, he hoped Herkimer would pour another. And when the telegraph operator immediately topped off his glass, a relaxed smile settled on his lips.

A Chinese man came up and offered Herkimer a pipe. He waved it away and instead pulled a cigar case from his jacket, which was hanging on a hook on the wall behind him. He offered Philemon a cigar and this time he accepted. Smoking with relish, they were soon leaning back against the cushions, and Philemon began to enjoy the subdued atmosphere in this cloth-hung basement. Gee, how he missed New York! He cast a sidelong glance at Herkimer. Maybe the guy wasn't so bad after all. He'd see what he had to say.

After they had stubbed out their cigars and had another vodka, the blond telegraph operator began to speak.

"I'm sure you already know the Pinkertons are in town."

"As a matter of fact, I found out from old Ben."

"Oh, you went to see him?" Herkimer grinned. "And you didn't get a hole in your stomach? That's amazing; the old man is as trigger-happy as an injun on the warpath, and most of the time he doesn't have all his wits." He circled his index finger beside his temple.

"And yet you believe his story about the night at the lab and the lightning strike?"

Herkimer shrugged his shoulders, unconcerned.

"Is that why the Pinkertons are here?" continued Philemon. "Are they here to solve the disappearance of Frederick Myers?"

"I don't think Frederick Myers interests them. It's something else." Herkimer turned and looked at him. "They've already interviewed me, by the way."

"Oh yeah? And what did they want to know?"

"It was just one of those guys and a purely chance encounter at that. The fellow was inconspicuous. A real mister 'seen-once-and-then-forgotten.' He asked me for directions on the street and then covertly showed me his badge, that 'we-never-sleep' bullshit. He told me to be discreet and walk on beside him, and quizzed me as we went. He wanted to know what I knew about the mad doctor's experiments, who all belonged to the research group, and if I had noticed anything strange."

"So have you?"

Herkimer fell into loud laughter. "Hahaha! You're quite a joker, Phil. Honestly! What a stupid question!"

Disgruntled, Philemon brushed a crumb off his sleeve.

"That's really droll!" Herkimer just kept talking, oblivious to his counterpart. "I just said, 'Strange things in Colorado Springs?' Hell, yeah! Of course there are strange things going on. It's like asking Jesus if he believes in God! Since this mad doctor has come among us, our once idyllic little town has become the new capital of weirdness! 'Visit Odd-City while it's still standing!' Shoot!" He shook his head in disgust. "What utter nonsense! Why is the Pinkerton guy asking me, of all people, if anything's odd? Surely I'm not the only one 'round here who notices what's going on. The thunder, the lightning from the faucets, the light bulbs that start glowing at night, just like that, and then the horses passing through—all this nonsense almost every day. The Pinks ought to be witnessing it for themselves. Those bastards!" Herkimer smacked the flat of his hand down on the tabletop, making a dull thud.

"And what answer did you give him?"

Herkimer put a finger to his nose. "I saw right through his little discretion maneuver, of course. First, he wanted to strike up a casual conversation with me, and then he wanted to ask about the things that really interested him."

"About the telegrams you send?" said Philemon with a knowing air.

"There you go, you're a bright one! I like that! Come on, let's have another drink." He refilled and they drank. Afterward, they slammed the empty glasses down on the table with a satisfied sigh.

"Ah, that's good!" Herkimer wiped his blond mustache and looked directly at Philemon. His gaze flickered briefly, but whether from alcohol, opium smoke, or excitement, Philemon could not tell.

"It was just as I suspected," Herkimer finally continued, slurring much more heavily. "Since I send the telegrams for the mad doctor—Mr. Palmer, by the way, had allowed him to do so at the beginning of his research stay here—the Pink unceremoniously asked me about his correspondence. He wanted to know what the doctor was saying, and who to."

"Well, did you tell him?" All at once, Philemon himself was burning to know what was in the telegrams. If Herkimer knew, and he certainly did, he might be able to give him a little help in solving the mystery of Frederick Myers.

"Of course not!" exclaimed Herkimer indignantly. "What do you think? I have a professional code, and that is secrecy. Under no circumstances am I to talk about what I transmit in the telegrams."

Philemon twirled the small glass thoughtfully between his fingers, wondering how he could persuade the telegraph operator to talk a little.

"Who might the Pinkertons have been hired by?" he asked, initially steering the conversation in another direction.

"I don't know."

"How many detectives are here in town anyway? And where are they lodging?"

"There are three of them, as far as I know," Herkimer said. "And they're all staying at Kensington Gardens, disguised as spa guests."

"And how would I recognize them?"

Herkimer let out an amused laugh. "You don't recognize the Pinks. That's why they're Pinks!"

"Well, well," Philemon said wryly. He pushed himself up from the pillows and leaned forward. He was inches from Herkimer's face when he asked, "You know, I don't understand all this. Why are you telling me, of all people? You don't know me at all. And besides, I work for that crazy doctor, which doesn't exactly make me a person you can trust."

"I'm just trying to warn you!"

"Warn?" asked Philemon skeptically, and all of a sudden, he turned his head, because next to them on one of the couches, a dreamer was stirring. The older gentleman sighed, turned on his back, and quieted down again. Opium smoke rose from his pipe like a djinn, clouding their vision. Philemon had to blink before he could see clearly again. The smoke of the opium poppy was unexpectedly strong. Or was it the Polish liquor? At any rate, he suddenly felt very, very tired. Still, he couldn't just leave now. He had to know what had been in the telegrams! He forced his eyes open and braced himself against the fatigue.

"Who or what are you trying to warn me about, Joe?" he inquired in a confidential tone. "About the Pinkertons, because they are after the doctor's inventions, or about Dr. Tesla himself, because he is most likely responsible for something that happened to one of his assistants?"

He saw Herkimer's gaze dart uneasily around the room, finally set-tling back on him. The telegraphist's water-blue eyes were red-rimmed, but something in their gleam had changed. They suddenly no longer seemed dazed by opium, but clear and perfectly sober, as if they were looking directly into the truth.

"Your doctor is a liar!" he growled a moment later.

"A liar?" urged Philemon. "Why?"

Herkimer bared his teeth in an inscrutable grin. "Because Fredrick Myers isn't gone and he isn't dead. He's still here!"

CHAPTER 38

May 27, 2011
Casablanca, Morocco
11:30 am

After arriving in North Africa and taking up quarters in a hotel, Ondragon met with his associate Achille Mercier at a small café in the Casablanca medina, where they enjoyed a second breakfast of strong mocha and sweet baklava.

"Tell me, Achille," he began, slightly miffed, after downing the first mocha. "Why did you book me into this hotel and not the Sofitel as usual?"

"*Je suis désolé*, Chief, the Sofitel was fully booked, even the suites. I thought something in a more traditional style would be okay for you too. Besides, it has a good view of the harbor. And that was your top priority, if I recall correctly."

"Yes, that's right. Normally, I don't mind a little local color either, but did you check out the rooms first?"

Achille raised his dark eyebrows, looking like a typical Frenchman being asked for directions but refusing to understand the halting tourist French.

"I have nothing against colorful tiles," Ondragon continued, "but my room is pink, Achille! Pink! With a frilly four-poster bed like in the Thousand and One Nights. It would be just the thing for Scheherezade and the Forty Thieves!"

"Ah, it's pretty, *n'est-ce pas*? I like it."

Ondragon refrained from making an allusion to an unwitting change in the Frenchman's sexual orientation. At least the breakfast at the hotel was okay and the room was relatively clean by Moroccan standards. And it did have a good view of the harbor. He would put up with everything else. He would only be there for a few days anyway.

"All right, let's get down to business. We have some work to do before the ship, the *Tethys II*, arrives here in seven days. Most likely, though, we'll have to take action before then. I suspect our man will disembark early. To come here to Casablanca would be hugely stupid of him."

"Is he stupid?"

"No, he hasn't given that impression so far. I still have the feeling that he's a freelancer, but he's not stupid by any means." Ondragon told Achille what he knew about the guy and showed him the photo he had taken outside the hotel in Fortaleza.

"French?" asked Achille.

"Definitely of French descent."

"North African?"

"Conceivably, with his looks."

"Where is he going?"

Ondragon appreciated his colleague's short, precise questions. The skinny Frenchman with the black hair was his right arm in Africa and southern Europe. And he could always rely on him. Achille had grown up in Paris. But not the Paris where the tourists went, the magical city of love! No, he came from one of the suburbs where the cars were constantly on fire. There he had learned—a white man among dark-skinned people—all the knowledge he needed to survive. Achille Mercier was Ondragon's French secret weapon, as clever as a Libyan desert fox, as cunning as an Algerian street dog, and as ruthless as a hungry hyena—to stay with the animal comparisons.

"There are two possibilities," Ondragon then said. "One is that our unknown friend—let's call him 'Monsieur Noire' for simplicity's sake—is aiming to get from Africa to France. His potential client, Groupe Hexagone, has its headquarters there. Although I would find it strange if he wanted to hand Pandora over in France. That he hasn't already done so in Brazil is strange enough, given how hot the stuff is!"

"As in *the* Groupe Hexagone?" asked Achille.

"Right, that one."

The Frenchman whistled softly through his teeth. "If that is indeed the case, then we have a powerful opponent."

Ondragon smiled grimly. "We can handle it all right. After all, wouldn't be the first time we pissed in the pond of one of the big boys, would it?"

"Damn right, *mon ami!*"

"So one possibility might be that the guy is aiming to get to France. The second, and I think this is the more likely, is he's aiming for Western Sahara, formerly Spanish Sahara."

"Western Sahara? Why?"

"Just a guess. It's to do with Pandora itself." Ondragon briefly told Achille about General Kammler's unfortunate journey and the secret cargo.

"So you think that stuff is still out there in the desert?" asked Achille.

"Might be," replied Ondragon. "You know the Sahara very well, Achille. Could something have survived there without ever being found?"

The Frenchman tugged at his lower lip. Then he nodded. "Depends, of course. If it's in a particularly secluded area, then it's possible. And by that I mean places that absolutely no one can tolerate. The Tuareg call that kind of place *tarart*—dry place. And if a Tuareg calls something dry, then it really is dry as shit! Do you know where this place could be?"

"Unfortunately, we haven't figured that out yet."

"But then why would this Monsieur Noire know about it? Has he already deciphered the code in the logbook?"

"Man, Achille, that's it! You've hit the nail on the head!" exclaimed Ondragon. "I hereby name you Frenchman of the Month!"

Achille looked slightly irritated, not knowing that he had unwittingly provided his boss with the keyword.

"I never thought of that before!" Ondragon slapped his thigh. He then pulled out his notepad and continued his train of thought to Achille while simultaneously writing everything down. "Assuming that Monsieur Noire was already in possession of the keyword *before* he stole Pandora, the contents of the box are probably not what he's after at all. It's probably the stuff that's out there in the desert. That would also explain why he still hasn't handed over Pandora. His mission is to recover the cargo of JU 390, not just to get the logbook! Groupe Hexagone has been very clever. They let a mercenary, who is expendable and can be sacrificed, do most of the work and then calmly collect the fruits of his labor." Ondragon paused briefly in his musings. He jotted something down, crossed it out again, and wrote something else underneath. Then he looked at Achille. "If that is indeed the case, and the guy already knows where to look, all we have to do is wait for him to leave the ship. We can track him into the desert via the BND's satellite surveillance. *He* will lead us to the treasure, not the code!"

"That's good. However, it would be better if we didn't rely so much on BND technology and cracked the code ourselves. Then we could get ahead of the guy," Achille interjected.

"That's already in the works. A physicist I trust is figuring it out."

Achille nodded, put the last piece of baklava in his mouth, and chewed it with relish, while Ondragon waved the waiter over and paid the bill. Afterward, they took a cab back to the hotel, where in the protection of the room they discussed how to proceed. They didn't need to worry about equipment. Achille had come to Casablanca in the Cessna Stationair that Ondragon had registered to the Frenchman through a Moroccan dummy company and which was always on standby for them. Weapons and all other military equipment were already on board. The Frenchman's task would be to get permission to fly through Algerian, Mauritanian, and Western Saharan airspace from the relevant authorities as quickly as possible. However, since they did not yet know where exactly their mission would take them and the political situation in Western Sahara, which was partially occupied by Morocco, was considered unstable, Achille would also have to try to obtain permission from the Sahrawi rebels who held the western part of the country. The Frenchman apparently had what he called a rather profitable relationship with the Sahrawi. Ondragon preferred not to inquire what the nature of the relationship was. That the whole thing had nothing to do with the Nobel Peace Prize was certain. Instead, he focused back on the plan. They couldn't make any mistakes now, or Pandora might disappear into the desert, never to be seen again. So Achille would take care of the flight path, communications en route, gasoline and water, and any gifts they would need to present on the ground. Ondragon himself had the easier task: he only had to get provisions and a metal detector.

Achille opened his bag, which he had been carrying all along, and handed his boss a Sig Sauer, holster, and ammunition. Satisfied, Ondragon weighed the familiar gun in his hand. It was the model he always used. It was a good thing he had set up stores all over the world. He still felt safest with his own weapons. He put on the holster and hid the pistol under a light linen jacket he had bought at the airport the day before. For now, that would have to suffice as a wardrobe for Casablanca, but he would have to acquire more clothing for the expedition. The desert called for a rather different kind of couture.

He sent Achille away and went to work himself. First, he made a flying visit to the dog forum to see if there was any news. Kubicki had set up a livestream for him with the satellite monitoring and was providing him with the essential information under the name Bulldogge77. There was still no news from the ship, which had moved just five hundred nautical miles from the Brazilian coast and was near the 33rd meridian. Three more days, and it would pass the Cape Verde Islands, one day after that the coast of Western Sahara, and one day later the Canary Islands. So they had enough time before it all kicked off, but only if everything went as Ondragon suspected it would. He could not rely 100 percent on this version. Monsieur Noire was unpredictable. They had to be ready to leave at a moment's notice if he were to disembark early. He hoped Achille knew exactly whom to bribe in the Moroccan authorities so that they could get their permits quickly. If necessary, they would have to travel without them. After all, it wouldn't be the first time.

All in all, Ondragon was confident that they would be able to keep up with the unknown man, at least as long as the BND's satellite surveillance was working. He felt the tingle of anticipation take hold of him again and rubbed his fingertips together in anticipation. The race had begun.

In the evening, he returned to the hotel, heavily laden after his errands. His room was overflowing with bags of clothing, provisions, and other desert-appropriate paraphernalia. He had purchased the metal detector from an outfitter for amateur treasure hunters and beachcombers. It was an older unit, but it worked perfectly. As he threw himself down on the bed and closed his eyes—not only to rest for a moment, but also to block out the frilly curtains if possible—his phone rang. Ondragon took a cursory glance at the display, pressed the button with the green receiver, and quickly closed his eyes again.

"Hello, Truthfinder! What's up? Did you crack the code?"

"I'm afraid not yet, Mr. O."

"So why are you calling?"

"Man, you're in a lousy mood."

"Indeed. And it gets lousier with every hour it takes to crack the code! We only have three days, five at most, to crack it. Maybe a lot less. I need to know what those numbers are all about."

"It sounds like you have Dr. No breathing down your neck!"

"Sort of."

"Okay, I'm calling because I checked the cross tattoo. At first glance it just looks like a geometric pattern, *but*—and here's the thing—at second glance it could be numbers!"

"What kind of numbers?"

"Roman numerals. They are mirrored on two crossed planes. The top one is two X symbols, that is, two tens. They probably form a twenty. Below that is a V, which is a five. Rad, isn't it? The symbol in the middle is a bit more complicated though. In any case, it's not a bar cross. If it's supposed to be numbers, then you could see an X and four Vs with a dash in each, so a one."

"Get to the point!" urged Ondragon impatiently.

"Okay, okay, I'm on it. So the symbol in the middle either gives us an impossible number to construct, or we just cross out three of the Vs and Is to the detriment of symmetry and get a fourteen or a sixteen!"

"Twenty, five, fourteen, sixteen? What does that mean?"

"I ran the numbers through a special symbolism program, but unfortunately they don't make sense. Neither do the sums of the digits. Nevertheless, we can assume that the cross was made by someone who knew exactly what he was doing."

"It means something, I can feel it," Ondragon murmured thoughtfully.

"What though?"

"We're going to find out! Truthfinder, could you check to see if a guy named Chester William Black or a Monsieur Noire is on your forum? Also look for other names that might have something to do with black or dark. I have my suspicions."

"Will do. Anything else?"

"Yes, explain to me as simply as you can what zero-point energy is all about."

"Now?"

"Yes, now!"

"Ooookay. As simply as possible, you said. Very well. There is the thesis that all space contains invisible energy that could be harnessed. This form of energy used to be called 'dark energy' or even 'dark radiation.' Nikola Tesla, I think, called it ether energy. Today it is called vacuum energy, free energy, neutrino power, or cosmic radiation, for example. But we'd better stay with zero-point energy, I like that term best. It derives from the fact that even at absolute zero, at zero Kelvin, energy must still be present. However, it is easier to explain it in a vacuum. Quantum mechanics assumes it is probable that something still exists, even in a vacuum, i.e., a space that is completely free of particles, that is to say, nothing, namely what are known as virtual particles. Here the Casimir effect comes into play, which we can use to prove the existence of zero-point energy. In the experiment, a vacuum is squeezed between two conductive plates; you compress it, so to speak. In addition, you should know that the quantum mechanical properties of the vacuum are wavelike. Between the two plates, at a defined distance, only virtual particles with certain wavelengths can move. Outside, however, an infinite number can move. This creates pressure on the plates from the outside, zero-point energy, which can be measured. However, most physicists believe that this is utter nonsense. They also say it is impossible to make zero-point energy usable."

"You believe otherwise, don't you?"

"Yes. Let's say I'm trying to figure out if this form of energy can't be converted into something useful after all."

"Okay, I got that," Ondragon replied. "And do you think it's possible Tesla could have invented an apparatus for converting space energy?"

Truthfinder was silent. Then he said, "It would be nice if he had. A dream that even I dare not dream. But alas, as far as that goes, I'm skeptical."

"Me too," said Ondragon, who didn't want to go into it any further. "Thank you for the explanation, Truthfinder. It would be good if you could get back to the code now."

"All right, Mr. O. I'll be quick about it. And I'll show the cross to a friend. He's a freak and knows more about symbolism than anyone."

"But only the cross! Not a word about the logbook or the code."

"Yeah, yeah, I get it."

"All right, get back to me as soon as you have something!" Ondragon hung up. The boy wonder could have thought of the symbolism guy earlier! He looked at his watch. It was half past eight. Now he needed a drink to help him come down. He left his room and took the elevator to the second floor. The hotel restaurant was there, but unfortunately, he discovered the establishment had no bar that served alcoholic beverages. So much for somewhere "traditional." Great, Achille, really, really great!

Slightly annoyed, Ondragon went down to the foyer and asked at the reception for a bar with European standards. They recommended the Golden Tulip, a hotel just a block away. Why hadn't Achille booked him in there? Suddenly, it dawned on him. This little rascal was likely playing another joke on him. Achille was known to do that that from time to time, although Ondragon had assumed he'd beaten it out of him on his last visit. Well, patience! He would think of a suitable revenge for this Frenchman.

By the time he sat down at the counter in the very fashionable jazz bar at the Golden Tulip and took his first sip of the sweet, tart whiskey sour, he was already feeling much better. And when he spotted the attractive brunette at the next table, the evening was almost perfect.

CHAPTER 39

August 21, 1899
Colorado Springs
the same night

Myers is still here?" asked Philemon, aghast.

Herkimer nodded eagerly. "I sent two telegrams for the mad doctor right away."

Philemon was secretly pleased. So now the man wanted to chat after all. He would hear what he had to say!

"The one dispatch talked about Mr. Myers being still here on site," Herkimer explained. "They'd had trouble 're-locating' him, but also had hopes that they could. A certain George Scherff—to whom the telegram was addressed—was to requisition a new assistant as soon as possible, he said, so that the doctor could continue his work here. It was only a question of time before the Röhnfeldt experiment would succeed again. Hence the urgent request for a new assistant with specific qualifications. That was on the fifth of July, two weeks before you arrived here, I guess."

Philemon nodded but in no way wanted to interrupt the telegrapher.

"The other telegram," Herkimer continued, "went to Boston, to a Mr. Albert Myers, 114 Beacon Street. There was nothing unusual in it, a description of the daily life in Colorado Springs and work in the laboratory. It was signed Frederick Myers and was posted four days after Ben's observations. However, that was after Myers had long since disappeared!"

A lump formed in Philemon's throat. He stared sadly into space. He did not want to believe what he was hearing. The doctor had lied to him! The two telegrams seemed to be irrefutable proof of that. But was it also true that Myers was actually still here? What did they mean, they were having trouble re-locating him? And why did the doctor mention the Röhnfeldt experiment in one of his dispatches? Philemon had first learned about it when he had read Tesla's notebook without permission. What was this sinister experiment? And why was the doctor conducting it in secret?

Philemon resolved to find out more about it as soon as he had the time. He turned to Herkimer, wanting to know more about the telegrams. "And was there any reply from this George Scherff?"

Herkimer considered the question. "Hmm, yes. A week later. It said he had found a new assistant. Then it gave measurements and a shoe size, and your name, Phil."

Philemon thought. George Scherff was Dr. Tesla's accountant and had conducted the interviews for Colorado Springs in New York. He had also selected him from the long list of applicants. Philemon remembered the questions Mr. Scherff had asked him. Most had been normal and had focused on his studies at Yale. Then he had wanted to know where Philemon lived, what his home was like, and what his preferred research fields were. Such things. Even the question about his health and his stay in a Swiss sanatorium a few years before had not seemed very strange to Philemon. It was only when Mr. Scherff had asked about the incident in his fraternity and whether he knew what principles and *true* loyalty meant that Philemon's mood had suddenly plummeted. Even though it was no secret, he had fervently hoped that the story about Chi Psi would not come up. He had reluctantly told Mr. Scherff about it and had hurried home after the conversation. All his hopes of the prestigious job in Dr. Tesla's laboratory were gone. He was all the more surprised when Mr. Scherff told him a few days later that he could pack his things and go to Colorado Springs.

Why me of all people? Philemon asked himself suddenly. *And what did "specific qualifications" mean anyway?* That sounded rather strange. But at the time he had thought nothing of it. Dr. Tesla was known to be a very unusual man. Why shouldn't he recruit his people in an unusual way? Today he knew that the doctor had chosen him because he was "specifically qualified." Whatever that meant.

"And what did you mean, Myers was still here?" he inquired of the telegraphist.

Herkimer looked at him seriously. "Myers has been seen. After old Ben told me he'd been struck by lightning!"

"Where might that have been?" asked Philemon incredulously.

"Top of Pikes Peak."

"On the summit? And who, pray tell, would have seen him there?"

"Hmm, I don't know their names, but they all tell similar stories. For example, two men saw a young red-haired fellow wandering among the rocks. He looked disoriented and they approached him, but he didn't respond. Four days later, a lady, a Colorado Springs spa guest, saw him on a trip up the mountain. He had caught her eye because he was standing motionless, staring off into the distance."

Philemon was skeptical. "How do you even know that was Myers? It could just as easily have been someone else."

"It's Myers. For sure! I knew him, after all. Met him a few times myself. That's how I know he has red hair!"

Aha, Philemon had not known that. But the matter still didn't quite make sense to him. "I wonder why no one took him down the mountain if he was obviously confused. He could have frozen to death up there. It gets damn cold at night. Or he could have been suffering from altitude sickness."

"I can only repeat what I heard, Phil. No one said they took him down with them. But apparently, he didn't freeze to death either, because he was spotted again just the day before yesterday. He was standing next to that funny tube thing you set up there."

"The tube thing is a receiving terminal."

"Whatever. Anyway, he's supposed to have been standing there staring at the thing all the time. People are already calling him the 'Ghost of Pikes Peak.' Real creepy, I can tell you!"

It is indeed, thought Philemon. However, he could not remember seeing anything of the sort when he had been up on the mountain with the others. "And has he ever been sighted down in the city?"

Herkimer shook his head.

"Do Dr. Tesla and his assistants know about this?"

This time the telegraphist merely shrugged his shoulders.

Philemon felt the uneasiness take a deeper root in him. They had to know. Why else would Tesla and the other two have been calling for Myers at night? He had supposedly been sighted for the last time the day before yesterday. That had been during the experiment!

"Thank you for the information," he said, rising a moment later. "I have to go now."

Herkimer blinked up at him, "I'm telling the truth."

"I believe you, Joe, and I owe you. But first I have to think about it. Adieu." He tapped his hat and left the smoky basement.

Outside, Philemon smoothed down his clothes. He snorted into his handkerchief to get the opium smell out of his nose and took a few deep breaths. He needed to digest what he had heard before he could get into bed and sleep. So he went back to Pikes Peak Avenue and walked aimlessly through the night.

Armed with a tool bag, Philemon took a carriage to Manitou Springs the following Sunday and got out at the valley station of the cog railroad. Together with a crowd of excitedly chattering spa guests from Colorado Springs, he waited for the train to arrive. Again and again, he looked around to make sure that no one was following him.

Dr. Tesla had been extremely pleased last night that Philemon had offered to inspect the terminal at the summit and had even given him the money for a ticket. He should, however, be careful not to work too long on the Lord's Day, he warned. Himself the son of a priest, the doctor could justify requiring himself to work on Sunday, but he did not want to prevent his assistants from going to church. Because religion was important, he said. It gave people ideals and encouraged good behavior.

Philemon grimaced. While he agreed with Tesla's view of religion, going to church here in Colorado Springs? No, thank you! Ten horses could not drag him to a place of worship here. He would likely have to wait until he was back in New York to receive his next communion.

The cog railroad train arrived and there was some jostling. The people coming down from the top got off and those who were going up got on. Philemon hurried to get a window seat on the windward side. That way he could enjoy the view and the fresh air during the ride without being disturbed by the smoke of the locomotive.

Panting and spitting clouds of soot, the train struggled up the fifteen-kilometer route; at the steepest hairpin bends only at walking pace—one could have walked alongside it. After half an hour, they reached the tree line and the landscape opened out into green meadows and scree fields. The sky was slightly cloudy, but the view was still breathtaking. Philemon could see across Colorado Springs to the spot on the prairie where the lab building stood—a tiny dark speck on the parched expanse of yellow.

At the halfway point, the air started to get thinner, and Philemon hoped not to get another headache like the first time they had set up the terminal. The only thing that would help against altitude sickness was staying hydrated and descending if it got too bad. He opened the water bottle he had brought with him and drank a few large, precautionary gulps. He had to equalize the pressure in his ears several times and it became noticeably colder. Shortly before reaching the summit, the train plunged into the clouds and the passengers made disappointed sounds as they were now denied the view. Philemon, on the other hand, did not mind; after all, he was not here for the panorama.

At the summit station, he got off with the other passengers and walked first through the haze to the Summit House. There he allowed himself a small meal and a few more sips of water. He then turned up his collar against the cold and descended the southeastern slope to the terminal, which they had surrounded with a barbed-wire fence to protect it from prying eyes. The sign they had put up read ATTENTION! DANGER TO LIFE! DO NOT ENTER! in insistent red.

Philemon set down his heavy tool bag and sat on a rock near the terminal. Listening to his own breathing and the whistling of the wind, he observed the terrain. No visitor had strayed this far. There was no movement anywhere among the rocks. Philemon shivered. He turned his head and looked at the man-size copper tube behind the barbed wire. So this is where Frederick Myers had been standing—if the good lady about whom Herkimer had told him hadn't been suffering a hallucination, which could happen to sensitive people at this altitude.

After a while, Philemon rose and climbed carefully over the fence. He felt a slight pressure behind his forehead. The beginning of a headache. So he didn't have much time to examine the area. He walked over to the copper tube with the mushroom-shaped dome and tapped his fingers against the cold metal. It sounded hollow. Then he checked the insulation of the wire coils around the tube and finally bent down to open the small door. He was seized by a sudden déjà vu and saw himself crouching in the tube, peering out through the slit.

He looked at his shoes, which were standing on white limestone. Could that be it? He quickly reached for the hook on the door and pulled it open. The inside of the tube was dark. Philemon ducked his head and climbed into the terminal. As he closed the door, the familiar feeling of trepidation instantly gripped him and he had to wait for his heartbeat to quieten. Meanwhile, from outside, he heard the high-pitched wail of the wind as it caught in the struts of the antenna. Resolutely, Philemon shook off his trepidation, bent his knees, and looked through the door slit.

Had he seen those bright stones? Had he had this buzzing in his ears and felt this cold on his skin? Goose bumps covered Philemon's arms, and the internal pressure against the top of his skull had also become stronger. Groaning, he rubbed his temples.

Suddenly, he heard a noise outside. The trickling of stones. Quickly, he lowered his hands and froze.

Was there anyone there? A summit visitor? Or was it Myers? Philemon peered through the slit once more but could see nothing. Damnation, he would have to leave the tube if he wanted to learn more. So he shook himself, quietly opened the door, and scrambled out into the open. Immediately, the wind tugged at his hat, threatening to blow it off his head, but Philemon was just able to grab hold of it and push it back into place. With one hand on his hat and the other on the collar of his jacket, he straightened up and turned around once. There was no one to be seen, only the misty wisps of clouds sweeping over the ridge and dancing through the rock garden like figures from the realm of fairies. If anyone had been there, they were either gone or hiding behind one of the countless rocks.

A whistle sounded in the distance. It was the signal that the train would be returning to the valley in a few minutes.

Since the pressure in his brain had now turned into a painful throbbing, Philemon decided to conclude his mission and get on the train. He gathered his things and went back to the mountain station.

On the way down, he propped his thudding head in one hand and squinted out from under the brim of his hat at the passing landscape. To distract himself from the pain, he contemplated the colors up here. Scree, as bright and faded as bone, alternated with barren, greenish patches of grass. Here and there were bold splashes of color from mountain flowers. A soft pink, a strong yellow, and a fiery rusty red.

Rusty red? Philemon startled out of his contemplation. Wasn't that the color of Myers's hair too? Hastily, he scanned the terrain. Could he see movement over there? There, in the thicket of crippled white pines?

Only a little later did Philemon see it. It had stepped out of the thicket and was looking around in fright.

A bighorn sheep with its young.

CHAPTER 40

May 28, 2011
Casablanca, Morocco
10:05 am

Ondragon was aware that several reasons were taking him into the desert. For himself, he wanted to seize the opportunity to solve this unusually tricky puzzle. For the BND, he wanted to get hold of Pandora (which was ultimately for himself again, since he wanted to see the Gemini file), and for Charlize, he had promised to seek revenge! They were three good motives, but the first one, he had to admit, was still the strongest. Curiosity was in his nature and there was nothing he could do about it.

Since he was going to have to wait around for an uncertain amount of time, he spent the second day in Casablanca feeling his way deeper into the city. He wanted to take it in with all his senses. He quickly discovered that he felt at home here. Not only because he spoke both national languages, but also because his European 6'2" figure could blend into the Moroccan *savoir-vivre* without anyone noticing. As he strolled the streets, he became one of many. In reality, he was nothing more than a chameleon who had mastered the art of deception, stealthily observing his surroundings from under his disguise. There was only one place left in the world, other than the city, where he could blend in this well: the desert.

Ondragon hailed a cab and asked to be driven to the old town. He had already bought all the equipment he needed the day before and could take his time today. He entered the medina through the large archway on the Avenue des F.A.R. and strolled through the bazaar at a leisurely pace. It was disappointingly shabby and nothing like the wonderful Khan el-Khalili bazaar in Cairo, where he had roamed as a ten-year-old and squandered his pocket money—much to his father's annoyance, of course. He suppressed the thought of his former master and looked somewhat listlessly at the merchants' wares. At a touristy stand with lamps made of colored glass, he bought a charming piece for Charlize. She loved this kind of oriental kitsch and would be delighted with this souvenir.

At a particularly busy corner with a tiny café and bric-a-brac stores, he stopped and watched in amusement as the merchants hustled and bustled, haggling with the helplessly gesticulating tourists. As he did so, a woman at a spice stall suddenly caught his eye. It was the brunette lady from the jazz bar. Throughout the evening, he had glanced at her furtively but had not approached her. She had looked over at him a few times, but had not revealed by any movement whether she had noticed him. Her companion from the evening before was with her again. He stood very close behind her, as if he wanted to protect her. However, the woman did not give the impression that anyone needed to be particularly concerned about her safety. She had quite a robust appearance, and an air of being able to look after herself, which immediately appealed to Ondragon. He had watched the two of them very closely last evening and tried to assess what they were doing here in Casablanca. Secretly sizing up people was his favorite pastime, and a good way of honing his people skills. He had mastered the art almost to perfection and was almost always right in his assessments. Almost always, that is, ninety-eight percent of the time. To his great annoyance, however, his gift failed him with regard to the remaining two percent. This irritated him and made him constantly strive to finally achieve 100 percent.

He squeezed himself into a shady corner and kept an eye on the woman and her companion. They hadn't noticed him and were haggling blithely with the spice merchant. Or rather, she was haggling, because the guy was standing back with a rigid expression and turning his head suspiciously in all directions. The woman was in her late thirties, Ondragon guessed from the fine lines around her eyes. Her tanned face and toned, slender body were evidence of a marked vitality. She wore cargo pants and over them a sand-colored tunic. Around her waist she had tied a heavy leather belt with a bag. Her dark brown hair, braided into a pigtail, was loosely covered by a scarf that was more of a statement than a correct Muslim garment. On her feet she wore not sandals like most tourists, but high desert boots made of coarse canvas. She looked like Princess Leia with Luke Skywalker by her side. All that was missing was Han Solo and the Wookie! Luke appeared to be a little younger and was in pragmatic expedition clothing: a khaki cotton shirt with the sleeves rolled up and outdoor pants with the legs zipped off. He also wore sturdy shoes and a baseball cap embarrassingly inscribed TOP GUN.

Cautiously, Ondragon worked his way through the throng toward her, picking up a few phrases as he passed. Surprisingly, the woman was speaking High Arabic to the spice merchant, confirming his impression that this was not her first time in an Arab country.

He strolled on, stopped at a neighboring stall, and studied the display, giving her a covert glance. She had now finished her business and was walking away with her companion, toward the large archway. Ondragon followed hot on her heels. He had nothing special in mind and was intending to trail her for fun. That was his second-favorite pastime: spying on people. He called it "city stalking."

While Leia and Luke stepped through the gate onto the busy Avenue des F.A.R. and walked along the sidewalk toward the harbor, Ondragon kept discreetly in the background. The more he observed the two of them, the more certain he became that they were either archaeologists or belonged to an NGO working here in Morocco or in one of the neighboring countries. More precisely, he had the feeling that, like him, they were waiting for something. Perhaps for the start of a mission. Unfortunately, he had to keep too great a distance to understand what language they were speaking. He had a hunch they were northern Europeans.

Unfortunately, nothing particular happened and he followed them to the Golden Tulip Hotel. They were guests here, he had already found that out yesterday, because they had their bill written on their room number at the bar. All the drinks were charged to one room: number 818. Were they sharing a bed? Ondragon didn't think so, because they didn't give the impression they were in a sexual relationship. Even if they were respecting the rules of etiquette of the Arab world by not engaging in physical contact in public, he assumed it was a purely business connection; Leia was clearly the boss and Luke her sidekick. The last Ondragon saw of the two of them was the guy holding the door open for her with a smile. Yes, he clearly had a crush on her, but it seemed a hopeless cause, because Leia merely smiled back coolly. So not sleeping together. He could have gone after them and checked it out, but he'd lost his appetite for the game and besides, he was ravenously hungry.

He walked through the side streets to Boulevard Mohammed V and treated himself to a sumptuous lunch of tabbouleh, hummus, and fish tagine at a Moroccan restaurant. For dessert, he had fresh dates, which he bought from a fruit vendor one street over.

He spent the rest of the day rouletteing haphazardly through various cafés, unobtrusively monitoring the livestream from the ship via his iPhone and risking the sugar rush from sweet mint tea and white nougat.

But the stuff helped him get through the tiring afternoon hours that hung oppressively over the Casablancan streets.

In the early evening, Ondragon packed the small backpack he had bought in Fortaleza and went over to the Golden Tulip. His hotel, how could it be otherwise, had no fitness room. For a fee, however, he was able to use the facilities of the hotel across the street.

The room was quite small but equipped with state-of-the-art machines. Ondragon completed the program that was specially designed to keep him fit on the road, working up a mighty sweat despite the air-conditioning. After an hour and a half of rigorous exercise, he relaxed for another twenty minutes in the steam room of the adjacent hammam and took a cold shower afterward to stimulate muscle regeneration. He shaved and put on a dark suit and white shirt, but without a tie and leaving the top button undone. He wanted to appear elegant, but also casual. A management consultant on a business trip. Then he reached for his backpack and went to the hotel's jazz bar, full of expectation. On the one hand, he was looking forward to a cool drink, and on the other, he was eager to see Princess Leia again. He hadn't been able to get her out of his head all day.

It was only moderately crowded in the bar and Leia was sitting with the guy at the same table again. They had two empty glasses in front of them and were having a moderately animated conversation, Ondragon diagnosed. He settled on a stool at the bar, making sure to leave the seat next to him empty, and ordered a Pimm's Cup, making a show of focusing on it. In reality, he was enjoying the stimulating tingle that brushed across his back whenever Leia looked over at him. Like a hand in a silk glove!

He felt almost as ridiculous as a teenager with a crush, wondering why he found this woman so provocative. It was her charisma. She clearly had the aura of a hunter about her. And he had a thing for hunters!

After he had half emptied his glass, he shifted his position at the counter and deliberately turned to the right so that he could see her better. There was now a new drink in front of her—a bottle of Beck's beer. He loved women who drank beer out of the bottle! She was leaning back in the lounge chair and had crossed her arms over her chest. A clear rejection. She was probably tired of her companion, who was still babbling at her, not realizing she wasn't even listening anymore. She no longer even nodded out of politeness, and instead her gaze began to wander around the room. Ondragon maintained an unconcerned expression and waited for their eyes to meet. The moment they did, his pupils went to work and held her gaze.

It was the first time they had looked directly at each other and this time he detected a clear emotion in her. Her eyes widened slightly and the corners of her mouth lifted a tiny bit. At least she seemed to regard him as a welcome change. But then she looked down and took a sip from her bottle. As she put the beer back on the table, her eyelashes slowly lifted and finally her gaze returned to him. It was much more intense than before, and obviously calculating.

Like someone who weighs up risks in seconds, Ondragon surmised, nodding at her. The warm tingling sensation intensified and flowed from his back into his legs. Even if the lady got up the next moment and disappeared to her room, the evening would have been worth it.

But she did not. Her gaze continued to rest on him. Now somewhat more mildly and more confidently, but there was also something else. Her posture had changed. She was now sitting in a relaxed posture in the chair, one arm casually resting on the backrest and one leg crossed over the other. She wore tight pants with a tunic over them. She had draped the headscarf around her neck, allowing her dark curls to fall over her shoulders. All that was missing was the laser cannon on her hip! Ondragon smirked cautiously. He still found his comparison to Princess Leia decidedly apt. However, the lady over there seemed like a much tougher and more emancipated edition of Leia. Star Princess 2.0, so to speak.

Ondragon finished his cocktail and pointed to the empty glass. She understood his sign, whispered something to her companion, and rose. The beer bottle in her hand, she approached him. She was only half a head shorter than Ondragon, and when she came within a few feet of him, first her aura invaded his, and then her scent. A hint of sandalwood and jasmine wafted into his nose.

She sat down on the stool next to him and said in English, but with an accent he was very familiar with, "Hello, how are you?"

So I was right after all, he thought. *"Mycket bra. Och med dig?"* he replied in Swedish.

A surprised smile appeared on her face. It was delightfully broad and a touch suggestive. "You're Swedish too?" she asked.

Swedish too? Hmm. He considered which tactic might work best and on instinct chose the variant that contained the greatest amount of truth. That was easier.

"It depends," he replied. "My mother is Swedish and my father is German. But I myself have lived in the States for several years."

Her lips formed an O.

That's right, that was his name!

"Paul Ondragon," he introduced himself and held out a hand to her.

"Malin Ysanter." She grasped his hand. Her handshake was as firm as a lumberjack's. "Ondragon, what an interesting name. Spanish?"

"Yes, my great-great-grandfather on my father's side was from the Iberian Peninsula," he replied, glad that he had his features so well under control, despite her surprisingly resilient greeting.

"Where did you grow up?" she asked, "From your accent, it sounds like Småland."

"My father was a German diplomat," he explained. "I was born in Stockholm, but we moved around a lot and lived in different countries. I was mostly only in Sweden in the winter, for Yule with my grandparents, who lived near Jönköping at the time." That was true up to this point. His grandparents had indeed lived at the southern tip of Lake Vättern. Let's see how long he could stick with the truth this time before he was forced to resort to one of his ersatz biographies.

"And where in the US do you live, if you don't mind me asking?" She took another sip from the bottle.

"In Los Angeles. And what about you?" he asked back to turn the conversation to his object of interest.

The Swedish woman named Malin emptied her bottle of beer and set it down on the counter with a smirk. She then ordered another drink from the bartender. Out of the corner of his eye, Ondragon registered Luke shooting over a jealous look, but he ignored the little squirt.

"I currently live in Gothenburg, but I grew up in a less sunny environment. I was born in Kiruna in the Arctic Circle where it's cold as hell, even in summer. That's also the reason I moved to southern Sweden. Slightly longer summers and milder winters." Malin shook herself as if a chill was coming over her. "I don't like winter much. I'm more comfortable with desert temperatures. And that's despite the fact that my grandfather used to drive herds of reindeer through the taiga!"

Aha, so in her veins flowed the blood of the Sámi, the indigenous people of Scandinavia. That probably also explained her dark hair.

"Then you must be here for the temperature," Ondragon speculated. "Are you on vacation?"

"Not exactly." Somewhat embarrassed, she ran her finger over the rim of the glass. "Actually, I'm a geologist working at the University of Gothenburg."

Damn! Geologist! He hadn't guessed that. That likely fell within his standard two percent error rate. But at least he had been close. After all, like archaeologists, geologists liked to dig in the dirt "So you're interested in rocks?"

Malin laughed. "No, more oil, gas, and ores. I'm a deposits expert."

"Then you're here prospecting or on a field trip with students?"

Again, she shook her head. "It's more of an expedition. And what brings you here to Casablanca?"

She wanted to distract him, he could tell. But he wouldn't let up. "Oh, it's all pretty boring; I'm traveling on business and I have meetings here."

"On business, well, well." She gave him an appraising look that indicated she didn't quite believe him. "What line of work are you in?"

"Management consulting." There it was, the first lie. Ondragon didn't let on. It was the same as always. By the third question at the latest, he was no longer a member of the honesty club. He sighed inwardly. Sometimes playing with secret identities was no fun. He leaned a little closer to her, breathed in her scent, and said in a low voice, "Now that I've told you about the full sad banality of my stay here in Morocco, I'd like to know what kind of expedition you're on."

She looked at him impenetrably. Then she turned her head and looked over at Luke for a moment. He was the picture of jealousy, and was obviously boiling. But only on the outside. On the inside, he was almost certainly just hiding a small, awkward pile of misery, despondency, and childish defiance.

Sorry, kid, but this evening is mine, Ondragon thought, the corners of his mouth lifting in amusement.

"I'm not just a geologist," Malin Ysanter said finally, "I'm also a hunter."

Ondragon almost choked on one of the cucumber slices from the drink. "A hunter? No kidding?" he asked.

Malin shook her head. "That's sort of my second job: big game hunter."

He had to digest that first. Ondragon did not believe in fate, but this was a damn strange coincidence. First that beautiful Ojibway Indian two years ago and now this irresistible woman from the far north! Why did he always fall for hunters, of all things? Were they his nemesis? In the guise of Diana, goddess of the hunt? Deeply enraptured, he drank the rest of his cocktail.

Meanwhile, Malin misinterpreted his silence and kept talking, as if she had to apologize for being engaged in such a martial activity.

"I learned to hunt as a child; my grandfather taught me. Today, hunting gives me the opportunity to observe and hunt rare and fascinating animals in the most remote regions of the world. As a geologist, you do get around a lot, but in the end that's not nearly as exciting as hunting."

"What have you shot, then?" asked Ondragon, finally breaking his silence. He was eager to learn more.

"Oh, I've had everything in my sights," she replied, "from grizzlies to walruses. But my favorite assignments are like this one. Capturing live animals and shipping them safely to another location. Because that's far more challenging than just shooting an animal."

"I can imagine. And what species are you after?"

She hesitated again. But then she revealed her secret. "I am on a mission to capture a white dromedary."

"Uh-huh, and what's so special about those?"

"My client is one of the richest men in the Emirates. He has heard about the special breed of the *Ebäydäg*, which is the name of the most perfect of all white dromedaries in the Tuareg, and now he absolutely must have a specimen in his collection. But not one bred in captivity, no, he wants a wild one! Unfortunately, these white ghost dromedaries are hard to come by. They are very shy and live in the deepest sandy deserts of the Western Sahara. They are actually very graceful animals and fascinatingly undemanding."

Ondragon did not think that dromedaries could in any way be described as graceful, but he knew all Arabs were infatuated with these beasts. Noble-blooded dromedaries were ranked above the Ferrari, the racehorse, and the hunting falcon on a sheik's list of must-haves. "And that's where you're going next?" he asked, as impressed as a management consultant could be. "Into the middle of the desert?"

"Yes, and I'm really looking forward to it. I love the desert! We just have to wait for the flight permits. Other than that, we're good to go."

Well, look at that, they not only had the same goal, they also had the same hurdle to overcome.

"Can I ask you something, Malin?"

"Go ahead," she replied readily.

"Is what you do always legal? I mean, is it always animals that are cleared for shooting anyway, or is it sometimes animals on the endangered species list?"

She lowered her voice. "Is your work always legal?"

He smiled subtly. "Not necessarily."

"Well," she said, "then you have your answer. However, this order has been approved by the highest authorities."

Ondragon smiled pensively. Just as he was wondering if she also hunted dragons, Luke got up from the next table and stomped out of the bar, obviously displeased. Total capitulation!

"And who is he?" Ondragon jerked his thumb toward the slamming door.

"That is Pelle Knatte, my pilot."

No wonder, he thought almost pityingly. With a name like that, you had lost before you began.

"I can fly our plane myself," Malin continued, "but I need both hands free for observation and shooting. In this case, with the tranquilizer gun. Pelle very often comes with me. He's a little too fond of me, I'm afraid, but he's a good pilot."

Top Gun, all right. Ondragon pushed his hand closer to hers. Malin had also moved closer to him and was almost touching his knee with hers, which had a fatal effect on his libido. The area between his belly button and thighs began to blaze. How long had it been since he'd had sex? Too long. Somehow his work had always been to the fore lately. Or rather, his obsession with solving problems. He wondered if she felt the same way. Malin Ysanter . . .

They looked at each other in silence for a while. The air between them crackled so loudly that Ondragon feared other customers might hear it and turn to look at them curiously. At that moment, any observer would have come to the same conclusion.

"Are we going to my room or yours?" Malin asked the classic question, looking at him meaningfully.

Ondragon lowered his head in surrender. In this case, he was happy to be conquered. After all, she was a huntress, and as was well known, they always went ahead of their prey.

"Are you into frills?" he asked.

She shook her head.

"Then let's go to your place." He placed four hundred dirhams on the counter and rose. He was glad she didn't want to go to his room, because he had remembered it was full of bags with dubious contents. Inventing a suitable explanation would have been difficult. He took Malin lightly by the elbow and led her to the elevators. When the door closed, they exchanged a look that would have made even the pope realize what they were about to do. Ondragon saw her lips twitch and felt magically drawn to them. He could kiss her now . . . but he held back. For now. The hunter needed to drag her prey to her safe refuge first.

His nerves like red-hot wires, he watched her open the door with her keycard and then insert it into the slot for the light. The overhead lights came on and she pushed the door closed with her foot. At the same moment she fell upon him.

The huntress threw her prey back against the wall, grabbed his hair, and kissed him directly on the mouth. Ondragon willingly let it happen, enjoying the feel of her hands sliding commandingly over his body. She was pretty strong and her movements were purposeful. With this woman, he knew he would have fun.

While she unabashedly grabbed his crotch and felt his erection, he tugged at her tunic. Fucking cumbersome garment! The Arabs knew why they wrapped their women in such ungainly bags! He pushed the fabric up to her belly button and it got stuck there. But Malin came to his rescue, pulling the garment over her head. Underneath she wore a lacy, light blue bra. A pleasant surprise, given her rather pragmatic wardrobe—as if she had set out to hook up with someone today. The thought twitched briefly through Ondragon's befogged brain but disappeared immediately, because he didn't care. She was a hunter, after all, and that kind of woman did that kind of thing. The sight was divine anyway, as she shook her hair, letting it fall freely over her bare shoulders. As she did so, her breasts swayed slightly in their provocative lace. Ondragon ran his tongue over his lips. It was time to switch roles!

He pushed himself off the wall and urged her toward the bed. In doing so, she did not behave quite as compliantly as he had hoped. She pressed both hands against his chest and braced herself against him. In the process, her mouth found his lips again and sucked on them hungrily. She then moved to his earlobes, then covered his neck with small bites. Cascades of pleasurable shivers coursed over his body. He moaned softly and finally she gave in to his urging and let herself fall backward onto the bed.

Without taking his eyes off her, he slipped his jacket off his shoulders, undid his shirt and pants, and completely removed his clothes. In front of him, Malin was lolling on the sheet like a feline predator. She still had her pants on, and after the change of roles, she now expected him to take them off for her. With pleasure! Ondragon bent down, grabbed her by the hips, and pulled her toward him with a jerk. After a few deft moves, she was free of her pants and, before she knew it, the pretty lingerie as well. Not at all shy, she presented him with her stunning femininity.

Ondragon threw himself on top of her and in his turn drove his teeth into her flesh. His desire built to unbearable levels as he savored every inch of her body, finally arriving at her nipples. Suddenly, he penetrated her hard. Malin threw herself at him wildly, fighting with him for the tempo of his thrusts. She screamed and writhed under him as if she was possessed and he was the devil incarnate. And when she came with a mighty tremor, he cried out as well, as she dug her fingernails deep into his back. Then he came too.

Exhausted, Ondragon rolled onto his back and stared blissfully at the ceiling. Next to him, Malin sighed contentedly and propped herself up on one elbow.

"For a management consultant, you sure have a fancy tattoo!" she said, jabbing her finger at the dragon writhing on his chest.

"Thank you," he replied simply.

Her finger traveled further down and found the spot where Kateri's arrow had struck him two years earlier. "And a hell of a lot of scars!"

CHAPTER 41

August 23, 1899
Manitou Springs
afternoon

After getting off the Pikes Peak train at the foot of the mountain, Philemon sat down on a bench in a small, well-kept park. Although alcohol and other sins were peddled in Manitou Springs, the place seemed no worse or more squalid than Colorado Springs. Nowhere did one see vagrants or drinking companions loitering in the streets. Nowhere did a slight girl tout her flirty charms to the men strolling by.

It's not the devil who made the booze, he thought snidely, *but man himself. We are already so depraved, there is no need for a devil.*

Philemon stroked his forehead. His headache was gradually subsiding. Even though altitude sickness had prevented further investigations on the mountain, he was determined to continue them down here. He needed to know if anyone had indeed seen Myers.

After half an hour, he rose and wandered into the next bar. At the counter, he ordered a double whiskey and drank it down in one go. Afterward, he felt brave enough to ask the bar owner about the ghost of Pikes Peak.

"What is this crap?" the man growled, leaning forward. "You'll drive away my guests with that kind of talk!"

Oh, how familiar it sounded to him! It was the same sermon as in Colorado Springs. This we-are-an-honorable-town drivel! How fed up Philemon was with it. He also leaned forward and whispered, "I know someone from your neck of the woods has seen him. Just tell me the name of the person and I'll be gone before any of your guests even notice me! Or I'll make a little round and ask everyone at the tables about it!"

"Are you one of those Pinkertons who hang around here all the time and startle people with their questions?"

"No, do I look like one?"

The host eyed him grimly. "Nah, the guy who was here was different, but he asked the same dumb questions."

"So are you going to give me the same dumb answers you gave him, or are you going to be a little more honest with me?" Philemon slid a twenty-dollar bill across the counter to the man. "You can keep the change!" He could literally smell the finish line.

The bar owner put a hand on the bill and pulled it unobtrusively toward himself. "There is no ghost here! Neither in the village nor up on the mountain! Understand? Now get out of here!"

"And my change?"

"I thought that was for the honest answer, pilgrim!" The host tilted his head and looked as if he was trying to convince Little Red Riding Hood he was not the Big Bad Wolf.

Philemon clenched his hands into fists and glared at the man. But there was no point in scowling. Without taking his leave, he turned and left the bar. As he did so, he closed his ears to the bar owner's mocking laughter that echoed behind him.

But he wasn't going to give up so easily. He continued through the eateries and bars, asking questions, inquiring at the haberdasher's and the general store, even asking the funeral director, who was smoking a pipe in front of his establishment. But no one would admit they had seen the ghost of Pikes Peak, or even heard a story about it. Either the stubbornness of the local residents was even more pronounced than that in Colorado Springs, or Herkimer had actually been spinning him a fairy tale. At least he now knew that the Pinkertons had also tried their luck here. Just as unsuccessfully as he, Philemon hoped.

Around three o'clock he boarded a carriage back to Colorado Springs. Once there, he went to a coffee house across the street from the Kensington Gardens Hotel, and while eating cookies and drinking black coffee, kept a continual eye on the hotel entrance. After three hours, he gave it up. His stomach couldn't take any more cookies, and all the coffee had made him feel quite twitchy. No Pinkerton had shown up outside the hotel, or at least no one he thought looked like one. He had wasted his time here; it had all been for nothing. Perhaps Herkimer was right after all, and these people were indeed particularly well camouflaged. Disappointed, Philemon returned to the Alta Vista, where he shut himself in his room.

On Monday morning, he woke early and in a better mood, which even the rain could not diminish. It hung over the city like a gray veil. As soon as Philemon had breakfasted, he hurriedly made his way to the post office. Under the protection of his umbrella, he wandered through the muddy streets. There was not much going on at the office. Philemon joined the line of the few people waiting by the telegraph operator's counter. Although Herkimer had offered him the use of his terminal in the railroad depot, the guy was too curious; Philemon's request was delicate.

When it was finally his turn, he slid the note with the message across the counter to the telegraph operator, an elderly gentleman with an expansive mustache. The man took it, went to the telegraph machine, and let his index finger dance on the Morse key for a while. A few minutes later, he returned. "You can pay at the next counter. Have a nice day."

"Thank you," Philemon said, and picked up the note again. He went to the counter, paid, and left the post office. Outside, he looked again at what he had written. It was addressed to his friend in New York, the only fellow student left, after graduation and the fraternity thing, whom he could ask for such a favor. Here in Colorado Springs, Philemon had not been able to find out anything about the Röhnfeldt experiment, since the public library, which they did have here, did not hold the appropriate technical volumes. He asked his friend to rummage through the books in the faculty libraries in New York for him and, if necessary, call in one of the professors. He had to know what this Röhnfeldt experiment was all about and hoped for an answer soon.

In order not to be late at the laboratory, Philemon took the carriage to the outskirts of town, where he got out and tore up the note. He threw the shreds out into the prairie. Then he opened his umbrella and continued on foot. Fine droplets dampened his shoes as he dodged the larger puddles. Thin plumes of rain streaked across the plain in the distance.

When he reached the lab, he slipped quickly inside. The warmth stored from the previous day welcomed him, and grateful for the cozy atmosphere in the lab, Philemon took off his jacket. He had just tied on his antistatic apron when Czito and Löwenstein stepped out of Tesla's small study. Of course they were here ahead of him again. Philemon wondered what invisible signal drew them to the doctor's office each morning. The two assistants approached him and greeted him cheerfully.

"Good morning, Phil," Löwenstein said. "Not the best weather, huh? But it's all the better for us. The doctor wants to repeat the last big experiment today. He wants to see how the terminal behaves in humid air, and maybe a little thunderstorm too. After all, we noted an increase in static energy in the atmosphere despite the falling air pressure. That would be fantastic!" The German rubbed his hands together in anticipation.

"Really?" asked Philemon, seeing the doctor coming out of his chamber as well. "I'll be happy to get back into the terminal if you wish, Dr. Tesla."

"Oh, thank you very much for your offer, Mr. Ailey. But I think you still need to recover from the strain of the last experiment. Even though you probably don't feel anything, your body will certainly remember the recent alternation and will need to settle down again. You know that every body, every type of matter—whether solid, liquid, or gas—vibrates at its own frequency. In the experiment, you were exposed to vibrations that threw your metabolism out of rhythm. And I think it is not advisable to repeat this procedure too often and too close together. Therefore, we will introduce a kind of rotation in which we will all participate. That way, someone new will always go into the terminal. Today, Fritz will take over." He pointed to the German engineer, whose eyes were glittering with excitement. Now Philemon knew why Löwenstein was so chirpy.

"All right," he agreed, a little soberly. Then he would probably have to wait a little longer before he would again have the pleasure of climbing into the tube and being able to test his Pikes Peak theory. He slumped his shoulders and set about his assigned tasks.

An hour later, they had set up the terminal outside. In the meantime, it had become even darker and a black weather front threatened heavy rain. Philemon saw lightning flashing from the clouds down to the ground.

Well, this could be fun, he thought, and was secretly glad not to have to go into the tube today. In this weather, it was downright suicide. No matter whether the terminal was a Faraday cage or not. All it took was a lightning bolt to strike the tube and the heat inside would roast Löwenstein!

Shortly afterward, his knees weak, he helped the German into the terminal. Did Löwenstein know what he was getting into? He looked at the engineer, who was smiling unconcernedly. Then he closed the door.

"You all right in there?" Philemon tapped the metal. He felt guilty for not trying to stop Löwenstein.

He knocked back from inside. "Yes!"

"Are you sure you want to do this?" shouted Philemon into the wind, which had abruptly picked up.

"Yes! Fresh, pious, cheerful, free! Go ahead!" Löwenstein's voice was muffled.

Philemon shook his head. The world-weary daredevil!

He quickly ran back to the lab and shook the raindrops off his clothes like a wet dog. When he paused, he saw the puddle in which he was standing. He guessed that was the work of the insulating shoe soles. Hopefully, they wouldn't all get a shock in this rain and fall down dead! Briefly, it occurred to Philemon that the doctor might actually be crazy. What if he really didn't know what he was doing?

Then God have mercy on us! said another voice in his head.

Without the others noticing, Philemon crossed himself and sent a prayer up to Saint Joseph, the patron saint of all engineers. Then he took up his position, which had been Mr. Czito's during the last experiment, and waited for Tesla's signal. Thunder rolled over their heads and the storm tore at the wooden walls. Was this a warning from Saint Joseph?

Clutching the lever of the high-voltage switch tightly, he braced himself against the gusts of wind that swept in through the open door. He winced as lightning struck the prairie and there was a loud crack. The thunderstorm was now directly overhead. What was the doctor waiting for? Philemon felt the hair on the back of his neck stand up. This was complete madness!

He was about to let go of the switch and tell Dr. Tesla of his concerns, when the doctor gave the signal. Philemon hesitated. He felt fear pulsing in the dark cavity of his chest and began to tremble. But as Tesla's stern gaze passed over him, he immediately pressed the switch. A high-pitched whirring and crackling sound traveled through the large coil in the center of the lab, and plasma-like extensions of bluish light twitched from the tip. There was a rhythmic banging, as if someone were being whipped.

Tesla raised his hand, and Philemon cut the power. The whirring and crackling died away, but not the thunder outside over the prairie.

What had happened to Löwenstein?

Someone should go out and check on him, Philemon thought. But Tesla lowered his hand again. In the dim light of the lab, he looked like the silhouette of an executioner bringing down his axe on the condemned man. Philemon groaned and completed the circuit. Again, the coil came to life, spouting eerie sparks of light. And again, it crackled and hissed as if the last hour had struck. Then the doctor raised his hand and Philemon jerked the switch up.

Please, let it be the last time, he silently pleaded, *otherwise I'll go out myself and free Löwenstein from the tube!* The roar above their heads slowly subsided; the thunderstorm moved away.

Tesla nodded at him, picked up the umbrella, and opened it. Then he stepped out into the rain. Philemon watched as he went to the terminal and opened the door. But he didn't get to see anything of Löwenstein. Instead, the doctor stuck his head into the tube, turned it left and right, and finally pulled it out again. Then he came back to the laboratory. With an impenetrable expression, he put the umbrella in the corner and said, "We must repeat the experiment once more."

Philemon closed his eyes at the strain and put his head in the crook of his arm. His clothes were still damp from the rain. *Please don't*, he thought, *please don't!* But the doctor insistently raised his arm.

Philemon grasped the lever. The doctor's arm fell, and as if in a trance, he completed the circuit. Like a Medusa with blue serpents of light on her head, the coil shone under the gloomy laboratory roof, its electrifying fingers stretching out in all directions. Philemon felt the tingling of high voltage on his skin, then saw Tesla give the signal and quickly lifted the switch. Arduously, he exhaled. He felt overheated and drained, as if he had completed a ten-kilometer endurance race. Exhausted, he lowered himself onto a chair. Only slowly did the cold sweat on his forehead dry, while his heart still performed one somersault after the next. He saw the doctor marching out to the terminal again. The rain had stopped and the first rays of sunlight were breaking through the cloud. They turned the rain-soaked prairie into a sea of glittering diamonds. But Philemon had no eyes for beauty; his gaze was glued to the doctor, who was about to open the door to the tube. To Philemon's great relief, Löwenstein rose from the terminal like a phoenix from the ashes. He saw the two men talking to each other, and Löwenstein shaking his head. Tesla's back tilted forward only a few degrees, but Philemon immediately noticed he was no longer standing quite so upright. It seemed as if a weight had settled on his narrow shoulders. Then Tesla turned around and came back to the laboratory with Löwenstein. Philemon would have liked to hug the German, he was so happy to see him safe and sound, but he controlled himself and merely slapped Löwenstein appreciatively on the shoulder.

Meanwhile, Czito was taking care of their physical well-being, and was serving them strong tea with lots of sugar. Gratefully, they all accepted a cup and sat down in the middle of the laboratory, each silently following their own train of thought. Philemon sipped his scalding-hot drink, while covertly watching the others. He noticed them casting meaningful glances at each other. It was as if they were speaking a secret language, without him being able to participate. Troubled, Philemon lowered his eyes and turned his thoughts inward. Now that all the tension had left him, his determination burned brighter than ever. If he ever wanted to know what this experiment was all about, he had to read the doctor's diary! But how could he get hold of a book that belonged to a person who never slept?

CHAPTER 42

May 29, 2011
Casablanca, Morocco
1:10 pm

Ondragon spent the next day sightseeing at Hassan II's mosque and later went to lunch at the Tahiti Beach Club on Boulevard de la Corniche. Achille was still busy with the authorities and all was quiet aboard the *Tethys II*. Likewise with Kubicki and the dog forum. Since he had fooled Malin into thinking he was a management consultant and had meetings to attend, he had to wait until the evening before he could meet her again.

After an exquisite meal taken overlooking the Mediterranean, he called Charlize to check on her. Fortunately, she was doing well enough to be released from the hospital in two days and fly back to LA. Ondragon was pleased and told her how they were getting on in Casablanca. As a precaution, he concealed his little affair of the night before.

"Any word on the code?" Charlize wanted to know.

"Unfortunately, no," he said.

"Hmm, that Truthfinder is sure taking his time deciphering it. I thought he was a number-crunching genius. The code can't be that complicated. After all, this Dr. Schuch didn't have much time to develop it either."

"That's true. But there you see how difficult even a supposedly simple code is to crack. Without the keyword, nothing works."

"I guess that's how it is," Charlize replied, sounding slightly disappointed. "Well, hopefully it'll work out in time."

"I hope so too. Because I have little desire to wander cluelessly through the desert."

"You'll let me know before you set out though, right?"

"Sure thing," he said.

"Aw, damn!" Ondragon heard Charlize slap her hand somewhere and there was a clatter. "I wish I was with you guys so I could kick that guy's ass myself!" So that's what was bothering her.

"I promise to make him suffer, okay?"

He heard a grumble and then an "Okay."

"Don't be vexed. I'm sending you a little something to cheer you up," Ondragon said. "A little package."

"That son of a bitch's balls, maybe?"

Ondragon had to laugh. "No. But you'll still like it."

"If you say so."

"Oh, Charlize. Don't fret. Get well and fly to LA; that's where you'll be most useful to me."

"All right, Boss. I'll pack my stuff as soon as I can. Good luck!"

"Thank you." Ondragon hung up. He left the beach club and took a cab to the hotel, where he booked a FedEx messenger to pick up the package with the lamp for Charlize. Afterward, he looked at his watch and decided to call Malin. He had gotten her number last night when he had said goodbye to her. A sign that she wanted to see him again? Not necessarily.

"*Hej,* Paul. Finished work already?" he heard her dark voice ask.

"Not quite," he replied, "but in a couple of hours. Shall we meet tonight?"

"Where?"

She did want to, then. Ondragon had hoped she would, but he hadn't been sure if the whole thing might have been a one-night stand. "I'll pick you up at six. Wear something pretty."

"Fine. So we're going out?"

"Yes. Let me surprise you, Malin."

"Well, I'll see you later. I'm looking forward to it, Paul." She said goodbye, sounding as if she was sincere. *Well,* Ondragon thought, *now it might turn into a two-night stand after all.* But he didn't expect too much from his encounters with women, because nothing long-term could ever come of them anyway. Because of his job, for a start. It was simply too risky for everyone involved. He had to remain independent and unblackmailable, the thing with Charlize was proof of that. But there was nothing wrong with a refreshing *amour fou.*

He dialed Achille's number.

"Nothing new, Boss. The office is still in gridlock," he said as he picked up.

"Hang in there. Raise the baksheesh if need be."

"Yes, I already have that in mind." Achille sounded slightly irritated. No wonder, given the stubbornness of the Moroccan authorities.

"Oh, and do you happen to know of a romantic restaurant here in Casablanca?"

"By romantic, do you mean expensive and impressive?" echoed Achille.

"Exactly. But not too pushy."

"Are you planning a little *aventure galante*?"

Ondragon could almost hear Achille grinning into the receiver. "None of your business!"

"I get it. You're not into frills, but you're into romance. Somebody should figure you out. But I don't begrudge you. Take your date to the Ocean View Cabestan, which has a great view of the lighthouse; you'll really get your money's worth. They also have a very fancy bar for afterward. Want me to reserve you a table for two?"

"That would be really lovely of you, Achille."

"De rien, chef. Et grand bien te fasse!"

After finishing the conversation, Ondragon got up from the bed and checked the equipment, which he had now stowed in inconspicuous duffel bags. Everything was ready; he only needed the starting signal—in whatever form. Then he went to the bathroom to freshen up for his rendezvous.

Malin was amazed when they entered the restaurant. Ondragon suspected that her expedition budget would not have stretched to such an exclusive location, and was pleased to see that she liked it. They were taken to a table overlooking the rocky beach and ordered a bottle of white wine, while outside over the sea the gulls flew into the pastel evening sky.

"Now, this is what I call palatial!" said Malin, impressed. "You really know how to wrap women around your little finger. One might almost think you had plenty of experience at it."

Ondragon gave a flattering smile but said nothing in response.

"Can I ask you a question first?"

He nodded.

"Do you have a Mrs. Ondragon sitting at home waiting for you? I mean, I don't see a wedding ring on your hand."

Ondragon had expected this question, though not so early. Malin seemed to be very direct. He tilted his head and asked back provocatively, "Would it bother you?"

"No."

"Me neither. But if it makes you feel any better, I'm single. My job is the relationship killer par excellence."

The waiter came with the wine and poured it. Ondragon tasted it and nodded to the waiter. They ordered their food and the waiter then left them alone again. Ondragon knew that this kind of meeting with a woman in a restaurant offered plenty of scope for conversation. Conversations in which he would be forced to lie. It was better, actually, to go to places where you couldn't talk so much, like discos or bars with a band. It was distracting. But today he had chosen the situation deliberately. He wanted to learn more about Malin and hoped to be able to steer the conversation in a direction that suited him.

"I'm constantly on the move, and I'm out of the country more than I'm at home. Hardly any woman would put up with that," he said lightly.

"Where have you been?"

"Oh, everywhere." He waved it off. "But I can't come up with exotic places like you've seen."

"What's the most exotic place you've ever been?" she asked.

Ondragon reflected. "The freeway on a Monday morning in Los Angeles, seven o'clock, almost empty! A once-in-a-century experience! So? Do *you* have a boyfriend?" he asked freely.

Malin's eyes lit up briefly. "I think my job is at least as incompatible as yours when it comes to committed relationships. But I don't want to give up the life it gives me. I get to meet a lot of interesting people." Her hand wandered across the table and rested on his.

Ondragon raised his eyebrows imperceptibly. With this woman, he really didn't need to worry about making the right moves; she took care of that all by herself. He clasped her hand and his southern regions began to make themselves heard. He wanted to feel more of Malin, to taste and smell her, even though he might never see her again. Precisely because of that.

"Then let's enjoy this evening," he said, raising his glass to her.

The food came. Ondragon had grilled lobster with chili lime sauce and Malin had a swordfish steak on an artichoke salad. As they ate, they talked casually about Malin's hunting adventures and Ondragon's experiences as a diplomat's kid who had moved to a different country every three years. As they did so, he kept catching himself gazing into Malin's eyes in fascination. She didn't seem to notice, but he wasn't sure.

After the meal, they ordered a light dessert of fruit sorbets and a mocha to go with it. Malin took obvious pleasure in it. She spooned up the icy confection with the enthusiasm of a child and left none of it on her plate. When she had drained her mocha afterward, she sighed contentedly and put the small cup back on the table. "That was really good!"

Ondragon smiled. "Yes, it was."

They looked at each other for a while, then she leaned forward. "Now will you tell me where you got all those scars?"

Ondragon was not especially surprised; he had sensed that this question was coming. He folded his napkin and laid it on the table. "Well, that's easily explained and no secret. I have very dangerous hobbies."

"And what would those be?"

Hunting Voodoo zombies, fighting forest monsters, taking out unwanted rivals, breaking into labs, things like that, he thought. Out loud he said, "Riding motorcycles, skydiving, skiing, surfing, golf . . ."

"Golf?"

"No, I was just kidding." He smirked. "But everything else is true. And you can do yourself a real injury."

She pursed her lips and nodded in agreement. But her eyes said something else. Ondragon had the impression that she had a permanent distrust scanner running in the background. Well, he couldn't blame her for that, because after all, he wasn't telling her the truth.

"Shall we have another drink at the bar outside?" he said, steering the conversation to another topic.

"I have a feeling your life isn't as boring as you pretend," she said without responding to his question. Her gaze continued to hold him.

Ondragon put on a surrendering smile and said, *"Touché."* He placed a hand on his chest. "Indeed, I can't complain that too little happens in my life, and I've seen more than enough of the world to have developed a certain detachment. But let's face it; if I'd shown that side of me from the start, you'd have thought I was horrible."

"Oh, you did show it! And you're terrible!"

Now Ondragon looked puzzled.

Malin looked back, unmoved. But then a mischievous smile crept over her lips and she let out a chuckle. "I didn't think you'd be so easily flustered." Her hand reached for his again. "You're not horrible at all, honest. I like you."

I like you. It echoed in his ears as he leaned in and whispered in her ear, "And I want you! Now!"

She smiled a little embarrassedly and squeezed his hand. Her lips brushed his cheek for a second. There was nothing more in public, but the signal was clear. The bar was forgotten. Ondragon hastily paid the bill and they took a cab to the Golden Tulip, where they disappeared into room 818. What happened behind the door this time was not quite as wild as the first time, but no less noisy.

A sound woke Ondragon from his blissful sleep and he had to get his bearings. Pleasantly surprised, he found he was still lying next to Malin. The sound came again. Somewhere his cell phone was vibrating softly. He stood up and searched for his pants in the tangle of clothes on the floor. When he found them and the cell phone, the ringing stopped. He looked at the display. Three missed calls from Truthfinder. Immediately, Ondragon was wide awake. Had the boy cracked the code?

He glanced at Malin, who was fast asleep, and quietly slipped into the bathroom. After closing the door, he pressed the "call-back" button.

"Gee, Mr. O, I'm glad to hear from you!" the young physicist reported excitedly. "Guess what? I got it!"

"What, the code?" asked Ondragon quietly.

"No, I'm afraid not, but we—that is, my acquaintance and I—figured out the meaning of the cross."

"Well, all the same." Ondragon settled down on the edge of the bathtub.

"It was really quite simple," Truthfinder said. "But our thinking was way too complicated and we didn't figure it out until later because—"

"Hey, get to the point! It's the middle of the night and I'm not alone!"

"Oh, sorry. All right, so . . . *shit*, now you've thrown me off." Ondragon heard Truthfinder typing frantically at the other end and rolled his eyes.

"So there you have it. The Roman numerals XX, V, and XIV stand for the twentieth, fifth, and fourteenth letters of the alphabet, respectively. So *T*, *E*, and *N*. When arranged in the cross, they make the word *Tenet*, which reads the same both forward and backward."

"Not at all!" Ondragon interjected indignantly. "What kind of nonsense is that? *Tenet*. I never heard the word before."

"Just you wait and see. I'm trying to explain!"

Truthfinder was right, he was too impatient. Ondragon apologized and let the young scientist continue.

"*Tenet* is a palindrome and forms the intersecting middle word of the Sator Square. That is a very old magic formula, the oldest image of which dates back to the first century CE. It is located in Pompeii, but that's just by the by. Wait, I'll send you a picture of it and you'll get a better idea."

A few seconds later, the cell phone beeped and Ondragon opened the image file. A square of words appeared.

"'Sator, Arepo, Tenet, Opera, Rotas,'" Ondragon read aloud. "Is that Latin? What does it mean?"

"There are many different interpretations of the square. There are two that are the most common. In one of them, the words are read one after the other from left to right, as you have just done. The translation is then: 'The sower Arepo holds with difficulty the wheels.' The second version—which is also the interpretation considered more probable among scientists—is read in a zigzag fashion and results in the following wording: 'Sator opera tenet—tenet opera Sator.' That is to say: 'The sower holds the works—the works hold the sower.' Figuratively speaking: 'The creator holds his creation.' So he preserves it."

Ondragon's *centrifuge* raced as Truthfinder continued to pontificate on the meaning of the formula. Two words in particular jumped out at him. *Wheel* and *sower.* The wheel of the sower! Hadn't Schuch written, *The wheel of the sower can only be turned back with difficulty?* It was confusing, because it created a connection between Monsieur Noire and the Nazi scientist that really shouldn't exist. Sator and Sower. What the hell did Noire have to do with Dr. Schuch? One had been born a whole century ago and had died in an airplane crash, and the other was almost certainly a young North African hired by a French energy company to steal the box from said plane. Ondragon's thoughts were almost doing somersaults. And what if there was a connection between the two after all?

"Truthfinder, have you tried the words from the square on the code? *Arepo* and all that?"

"Yes, yes, for ages."

"And?"

"Nothing."

"Shit!" Nevertheless, Ondragon had the feeling that the only place the two strands would converge had to be that mysterious place in the middle of the desert. Where the Junkers' cargo had been unloaded, where Schuch had witnessed Kammler leave three of his colleagues behind, where their unknown Monsieur Noire was headed, on behalf of one of the largest energy corporations in the world!

"We don't have much time!" urged Ondragon. "Keep trying to find out why someone might have that kind of cross or square as a tattoo!"

"Okay, Mr. O. I'll get right on it. I'll be in touch."

Ondragon hung up and stared thoughtfully into the dark bathroom for a while. Then he got up. He had to go back to his hotel, where a lot of work was waiting for him. Time was too short for him to rely solely on Truthfinder's research. He couldn't let Groupe Hexagone get ahead of them. He would get Charlize involved too—he sent her a quick text message. He then opened the door and winced in shock, for Malin was standing before him. She was wearing a hotel bathrobe and yawning. He, on the other hand, was still naked. He quickly pulled a towel around his hips.

"Who were you talking to?" she asked sleepily.

Ondragon raised his cell phone. "Oh, that was my associate; there are new developments with a client."

"In the middle of the night?"

He sighed. "Yeah, these things happen. Besides, it's only six o'clock in the evening in the LA office."

"Right." Malin looked down at her hands. "Then I guess you have to go now."

"Hmm, unfortunately."

She knitted her fingers together self-consciously. "We're flying out in the morning. The permit has arrived."

Ondragon remained silent. He had to come to terms with it. They were two loners who had converged for a brief moment and were now going their separate ways again. "Well, that's the way it goes," he said, pushing past her into the room and getting dressed.

After gathering everything and making sure he had left nothing in the room, he went over to the door. He reached for the handle and pushed it down. He hesitated, then turned around to face her one final time. His hand slipped into the inside pocket of his jacket, and without thinking about whether it was sensible, because it wasn't, he handed Malin one of his business cards.

"Call me if you're ever in LA."

She took the card and raised an eyebrow skeptically. "I think you mean if *you're* ever there."

Ondragon wanted to say something in reply but changed his mind and quickly left the room.

CHAPTER 43

August 24, 1899
Colorado Springs
toward evening

After they finished their tea, Philemon and Löwenstein dismantled
the terminal together and took it to the laboratory building. There they
stowed it in a corner, where Philemon rubbed the copper tube dry so that
it would not oxidize. Then he covered everything neatly with a wax cloth.

"Thank you very much, Mr. Ailey. You can go ahead and call it a day.
We'll see you again tomorrow," Dr. Tesla called out to him, and Philemon
nodded. What was going on with Czito and Löwenstein? He looked over
at the two assistants begrudgingly. Apparently, they were allowed to stay.
Philemon bit his lip. Although Dr. Tesla had only recently made him a
full-fledged lab assistant, it hadn't put a stop to the secrecy. Anger boiled
up inside him. Did they really think he was that stupid? Didn't they realize that he had long been concerned about what had happened to Myers?

Once again, he turned away in disappointment, seeming to obedi-
ently bid farewell to the others, who were already on their way to Tesla's
study. He stepped out onto the wet and glistening plain. Crickets were
chirping after the rain, and the air smelled of damp earth. It seemed as if
the prairie were taking a deep breath after the long drought.

But Philemon had no intention of going back to the town. He noisily
closed the door to the laboratory building so that everyone would hear
and walked a few steps to the fence, then turned around and crept back.
Quietly, he circled the building until he came to the spot behind Dr.
Tesla's study. The lab walls were made of comparatively thin wooden slats;
perhaps he might hear what was being said inside. He put his ear to the
rough surface and listened. He could indeed hear voices, but not clearly
enough. He moved rapidly to another place, but that was no good either.
He looked at the wall and found a gap at the level of his navel. He went
down on his knees and put his ear to it, feeling no remorse whatsoever,
for those inside were, after all, the ones who were keeping a dark secret.
Through the gap, he could easily distinguish the voices of the three men.

They were talking in nervous tones. Clearly, something had upset them. Only what?

Dr. Tesla: "You were there, Fritz! Didn't you see him?"

Löwenstein: "No, I didn't see him."

Dr. Tesla: "But that's not possible! He must be there."

Löwenstein: "I can't explain it either."

Dr. Tesla: "Hmm, then I guess I'll have to recalibrate the frequency spectrum for the solute in the ether solvent."

Silence. Then a sigh—from whom, Philemon could not tell.

Löwenstein: "Might Philemon have seen him? I mean, he's been gone long enough. Maybe he just doesn't dare tell us because he thinks he had hallucinations. I felt the same way the first time, until I realized what was going on."

A growl—from Czito.

Dr. Tesla: "Possibly. I've already wondered about whether it mightn't be a good idea to finally let him in on it completely. He is a reliable young man and has long suspected something, I feel. His file, which Mr. Scherff sent me, proves to us his specific qualifications. His most outstanding characteristic is his extraordinary loyalty. He practices it to the point of self-sacrifice."

Löwenstein: "You mean the student union incident?"

Dr. Tesla: "Exactly. Surely his behavior in this matter shows us that he is capable of keeping a secret, even if it causes him great distress." Another growl from Czito.

Philemon suddenly became hot under his clothes. Was that really the reason he had been chosen? That tiresome story about the experiment going wrong at the university and the Chi Psi student association? He bit his lip; he was embarrassed these three men were discussing it. He and a few fellow students had made a mistake back then, and had paid dearly for it. The irony of the fact that it was this circumstance of all things that had brought him here could hardly be surpassed.

Löwenstein: "Well, I don't know if he can handle it. We'd do better to wait."

Dr. Tesla: "You are right, Fritz. He has not been with us long enough for us to have complete certainty about his trustworthiness. We will continue to wait and see. Perhaps we will never be able to initiate him. If that is the case, unfortunately we will have to part with him. But now back to our problem. We must succeed in tracking down the divergence in which Frederick is trapped. Only then can we modulate a loophole for re-localization."

Löwenstein: "I agree. But at least this time the transmission succeeded completely. We had hardly any noise, as in the experiment before, when Philemon volunteered. So the Röhnfeldt effect seems to be controllable after all. You can see it from me. I'm completely unharmed."

Dr. Tesla: "In future, we must direct our attention toward an even higher constant of the frequency spectrum. Just because the experiment was successful with you, Fritz, does not mean it will be successful with me or with Kolman. The noise must be eliminated completely. I plan to reconfigure the attenuation frequencies once more. And in a few days, I hope, the components from New York will arrive; those I ordered by telegraph from Mr. Scherff. They will give us greater opportunity to control the frequencies and signals more precisely. We must be able to determine the precise vibration spectra of all bodies before a transmission. The world system *must* ultimately be multipersonal, otherwise our research here has been in vain!"

There was silence.

Then Dr. Tesla again: "Nevertheless, I think we are on a good path and should continue down it. One failed transmission with Mr. Myers, one with Mr. Ailey that can certainly be called a success, and another excellent one with Fritz. I see some progress there."

Czito: "If you wish, I will try it next, Doctor!"

Dr. Tesla: "Kolman, my dear fellow, that is too kind of you. I'll get back to you on that when the time comes."

Someone was hemming and hawing.

Dr. Tesla: "Yes, Fritz? What's on your mind?"

Löwenstein: "I'm worried, Doctor. Not just about you. There are strange things going on here in Colorado Springs."

Czito: "Yes, the Pinkertons are out and about."

Dr. Tesla: "Oh, I already know that. That doesn't scare me."

Czito: "But they're asking people about you, Doctor."

Dr. Tesla: "So what? What can these simpleminded devils tell them? I am much more interested in whether they have talked to you too, gentlemen."

Czito and Löwenstein together: "No, sir."

Löwenstein alone: "The snoopers obviously haven't dared do that yet. They know for sure they won't get anything from us. But what if they approach Philemon? Or have already done so? And what if the Pinkertons hear about the thing with Frederick?"

Dr. Tesla: "They won't get much about Frederick. The rumor about his vaporization after a lightning strike is too persistent for that. And that, as we all know, is absolute humbug. But the point about Mr. Ailey is quite a serious one. Just recently I had a conversation with him regarding information dissemination in this town, but it couldn't hurt if you, Fritz, took another run at it. Keep an eye on our young friend, just in case those pesky snoopers sneak up on him with their highly unsportsmanlike methods. These people are like blowflies!"

Löwenstein: "I'm afraid they won't rest until they get what they want."

Dr. Tesla—very sharply: "But they won't get it. Never! Because everything there is to know about it is here in my head and in this little book that I always carry with me. Even you each know only a part of it—for your safety, gentlemen. Without my knowledge, however, all the devices here are worthless!"

Thoughtful silence.

Dr. Tesla: "Let's not quibble any longer about these detectives now. They are a nuisance, but by no means dangerous. We'd better get to work on the last experiment. I want a detailed report from you, Fritz. Kolman can help you with that. Meanwhile, I will make new calculations. Get to work, gentlemen, the night is still long!"

Philemon had heard enough. Enough to be altogether emotionally confused. He began to stand up, but he realized that his legs had become completely numb due to the crouching. Only slowly did life return to his tingling limbs, and a little later Philemon stalked away stiff-leggedly through the twilight.

It bothered him that Dr. Tesla still did not trust him. On the other hand, Czito and Löwenstein apparently didn't know everything either. At least that's how it had sounded. And the three men seemed to consider him trustworthy enough that they were thinking about letting him in on it. And they had actually admired his loyalty. Philemon himself did not even know whether he was capable of such extraordinary loyalty as they demanded of him.

But his heart already knew the answer.

No matter what he or Dr. Tesla might do now, his loyalty had long since attached itself to his new master. The three men in the lab were right. He would rather die before he revealed even the smallest splinter of the secret. Even if the splinter drove itself deeper and deeper into his own flesh!

CHAPTER 44

May 31, 2011
Casablanca, Morocco
9:21 am

The day after Ondragon and Malin parted ways, Achille too finally received permission to fly into Moroccan-occupied territory in Western Sahara. Ondragon decided to break camp in Casablanca and fly to Laâyoune, where they would be significantly closer to the action, in case Monsieur Noire had the idea of landing on the coast. He instructed Achille to get the plane ready for takeoff and threw on his gear. At the reception desk, he ordered a large-capacity cab and several hotel employees to carry his extensive luggage.

Two hours later, slowed down a bit by rush hour, he reached the no-customs Tit-Mellil airfield outside of Casablanca. The luggage was picked up by a small runway car and brought to the plane together with Ondragon. Achille was already waiting for him.

"We can head right out," said the Frenchman. A cigarette was hanging casually from the corner of his mouth.

"What about the other overflight permits?"

"We only have those for Western Sahara and the rebel areas."

"Algeria?"

"They're not issuing permits to private citizens right now. Because of the war in Libya, it's too sensitive. They don't want to be blamed if Gaddafi manages to flee the country. We don't have anything from Mauritania either. But they are just being stubborn." Achille threw the cigarette butt away and stamped it out with his desert boot.

"Good, then we'll bypass Algerian airspace for the time being." Ondragon heaved his travel bag into the fully loaded plane. "Let's go over the list again." He pulled out a clipboard. You had to be well prepared for a trip to the world's most hostile desert.

Achille got onto the plane alongside the luggage. "Ready for takeoff!"

"GPS?" asked Ondragon.

"Check!" shouted Achille.

"Generator and batteries?"

"Check!"

"Gas, water, satellite phone, and Toughbook?"

"Check!"

"Metal detector? I got it, so check! Just like provisions for two weeks. Check. Tent and equipment?"

"Check!" exclaimed Achille. "All on board, so is the hardware, the Snake, and the gifts."

"Okay." Ondragon checked off one item after another. And after they were through with the list, the one for the plane followed. Half an hour later, everything was checked, stowed, and strapped down, and the two men were secured in the cockpit. Achille took the first shift at the controls. At 12:30 pm sharp, they took off and the Frenchman steered the Cessna in an elongated arc to the southwest. Twelve hundred kilometers lay ahead of them, and Ondragon hoped to cover the distance in four hours, reaching their preliminary destination of Laâyoune, the capital of Western Sahara, before sunset.

While Achille followed the coastline, Ondragon studied his notes on the Sator Square. After saying goodbye to Malin, he had spent the remaining hours of the night working with Charlize and Truthfinder to find out everything they could about it. The square had turned out to be one of the oldest magic formulas in the world and had always been considered a protective amulet against epidemics and other calamities, but it also supposedly helped ward off fires or thieves. But that was just superstition and didn't get them any further. Perhaps there was more of a connection to the Knights Templar, who were said to have used this square as a secret talisman after their order was broken up in 1312, though they used the words *Satan, Adama, Tabat, Amada Natas.*

Ondragon pondered. The two words, *wheel* and *sower*, that appeared in both Schuch's report and the Sator spell just kept on bugging him. The wheel of the sower. The Creator preserves his creation. It could not be a coincidence. This cross tattoo on the unknown man and the notes from Dr. Schuch! He quickly turned to the page where he had drawn the square, the cross, and Schuch's eight number squares side by side and immersed himself in them.

When he emerged from his thoughts an hour later, he was no smarter than before. It was like a jinx. The key to the code remained elusive. Gritting his teeth, he slapped the side of the notepad. "Shit, dammit! I'm going crazy over this!" He closed the notes and stared at the yellowish shoreline below them. This puzzle had him fooled.

"How long to Laâyoune?" he finally asked.

"Two hours."

"This guy cannot get away, do you hear? Otherwise, the secret of Pandora will disappear with him, forever!"

"Sure, Chief!" replied Achille above the hum of the plane's engine, maintaining a steady course along the coast.

They landed in Laâyoune just in time, before dusk set in. Ondragon was glad, because although the airport of the city had an asphalt runway and state-of-the-art guidance systems, it was still in the middle of nowhere and would have made a night landing risky. Not because of the heavy air traffic, rather because of the darkness here, which seemed particularly compacted. It would be even more fun later, when they might have to land on unpaved runways. But Achille was an experienced bush pilot. He knew the quirks of sand and rock.

Once they had taxied in, they pulled into their assigned parking position in front of a corrugated metal hangar and got everything ready for the night. They would sleep on the plane. With the kind of cargo they were sitting on, it was better to take good care of it. It was not only thieves whose eyes would widen at the sight of their extensive weapons arsenal; so would the eyes of any overly curious guards or airport inspectors. Here, the stuff would only be secure if they stayed close to the aircraft and took turns keeping watch.

Fortunately, only one sentry took an interest in them. He drove by in a jeep and walked once around the plane, checking. Since the Cessna had Moroccan markings and Achille could chat with him in his best Maghrebi Arabic, the guy was finally satisfied with a few dirham bills and went on his way. As the lights of his jeep were swallowed by the darkness of the desert night, it fell dead silent outside the hangars. They would probably not have to reckon with much aircraft noise here. Ondragon assigned Achille the first watch and himself the early hours of the morning. He made himself comfortable in the pilot's seat, picked up the satellite phone, and called Kubicki and Charlize to let them know his new location. He then turned out the light and closed his eyes while beside him Achille stared out into the darkness, pistol in hand.

*　*　*

Before dawn, Ondragon received a call from Kubicki.

"It's happening. Mr. Unknown is disembarking," the BND agent informed him.

"Where?" asked Ondragon.

"About twenty nautical miles off the southern coast of Western Sahara, but still outside the twelve-mile zone."

"Do you have him in your sights?"

"Yes. For now, anyway. He is heading—presumably in a boat—toward the coast. It's still too dark to make out anything more specific. All we have at the moment are the infrared images."

"Is it even him?"

"I guess so, who else would it be?"

Ondragon remained silent. There were several other possibilities, he thought.

"Do you have any idea what he wants in Western Sahara?" asked Kubicki.

"You tell me," Ondragon returned the question.

"I think he might want to go to the Junkers' landing site in the desert. We have a suspicion the plane was supposed to have made a stopover there somewhere."

"And how does our unknown know where to go? Does he have a suspicion too? This is pure speculation."

"He has the logbook, of course."

"And does it say where the Junkers landed?" asked Ondragon, to probe how much the BND knew about the logbook.

"That's what we hope, at least" Kubicki replied, without giving anything away. "And that's why we absolutely have to stay on this guy! He's our only lead. But it's going to be tough. I'm afraid we'll lose him as soon as he lands in Dakhla or Boujdour and disappears into the crowds in the city."

"We should avoid that at all costs and take action before then, if possible. We are about a forty-minute flight from Boujdour and an hour and a half from Dakhla. I suggest we fly to Dakhla first; that's closest to our unknown man. If he does go ashore on the uninhabited coast farther north, or to the south of Dakhla, we'll get airborne again. All I need from you is a precise indication of where he's going to land. Give me the coordinates. And, in spite of everything, keep the tanker under surveillance. Just in case."

"All right," Kubicki said, and hung up.

Half an hour later, the eastern horizon gradually brightened and the impenetrable darkness gave way to a diffuse twilight in which they could just barely make out their hands. Another fifteen minutes later, the tower approved their takeoff, and they were in the air as the sun was sending the first of its rays over the horizon. Achille took the controls so that Ondragon could communicate with Kubicki uninterrupted.

We're still in the green, he thought, *we still have everything under control. But that could all change very quickly.*

CHAPTER 45

June 1, 2011
Western Sahara
8:03 am

The satellite phone rang when they were just outside Dakhla.

"Target's going ashore, south of the city, but on the side of the peninsula facing away from the sea, where Dakhla is located. The coast is flatter there. He's mooring at the point where the causeway leads across to the port terminal. Seems to be alone so far. Wait. He's leaving the boat and going to a building, a warehouse. Now he's gone inside. Crap! Now we can't see him."

"Maybe he has a car there," Ondragon said.

"Possible. There he is again! A vehicle's leaving the hall. A sand-colored Land Rover, old model, no license plate. It's heading toward town on Route du Port. Steiner, zoom in!" Kubicki fell silent and Ondragon listened intently. He heard the tapping of a computer keyboard and the murmuring of voices. Meanwhile, Achille was preparing to land at Dakhla airport, which was in the north of the city, several kilometers from Monsieur Noire's current location.

"Five minutes to touchdown," Ondragon said into the silence on the other end.

"Okay. Target is now in the city. He's continuing north."

"We've landed," Ondragon told him, "and we're heading for the parking position. I hope we can get through the controls without much delay!"

"Target turning right onto Boulevard Mohammed Bahnini."

"We're here. Get out now." Ondragon jumped out of the cockpit and saw that a jeep with soldiers was coming toward them, just like in Laâyoune. He indicated to Achille that he should handle it and pressed the phone to his ear again.

"Target is turning," he heard Kubicki say, "to the left this time. He's continuing north in your direction. Maybe he's going to the airport because he has a plane waiting there."

"We'll check it out." Ondragon watched as Achille showed one of the soldiers his fake Interpol ID. Morocco was affiliated with Interpol and would therefore have to give them safe passage. The BND was lucky to have hired him for this job, Ondragon thought; he was well prepared for something like this. Who knew how long the BND would have taken otherwise?

The soldier studied the ID card. Longer than usual. Then he gave it back and asked Achille a few questions that Ondragon couldn't understand because he was standing too far away. But the Frenchman responded with authoritative gestures. The soldier seemed to give it some thought and finally nodded. He indicated to Achille that they should follow him.

"Target is making another turn," Kubicki said over the phone, "right, onto Avenue Tinghir."

Ondragon let his eyes wander over the tarmac and the parking positions in front of the small terminal. The air above the hot sandy surface shimmered, conjuring up a mirage over the asphalt runway, but he couldn't see a small private plane standing by anywhere. There was not even a large passenger jet in this godforsaken place. Just a few vultures, circling.

"There is nothing to see at the airport," he relayed to Kubicki.

Achille came back and rubbed his nose. "They swallowed it," he said. "They want us to get in the jeep with them and they'll take us out."

"Target is stopping!"

Ondragon signaled to Achille to stop talking and listened to Kubicki.

"Target has left the car. He is going into a building. It's on the corner of Boulevard Bahia Aini and Avenue Tinghir. Across the street is an orphanage."

"Give me the coordinates!" As Ondragon spoke, he locked the Cessna carefully. He would need Achille on the hunt for Monsieur Noire and they would have to leave the plane behind and trust to luck. Hopefully, no one would tamper with it in their absence. He and the Frenchman walked over to the jeep with the soldiers, nodded to them in greeting, and got in. They drove off and Ondragon felt the wind glide pleasantly over his sweaty skin. He noted the coordinates Kubicki had given him and entered them into the GPS device. One of the soldiers watched him curiously, but Ondragon ignored him.

"Target is still in the building," Kubicki reported.

Ondragon activated the GPS unit's locator and looked at the digital map. "That's less than three kilometers from us," he replied. "We're on our way."

"Roger that. We'll keep you posted."

The soldiers dropped them off at a small side terminal for private passengers, where they were allowed to pass through the controls unmolested. Outside the airport building it was as empty as it had been on the tarmac out back. No cab for miles, not a soul to be seen, and in the middle of the day, at that! Ondragon sighed. Well then, they would just have to try Shanks's pony.

He hurried off, still with the phone to his ear. Achille followed him. The sun burned the tops of their heads and parched their throats after only a few minutes. Fine dust blew through the streets and settled on their tongues like a sticky film. Ondragon was soon out of breath, although he was actually in good shape. He remembered the First Rule of the Desert from his friend and former mentor, Roderick DeForce: "In the desert everything is worth half as much! Even a water pouch, because you need twice as much of it."

Since Kubicki was silent on the other end of the line, Ondragon assumed Monsieur Noire was still in the building in question. At a run, he followed the directions from the GPS. When he reached the street with the orphanage and the building with the old Land Rover parked outside, he stopped. Pressing himself against the wall of the house, he told Achille to stay back.

"Reached buildings," he relayed to Kubicki.

"Good. Target is still inside. At least, no one has left from visible exits. No idea if there are any secret routes inside."

"I'll take a look around." Ondragon eyed the building. It was a multistory concrete block with an open, flat roof and the rotten plaster typical of the region, with garlands of laundry on the balconies. It was obviously a housing complex for several families. The traffic on the street was moderate and the few passersby who were around were not interested in them. The house was at the end of a block, with only its north side directly bordering the next building. If there was a hidden entrance, that would be where it was. Ondragon ruled out an underground passage because of the nature of the terrain. As Porky Pig once said, "Never build your house on sand." Or was that Jesus? No matter.

He put a hand on the phone's microphone so Kubicki couldn't hear. "There are likely two entrances," he told Achille. "One we can see out here and the other is certainly on the other side, in the alley that runs along behind the building. Since we don't know which unit the guy is in, we'll have to work our way up from the bottom. Use the Interpol badge to get us in. I don't want monsieur to slip through our fingers. Clear so far?"

"Clear!"

Ondragon took his hand off the mic and informed Kubicki of his plan without giving details. He instructed the BND man to keep an eye on all entrances and the roof via satellite, and to call it in if the unknown man made a run for it. Kubicki agreed and remained on standby.

Ondragon attached the phone to his shirt with Velcro and drew his gun. Together with Achille, he ran over to the building and they entered it separately, one from the front and one from the back. As expected, both entrances converged in a stairwell. Such houses were utilitarian and usually built with as little expenditure as possible. They crept up to the apartments on the second floor. There were only four doors. Ondragon hoped the same was true of the other two floors. That way they only needed to check twelve units. Twelve units where everyone from Gaddafi to Popeye could be hiding. And, of course, their great unknown.

Ondragon pounded on the first door.

"Police! Ouvrez la porte!" shouted Achille, making as much noise as possible. Maybe they would startle Monsieur Noire and he would do them a favor and leave his hiding place early.

The door opened tentatively and a veiled woman looked out.

"Oui?" she asked, *"Mon mari n'est pas là. Qu'est-ce qu'il y a?"*

Achille showed his ID and pushed past her into the apartment with the words *avec votre permission.* Then, wordlessly, the Frenchman searched the three rooms, where two small children were squatting. The woman let him, looking anxious, while Ondragon waited in the doorway to watch the hallway.

"Clean!" exclaimed Achille, finally reappearing. He said goodbye gallantly and stepped out into the hallway. The door immediately closed behind him and they went to the next one. It was the same picture everywhere. Frightened women with children, or old people. Mostly too many people in too little space, but no Monsieur Noire.

In the meantime, there was a strange silence in the house, as if all the residents were in a state of rigor mortis. When they reached the top corridor, questioning faces were already looking out at them from two of the doors. Achille combed the apartments and Ondragon kept watch. He had positioned himself by the stairs to the roof, to block the escape route.

He felt a sudden warning prickling in his neck and instinctively threw himself to the side. At that same moment, he heard the characteristic pop of a gun with a silencer. Whining, the bullets smashed into the wall opposite the staircase and plaster clattered to the floor. Then Ondragon heard a door click and a bright light shone down on the stairs.

"Target fleeing over the roof!" he heard Kubicki shout through the phone on his shirt.

Ondragon got up and stormed up the steps to the roof. Carefully, he opened the door. Again, he heard gunshots. *Pop, pop.* Two holes burst open in the metal door above his head.

"Damn it!" he hissed into the phone. "Where is he?"

"He's on the neighbor's roof, running north. You can go after him now," Kubicki said.

Ondragon stepped onto the roof holding his gun, and looked around searchingly. Seeing no movement in his immediate vicinity, he ran in a crouch to the low wall that bordered the roof of the neighboring house and risked a look over. He saw the man fleeing across the rooftops.

Achille had now arrived. Ondragon told him to run down quickly and try to intercept the guy on the road, then rushed over the wall and took up the pursuit of the stranger, who already had a lead of about fifty meters and was jumping smoothly over the obstacles.

Ondragon did his best, but the guy was good. He was probably doing parkour or something. Despite this, he had few opportunities to get off the roof, because the block consisted of no more than six buildings and was isolated from the other buildings, so he would eventually be stopped by a precipice. Then he had only the stairways, or he would have to spread his wings.

No sooner had Ondragon had the thought than the guy disappeared.

"Target in the fourth building!" said Kubicki.

Alert, Ondragon walked to the spot and looked down into a black hole: an open staircase leading downward. He had two choices now. Either he followed the guy and risked being ambushed somewhere and shot at down there, or—ah, screw the second option! Ondragon ducked his head and stormed down the stairs with his gun at the ready. He paused for a few seconds in the first corridor to let his eyes adjust to the darkness. He heard hurried footsteps in the stairwell below. Monsieur Noire was moving extremely carelessly, making enough noise for ten! Quickly, Ondragon took up the chase, taking several stairs at once. In between, he kept pausing briefly, listening to the stairwell with bated breath. He heard a door being yanked open at the bottom, took the last two flights of stairs, and stopped, gasping for breath, behind a corner, to be sure his opponent wasn't waiting for him there. But the short corridor to the front door was empty. Without hesitation, Ondragon leaped out the door and looked around the street. It was also completely empty. Achille appeared in the distance; he had probably run around the block once and was now coming toward him.

"Where is he?" Ondragon asked Kubicki on the phone.

"I don't know," the latter replied. "We haven't seen anyone leave the building!"

"Shit!" Ondragon signaled to Achille to turn around and ran back into the building himself. As quietly as possible, he entered the stairwell and waited for a noise to indicate where the guy was hiding. Monsieur Noire was playing cat and mouse with them, crisscrossing through the block. But Ondragon was at least as good at this game.

Like a hunting dog picking up a scent, he stalked the lowest hallway, sniffing into all the nooks and crannies. He assumed the guy hadn't fled upstairs. He had already used the roof and discovered that it wasn't a good escape option. If he was in the building, it was down here in one of these four apartments.

Ondragon crept to the first door, cautiously put his ear to the wood, and tried to feel for vibrations with his fingertips. But all his sixth sense perceived was busy everyday life behind the door. The clattering of pots in the kitchen and children squawking in the living room. He went to the next door. Here was the absolute silence of an empty apartment. No one was at home. Behind the third, an Arabic docu-soap was playing on TV, and behind the last, a woman was talking loudly. She was laughing, probably talking on the phone with a friend. Ondragon frowned and finally returned to the door with the silence. Again, he put an ear to it. The silence sounded piercing, almost suffocating and charged with energy. There was a tingling under his fingertips. He eased away from the door, raised his weapon, and took a step back.

I'm home! he thought with some glee, and fired at the door. The lock shattered and with a single kick the door was open. In the style of the best special forces raid, Ondragon ran through the apartment, checking every room. In the living room he found a woman cowering on the floor, trembling with fear. He spotted movement on the balcony out of the corner of his eye and shot through the window without hesitation. Glass shattered and a scream rang out. A shadow fell into the depths. Ondragon rushed to the balcony and peered over the parapet. About ten feet below, the guy was lying face down on the asphalt, moaning. Blood was running from a wound on his back. He had dropped his gun; it was lying in the street a few steps away from him. Achille was standing next to him, pointing his pistol at him. It was stupid to play cat and mouse with two cats.

With a triumphant grin, Ondragon pushed back from the balcony railing and ran down to the street. There he bent over the guy and turned him around. His initial elation stuck abruptly in his throat when he realized who they had there. It was not Monsieur Noire, but merely a young man who looked a hell of a lot like him!

Enraged, Ondragon rose and kicked the guy in his wounded back. Ignoring the man's cries of pain, he then snatched the satellite phone from the Velcro and tried to talk to Kubicki, but the connection was broken. Cursing, he dialed the number.

"What is it? Isn't that the guy?" asked Achille uncomprehendingly. Ondragon raised a hand to silence him.

When Kubicki picked up, his anger finally found an outlet. "You idiot! You've been chasing the wrong guy all along! Son of a bitch! This is just a decoy!" Ondragon didn't care what the BND agent thought of him. He had no desire to work with this amateur anymore!

"A decoy? What?" Kubicki sounded surprised. "But . . ."

"What about the boat? Is our man still there?"

"No, there's no one there," Kubicki stammered. "We've been watching it the whole time. The target was always alone—he got off the tanker alone, and he went ashore alone."

"Then the whole thing is a red herring, and he was either hidden in the boat and swam ashore earlier, or he switched places with the decoy here in the building."

"The second may be the case; we have no evidence for the first at all. We monitored everything completely. He can't have swum either. That would be outright suicide. The coast is a continuous cliff for thirty kilometers, with a dangerous current. Besides, we haven't seen anyone. And no fishing boat that could have picked him up."

"Then he must still be here in the building." Ondragon heard the sound of an approaching siren. Someone must have alerted the police about the gunshots in the block. "Damn it! We've got to get out of here, the cops are moving in. Keep an eye on the building via satellite, Kubicki. I want to be notified of any activity." He ended the call and put the phone away. The wailing sirens grew louder.

"What do we do with him?" asked Achille, nudging the injured man with the tip of his foot.

Ondragon bent down and rummaged in the pocket of the guy, who was writhing in pain. When he pulled them out again, he was holding the Land Rover keys. "We'll take him in and question him a little!"

A smile flitted across Achille's lips. "You mean an Arab interrogation, Chief?"

Ondragon nodded grimly.

"Fine," the Frenchman replied, grabbing the man roughly under the armpits and dragging him to the vehicle.

CHAPTER 46

Clandestin steered the off-road vehicle over the sandy track, heading east. The moon had already risen there, a white disk above the horizon, although it would still be some time before sunset. In the rearview mirror he saw the cloud of dust he was leaving behind him like a signal flag. From the air, it would be hard to miss. But it didn't matter at the moment. The German was still busy in Dakhla and it was not certain he would even be able to pick up the trail, or whether he would even know where to.

Clandestin dodged a rock and steered the vehicle back onto the narrow strip of road, which was only recognizable by a few tire tracks. But even they would be blown away by the wind in a few hours. And once night fell, he would be completely invisible. In the desert, everything worked in his favor.

Clandestin opened the window a tiny crack and breathed in the smell of the desert. The fresh note of loose quartz sand, the metallic aroma of the desert varnish on the weathered stones, and of course the bewitching scent of water when you approached a guelta or an oasis. Clandestin could literally smell water. In this he was as unerring as a dromedary. A smile spread across his lips. By tomorrow night, he would have completed his mission . . . if all went well. He would spend the night in the desert and in the morning Masut would pick him up by plane.

He rolled the window back up and focused on the track. The sun's light gradually turned to liquid bronze, casting an otherworldly glow over the distant hills. He dodged another rock that lay in the sand like a severed head, and his thoughts inevitably returned to the German. Mr. Big would give Achmed quite a run for his money, he suspected. But Achmed was one of them. He would sacrifice himself for them if he had to. He had bent to Yaqub's will. They all bent to Yaqub's will. For Yaqub was a wise man and knew what fate had in store for them. And the destiny of Achmed was to sacrifice himself for his brothers. The Creator would welcome him with open arms.

CHAPTER 47

June 1, 2011
Dakhla, Western Sahara
5:40 p.m.

Achille kicked the man in the side until he woke up again. The prisoner was barely whimpering—he had no more strength for it—and stared at them blankly. His face was puffy from the Arab interrogation and snot and blood were running from his nose.

They had taken the guy out into the desert, looking for somewhere quiet, which hadn't been hard, because this land was deserted. Withered and flat like a fried egg . . . like a burned fried egg.

"I'm going to ask you one last time: Who do you work for?" asked Ondragon in Arabic.

"My name is Achmed and I serve the Creator alone."

He had been repeating this sentence for an hour now. Unfortunately, it was the only thing they had gotten out of him, despite the agony they had caused him. The guy was tough, that was for sure. Ondragon remembered his last torture session. Back in New Orleans, it had been a DeForce mailman he'd taken to task. Sometimes you had to do what you had to do.

"You heard my boss," Achille purred softly. "He wants to know who your client is. Are you also part of Groupe Hexagone? Who is your accomplice and where is he? Well?"

"My name is Achmed and I serve the Creator alone," the guy whispered.

"*Fils de pute!* What does this tattoo mean?" Achille angrily rammed his fist into the pit of the prisoner's stomach, eliciting a loud cry. On his neck was a small cross whose resemblance to Monsieur Noire's tattoo was unmistakable. It seemed as if the great unknown was leaving indirect traces through this symbol, like a scavenger hunt.

"Well, what is it? I'm waiting!" said Achille, looking into the prisoner's dull pupils.

"My name is Achmed and I serve the Creator alone."

* * *

Annoyed, Achille looked up. "Damn it, Chief, it would have been better if we had tried a truth serum."

"You know I don't work with that kind of stuff," Ondragon countered. "It's unpredictable, and you never know if they're lying. Besides, I've found that threatening to remove a body part is much more effective."

"Well, let's finally cut something off him! Or I'll poke his eye out with this! What do you think of that?" The Frenchman raised the rusty screwdriver they had found while searching the Land Rover, but Ondragon held him back.

"No, Achille, I want to try this again." He bent over the prisoner, but before he could force him to look him in the eye, the satellite phone rang.

Cursing, Ondragon let go of the guy and, turning his back to Achille, snapped into the phone, "What is it?"

"Kubicki here. Unfortunately, there is still no news from the building surveillance. Where the hell are you? It'll be dark soon and then the guy will slip through our fingers!"

"We're interviewing his accomplice right now."

"And?"

"He's tight-lipped."

"Torture him!"

"Already have. He won't say anything!"

"Then threaten to kill him. That always works."

Ondragon ground his jaw irritably. Kubicki's smart-ass attitude was really getting on his nerves. He should come here himself and beat the shit out of the guy. But that's how they were, the fine gentlemen of the secret service, always giving orders and never getting their own hands dirty. Ondragon was just about to give the BND man an appropriate answer when suddenly a shrill scream sounded behind him. Startled, he whirled around and stared in bewilderment at the Frenchman, who had drilled the screwdriver into Achmed's bullet wound and was digging around in it with a diabolical grin. Blood gushed out and suddenly Ondragon felt sick.

"Man, Achille!" he shouted, leaping toward the Frenchman. "Have you gone insane? Stop that at once!" He grabbed him by the collar and dragged him away from the prisoner, who was screaming like a banshee.

"But, Chief, everything else was useless. I was sure he would blab!"

"But he didn't, did he! Hell, what's gotten into you?" Ondragon glanced at Achmed, who had stopped screaming. His head was lying on its side and his eyes were open. Had he passed out? His blood was everywhere. On his clothes, in the sand, even on Achille's pants. The Frenchman must have hit an artery. What a mess! "Damn it, Achille! If you disobey my orders one more time, you're fired! Do you understand?"

"*Oui, oui, bien compris,*" Achille said, tossing the bloody screwdriver away.

Ondragon bent down and felt for the wounded man's pulse. His lips pressed together, he rose. "He won't say anything more. He's dead," he stated, looking reproachfully over at the Frenchman. "You've done a great job! Now we have no more cards to play! He was our only link."

"Sorry, Chief." Achille looked guilty.

Ondragon sighed and looked around. "We can't just leave him lying here. I don't want the vultures to get him." He went to the Land Rover and took out the folding spade they had found there. He tossed it to Achille. "You dig a hole for him. But hurry!"

The Frenchman caught the spade and while he dug grimly in the desert sand, Ondragon stared at the flat horizon, behind which the sun was setting at that moment, glaring red. *Now we will indeed have to search the haystack*, he thought resignedly.

Without exchanging a word, they drove back to the city. As they headed through the desert, Ondragon picked up the conversation with Kubicki that he had broken off, telling him about the loss of their prisoner. Fortunately, the BND agent did not comment.

"The unknown man is still invisible," he said instead. "No one suspicious has left the building yet."

"Then we've lost him! At least we will have by the time it's completely dark; he'll be impossible to spot, if he's ever even been in that building!" Ondragon took a deep breath to calm himself. They could have done with a lot more people for this operation, not a Big Brother figure watching from space but otherwise incapable of helping. "Has anything else happened at the port or on the ship?" he asked Kubicki.

"No. And there hasn't been much movement on the airfield either. No idea where the guy is hiding."

Ondragon did not know what annoyed him more: the failure of the BND, the rash actions of Achilles, or the cunning of Monsieur Noire, who had set him up again. "Stay on the building anyway. Maybe something will go down there," he said to the BND agent, ending the conversation.

After that, he put his hands in his lap and plunged into the darkness of his thoughts.

When they reached Dakhla, the traffic was unusually busy. It seemed as if the city had awakened from its rigor mortis as the sun's glow had been extinguished. Achille maneuvered the Land Rover through the flood of cars to the airport and simply left the car by the roadside.

At the hangar, they first checked to see if the Cessna had been opened and searched. But the locks on the doors were untouched and the load was still intact. They had probably taken the police ID seriously and kept their hands off what they assumed was Interpol property.

Exhausted, Ondragon and Achille climbed into the cockpit, sat back, and considered how to proceed. They were literally high and dry.

"What are our options?" asked Achille. He now sounded as frustrated as Ondragon felt.

"Besides a presumably fruitless nighttime stakeout of the building and some pointless poking around in the desert, really only one."

Achille turned his head and looked at him questioningly.

But instead of answering, Ondragon dug out his cell phone and dialed a number.

"Hey, Truthfinder, any news? We could really use a little cheering up right now."

"Um, yeah, I'm still at it, Mr. O. I don't know either, but I can't crack this fucking code!"

"Keep trying! And let us know right away if you have anything, no matter what time it is. Got it?" Ondragon hung up before Truthfinder could say anything else, and irritably took his notepad out of his pocket. He showed Achille the number boxes, the cross tattoo, and the Sator Square. The Frenchman took the pad and looked thoughtfully at the notes.

"Hmm, the tattoo of this Achmed and the unknown actually are identical. But I've never seen this one before." He pointed to the number boxes. "And this is what this scientist did before the plane crashed?"

Ondragon nodded and rubbed his eyes tiredly. "Dr. Schuch didn't have much time, but the code is still tricky."

"Hmm," Achille said again, staring at the numbers. "May I?" he finally asked, holding up a pen.

"Please, don't feel you have to. I've been racking my brains and so has my physics genius, but if you find something, that would be goddamn great." Ondragon laid his head back against the seat and closed his eyes. He had a feeling that Mr. Unknown was a long way off. The bubble had burst, his motivation was failing. A little nap would clear his head. Ondragon felt his limbs grow heavy and sleep overtook him like a predator.

He woke up. Something was poking him in the shoulder. It was Achille and his pen. The Frenchman looked at him with tired eyes. Ondragon sat up and looked at the clock. Half past two in the morning. It was time Achille got a well-earned rest.

"So did you get anything from it?" he asked without much hope.

Achille shook his head and handed the pad back to him. Ondragon glanced at his efforts and his eyes widened in surprise. What had his French secret weapon been drawing? He clutched the pad with both hands and stared at the scribble.

"Achille!" he finally exclaimed. "You . . . you're brilliant!"

The Frenchman gave a start. "Really?" He scratched his head. "I was just trying out a few things. And because you said this Dr. Schuch was German and a Nazi, I played around with swastikas a bit . . ."

"Yeah, but that's genius!" repeated Ondragon enthusiastically, slapping his hand on the drawing. "I bet that's the solution!" He picked up the cell phone and called Truthfinder.

"What is it?" the young physicist asked, audibly irritated.

"I've got something!" said Ondragon excitedly. "Take the number squares and put a swastika over them. Could the numbers inside the cross tell us something?" He heard typing noises and Truthfinder muttering something to himself on the other end. And then a gasp of astonishment.

"What is it?" asked Ondragon, strained to breaking point.

"Awesome, Mr. O!" Truthfinder's Mickey Mouse voice reached an unimaginably high frequency and Ondragon had to hold the cell phone away from his ear slightly.

"I think we got it!" Achille could now hear the screeching from the phone as well. "That's it! That's it! Wow . . . just awesome!"

"Now tell me, what is it?" urged Ondragon.

"The squares, I mean, the numbers in the swastika, if you make a checksum from them, they each make a number. And if you read those in sequence with the others . . . wait, I'll change something else." Ondragon heard the typing again.

"Eureka, Mr. O! We've done it! We cracked the code!"

Ondragon rolled his eyes. "Hello, Earth to Truthfinder! Tell me already, damn you!" He shouted into the mouthpiece to bring the teenager down from his euphoria.

"Oh yeah, sorry. So . . ." Truthfinder exhaled and inhaled noisily, then said a little more calmly, "They're coordinates!"

"Right, then. What are they?" Ondragon placed the pen on a clean page of his notepad.

"Twenty-five degrees, twelve minutes, and eight seconds North, and twelve degrees, eleven minutes, and twenty-one seconds West!"

Ondragon noted the numbers and asked, "Where is that? Can you look it up on your computer? It's faster than putting it into the GPS and it'll also save our batteries." He gestured to Achille to hand him the map of Western Sahara, unfolded it, and ran his finger along the meridians. Achille held up the lamp so they could see better.

"Well, that's in the middle of the desert," Truthfinder said. "About two hundred and fifty kilometers east of the coast. There's a tiny oasis nearby. It's called Guelta Raa'd. The target is in a sand basin south of the mountains. On the satellite image, it looks like dunes."

Ondragon found the spot and marked it.

"This is rebel territory," Achille said.

"Is that good or bad?"

Achille shrugged. Ondragon mentally calculated how long it would take them to get there. The flight would take less than two hours. That was good. Their invisible opponent couldn't be any faster.

"Man, Mr. O!" reported Truthfinder over the phone. "That's unreal! How did you come up with that?"

"It wasn't me," Ondragon admitted, "it was a friend of mine."

"Then tell your friend he's a genius!"

The corners of Ondragon's mouth twitched. "Did you hear that, Achille? You're a genius, even though I did want to smash your face in earlier!"

"Mon Dieu." The Frenchman raised an eyebrow.

"What are you going to do now?" asked the young physicist. He still sounded totally overexcited and his pubescent body had released so many endorphins, he would likely not get a wink of sleep.

"Well, we'll fly there," Ondragon said casually.

"Madness! You know what? You're a real mythbuster! Let me know when you find something? Yes? Please!"

"I'll do that. And thank you for your help, Truthfinder. I owe you one."

"No big deal. Working with you was a lot of fun, and you can forget the reward. I've had a real, genuine adventure. That's priceless!"

Ondragon smirked at a physics nerd's idea of an adventure, sitting in his chair in front of his computer at home. "Okay I've got to call it a night. Speak soon."

"Yo, Mr. O! And find Tesla's wonder machine! Maybe it'll be a second Wardenclyffe Tower!"

"A what?"

"Tesla's transmission tower. He had it built in 1901, on Long Island. It was supposed to transmit energy wirelessly, but it was torn down before it was completed. Some people claim it was a free-energy converter."

"And what did it look like?"

"Look on the internet under 'Wardenclyffe,' and you'll see it."

"Okay, thanks." Ondragon hung up and did as Truthfinder had suggested. When the image of the tower opened, realization hit him like a bolt of lightning.

"Oh my goodness! Of course! Now I know why it's called that!" he groaned with glee. "I've solved the puzzle!"

"*Pardon?* Which puzzle do you mean, Chief?" asked Achille, looking at him uncomprehendingly.

"Well, I now know why the Nazi secret project was called The Bell!"

"You do?"

"Yes. Look here!" Ondragon showed Achille the Tesla tower. It had a bell-shaped dome made of copper. Above it was written WORLDWIRELESS, in crooked lettering. "That's why! It's the shape of the dome. It must have looked like an alien aircraft at the time. A UFO. And some people then invented a UFO theory from that."

"*Bien*, and how does your enlightenment help us now?"

"Achille, we now know what we're looking for!"

"Oh, that's helpful," the Frenchman replied cynically.

Ondragon grimaced. "Don't you get it? That was what was on the plane!" He pointed to the picture. "For sure."

"This tower?"

"No, much more than that!" replied Ondragon with a grin. "Tesla's world system!"

CHAPTER 48

August 26, 1899
Colorado Springs
noon

Two days later, a courier drove up in a carriage. The coachman seemed very bad-tempered, but the fact that he had driven out to the laboratory despite his fear could only mean that the courier had offered him a princely fee. Philemon and Löwenstein helped the messenger unload a large wooden crate marked CAUTION FRAGILE! and carried it into the laboratory. Afterward, the man spoke briefly with Dr. Tesla, secured a written receipt that the shipment had been received, and boarded the carriage. With that, he took his leave and hurriedly drove off.

Philemon looked at the box curiously. Were those the special components the doctor had spoken of in the conversation he had overheard? He looked over at Dr. Tesla, anxiously expecting to be sent away again, but to his surprise he was allowed to witness the opening of the box. He watched attentively as Löwenstein took a large screwdriver and pried open the lid. The crate was filled with sawdust. Carefully, Löwenstein rummaged around inside, revealing a dozen boxes, each the length of an arm. He blew away the shavings and reverently lined up the boxes side by side on the floor. He then left it to the doctor to open them. Tesla lifted one of the boxes and pulled off the lid. Philemon craned his neck to see what was inside. He spotted a glass cylinder on a bed of absorbent cotton. It was twice the size of a conventional wine bottle. The doctor took out the cylinder and turned it back and forth in front of the light.

"An excellent job," he said, and passed the cylinder to Löwenstein, who also examined it thoroughly. When the strange object finally reached Philemon, it almost slipped from his fingers, he was so nervous. He caught it just in time and felt the adrenaline bubble hotly in his limbs.

"Careful, Mr. Ailey! These components are worth a fortune!" said Löwenstein reprovingly. Philemon blushed. He looked cautiously at the mysterious object. It consisted of a hand-blown glass cylinder and a base from which protruded several polished contacts. The inside was filled with a fantastic jumble of wires, grids, metal plates, and even smaller glass tubes.

"Looks a little like a big light bulb," he finally stated.

Tesla laughed softly. "Indeed. But my design here is inspired rather by Professor Lenard's high-frequency ray tubes and Sir William Crooke's Maltese cross tubes. I have developed their inventions for my own purposes, and I am calling my objects simply cathode ray tubes until I can think of something better. Do you see those little pins and the metal mesh inside?"

Philemon nodded. "And what do you propose to do with them?"

"Well, for our experiments it is essential that we are able to modulate frequencies precisely. Our oscillators are too imprecise and far too inert in the ranges we are now exploring. These tubes respond at lightning speed; all you have to do is increase or decrease the voltage. So now let's insert the tubes into the apparatus." Tesla pointed to the brass cabinet on the back wall of the lab. It was several meters long, and Philemon had previously assumed it was part of the oscillator. Löwenstein pulled out a bunch of keys and opened the various padlocks attached to it. Then he pulled open the doors, and Philemon's eyes widened as he saw that behind them a row of tubes had already been installed. He was even more surprised, however, when he saw the large clock embedded in the base with the tubes.

Was this another mystery that was being revealed to him? Was this finally the hoped-for initiation of which the doctor had spoken, or only a test? Another step along the stony path of establishing his trustworthiness? Whatever the case, Philemon thought, at least he now knew why the cabinet had always been locked. No one was supposed to see the tubes and the secret heart of the lab. Suddenly, Myers's sketch came to mind. It too had shown an oblong box with a series of numbered circles. Were the circles perhaps the tubes? And the dial the clock? Viewed from above, the sketch could well represent this cabinet-like apparatus.

While Philemon was still thinking about it, the other two assistants carefully removed the old tubes from the sockets and inserted the new ones in their place, Tesla insisting on a certain order, which made no discernible sense to Philemon. Then they closed the cabinet again and wiped their hands. The old tubes disappeared into the boxes and the boxes into the wooden case, which Löwenstein carefully nailed shut again. Then he and Czito dragged the box into Tesla's chamber and spread an oilcloth over it.

What a pity, Philemon thought angrily. Now it would be difficult to get to it. He would have liked to take a closer look at those tubes. But now he would once more have to be patient and wait for a suitable opportunity. It was about as likely as him taking a look at the notebook the doctor carried with him day and night.

CHAPTER 49

June 2, 2011
Western Sahara
just before sunrise

Barely discernible, the expanse of the Saharan night slid by beneath them. Although it was pitch dark, Ondragon gazed steadily out the side window of the cockpit. They had taken off long before dawn, and he could only hope this might allow them to elude the satellite-based eyes of the BND. He had a bad feeling about the BND. Something told him that it was better to disappear and go undercover from now on.

Despite his lack of sleep, Achille had insisted on wearing the imaginary pilot's cap and was steering the aircraft eastward, following the coordinates on the GPS device. Deeper and deeper they flew into the vastness of this seemingly endless sandbox. Soon the sun would rise and the Guelta Raa'd would come into view. The guelta was a special kind of oasis: a natural cistern in the rock, filled with water. It was known that people had settled there temporarily, but for centuries the rocky guelta had been used mainly by passing nomads. In this case, by the Sahrawi tribe, because they were located behind the border wall that marked Moroccan-occupied territory. Achille didn't know whether there were Popular Front rebels there, but he was confident he could avoid a confrontation with them.

Ondragon glanced at his cell phone. To avoid being tracked, he had taken out the SIM card—they had no reception here anyway. The only connection they now had to the outside world was the aircraft radio, which was also switched off, and the satellite phone, which could not be tracked. Ondragon ran through the equipment again in his mind. They had enough fuel for the return flight and enough water and supplies for two weeks. Before they had taken off from Dakhla, he had even thought to let Charlize and his Middle East associate Dietmar Hegenbarth know, because the second of DeForce's admonitions was: "You only need two people. But you have to trust them implicitly. Always tell them what you're doing! This is especially true when you go into the desert."

Ondragon smiled; the rules for predominantly arid operational areas were still so clear in his mind. Yet it had been fifteen years since he had worked for DeForce and had been a mailman himself. But Roderick DeForce had drilled them into him down to the last period. The desert was an extreme place and had to be paid extreme respect—that was rule number three!

Ondragon tore himself away from his memories of DeForce Deliveries and opened the notepad. Once he had explained to Achille that of course the entire tower had not been in the Junkers' cargo hold, only parts of it, the Frenchman had understood. But even the dome would have been too large to transport in the plane, and Ondragon therefore believed General Kammler and the four scientists had taken only the associated technical equipment out of the country. The guts of the tower, so to speak, made of circuits and coils. And the tower in Ludwigsdorf had been destroyed by Kammler for two reasons. First, so that it would not fall into the hands of the enemy, and second, because he knew that there was another somewhere else.

Namely here in the desert!

This had been the Nazis' secret research station. A second Tesla tower! The reception terminal for the first tower in Silesia. It was the realization of Tesla's dream: a system that guaranteed free energy and communication for everyone. Except that the Nazis had a different purpose for it than to give it as a gift to all mankind. And even today, the world system would be a real nightmare for any energy company. No wonder Tesla had been prevented from working on the invention back then, and no wonder Groupe Hexagone was so keen on these devices. It would be the key to a new age. Clean energy for zero cents! That would attract the attention of any energy supplier, though not in a positive way. The energy business was dirty, and it was going to stay that way, because dirty made more money. Hexagone would lock away the key to a better future, or even destroy it completely, so that it would never fall into the hands of anyone who knew what to do with it. The same was true of the BND. It was obvious what the German secret service intended to do with Tesla's invention. They wanted to finish what the Nazis had failed to do. But with what aim? For Ondragon it was clear that it could not be good. After all, intelligence agencies almost never had noble intentions. They were organizations whose daily bread was deceit and fraud.

He slammed the notepad shut. He knew he would still have to choose a side once he found the thing and took out his adversary. He looked outside, where dark rock formations were appearing in the sand in the first light of day. The Guelta Raa'd had to be down there somewhere. The highest point in the landscape was just seven hundred meters and the few rocks beneath them were a joke. Only they couldn't land between them, so first they had to find a suitable runway. Next to him, Achille kept looking alternately from the GPS to the compass and out the side window.

"We'll be right there!" he said over his headset, and Ondragon nodded.

A little later they flew over the guelta and made several circles over it to survey the territory. There were one or two mud huts and tents down there, and even a few hardy trees. Countless dromedaries and goats crowded around the waterhole, which stared into the sky like a black eye. A handful of people noticed the plane and looked up at them. Sahrawi rebels? Some of them waved. No one fired at them. The oasis seemed a peaceful place. They turned and flew over the ridge, behind which a wide sand basin opened up. Majestic dunes undulated like a yellow sea.

"Six kilometers to the destination and from there it's only fifteen to the border with Mauritania."

"Okay, then we should make sure we don't overshoot it too much. Things could get tricky otherwise."

"Indeed. I get on very well with the Sahrawis, but it's best not to tangle with the Tuareg.

"Seems like an explosive region."

The Frenchman nodded and flew over the dunes, some of which towered up to two hundred meters, forming harmonious wave patterns.

"It should be over there." Achille slowed down and pointed downward.

"There?" asked Ondragon incredulously. "But there's nothing!"

"*Sacré bleu* . . . I don't know either, but the GPS is telling us we've reached our destination."

"Well, that's just great! And you can't land here either!" Ondragon stared at the mountains of sand below.

"Maybe the tower has been swallowed by the dunes," suggested Achille.

"Or the coordinates are wrong!"

"I see a flat area over there where we could land." Achille pointed to a larger area that was free of dunes.

"Mark the spot," replied Ondragon "Before we land, we'll fly a few laps around the target; maybe we'll find something somewhere else."

"Roger." Achille put the Cessna into a gentle turn, and they flew several loops over the sea of dunes. But nothing caught their eye: no irregularities in the natural regularity of the dunes, no remains of buildings or other evidence of human presence, not even animal tracks. The desert was desolate and empty. Wresting the secret from it would be more difficult than he had expected.

Fifteen minutes later, Ondragon realized that there was no point in continuing to circle. They would land at the spot Achille had chosen and set up camp there. Thanks to the aerial reconnaissance, they at least knew that there was not a soul for miles. And if there really was a treasure hidden down there, they had it all to themselves.

After Achille had set the bird down as lightly as a feather and decelerated abruptly because the runway was quite short, he turned off the engine and the propeller came to a halt with a stutter. Immediately, the silence of the desert descended upon them. All that could be heard was the crackling of the hot engine and the whispering of the eternal wind. From the shelter of the cockpit, Ondragon gazed out at the dunes, which, now that they had a worm's-eye view, rose into the sky like sharp-edged silhouettes. He nibbled pensively on his dry lower lip. The mere sight of the sand mountains sent his body into a state of thirst. But Ondragon knew how to control himself; after all, the desert was his second-favorite working environment after the concrete wasteland of the city.

He exchanged a glance with Achille and they got out. In the shadow of the plane's wings, they contemplated their surroundings and finally set about making camp.

They had erected the tent, or rather a functional shelter made of light cotton sheets, within a few minutes. Satisfied, Ondragon noticed that Achille's every move was perfect. The man was as used to camping in the desert as he was. Ondragon stretched his back and inhaled the hot air through his nose. Forty degrees in the shade and a wind like a hot air blower. Could there be any better weather?

Next, they stowed half of their supplies and equipment in the tent. The rest stayed on the plane in case they had to drop everything and haul ass. Finally, they assembled the Snake Scooter. This was a solar-powered ultralight buggy, a NASA reject Ondragon had bought from the agency a few years back. The vehicle was unsuitable for the moon because it was too light, but it was worth its weight in gold in the desert. It would serve well as a camel substitute.

Ondragon seized the opportunity to take the Snake for a test drive. He drove up to the nearest dune and stopped on the crest to scan the surrounding area with binoculars. To the east and south lay a wide-open expanse: a reassuring, flat nothingness where an approaching enemy would be immediately apparent. On the other hand, the situation to the west and north was different. Behind the humps of the dunes were the dark rocks of the guelta. There was water there, and people. The enemy would almost certainly approach from that direction. Ondragon got back into the Snake and returned to Achille, who in the meantime had prepared a small meal.

"What's to see?" he asked after Ondragon had grabbed a sandwich and taken a hearty bite.

"Sand," he answered with his mouth full. A few grains crunched between his teeth. Already the sand was everywhere. In an hour at most, it would be in the most impossible places. For this reason, Achille had covered the hood and propeller of the Cessna with a waxed canvas to protect against the inevitable sand, which trickled steadily into everything.

After Ondragon had fortified himself, he described the arrangements to Achille. They would work in two shifts. One would keep a lookout and the other would go in search of the tower. And the same at night. They would keep in touch with each other via radios.

Ondragon headed out first. He took the map, the GPS, and enough water with him. He attached the metal detector to the Snake so that it would inform him of anything underground as he drove. If the tower was modeled after Tesla's Wardenclyffe Tower, it would be at least forty-five meters long. Maybe it was peeking out of the sand at a spot they hadn't been able to see from the plane.

"Do you think it's still standing, the tower?" mused Achille.

"I hope so. Because otherwise we'll still be searching here long after humans have colonized Mars!"

Achille smiled wryly.

"Well, then. *Bonne chance!*"

"*Merci.*" Ondragon sat down in the Snake, pushed the fabric of the turban over of his face, and drove off, waving.

CHAPTER 50

September 12, 1899
Colorado Springs
afternoon

In the past weeks, they had repeated the experiment every damn day—except Sundays, of course. Again and again, they had set up the terminal in the morning and taken it down in the evening, sometimes in the sunshine, sometimes in the rain. But Philemon had never been permitted to climb into the terminal; it was always the other two who took part in the experiment. Even the doctor had climbed into the tube several times in order, as he had said, to finally try out the experiment on his own body.

So much for the supposed initiation, Philemon thought glumly. On the contrary, things were even worse than before, because since that day when the doctor had shown him the cabinet with the tubes, Tesla and his two cronies were more secretive than ever. The doctor monitored every experiment meticulously and then disappeared without a word into his chamber, where he stayed all night. Only very rarely did he make an appearance at the hotel.

It will certainly be the same today, Philemon thought. But perhaps that was just as well, because it suited what he had in mind. As so often before, he stood at the main switch of the large transformer and waited for the signal from Löwenstein. Dr. Tesla had retreated to his observation post at the open door and was gazing out with a fixed expression, with Pikes Peak like a gray giant in the distance. Philemon felt himself sweating, but that was more due to the hot, muggy air that hung over the prairie than to his fear, which he had long since shed. This was now the twelfth or thirteenth repetition of the experiment and it had become routine. On each run, they shot energy in the form of Tesla's specially modulated scalar waves from the laboratory to Pikes Peak, and each time the instruments apparently recorded everything. Philemon still had not seen the recordings. For some reason, Tesla and the others were keeping them from him.

For today's experiment, Czito had personally gone up the mountain to monitor it from up there and then immediately bring the recordings back with him. Philemon did not believe Tesla had any doubts about the precision of the instruments there. He just wanted to make sure that the results remained secret. The doctor had seemed sad in recent days, somehow, as if a cloud of sorrow had crept over his ever-sparkling mind.

Philemon saw Löwenstein looking at the chronometer they used in the laboratory to measure time, and shortly afterward the German raised his hand. So it had to be almost twelve o'clock; the time agreed upon with Czito. Their eyes met, Löwenstein nodded, and lowered his hand. With a determined jerk, Philemon closed the switch. Darkness fell in the laboratory and lightning began to flash across the room from the tip of the coil. But Philemon had long since grown accustomed even to this. He could hardly hear the thunder and crashing through the cotton plugs in his ears. Instead, he thought he could clearly feel the rhythmic pulsation of the scalar waves on the front of his body. It felt as if he were standing in the sea and the waves were lapping against his chest, powerful and penetrating at the same time. At this frequency, scalar waves were completely harmless, Dr. Tesla had explained. They even had a beneficial effect on well-being and he was thinking of developing a medical apparatus for the treatment of various physical ailments. This had briefly caused amusement among the other two assistants. Löwenstein and Czito probably still vividly remembered the whimsical effects of Tesla's sleeping apparatus.

Löwenstein's hand rose and Philemon opened the switch. The light came on and the noise died away. Dr. Tesla's expression was unchanged. He did not even blink. He was probably already going over in his mind what he would later record in his study.

"Gentlemen, I'm going to the terminal now. Löwenstein, do everything as I have explained it to you!"

"Yes indeed, Doctor!" exclaimed the German.

Philemon watched as Tesla marched outside and crawled into the terminal. As the small door closed behind him, he looked over at Löwenstein. The German engineer's hand lowered, and calmly, Philemon closed the circuit. After all, this was not the first time that the doctor had participated personally in the experiment, and nothing had ever happened before. At least not since he had been involved.

Philemon waited like an old hand while the lightning flashed through the lab and the scalar waves rippled through his body. Then Löwenstein's hand lifted again and he cut the power. Immediately, his eyes darted over to the terminal, and his heartbeat quickened as nothing stirred. But then the door opened and Dr. Tesla came out. Reassured, Philemon saw him stretch his long limbs and come sauntering over to them. He seemed to be in a much better mood than before and winked merrily at Philemon as he walked past him into the lab.

"Enough for today!" he shouted, and Philemon pulled the plugs from his ears. "We'll break off here. You can dismantle the apparatus." Then he disappeared into his chamber.

Philemon helped Löwenstein dismantle the terminal. Again and again, he cast a furtive glance at the German. Should he ask him about it now? He was uncertain. Two days ago, he had received an answer to his telegram, and he could hardly wait to confront Löwenstein with it. What his friend in New York had found out about the Röhnfeldt experiment after some research was extremely disturbing, and he absolutely had to talk to someone about it.

They dragged the large copper tube into the laboratory and covered it with the oilcloth. Löwenstein also looked as if he was under great strain. He was not very talkative, which was unusual. Philemon wondered if something had happened that he didn't know about. Had the problem with Myers intensified? Or perhaps it had to do with the records from the gauges on the mountain, the ones that had been withheld from him? Philemon suppressed a sigh and went over to help Löwenstein deactivate the capacitors. He would never find out unless he mastered himself and asked the German about it. They pulled the wire clips off the contacts and put them carefully aside. No current could flow between the capacitors and batteries. At best, the batteries would be dead the next day, but at worst, there would be a spark and the laboratory would burn down.

When they had finished cleaning up, they pulled off their rubber gloves and washed in the rain barrel outside the building. Then they returned to the lab, where they sat down at a table and drank cola. They had sunk the bottles into the rain barrel to cool. Löwenstein grinned and toasted with Philemon. They made satisfied noises as they set the bottles down again.

"A real tasty swill you Americans have invented there!" said Löwenstein, leaning back in his chair. "Well, let's wait for good, old Czito. I'm curious to see how fast he can make it here on his short, stubby legs."

Philemon laughed and took another sip of the sweet drink. It was the perfect moment, he thought. He had to take advantage of this friendly mood. He looked at Löwenstein, who had finally seemed to relax a little, and gave in. He who never asks questions will die stupid, his uncle had always said, and he had been a reporter for the *New York Times*. He set his empty bottle on the table and leaned forward. "What do you think the records Czito is bringing will show? I'd love to see them sometime."

Löwenstein's expression shifted slightly and his smile suddenly didn't seem quite so open. "Well," he said, leaning forward again, "I'm afraid I can't say anything about that. Dr. Tesla is evaluating the results without us."

"Why do we keep repeating this one experiment?"

Löwenstein raised his shoulders and his fingers played with the bottle on the table in a preoccupied manner. Clearly, the questions were making him uncomfortable.

Philemon held the German with his gaze. "Why? After all, it has been proven that Dr. Röhnfeldt was mentally ill."

Löwenstein looked up in surprise. "How do you know Dr. Röhnfeldt?"

"Dr. Tesla must have told you that he caught me in his chamber with his notes."

A hint of blush settled on Löwenstein's cheeks, telling Philemon he was on the right track.

"Before I came here," he continued, "I had never heard of Dr. Röhnfeldt. But after I came across that name in Dr. Tesla's notes, I began to make inquiries. What I found out is extremely interesting." It was indeed, if not completely crazy! "Dr. Felix Röhnfeldt was a respected physician from Berlin, his medical specialty the human anatomy. He was also a supporter of the ether theory and an admirer of Luigi Galvani's discovery of 'animal electricity.' You know, the experiment with the frog's leg that started to twitch when an electric current was run through it. Dr. Röhnfeldt wondered whether this could also be done with the human body and initially devoted his private work to the question of what effects electric currents could have on humans. Similarly, Dr. Tesla had millions of volts flow over his own body to prove that his alternating current was harmless, contrary to Edison's claim. But Dr. Röhnfeldt came up with a much crazier idea. He wanted to test whether electricity could be used to dissolve matter and solidify it again elsewhere in space. He called this 'transportation of matter dissolved in ether,' or 'the Röhnfeldt experiment.' Allegedly he succeeded in transporting some inanimate objects, yes, even a canary—if you believe it. But he did not show this experiment to anyone. He wanted to make absolutely sure that his invention worked perfectly before he presented it to the public. His fear of being laughed at was too great, and so he always conducted his experiments in secret. But one day he thought his experiment was ready, and he persuaded his wife to participate. He stood her in front of his transporting apparatus and directed the electron stream at her. And sure enough, she disappeared before his eyes. Just dissolved." Philemon emphasized his narrative by making his fingers dance like a magician. Then he became serious again. "But what reappeared a little later elsewhere in his laboratory bore not the slightest resemblance to his beloved wife. It seemed as if someone had taken her body apart and put it back together wrong. A pile of dying flesh. Dr. Röhnfeldt lost his mind and was found kneeling next to his dead wife with disheveled hair and a vacant stare. He was tried and convicted of murder. However, he was not hanged, but locked up in a mental institution as an object of study. His laboratory equipment was sold, his records destroyed, and with them all the evidence of what he had done. A few years later, he died in his cell. By then, all memory of him had long since been erased. Only one rumor persisted: that a certain Dr. Felix Röhnfeldt is supposed to have dissolved his wife during an experiment. The Röhnfeldt effect!" Philemon leaned farther across the table. "That's what Dr. Tesla calls it in his notes too. And now tell me that there is no connection!"

"No, it's not like that!" Löwenstein defended himself. "It's not the Röhnfeldt experiment we're conducting here. God forbid! Dr. Röhnfeldt's theory was completely wrong. Dr. Tesla, however, knows what he is doing. He is concerned with something completely different. He only named this series of experiments because Röhnfeldt had inspired him to conduct them. He will give it its own name later before he presents it to the public. But only when he can be sure that it can be carried out successfully."

Philemon let out a bitter laugh. "Just like Röhnfeldt!"

"No, not at all. Dr. Röhnfeldt overlooked a crucial factor in his experiments, a quantity he could not control. You know that the ether is filled with unused energy, what Dr. Tesla calls 'dark cosmic rays.' He recognized their influence on the experiment and factored them in."

"But only after something happened to Myers!"

Löwenstein glanced at the closed door to Tesla's study, as if seeking help. But nothing stirred behind it.

"What happened to Frederick Myers?" Philemon pressed. Now it didn't matter what Löwenstein thought anyway. "Myers fell victim to the

Röhnfeldt effect, didn't he? Dark cosmic rays or not. You re-created that German doctor's original experiment!"

Löwenstein turned and regarded him, clearly petrified. His face was so pale, it was as if he had never seen the sun.

"I know you're looking for Myers," Philemon whispered. "He disappeared during the experiment three months ago and has not returned. I wonder though: Is that luck or bad luck? After all, he could have suffered the same fate as Röhnfeldt's wife!"

Löwenstein's whiskers began to tremble.

"You" —Philemon jabbed a finger in the direction of the German— "have allowed the experiment of a mad doctor to be repeated and a human being to be harmed! You are to blame for Frederick Myers's death!"

Suddenly, a voice rang out from the depths of the laboratory. "Let he among you who is without sin cast the first stone!"

Startled, Philemon jumped up and stared with wide eyes over to the large coil from whence the voice had come. A tall figure was standing there in the darkness.

"Isn't it a little self-righteous to judge so harshly," it said, "when the same could well be said of you, Mr. Ailey?"

He saw the doctor's pale face emerge slowly from the shadows. He was looking over at them, a ghostly glint in his eyes.

"Doctor . . . why aren't you in your study? I saw you go in earlier!" The question was somewhat stupid, but Philemon could think of nothing better at that moment.

Löwenstein had also stood up in the meantime and was looking at him.

"I . . ." Philemon's voice failed and now a flush of shame shot up his face. It burned on his skin like fire.

Dr. Tesla stepped out of the shadow of the coil and moved over to his German assistant. Almost solemnly, he folded his gloved hands in front of his body. Philemon was trembling all over and suddenly there it was again, the fear! The fear of having gotten into something here, from which he would not come out alive. These men had already brought misfortune on an assistant once, and they would do it again if he got in their way!

The doctor frowned slightly and tilted his head to one side. "What is wrong with you?" he asked, as if he had no idea how menacing he seemed. "Are you not feeling well?"

Philemon would have liked to laugh at the absurdity of this moment, but his fear of these two men was too great for him to make a sound. He backed away from them and tried to put more distance between himself and the doctor.

"Your mistake at the time, by the way, was to stand too close," Tesla said suddenly. "That's why it failed, your experiment."

Philemon blinked in confusion.

"The experiment in the Yale University lab. The unauthorized experiment, mind you. If you had taken into account that air is a conductor, then you would have succeeded and . . ."

". . . and my fellow student would still be alive. It was an unforgivable mistake," Philemon continued dejectedly. Now he knew what the doctor was talking about. He bowed his head in dismay and at the same moment the past, which he had so carefully tried to suppress, swept over him. Like a magic lantern, the images of that fateful night in New Haven processed before his mind's eye. Three of them had entered the university laboratory: Elias, Robert, and himself. Students of electrical engineering, heads full of fluff and equipped with the arrogance of youth, and proud members of the student association Chi Psi to boot. It was Robert who mustered the courage to stand on the metal plate that Philemon had constructed and wired to the large coil, and at Robert's signal, Philemon flipped the switch. Several thousand volts flowed through Robert's body and sparks shot from his hands, just as in the legendary demonstration by the famous Nikola Tesla, whom they were all trying to emulate at the time. Robert, surrounded by a blue corona of small lightning bolts, was still smiling, they were all still smiling. But then a loud bang sounded and with it a discharge of sparks came loose from the coil. Why they had placed the coil right next to the metal plate, Philemon no longer knew. In any case, it had been a big mistake. The lightning that had come so suddenly struck Robert in the face. He fell from the plate with a scream, and writhed on the ground. The smell of burned flesh rose to their noses . . . and suddenly they no longer felt like gods. They looked down in horror at the screaming Robert, at his smoking hair and the blood on his hands, which he was smashing into his face. To their good fortune, the faculty janitor heard the screams and immediately went for help. That was why Robert had escaped with his life. His face, on the other hand, would forever be a horrifying mask of clotted tissue and blind eyes. A monster that made everyone catch their breath involuntarily when he entered the room.

But the incident had harsh consequences for them as well. The university demanded an explanation, which all three refused to give because they were abiding by the code of their fraternity. The code was Chi Psi's pride and joy and dictated that they stick together forever; true gentlemen who stood by their word even if the devil himself should lead them into the temptation of sweet betrayal. But Chi Psi saw things differently in this case and expelled the three troublemakers from its protective circle. The university was also implacable. It suspended the young men from lectures. For Philemon's parents, this incident was a disgrace that made them the talk of all the other respectable families in the neighborhood, and they sent their wayward offspring to Switzerland on the pretext that he was suffering from a lung ailment. After a year of penance, his parents convinced the dean of the university of Philemon's rehabilitation, and he was permitted to continue his studies. Of the three who had participated in the ill-fated experiment, he was the only one to graduate. Elias never returned to the university. Instead, he became an employee at the General Electric Company and married a pretty girl from New York. To this day, he was Philemon's only real friend. Robert, on the other hand, no longer saw any meaning in life and hanged himself in his little apartment a year later.

Saddened, Philemon now looked up at Dr. Tesla. That was it now, his whole sad story. Of course, the doctor, Löwenstein, and Czito had known it before he had come to Colorado Springs. That had been his "specific qualification." He sighed and hung his head. Heavy guilt flowed over him, pushing him to the floor. No, farther down. It pushed him down to the bottom of the sea, poured lead over his feet, and trapped him where the pressure was highest. He was dead. Buried alive. And he wished he had a rope like Robert.

"But what about you?" the doctor asked good-naturedly. "There's no reason to despair, Mr. Ailey. Don't give up on yourself. Sit at this table with us and hear what I have to say. I promise you it's nothing that will weigh on your conscience." Tesla looked at him invitingly and slowly extended an arm toward the table.

Philemon hesitated. He saw the doctor's shadowy gaze. The line between genius and madness was notoriously thin. Dr. Felix Röhnfeldt had also stumbled over it and finally fallen into the darkness on the wrong side.

"Please, Mr. Ailey," Tesla repeated. All at once, his gaze filled with deep sadness, and Philemon felt a twinge in his heart. It was that sadness that made him sit down at the table.

For a while, the three men looked at one another, silently absorbed in thought. And when the doctor finally began to speak in a low voice, it seemed as if the whole world was holding its breath, listening to this man's words.

CHAPTER 51

June 2, 2011
in the desert
morning

Ondragon stopped the Snake on the crest of a dune and fished for his water bottle. He took a small sip and wiped the sweat from his eyes with a loose end of the turban. Systematically scanning the dunes with the Snake, map square by map square, was not easy, despite the GPS. Unfortunately, the metal detector had thus far remained silent, either because there really was nothing here, or because the tower was buried too deep in the sand. Ondragon hoped neither statement was true, and resolutely adjusted his sunglasses. Then he continued. Whirring, the Snake worked its way down the dune and up the next one. It went on like that all the time. Down and up, like a roller coaster.

"What's that?" he said to himself a little later, and stopped. He was looking at a wide strip of churned-up sand that stretched through the dunes. It looked as if an entire company of soldiers had marched along here. Ondragon followed the trail for a whole kilometer until he finally came upon its origin. Well hidden in a dune valley, more than a dozen dromedaries were huddled together. Curiously, they craned their necks and eyed the visitor. Ondragon noticed that some of the animals had unnaturally light coats. They were as white as snow.

Malin's ghost dromedaries! His heart performed a little somersault. It was a pity she wasn't here now. It would have made her happy for sure.

He pulled his small camera out of his pocket and took some pictures. He would send the pictures to Malin later, telling her where he had seen the animals. With a smile, he turned his back on the dromedaries and continued the unedifying search for the tower. He wanted to cover at least one square of the map today.

Suddenly, Ondragon sat up.

He turned his ear to the wind. He could hear engine noises. He quickly jumped out of the scooter and scanned the sky and the desert with his binoculars. A gust of wind blew grains of sand into his face like tiny needles, stinging his skin. Ondragon pushed the fabric of the chèche-turban back over his mouth and nose for protection.

But the wind also brought something else: a low-frequency, barely perceptible hum, clearly from an engine. Ondragon strained, squinting into the sky, where he saw a split-second flash. Sunlight reflecting off a shiny surface! Probably the window of an airplane. He raised the binoculars and made out a small plane flying low over the crest of the mountains, descending lower and lower. It looked like it was going to land near the oasis. Ondragon's heartbeat quickened. Was that Monsieur Noire? He followed the flight of the strange machine, which was now so low that the ridges of the mountains seemed to tickle its belly. Then it dived between the rocks and was lost to view. Ondragon looked up. He could not remember seeing a runway there as they flew over. It was a mystery to him anyway how the much larger and heavier Junkers had been able to land and take off again here in the sea of dunes. Suddenly, another thought occurred to him. Maybe the Junkers had not landed here at all, but over there. Maybe Schuch's coordinates were incorrect, and they were looking in completely the wrong place!

Ondragon ran back to the Snake. If that was indeed Monsieur Noire, then it was time to get a move on!

CHAPTER 52

June 2, 2011
in the desert
morning

Clandestin stepped out of the plane and saw Yaqub coming toward him. He spread his arms and stepped into the older man's fatherly embrace. When they let go of each other, Clandestin kissed him on both cheeks.

"*As-salamu 'aleikum*, Master Yaqub."

"*Wa-'aleikumu s'salam*, Clandestin." Yaqub smiled. His white beard shone like snow against his brown skin, lending him a dignified air. "Did you bring the treasure?" he asked.

With a proud smile, Clandestin pulled the two items from his belly band and presented them to Yaqub.

"Praise be to the Creator. Both can now return to the place where they belong: in the bosom of the Brotherhood." Yaqub took the book and the medal like two precious relics and stroked his fingers over them devoutly. "I thank you, Clandestin, for making the arduous journey to fulfill our vow."

Humbly, Clandestin bowed his head. "I must thank you for choosing me for this honorable task, master."

"What about Achmed?" Worried wrinkles appeared on Yaqub's forehead.

"I think he is dead. Otherwise, he would have sent me a message long ago, as we had agreed."

Sadness settled into Yaqub's gaze. "Was it the German?"

Clandestin replied with anger in his belly. "I'm afraid he's closer on my heels than we would like."

"Then he must have been on the plane I saw this morning. It landed out in the dunes."

Clandestin looked up, startled. "An airplane? But how did he know where I was going? I don't understand! He must be in league with the devil."

Yaqub put a comforting hand on Clandestin's shoulder. "Whoever he's in league with, he seems very talented. And tenacious. Not a bad quality for a man whose destiny is to wrest secrets from the world."

Clandestin shook his head in despair. "His presence here is entirely my fault. I failed to shake him off. Please, punish me if you wish, master."

"Nonsense, you did what you could. This stranger is just another test for us. We will overcome that too. Trust me. Come, let's go to the Room of Silence and pray for Achmed, who sacrificed himself, and for the Creator's blessing, that we may be armed."

"The German is out in the dunes, you say?" Clandestin looked over at the plane he had come in. It was being turned around on the runway by four brothers and covered with a camouflage net. The runway, barely visible, was located in an inaccessible valley among the rocks, several kilometers from the guelta. The valley was taboo for the inhabitants of the guelta and no one was permitted to enter it. It had its own source of fresh water and could only be reached by a narrow path or by a small plane— the perfect hiding place.

"Then he's close by," he said anxiously.

"Not close enough. Do not worry. The desert will help us and bring him to his knees. It will devour him as it has devoured all other invaders. No trace of him will remain. Now come."

Clandestin allowed Yaqub to lead him through a barely visible entrance in the rock, into the extensive cave system, which contained countless passages and chambers as well as their modest dwellings and the Room of Silence. As Clandestin entered the cavern hewn out of the rock and saw the bronze cross on the altar of the Creator, he fell reverently to his knees. Touching the ground with his forehead, he inhaled deeply, smelling the familiar aroma of damp clay and incense, and began to quietly recite the magical verses. Old Yaqub joined in his prayer and their murmuring voices floated around the room. Clandestin felt his strength being renewed. He was at home, in the circle of the Brotherhood. Different laws prevailed here than in the world outside. The German was an intruder. He would have to leave. Or die.

CHAPTER 53

June 2, 2011
in the desert
noon

Hastily, Ondragon told Achille about the strange plane and then packed what they needed for a reconnaissance flight over the mountains. He had a gut feeling that they had no time to lose.

A little later they were sitting in the cockpit and Achille was turning the ignition key. The engine started without a stutter. The Frenchman checked the oil pressure and placed both hands on the joystick. Then he released the brake and opened the throttle right up. The machine bounced across the sand like an angry bee. Ondragon involuntarily tensed in his seat. The dune at the end of the short runway came ominously closer, and he squinted his eyes as the Cessna's nose lifted just before they reached it and the plane shot into the sky. As it did so, it grazed the sand with one tire, but Achille expertly caught the craft's landing gear and pulled it up mercilessly. Ondragon's breath caught as at least two Gs pushed him back into his seat. Despite the pressure on his ears, he could hear the Cessna's fuselage cracking and groaning. Why did he keep doing this to himself?

When they reached an altitude of seven hundred meters, Achille reduced their speed. The engine became quieter and the vibrations subsided somewhat. Ondragon too had regained control of his involuntarily accelerated breathing and pointed to the dark rocks below. "Go over there. I want to investigate that oblong valley."

"On it!" The Frenchman put the Cessna into a turn and a little later they were flying over the valley. Ondragon tried to look through the binoculars, but they were going too fast.

"Can you turn around and fly over the valley again, lower and slower?"

"Oui, mon Capitaine!"

Achille flew a long loop over the other valleys and Ondragon took the opportunity to inspect them. But here too he could not see anything conspicuous. No alien aircraft, anyway. Achille went lower, and as they traversed the valley in question, Ondragon thought he spotted something.

But suddenly the Cessna's engine began to sputter. Achille pulled the plane up and got it over the ridge just before all the instruments failed. More amazed than horrified, Ondragon watched as the propeller stopped with a jerk and the Cessna went into a dangerous dive.

"What the hell is going on?" he screamed, holding onto the seat. Now he was horrified!

"I don't know," Achille gasped, concentrating on controlling the small plane. But the dunes on the ground were getting closer. The Cessna was going much too fast. If they were lucky, it would crash-land, but only if they were lucky. Otherwise, the vultures would get an unexpected feast.

The Cessna lowered its nose and began to lurch. Achille pulled with all his might on the joystick.

This is it, thought Ondragon. *This is how it's going to end. Not pretty, but heroic at least.*

But before they hit the top of the first dune, Achille managed to pull the plane up a little and get it into a balanced glide. Of course, they were still going too fast, and when they touched down for the first time among the dunes, the Cessna bounced uncontrollably off the ground and across the sand. In the end, the plane buried its nose into a high dune. Metal crunched and glass shattered. Ondragon was thrown abruptly forward and lost consciousness.

CHAPTER 54

September 12, 1899
Colorado Springs
afternoon

Philemon burst into tears and allowed them to stream down his face. A torrent of diverse emotions flooded him. Tears soaked into his shirt, his hands, and the tabletop in front of him. Trembling, he looked at Tesla. He was electrified by what the doctor had just told him. He had forgotten the negative effect of the Röhnfeldt experiment, for something much greater had taken its place. Tesla had discovered something Röhnfeldt had overlooked. A hidden energy source, which had always been there. But no one had ever noticed it before. It was the greatest discovery of all time!

"Doctor," Philemon said, his eyes filled with tears, "why haven't you revealed this to the whole world long ago? Your discovery would change everything!"

"Because I fear people will not realize the greatness of my invention and may misuse it for evil purposes. That's why it has thus far remained such a well-kept secret. And I want it to stay that way for the time being, Mr. Ailey. Will you swear to me that it will?"

"Yes, Doctor, of course! I swear on my life!"

"Good." The great inventor looked down. All at once he seemed tired and worn out. "I too have made mistakes," he said quietly. "And the one with Mr. Myers is of course one of them. But it's the mistakes we learn from, my young friend, not the successes. Only those who face their mistakes can accomplish what others despair of." Tesla rose reverently, and the magic of the moment was broken. Without another word, the doctor went into his chamber and closed the door behind him.

For a moment, Philemon looked thoughtfully at the door and then at Löwenstein. The German nodded at him knowingly, and from that moment on Philemon knew that he was one of them for good.

* * *

Philemon hurried to get back to the hotel, because his secret notes were awaiting him there. Today had been eventful and he had a lot to write down. Besides, he had to check something urgently!

He was passing China Jim's store when he realized someone was standing in the dark gateway. It was Joe Herkimer. The telegraphist almost gave the impression he had been waiting for him.

"Evening, Phil," he said good-humoredly, "how are you? Haven't heard from you in a while. Everything all right out there in the lab? You look so weary." Herkimer had hooked his thumbs in the pockets of his vest and was rocking back and forth on the heels of his shoes.

"Yes, everything is all right. We have a lot of work," Philemon replied curtly, and made to continue, but Herkimer stepped out of the entrance, blocking his path.

"Did you hear? The Pinkertons left today."

"Really?" replied Philemon, secretly admitting he was surprised by this news. "Then it seems those guys finally got what they wanted. Whatever it might have been."

Herkimer smiled. "I received and forwarded a telegram. It came from Chicago and was an instruction to the leader of the Pinkerton detachment here in Colorado Springs. It said all detectives were to return to headquarters immediately. Do you want to know why?"

"Yes, of course," Philemon said with a sigh.

"But first, tell me if you've found out anything new about Myers."

Philemon shook his head. "Unfortunately, no. I've been to Manitou Springs and asked around everywhere, but nobody there claims to have seen any trace of a ghost, not even on Pikes Peak." It was a weak excuse, but he couldn't very well tell Herkimer the truth after he had given Dr. Tesla his word of honor moments before. It was now clear to him that Herkimer's story was true. Myers had indeed been seen on the summit, and Philemon knew why. But he would keep as silent as the grave. He would never again speak to a stranger about the doctor's work. Never! Not even if he was tortured!

"That is unfortunate," Herkimer replied. "But you'll continue to keep me informed, will you not?"

"Naturally," Philemon lied. "Now, will you tell me why the Pinkertons are gone?"

Herkimer stepped close to him so that Philemon could again smell that cloying odor on his clothes, the breath of opium pipes. "The Pinks," he whispered, "have been taken off the case because the client no longer feels it necessary for them to snoop around here. Apparently, he received the information he was after about the doctor in the last few days."

"And who is this sinister client?" Philemon asked. At the same time, he wondered what kind of information Herkimer might be referring to and whether one of them had unwittingly let something leak out of the lab.

"Well, there is no client, unfortunately. Not in that sense, at least," Herkimer explained. He shoved both hands deep into the pockets of his coat and hunched his shoulders. "Rather, it's a corporation that's behind it."

"A corporation? Which one?" Philemon had already suspected something like that. His suspicion immediately fell on the General Electric Company of Thomas Edison, Tesla's bitterest opponent.

"It was the R. E. Olds Motor Car Company!" the telegrapher whispered, looking around nervously. But there was no one to be seen on the darkened road.

Philemon frowned. What did a car manufacturer have to do with Dr. Tesla? Or with his work? Well, he would find out at another time, but now he urgently needed to get back to the hotel! "Thank you very much for your confidence in me, Joe," he said kindly, tipping his hat. "But I must be on my way now. Have a restful night . . . or will you indulge in another of Buddha's dreams now?" He winked at the telegraph operator and nodded toward the entrance of the opium den.

Herkimer laughed and apologetically pulled both hands out of his coat pockets. As he did so, a small card fell out and drifted to the ground. Herkimer made to bend down, but Philemon was faster. He took a cursory glance at the card and stumbled.

"'We never sleep,'" he read aloud. "'Pinkerton's National Detective Agency.'" He looked questioningly at the telegraph operator.

"Oh, I must have got it from that guy. You know, the one who quizzed me. Give it here, I don't really need it anymore." Herkimer plucked the card from his hand, quickly tore it into tiny shreds, and then tossed them onto the pavement behind him with a carefree shrug of his shoulders. "Should have done that long ago. Water under the bridge. Stay well, Phil, and until next time." He turned and walked through the gateway into the backyard. When he was gone, Philemon bent down and picked up a few of the snippets. He tried to put them together, but Herkimer had done a great job; the name written on the back was indecipherable.

Philemon looked thoughtfully at the snippets for a while, then dropped them on the street and continued on his way to the hotel. When he arrived at his room at the Alta Vista a little later, he quickly locked the door and opened the closet. Finally, he could look up what had been bothering him all the way back. He retrieved the note from Myers from the clothes rack, smoothed it out on the top of the small secretary, and stared at the writing. It was as if he were wearing magic glasses, for suddenly he understood all that Myers had recorded there, what thought he had been trying to capture.

Philemon looked at the numbers of the calculation, at the result with the many exclamation marks. It was not a closed circuit, as Maxwell, Helmholtz, and all the other weighty men of science claimed! Quite contrary to their proclamation, there was something else: an open system. Open for energy from the ether! It was fantastic! Almost *too* fantastic, but Philemon knew it could become a reality. With Dr. Tesla's invention! And Frederick Myers's equation was the proof. But only for those who were willing to break away from the universal laws of physics. And who would that be? Who among the great lords of science was willing to risk his reputation and renown to create something new? The doctor was, in any case. And he, Philemon, was too!

Resolutely, he folded up the note from Myers and put it in his pants pocket. No matter what other people might say about them behind their backs, he was ready to stand in opposition to obtuseness. Together with Dr. Tesla, Mr. Czito, and Mr. Löwenstein, he would take heart and defy all the adversities that were coming their way!

CHAPTER 55

June 2, 2011
in the desert
afternoon

Ondragon opened his eyes and abruptly felt pain. The seat belts had held, but they had cut deep into the flesh on his chest and neck. He carefully unbuckled his seat belt, turned his head, and felt the rest of his body. It seemed everything was still attached. He turned to Achille, still unconscious in his seat, and felt for a pulse. The Frenchman's heart was beating slowly but steadily. Relieved, Ondragon bent down and checked to see if Achille was injured. Apart from a heavily bleeding laceration on his forehead, he could not find any external injuries and finally struck the Frenchman on the cheek with the flat of his hand.

"Hey, wake up! We're here!"

Achille's eyelids flew up. Confused, he looked around. "What? We're here? Ouch . . . *putain de merde!*" He wiped his forehead with his hand and stared at the blood on his fingers.

"It's nothing bad," Ondragon reassured him. "Probably just a mild concussion. Otherwise, are you okay?"

Achille unbuckled his seat belt and moved his arms and legs. "Seems so," he then said.

"I guess the devil didn't want to take us yet," Ondragon joked, turning to the side window, half of which was covered with sand. "I don't think we can get out this way." He climbed to the back, opened the sliding door of the hold, and jumped onto the sand. Achille followed him and groaned loudly when he saw the extent of the damage. The Cessna was stuck in the dune up to the pilot's cockpit, the landing gear had buckled, and the engine had been pushed backward by the impact. The propeller was gone.

"Oh, my baby! My beloved baby!" Achille cried, wringing his hands.

Ondragon raised his eyebrows in amazement. He hadn't realized how attached the Frenchman was to the machine. He put a comforting hand on his shoulder. "We'll get it fixed. Even if we have to fly in spare parts.

What's worse right now is that we're stuck here. Our camp is too far away to walk. I guess we'll have to spend the night." He looked around. The tracks of their crash-landing were visible for miles, stretching from the flat strip of sand in front of the mountains to the dunes. He raised his head and looked over to the rocky ridges. Monsieur Noire was probably squatting up there somewhere now, laughing to himself.

Ondragon uttered a silent curse and rubbed his aching neck. All in all, they had been lucky. They were alive. But it was strange that the Cessna's functions had failed over the valley. Something wasn't right there, and Ondragon wondered if there might be a device that caused airplanes to crash.

After a while, he turned his gaze away from the mountains and looked at Achille, who had sat down in the sand and lit a cigarette. Now they had to salvage what they could from the wreckage and set up a makeshift camp before nightfall.

Two hours later, they were sitting dejectedly by a small dromedary dung fire, waiting for nightfall. The crash-landing was still in their bones and neither of them felt like talking. As a substitute for a tent, they had stretched a sheet of fabric over the wing of the Cessna, so at least they didn't have to spend the night in the open air. In addition, Ondragon's precaution of leaving half the equipment and supplies in the plane for emergencies had proved very useful, and they were reasonably well supplied with food and water. The Cessna, however, was a total write-off. With aching limbs, they had dug the machine out of the dune and found that the engine had suffered irreparable damage from the impact. At least it wasn't worth repairing the thing here in the desert. Too bad, Ondragon thought, but when they were back in Morocco, he would buy Achille a new machine. First, however, they had to get this damn job done! And hopefully they could do that without a plane.

A distant sound caused both men to snap out of their lethargy. Ondragon put a finger to his lips and craned his neck. It was clearly an aircraft engine again. The hum grew steadily louder. Was it Monsieur Noire taking to the air again from his secret landing place?

Ondragon told Achille to stay with the plane and ran up the dune. His heart almost stopped when an airplane thundered overhead at low altitude. Instantly, he went down on his knees, drew his pistol, and aimed at the plane.

Did Monsieur Noire want to startle them and find out what they were up to? Or did he want to finish them off now? Ondragon shielded his eyes against the low sun and tried to decipher the aircraft's markings. But the plane was too far away now, and he'd left the binoculars with Achille. He saw the plane make a turn and set course for him again. What if the occupants fired at him? Ondragon took to his heels and charged back toward the wreckage of the Cessna. At his back, the alien plane sped up, flying low over the dunes. The engine roared into the silence like an angry rocket. Ondragon ducked as he ran, and the shadow of the plane flitted over him. Now he knew how a field mouse felt when a buzzard circled overhead. He quickly ran into the shelter of the plane's wings, where Achille was also hiding.

"Who is that?" asked the Frenchman.

Ondragon shrugged his shoulders and peered at the sky from under the wing. The engine noise grew fainter, only to swell again a moment later, and then the plane shot over the dune, its engine roaring. Then it turned off and finally Ondragon could read the identification.

SE-MAX.

That was . . .

Suddenly, he jumped out from under the wing and let out a joyful laugh.

"Hey! Are you crazy?" the Frenchman yelled after him. "Get back under cover, Chief!"

But Ondragon only laughed more heartily and began waving at the machine, which meanwhile was wobbling its wings and making another arc. "That's Luke Skywalker!" he shouted.

"Who?" asked Achille.

"Well, Luke!"

Achille shook his head as the plane slowed and began its approach not far away. It was a large Cessna Grand Caravan, a spacious cargo plane.

A faraway smile settled on Ondragon's lips. Now they would meet one more time. He felt a brief sensation of doubt. Maybe the hunter didn't want to see him at all. She might not have recognized him; after all, she didn't know he was here. Ondragon scratched his chin and noticed that he looked very wild with his three-day beard. But even more urgently, he would quickly have to come up with an explanation as to what he, as a management consultant, was doing here lost in the desert.

No matter. Whether she wanted to see him or not, he and Achille were now getting some unexpected help. Ondragon squinted, peering into the distance, where the Swedish plane was gradually coming to a halt.

"And who, pray tell, is this Luke?" asked Achille, who had come up next to him and was likewise looking at the plane.

"Our rescuer," Ondragon replied simply. He saw the doors of the Grand Caravan open and two figures jump out. They put on their hats and waved. Ondragon waved back and then smelled his armpit. He grimaced, shuddering. Hopefully, Malin was also into animal scents.

CHAPTER 56

September 13, 1899
Colorado Springs
morning

Elated, Philemon made his way to the laboratory. He was still very much animated by the events of the previous day. Unconsciously, his hand felt in his pocket for Myers's note and he was reassured to find that it was still there. He tapped his pocket with a smile. He then looked up at the sky, closely. It had become noticeably cooler overnight, and clouds threatened rain showers on the horizon. Philemon hurriedly marched out into the prairie, his eyes fixed on the laboratory building. But already from a distance he could tell that something was wrong.

There were far too many people around. Philemon quickened his pace to a run. His heart pounding, he arrived at the laboratory and looked around. Strange men were hurrying in and out. Some of them wore the uniform of the local police.

"What's going on here?" he asked the next person who came out of the building, keeping an eye out for Dr. Tesla and the others.

"A fire broke out during the night," the constable replied.

"A fire?" Only now did Philemon notice the charred roof beams. "But how can that be?"

The constable shrugged his shoulders. "With all the strange equipment in there, it's no wonder, if you ask me."

"Has anyone been harmed?" Philemon's gaze darted back and forth. Where was Tesla? Had he not been in his chamber when the fire broke out?

"No, as far as we know, no one was hurt," the constable replied. "The lab was locked when we and the fire brigade arrived. No one was inside."

Philemon stroked his mustache nervously and looked up at the blackened roof beams again. "Thank you," he said, and ran quickly into the building.

"Be careful, it could collapse!" the constable called after him, but Philemon did not care. He looked around the inside of the laboratory. All the apparatus was covered in soot and the cables on the walls were scorched. The fire must have spread from the roof, but seemed to have been extinguished before it could spread to the entire facility. Philemon looked up at the gray sky through the roof beams.

"Doctor? Löwenstein? Czito? Where are you?" He ran to the small study. But there was no one there either. The furnishings were scattered all over the place. The doctor's notebooks and all his working materials. It looked as if someone had been looking for something in particular and had swept everything off the shelves. The box with the tubes, however, was still there. A thin layer of ash covered everything here as well. Philemon smelled smoke and something else. Gasoline? Oil? He quickly turned on his heel and ran back into the laboratory. The cabinet was open and all the glass cylinders were in pieces. But whether they had cracked in the fire or been smashed on purpose, Philemon could not say. He looked out the back door and finally spotted the three scientists. They were standing at some distance from the building, looking out at the prairie with petrified expressions.

"Dr. Tesla!" shouted Philemon. "Dr. Tesla! What happened?"

When he reached the three men, Löwenstein turned to him. There was resignation in his eyes. "A fire," he replied. "We suspect it was set by someone."

"Then it was petroleum I smelled after all," Philemon confirmed agitatedly. "The arsonists surely were aiming to accelerate the fire. The tubes have been destroyed. Also, your study was ransacked, Dr. Tesla. Someone was looking for something! What about your notebook? The one with the gold circle on it. Do you still have it?" All at once Philemon felt nauseated. Nauseated by the wickedness of the world.

Dr. Tesla blinked. He looked sad. He ran a gloved hand over the black cutaway he was wearing today. "It's here," he said softly, tapping a bulge at the level of his chest, "with me. I always have it with me. I said that before. I"—his voice faltered —"I think I may need some rest now . . . Yes, a little sleep might do me good." He swallowed and swayed slightly. Löwenstein took a quick step toward him and offered his hand for support, but Tesla declined with a grateful nod.

It pained Philemon to see the doctor like this. To see how he suffered at the knowledge that the people out there did not return his unconditional love. And it hurt to see how his generosity was repaid with nothing but resentment and disgust.

"It must have been those Pinkertons!" he said angrily. "Those sneaky dogs! Those damned snoopers! Their departure was probably just a deception." He choked down the lump in his throat, feeling helpless and filled with shame, while the doctor stood, his back bent, filled with exhaustion and disappointment.

Then he sadly turned his eyes away. It was the unreasonableness of people, the narrow-mindedness and stupidity in this world, that prevented wonderful things from happening. "I'll take the doctor to the hotel now," Löwenstein said, breaking into his thoughts. "He can rest there. You and Czito stay here and see what can be salvaged of the laboratory. Our work here is not done yet!" He directed Tesla along the path, which he willingly followed.

For a long time, Philemon watched the two walk slowly side-by-side across the prairie toward the town, then he followed Czito into the ruined building.

"Where was the doctor when the fire broke out?" he asked the Serb, who had begun to wipe the ashes from the apparatus with a cloth. "Wasn't he in his chamber tonight?"

Philemon glanced over at the small study and then looked around the lab. He noticed that the terminal was gone too. Searching, he walked around the room. "Where is the terminal?"

"Outside," Czito grumbled without looking up.

"Outside? Why wasn't it inside during the fire?"

Czito shrugged his shoulders.

"But we brought it in yesterday after the experiment. I know that for sure."

"Then someone got it back outside again. Maybe the fire department."

Philemon frowned. He went to the back door and looked out. There it stood, the terminal. Lonely and alone in the prairie. He had probably not noticed it before. He scratched his head pensively. Why would the fire department want to move this apparatus, of all things, outside? The copper tube didn't even look valuable.

"Could the doctor have taken the terminal there?" asked Philemon Czito.

The little Serb looked up from his work. "The doctor? All alone?" He grunted in amusement. "No way!"

Philemon agreed. Löwenstein and he had had difficulty moving the thing together. "This is really strange," he muttered, walking back into the lab. "Don't you think so?"

Czito rolled his eyes. "Mr. Ailey, you should have noticed by now that there are all kinds of strange things going on here."

Philemon had to grin. That was true!

"Come on," Czito finally said. "We've got work to do. It looks like most of the equipment is still operational. Dr. Tesla will want to continue his work as soon as possible, and we should cover the roof before the first of the rain."

Philemon followed the potbellied Serb and set to work. His anger had given way to a far better feeling. Defiance.

If the doctor had the strength to continue, so did he!

CHAPTER 57

June 2, 2011
in the desert
afternoon

With her obligatory shadow at her side, the tall Swede marched up to them. Luke Skywalker was wearing his Top Gun cap pulled low over his face, and Malin had a wide-brimmed cloth hat. Her hair was fixed in a braid that fell down her back.

"Hello, do you need help?" she called out to them in English, pointing to the upturned tail of the crashed Cessna.

"Yes!" Ondragon shouted back. And a little more quietly, "You could say that." He regarded her with a degree of suspicion he had not felt a few minutes ago. Why had she shown up in this godforsaken place now, of all times? Had she really come for the white dromedaries, or was she possibly a diversionary tactic of Monsieur Noire? Were the two of them working together? Could that be? And why had the thought only occurred to him now? Ondragon realized he had criminally neglected his own suspicion scanner when it came to Malin. He would have to make up for it urgently.

Meanwhile, the Swedish huntress came closer with long steps. But suddenly she stumbled and stopped abruptly.

"You?!" she said, looking at him puzzled.

Ondragon played the embarrassed one. "Yes, me."

The suspicion he was already familiar with crept into Malin's gaze. And he noticed that she kept a distance of five steps from him. Exactly the distance that made it impossible for an attacker to approach in one bound.

Apologetically, he raised both hands but stayed where he was. Because not only was Luke wearing a pistol on his belt, so was Malin. And who knew whether they would use their weapons in a situation that must understandably seem strange to them.

"I . . . well, I have an explanation," Ondragon said in a neutral tone. He felt Achille's gaze, but he had little desire to answer the Frenchman's unspoken question. But Achille seemed to understand what was going on, because he began to grin broadly.

"Well, well, an explanation," Malin repeated. "I'd like to hear that." She folded her arms over her chest and waited.

"I'm sorry," he finally said contritely. "I didn't tell you the truth in Casablanca. I'm not a management consultant . . . or rather, I am, but a special kind of one."

Malin still looked skeptical. Her dismissive attitude had not changed one iota. Mr. Top Gun was also staring at him extremely suspiciously.

"I do jobs," Ondragon continued carefully, "for certain people and—"

An alarmed light came into Malin's eyes and before he knew it, she had drawn her gun and pointed it at him. It was a Desert Eagle, the most powerful handgun on the market. The woman only went for the best.

"You're trying to screw me over, you son of a bitch!" she snarled.

"What?!" groaned Ondragon. "No! No way!" He laughed sheepishly, try-ing to defuse the situation. But Malin didn't go for it. She raised the hand with the pistol and aimed it directly at his face. "Don't think you can fool me. I know what you're up to. But you're going to leave well enough alone."

Luke had also reached for his weapon, but the young pilot seemed far more uncertain. His arm trembled and his gaze darted unsteadily back and forth. Out of the corner of his eye, Ondragon saw Achille reach into the back of his belt, where his weapon was hidden.

"I can get them both for you, Chief," he whispered. "We can dispose of their bodies just fine. They'll never be found in the dune. And we'd have a new plane."

After what happened with Achmed, Ondragon knew all too well that Achille was serious. But he cared about Malin and didn't want anything to happen to her, even if she might already hate him.

"Wait!" he shouted, taking a step forward to prevent another blood-bath. "Listen up, everyone!"

Achille cast a questioning glance at him, but Ondragon ignored it and turned to the Swedish hunter. "Malin, believe me, I'm not trying to rain on your parade. I couldn't care less about your white dromedary. I'm here for a completely different reason. If you put the gun away and calm down, I will explain, but only in private. That's the condition!"

Malin seemed to be thinking. Her lips were pressed together into a thin line. Her eyes were fixed on him. Then she lowered the pistol. "All right, I'll give you exactly one chance!" she said, putting the gun away.

Ondragon nodded in relief and pointed to the makeshift tent. "We have shade and water, and if you want, I'll make you a mocha too."

"Save the pleasantries, I just want an explanation!"

"Okay, okay, all right."

They went to the tent, where Ondragon held open the entrance for her.

"Be careful, Malin!" shouted Luke after her in Swedish.

"I'll be okay, Pelle!" Malin replied without turning to look at the pilot, and stepped into the tent. Before Ondragon followed her, he signaled to Achille to watch Luke. Inside the tent, he offered Malin a cup of water, which she accepted after some hesitation and drank thirstily. Then they sat down opposite each other on the mats. Ondragon was tense, searching for the right words. He knew he would only get anywhere with Malin by telling the truth. However, he would have to slim it down by a few critical pounds. Truth *light*, so to speak.

In contrast to the long-legged Swede, who sat there with a stiff back, he leaned back in a decidedly relaxed manner and tilted his head to demonstrate that he had more peaceable intentions.

"Well, here we are," he finally said. "Never thought we'd meet again. Especially not here in the desert. But before you freak out again, let me be the first to tell you that I'm very happy about this. Honestly."

Malin looked at him fixedly, not even blinking.

"Okay, you're not happy. Then I'll try to explain the situation to you now. First, though, I have to tell you that my assignments are usually subject to the strictest confidentiality."

Malin screwed up her face contemptuously, as though she could see through his lame excuse.

"There's something hidden out there in the desert," Ondragon continued unperturbed, "that my client really wants. And by that I mean, *really*, absolutely must have! So he has commissioned me to procure this object for him. In certain circles, I am known for fulfilling such wishes." He raised a hand to stifle an objection from Malin. "Of course, some of the things are illegal, but we already talked about that, and I don't think either of us is any more virtuous there. So let's stop throwing accusations at each other. I would find that, well, a little hypocritical."

He saw Malin nod. A first approving reaction.

"The thing is," he continued, "I solve problems. All kinds of problems. You might call me a fixer. And my business is booming—believe it or not. After all, each of us has a problem or two that we'd like to get resolved. I bet even you have one." He winked at her. "But I digress. Back to my mission. What I'm looking for is hiding here somewhere in the dunes. And it's very important that I find it. The fate of a number of people depends on it." *If not the fate of all of us*, Ondragon thought silently.

Malin relaxed her stiff posture a little and let her gaze travel around the tent. "And what is it?" she finally asked. "This thing you're looking for?"

"If I tell you, I'll be putting my reputation on the line. Discretion is my watchword."

Malin raised an eyebrow and suddenly laughed out loud. "You should hear yourself talk. That sounds really stupid! You're chasing around the desert dressed as Indiana Jones and it's probably the Ark of the Covenant you're after. Or the Holy Grail? Uh, how mysterious! But you don't seriously think I'm buying your story, do you?"

"I thought an adventurer like you would understand."

"Tell me what you're looking for, and I'll think about whether I believe you."

Ondragon raised both hands apologetically. "I can't. I'm sorry."

"There you have it! Screw your discretion! I think you're just stalling. This is all just a tactic to hide the fact that you're after the *Ebäydäg* too. You want to collect the money for it all by yourself! Boy, was I stupid to get involved with you. That was a weak moment. But it won't happen again." She was about to reach for her gun, but Ondragon sprang forward in a flash and threw himself at her. With one hand he stopped her from drawing the pistol and pressed the other to her mouth. For an instant, Malin was surprised, but then she resisted so fiercely that she almost threw him off. She was very strong and Ondragon had to use all his strength to hold her down.

"Now you listen to me!" he hissed in her ear. "I don't want any of your fucking camels! I can't stand the critters! But if you'll keep still, maybe I'll be nice enough to tell you where I saw one of your *Ebäydäg*!"

The Swedish hunter stopped struggling. But her eyes were still sending out hot sparks. He knew it made her furious that he had her in his power. She made a muffled sound under his hand.

"Was that consent?" he asked.

She nodded.

Carefully, he took his hand from her mouth.

"You should take another shower!" she hissed at him. "Now get off me! I won't scream. But this better not be a trick!"

"It's not a trick," he said calmly, but Malin just gave him a nasty look.

"Okay," he replied placatingly, "I'll tell you part of my assignment so you'll finally believe me." He took out his notepad, flipped to an illustration, and showed it to her. As he did so, he saw Malin's expression brighten a little.

"You're looking for a plane?" she asked.

Ondragon nodded. The lie was close enough to the truth. "Yes, but not just any plane. See, it's an old Nazi plane, a Junkers, that crashed over the desert here at the end of World War II."

"And your client wants you to find it and bring it to him? How is that going to work? That thing is way too big."

"That's true. But he doesn't want the airplane itself, he wants something that's *inside* it."

"And what is that?"

Ondragon twisted the corners of his mouth regretfully.

"Oh, of course: secret," Malin said mockingly, and a first smile appeared on her lips. "Is it at least valuable?"

"That's in the eye of the beholder," he countered. "Personally, I wouldn't go to all that trouble for the old junk. But anyway, at least I'll get my money's worth." He looked at her seriously. "By the way, it would be nice if you didn't tell Pelle Knatte about this. After all, it's about . . ."

". . . your professional honor. Point taken." She pretended to spit on her hand and then held it out. "I solemnly swear not to reveal anything I just learned from you!"

Ondragon nodded gratefully and relaxed.

"I'm sorry I didn't believe you," Malin finally said a little meekly. "But I really thought you were trying to steal the job from me." She laughed as if she herself now considered her previous distrust absurd.

He waved it off generously. "It's already forgotten. I shouldn't have told you in Casablanca that I was a boring management consultant. My fault."

For a while they sat there.

Then Malin leaned her head to one side and asked with a saucy grin, "And now will you tell me where you saw the white dromedary?"

"Not until you do me another favor."

Malin narrowed her eyes. "You're a fucking haggler, you know that?"

"I know." Ondragon pursed his lips.

"All right," Malin sighed, "out with it."

"As you may have noticed, we're in a bit of a jam here. We had a little accident and now our plane is screwed. As you can see. But don't worry, we'll get ourselves out of here. So you don't have to take us as hitchhikers. But unfortunately, I don't have any way of doing a final aerial reconnaissance now, which I would still need in order to locate the plane wreckage. I've narrowed down the area and I'm sure that—"

"I get it, you don't have to say any more. I'll lend you Pelle Knatte and his flying machine, but only if we can start looking for the dromedaries at the same time. Anything else?"

Ondragon shook his head. They looked at each other. Then he took out his camera and showed Malin the pictures of the white dromedaries.

CHAPTER 58

June 2, 2011
in the desert
evening

They're actually *Ebäydäg*!" exclaimed Malin excitedly. "A whole herd of them. Wow! Where did you see them?"

Ondragon gave her the coordinates.

"When was that?"

"This morning."

"Today?" Malin jumped up. "Then let's go!"

He looked at her in wonder. "But the sun is about to set. We'll never find those critters in the dark."

"Oh yes we will. Even more easily than in daylight."

Now Ondragon rose as well. "I see, and how, may I ask?"

"We have an infrared camera on board. We use that to track them."

Of course, Ondragon thought, using a camera that could detect heat sources. Heat that every living being gave off. It showed up as a red spot on a blue background. That was how they had monitored Monsieur Noire via satellite. And perhaps something else could be located in this way: a large metal dome, heated by the sun, hidden under the sand. But that only worked if the layer of sand above it wasn't too thick. It was a possibility; he had to try it!

"At night, the ambient temperature cools down to the point where it no longer exceeds the animals' body heat," Malin further explained. "Then the animals are warmer than sand and the air again."

"I see. And by day you search the desert by eye?" asked Ondragon, not letting her know that he knew how infrared tracking worked.

"Yes. But I don't want to wait until tomorrow. Dromedaries can wander a long way, you know. And they may have already moved several dozen kilometers from that spot. So we shouldn't waste any time!" She turned around and went to the tent exit.

My word! Ondragon thought, and followed her. Outside, he saw that dusk had already begun to fall.

"Pelle, get the plane ready for takeoff! We're going up right now!" Malin shouted to the young pilot, who was still standing in the same spot, looking at Achille like a mouse watching a cobra. Seeing his boss, Luke broke free of his stupor with relief and ran over to the Grand Caravan.

"Uh, I have a small question," Ondragon said with slight discomfort "How are we going to land in the dark? We'll never find the runway again at night."

"No problem," Malin replied, unconcerned. "We'll mark it with the electric flares we brought. Besides, Pelle can land anywhere, anytime!"

Well, if she said so. Ondragon went with her and Achille to the big Cessna and helped Pelle unload the equipment. In no time they had the tent of the two Swedes set up and the runway marked out with the lamps.

The three of them boarded the plane a little later. Achille stayed behind to watch the camp and later to check that the beacons were working.

Pelle stepped on the gas, and without its heavy load, the Grand Caravan rose quickly into the violet sky, which was so clear you could see for a hundred kilometers. The first stars were already visible on the eastern horizon and in the fading light the sharp lines of the dunes blurred into a velvety drape.

Meanwhile, Malin explained that the weight of the machine would change considerably once they had the dromedary, which could weigh up to six hundred kilos, on board. Ondragon already felt sorry for the beast, although Malin assured him that in its stunned state it would not notice anything. Well then . . .

They flew a few wide loops over the desert until the sun was finally gone and night was creeping over the sea of sand. Soon everything was dipped in a dark, inky blue.

"Are you ready for the hunt?" asked Malin, full of joyful anticipation. It seemed to be her ritual battle cry.

"Ready!" shouted Ondragon into the mic of the on-board radio they were all hooked up to. Since Malin was sitting up front in the copilot's seat, keeping an eye on the infrared camera transmission, he had been forced to take a jump seat in the back of the hold. He looked out into the night. Somewhere down there, the dark mass of the mountains lay shrouded in mystery. Was Monsieur Noire also crouching there, looking up at them? Had he already found the treasure? Would it be dangerous to fly over the mountains again? All these questions ran through his mind as they glided over the dunes in complete darkness. Pelle was now relying on the instruments alone but seemed to have things well under control. Gradually, they approached the point where Ondragon had seen the dromedaries. The screen of the infrared camera remained dark.

"We'll start circling now and hopefully track down the herd with that," Malin explained, and at her command Pelle turned the joystick. The Grand Caravan settled ponderously into a turn. Ondragon peered at the screen. He felt like he was in the movie *Das Boot*, where everyone waited tensely for the *ping* of enemy sonar. And then suddenly it came. The *ping*. In the form of a red dot.

"We've got something!" exclaimed Malin excitedly. "That could be them." She gave Pelle some quick instructions and the pilot turned to fly over the spot again. His circles became smaller and red dots appeared again.

"Unmistakable! There are animals down there! Tighter circles, Pelle," Malin ordered.

But maybe they were people, car engines, or power generators, Ondragon thought. How could they be so sure that they were dromedaries?

Malin slid open a small opening in the side window. Fresh air rushed into the interior of the plane and for a short time it became even louder. Ondragon saw the Swede pick up the rifle and slide the barrel through the opening.

"This is a pneumatic stun gun," she shouted. "I'm going to shoot some micro transmitters into the herd with it now. The animals are nice and close together now, forming one big target. I'm bound to hit one of them and then we can search for the herd tomorrow in daylight, using the tracking device."

Ondragon was not surprised by this plan; after all, he had not assumed that they would beam the dromedary into the plane at night. He watched intently as Malin fired several times into the night, apparently randomly. He saw some red dots on the screen detach themselves from the large spot and move away. Then they stopped.

"That shows I got at least one animal," Malin said. She put the rifle aside and closed the opening. "When they get hit, they get spooked and run away from the others."

Ondragon was still not quite sure whether this hunting method complied with international animal welfare regulations, but he was happy for Malin, as she seemed to be completely absorbed in the rush of the hunt. Of course, he too knew how it felt to be so close to the finish line.

Pelle Knatte swung the Grand Caravan away and they left the dromedaries to themselves again.

"So where do you want us to look for you now, Mr. Ondragon?" asked Malin good-humoredly over the radio.

"If we could fly parallel to the mountain ridge, that would be great."

"Just great or fantastic?" she inquired, turning to face him. In the dim light of the instruments, her eyes gleamed mischievously.

Ondragon smiled and instructed Pelle to fly parallel to the ridges. But no red or even yellow dot appeared on the monitor, and at the end of the mountains Ondragon had Pelle turn the aircraft around to fly back five hundred meters away from the previous course.

But the monitor remained dark.

Ondragon began to ponder. Had the dome under the sand already gotten too cold for infrared detection? Had they wasted too much time looking for those fucking dromedaries? Or—and this was the worse thought—was the tower not even down there?

With each unsuccessful loop they flew, Ondragon felt his motivation plummet toward zero. Unable to do anything about it, he was overcome by a dull resignation. It was pointless, he thought. Everything they were doing here was completely pointless. They would never find the tower. He leaned forward and was about to tell Malin that they could head off, when she turned to him and said, "There's something there!"

Straining, Ondragon looked at the screen, but he could only make out a diffuse cloud of slightly lighter blue against the dark background. The next moment it disappeared because the airplane had passed over it.

"I'd like to see that again," Ondragon said. "Can we do another circuit?"

Pelle nodded, and when the barely perceptible cloud reappeared on the screen a few minutes later, Malin bent over and put her fingertips on it, as if that would help her feel the hidden heat source. "Hmm, there's something there. It's emitting very minimal heat."

"Could that be what I'm looking for?" asked Ondragon innocuously, but his insides quivered with tension.

"It's possible. But it could also be that the texture of the sand is different there and is retaining more heat."

No matter, Ondragon thought, it was the only clue. "Quick, the coordinates," he demanded, and with nervous fingers typed the numbers Pelle gave him into the GPS. The result was clear; if that was indeed the dome of the tower down there, then Schuch had made a mighty error in his notes and consequently looked for it in the wrong place. The tower was much closer to the mountains.

"Okay," he said to Malin. "That should do it. We can head back to camp." Ondragon turned off the GPS and could hardly wait until they landed. Were they close to their destination? Or would they just be poking around unsuccessfully in the sand again?

CHAPTER 59

June 2, 2011
in the desert
night

After they had landed unerringly on the runway with the help of the beacons, Ondragon immediately rushed over to Achille and told him what they had found.

"That's something, at least," the Frenchman said, stroking his chin. "Shall we go right now?"

"If it is indeed the tower, we should be on our way as soon as possible, before someone else gets in our way."

"By someone, do you mean Monsieur Noire or them?"

Ondragon looked over at Malin and Pelle, who had lit a fire outside their tent. "No, those two have what they want. They won't bother us now, and they won't break camp until morning to catch their white dromedary. Come on." He pulled Achille into the shadow of the crashed Cessna so they could discuss their excursion undisturbed. Besides a potential adversary, there was another argument for a quick departure: the advantage of night. As long as it was dark, they would be protected from prying eyes.

"I hope we can dig down to the tower with our limited excavation equipment," Ondragon said. He climbed into the Cessna's hold and looked through the equipment. "It looks like all we have is a shovel and a pickaxe."

"Bah! I have something much better! If need be, we'll blast our way out with my little friends here!" Grinning, Achille juggled three hand grenades.

"I don't think we should make any unnecessary noise for the time being," Ondragon warned sternly. He knew the Frenchman wasn't kidding this time either. "Put those things away!"

"And what if it's not the tower in the sand?" asked Achille.

"Then *I'll* use the hand grenades!" Ondragon grinned, but quickly grew serious again. "There, now quickly pack everything up and don't forget the lamps."

"All right, Chief. But tell me, do you mind if I go over to those two cuties later, after we've finished the tour? I have a hunch the woman adores me. Maybe she'll let me have a go."

Ondragon gave Achille a nasty look. "You keep your illegal fingers to yourself, understand?"

Achille raised his brows indignantly, then a brazen smile spread across his bearded face and he pointed a finger at Ondragon. "Just as I thought. The mademoiselle is your sweetheart! She's the one you wanted the tip about the romantic restaurant in Casablanca for. So did it work?" Laughing, he waved it off. "Oh, of course it did. It always does." He giggled like a little kid, and Ondragon turned away, annoyed. The crazy Frenchman really got on his nerves sometimes.

In order not to lose any more time, he gathered everything they would need for the excavation. They couldn't take much with them anyway, since they had to go on foot.

A little later they were ready and stepped out from behind the Cessna. It had become cool and the firelight from the other camp shone invitingly. Even though he didn't usually have a sentimental streak, Ondragon wanted to say goodbye to Malin. After all, he didn't know if they would be back here by dawn.

With the equipment strapped to his back, he walked over to her and Pelle with Achille. As they stepped into the glow of the campfire, Malin looked up. A smile appeared on her tanned face and her eyes lit up. She rose and moved toward them with a welcoming gesture. "Hello, you two, come and take a seat! We're just talking about how much you've helped us, Paul."

Ondragon smiled sheepishly. "Sorry, but we're leaving now."

Her eyes widened. "Now? In the middle of the night?"

"Only the early bird catches the worm," he said with a wry grin.

"But the second mouse gets the cheese!" added Malin. "We're not going to make a run for it until just before sunrise. We want to locate the dromedaries from the air and then find a closer landing spot. If I manage to capture an animal, then we can leave this desolate area as early as tomorrow."

"And where does the expensive cargo go next? Directly to the Emirates?" Ondragon politely inquired.

"No, first back to Casablanca, where the animal will be quarantined. It will travel on a few weeks later. The transport will be taken care of by others, however. But my client will likely take the opportunity to have a look at the animal in Casablanca. Keep your fingers crossed that everything works out."

"I will." Indecisively, Ondragon stood there. "Okay, then let's . . ." he said then and was about to turn around, but Malin held him by the arm. She took a step toward him, and Ondragon, already startled, thought she was going to enact a schmaltzy farewell scene and kiss him; but she leaned forward and whispered something in his ear. A quiet expression of astonishment came over his face. And when Malin stepped back again, he was glad he had joined her at the campfire after all.

"I think I could work with you more often," she said, extending a hand.

Ondragon gave her a high five. "The pleasure was all mine."

"Well, *hej do*, Paul."

"*Hej do*, Malin." He gave the Swedish hunter one last look and then walked away with Achille.

"What did she say?" the Frenchman asked as he walked out into the desert night.

Ondragon turned his head. "Oh, nothing special. She only invited us to Sweden for a gangbang in her cabin by the lake."

"Really?"

Ondragon twisted the corners of his mouth mockingly. "Of course not!"

"*Quel dommage!* What a shame. But she's a beauty, admit it."

"I'm certainly not going to talk to you about that." With a knowing smile, Ondragon trudged ahead through the sand. They had a few miles of strenuous walking ahead of them, and Ondragon could already feel the thrill of the chase pulsing in his veins.

They headed directly for the target coordinates indicated on the GPS device. They walked in single file, taking turns to follow in each other's footsteps to conserve their energy. The moon had already risen, and in the bluish-black night the sand mountains looked like enormous waves frozen in midair. Ondragon strove to stay in the shadows, so they would not be seen so easily from the mountains.

An hour later, panting, they reached the place where, according to the GPS, their long-awaited treasure lay dormant. Ondragon put his head back. The dune was about fifty meters high and ran parallel to the ridges less than a kilometer away. Exhausted, he dropped the gear on his back to the sand and retrieved his water bottle. After a few deep swallows, he tossed the pickaxe to Achille.

"We don't have much time for a break. It's best to start digging right here at the back," he instructed. "But be careful, the sand is loose and slides easily."

They began the sweaty work, digging their way several meters into the dune below the crest. The sand kept caving in and it was almost a Sisyphean task to maintain a hole at least one meter in diameter.

After half an hour of toil, Ondragon straightened up. It was no use, he thought. They would never find anything in this place. They had dug much too deep. The tower had to be hidden in a much shallower place.

Or there is no tower at all! teased the little voice in his ear. *Maybe Malin is right, and it's just different sand!*

He glanced at the clock. It was already two in the morning! So they didn't have much time until sunrise. Ondragon breathed deeply for a while and listened to the desert. In the silence, only Achille's blows with the pickaxe and his strained panting could be heard.

"Hey, Achille! Stop it," he finally called over to him. "Let's try somewhere else!"

The Frenchman looked up and stretched his back. "Man, Chief! I feel like I'm doing hard labor!"

Ondragon laughed. It was a little like that! He moved twenty meters away from the first spot and plunged his shovel into the sand again. It was even looser here and trickled back incessantly into the hole, which hardly got any bigger. Cursing, Ondragon dug faster and suddenly he heard a dull sound. As if he had struck something hollow.

"*Mon Dieu*, you've got something!" exclaimed Achille, wiping the sweat from his brow.

Ondragon felt his heart rate suddenly skyrocket and hurriedly continued shoveling. When he had removed the sand from the spot, he looked at a dark, slightly curved surface with bulges the size of a head. Hastily, he took out his notepad and flipped through it in the light of the headlamp. When he found the picture, he showed it to Achille. It was the crude drawing of Tesla's Wardenclyffe Tower. The pockmarked texture of the copper dome was unmistakably the same as the one here at their feet!

Achille raised a thumb in the air and Ondragon grinned broadly. They had indeed found the tower! Now they only had to try to get inside.

Ondragon reached for the pickaxe. The copper sheet of the dome couldn't be too thick. Although he was sorry to destroy the evenly sculpted surface, he struck at it. There was a splintering crunch as the tip of the pick penetrated the soft nonferrous metal. The copper squeaked as he levered the tool out again and drove it in again at another point. After a while, he had a circle of holes, which they could push inward at one end like a shield. Beneath it, blackness yawned up at them. Ondragon shone his light into the dome and let out a surprised sound.

"Madness! Look at that!" he said to Achille, pointing the lamp into the opening. Myriads of tiny lights shone back like a giant disco ball! They were small concave mirrored surfaces of glass that reflected the light from Ondragon's lamp and gave the impression of an infinite vault of stars. From a hole in the floor of the dome protruded countless wires, stretching in all directions like the branches of a tree.

Like frozen lightning, Ondragon thought, turning to Achille. "I'll go in alone. You wait here and keep watch. We'll use the radios to keep in touch. I'll take a look around and then come back. Let's see what Schuch and Kammler left here!" Ondragon checked his equipment and crawled legs first through the sharp-edged opening.

Inside, he slowly shimmied down to the translucent floor and made one circuit, stooping, of the hole in the center from which the mighty tree of wires protruded. The individual fibers led to the reflective surfaces in the domed roof. Impressed, Ondragon turned his head. This was indeed Tesla's miracle apparatus!

The tingling in his nerves increased and the euphoria was bubbling in his bloodstream. They had found the treasure! It had lain here in the desert for over sixty years and no one had discovered it. And now here it was! The feeling was so overwhelming that it almost knocked Ondragon off his feet. At that moment, he knew why he loved his job.

Carried on a wave of happiness, he walked around the curved floor until he found a hatch. With both hands, he pulled it open and peered down. Like a fortified medieval tower, a spiral staircase of steel led down into the impenetrable darkness. Ondragon stepped tentatively onto the first step, bent over the rickety railing, and shone his light into the gloomy core. His eyes widened in astonishment as the light shone down on a tall copper pipe wrapped in several coils of wire. It loomed up in the center of the tower, and from its tip extended the thick strand of wire that disappeared through the hole in the dome at the top. This had to be a gigantic coil, Ondragon thought in fascination, and reached out a hand, thinking he could feel heat. Was it emanating from the giant tube? Strange. Surely the coil could not have been in operation. Maybe it was just an illusion. It was much warmer in here than outside anyway. He bent down and picked up a screw from the stairs. Listening, he dropped it into the depths. It took a few seconds for the piece of metal to hit and emit a bright clang. There was more metal down there. And perhaps the secret cargo of the Junkers!

Carefully, Ondragon took one rusty step after another, spiraling downward. As he did so, he noticed that the walls of the tower were octagonal like the one in Tesla's architect's drawing. The lower he got, the more the giant coil towered over him. Goose bumps rose on his body. He was about to enter something he knew only from a hundred-year-old picture. Something that was not supposed to exist. But the tower was there, even if it had not been built by Tesla himself, but by Nazi scientists. It was real. Had it also functioned?

Ondragon reached the bottom step and let the light of his headlamp wander. He felt a slight sense of disappointment. There was nothing special down here except the concrete foundation of the tower, the wooden base of the coil, and some apparatus connected to the coil by thick cables. Nothing was lying around untidily; everything looked as if it was in its intended place. There were no hastily stacked boxes or other materials anywhere to be seen. Ondragon walked around the apparatus and searched it; it consisted of large boxes with switches and relays. But again, he found no evidence of any possible cargo from the Junkers.

His radio crackled. "Hey, Rattlesnake? Are you all right?" he heard Achille ask.

"Yes, everything's okay," he replied.

"What did you find?"

"A huge coil and what looks like the control boxes, but nothing that could have been on the Nazi plane. I'm going to keep looking for a while more. Over." He shone his light around the room again and stopped at an alcove. There was something there! Stooping, he walked toward it and recognized a door. He put a hand on the knob and pulled. The door was not locked. But before he could open it completely and see behind it, the light in the tower suddenly went on! With a jerk, Ondragon raised his head and looked up. There were about twenty old-fashioned light bulbs hanging from cables and shining so brightly that he had to squint his eyes.

What the hell . . .? Why was there electricity here? And where was the switch? He hadn't touched anything except the door.

"Rattlesnake, is that you?" asked Achille from the radio. "I can see light. Are you coming back up?"

Ondragon wanted to answer Achille, but all of a sudden he felt something drill insistently into his neck. Cold metal. He froze and slowly raised his hands. And when he heard a familiar voice a moment later, he knew that someone else had beaten him to it.

CHAPTER 60

June 3, 2011
in the tower
night

Salut, *ça va?* Mr. Ondragon," the voice purred behind him in French. "As the saying goes, you always meet twice in life."

Ondragon would have liked to turn around and ram his fist into the bastard's face. But he didn't dare move and instead ground his jaws in rage.

"You really are persistent, I'll give you that, Mr. O. But this is the end. You've really gotten me into trouble, and I can't let you put our secret in jeopardy."

Ondragon let out a snide laugh. "*I'm* putting the secret in danger? And what are you doing? Selling it off to the energy company that puts in the highest bid! *Monsieur Noire*—I can call you that, can't I?"

The stranger cleared his throat quietly while Ondragon considered how he might get out of this predicament. How had the guy gotten into the tower? Through the door? Was that a way out?

"You are a bright one. My name is in fact Noire, Clandestin LeNoire, to be exact."

"Clandestin? Your name really does mean 'dark secret'? Seriously?"

"My parents had a certain degree of black humor." The stranger, who was now no longer unknown, laughed.

"Very funny!" Ondragon barked back and peered at the door. What was behind it? And could he possibly escape through it?

"I know what you're trying to do, Mr. O. But it's useless. There is not the slightest chance of escape, so don't even try. That door does not lead to freedom. So please be sensible and put your hands behind your head. And this . . . You will have no need of this."

Ondragon felt LeNoire pull his gun from his belt.

"Fine, and now I will take you to my leader. He will decide what to do with you."

Leader? Had Ondragon heard him correctly, or had LeNoire said client? Both words sounded similar in French. Thoughtfully, he raised his arms and put his hands to his head. Was someone from Groupe Hexagone here who wanted to finish him off in person? Well, he was bound to find out if he did what LeNoire asked.

"I'm going to remove my gun from your neck," the latter said. "And you will walk nicely through the door. But no false moves—I'll be close behind you. You'll see, there's only this one way."

Ondragon felt the pressure on his neck ease and took a first step toward the door. If he was quick enough, he could turn around and ram his head into LeNoire's stomach. Or he could just drop backward and smash his feet into his chin. The guy was no rookie though, Ondragon knew that; surely, he would anticipate it and simply take him out.

He slowly reached out and pulled the door open. Behind it, a dark corridor appeared. It seemed to be endless. Long and narrow. So narrow that two people couldn't walk side by side. LeNoire would hardly miss if he fired at him, Ondragon thought grudgingly. The miserable son of a bitch was right, this was the only way. He heard the radio crackle in his breast pocket, but no communication came through. Was Achille still up there on the dune? Would he follow him? He hoped so! Because the Frenchman was his only chance of getting out of here alive.

"What is it? Move!" urged LeNoire. "We don't have forever."

Ondragon hesitated but then saw that there was no point in resisting the inevitable and stepped into the corridor. He heard LeNoire follow him, though the floor of the hallway was covered with sand and muffled their footsteps. But the man's presence was an unmistakable hot pulsation, pushing him farther and farther into the hallway. By the light of his headlamp, Ondragon saw that the walls were boarded with rough planks and thick wooden beams propped up the ceiling every twenty paces. Certainly, it would not have been easy to dig a tunnel under the sand and maintain it for so long. Another masterstroke by the builders of this facility at the time! Where did it end? Might the Junkers cargo be there? Or the men from Groupe Hexagone?

They trudged down the tunnel for an eternity, and because Ondragon soon grew tired of the silence, he began asking LeNoire questions. Maybe he would get an answer.

"What is Hexagone paying you for your services? Can you retire on it afterward, or will you accept more assignments?"

Ondragon could hear his opponent's breathing behind him. It was fast and regular. However, there was no answer. But Ondragon did not let up.

"How did you manage to escape us in Dakhla? Were you even in the building? I tend to think not. You switched roles earlier in the hall at the port. Didn't you? Clever. Really. I fell for it."

LeNoire still did not reply.

"And then that Achmed. Babbled like a parrot: *My name is Achmed and I serve the Creator alone.* What nonsense. That kind of thing—"

"Shut your goddamn mouth!" blurted LeNoire abruptly.

Aha, so the guy could be provoked after all. Ondragon immediately went one better. "This Achmed, was he your friend? If so, I am sincerely sorry to inform you that he is no longer with us. *Je suis très désolé!*"

Ondragon felt a kick in his back and stumbled. He had to try hard not to sound astonished. "Hey, hey, why are we being so rough all of a sudden?" he said, laughing playfully. But LeNoire didn't seem to like the irony, because he gave him a second kick and hissed, "If you don't shut up already, I'll do to you what you did to Achmed!"

"Ooh, I'm scared . . ." Before Ondragon could draw the guy out any further, they unexpectedly came to a door.

"Oops, look at that. Already there. Shall I open it?" he asked, pointing to the closed passageway with a raised elbow. They had covered close to six hundred meters in the tunnel. Ondragon had secretly counted his steps.

"Open the door!" LeNoire ordered, the force of his hatred blazing hotly into Ondragon's back. With both hands he pried open the door, walked through, and stopped on the other side in surprise. A large hall opened up before him. A cave with several rows of light bulbs hanging from the high ceiling, bathing it in bright light. The cavern was empty except for a tangle of cables, man-size metal boxes . . . and a dozen hostile men staring at him with folded arms.

"Heavens! That's what I call a welcome committee!" said Ondragon, looking back belligerently. Which one of them might be the man from Hexagone? It seemed a bit strange to him that the guys were all dressed in a traditional *derra'a* and turban. They looked like the inhabitants of the oasis. Slowly, Ondragon turned in a circle and looked each of the dark-skinned men in the face, but none gave the impression of having come from the office of an energy company in Paris. Still, he sensed there was something special about the gentlemen. He completed his turn and finally dared to look his adversary in the eye.

Clandestin LeNoire seemed quite different from when they first met. Not quite as menacing and much smaller. Like the others, he wore a light blue robe with a white turban that made his narrow face appear even darker. On his left wrist shone the bracelet that Ondragon had found strange even then, and his coal-black eyes were glittering with undisguised disgust.

"Prepare yourself to go before the Creator!" said Clandestin, baring his gleaming white teeth. But it was not a smile. Ondragon noticed that Clandestin's gaze was fixed on something at his back. Quickly, he turned around and saw one of the guys standing behind him. He was holding a pistol-like device in his hand. But before Ondragon could back away, the man wordlessly placed the device on his chest and pulled the trigger. A short pain flashed through Ondragon and then he was enveloped in blackness.

CHAPTER 61

October 6, 1899
Colorado Springs
morning

Czito and Philemon looked at the clouds of smoke billowing past the windows. They were sitting on the Pikes Peak cog railroad train, riding up to the summit. Both felt the curious stares of the other passengers. This was not surprising, as they were a curious sight. The Serb had a backpack and a metal box on which one of Tesla's cathode ray tubes was perched, and Philemon held a gramophone tightly in his lap, the horn sitting beside his head like a large, flower-shaped ear. Today the all-important experiment would take place, at twelve o'clock sharp. Philemon felt his body vibrating with excitement.

Just three weeks had passed since the fire. Three weeks in which they had rebuilt the laboratory and returned it to operation. The damage to the building had not been too great and the equipment had been largely intact. The rest had been repaired by Czito, Löwenstein, and Philemon with tireless diligence. They all agreed that they were keener than ever to continue their work after the cowardly attack. They would show the residents of Colorado Springs that they could not be so easily intimidated, and they would also show the Pinkertons, or whoever had set fire to the lab. The hours spent together rebuilding had made the bond between the three assistants even closer, so much so that now they only had to exchange a glance to understand one another. This filled Philemon with pride. At last, he had arrived in the inner circle of Tesla's confidants; at last, they accepted him as one of their own.

He looked out the window at the barren mountain landscape. The smoke from the locomotive wafted over them in dark swaths, dissipating farther back. The sun was shining, but it had become noticeably colder. The closer they got to the summit, the more the temperature dropped.

When they finally reached the top, they left the mountain station and the usual daytime guests behind and marched with their experimental equipment to the terminal, which still stood unchanged behind the fence of barbed wire.

With the weight of the gramophone in his arms, Philemon quickly became breathless. The thin air was still affecting him and he hoped the headache would hold off a little today. Once at the terminal, they unloaded the equipment and caught their breath. Czito looked at his pocket watch.

"There's half an hour to go before the experiment starts. We should get everything set up. It's not much, fortunately." The Serb set about positioning the box with the cathode ray tube on a rock several steps away from the terminal. He then retrieved a roll of cables from his backpack and connected them to the box.

"So now let's set up the gramophone. It's best here." Czito pointed to a flat patch of rough pasture not far from the stone. "The cables should be long enough. And make sure the turntable is level."

"Yessir!" replied Philemon, offsetting the slope of the hillside with a small stone he wedged under the front edge of the gramophone. Out of the corner of his eye he saw Czito smiling broadly under his black mustache.

"Today we will see, Phil," the Serb said. "God willing, we're going to witness something truly great."

Philemon nodded, eager and excited. Czito looked once more at his watch.

"Fifteen minutes!" He bent down with a groan and picked up the two cable ends. Then he plugged them into two temporary sockets that the doctor had mounted on the back of the gramophone case instead of the usual crank for the drive spring. Now both devices were connected, the cathode ray tube and the gramophone. Dr. Tesla had devised this assemblage and put it together himself. The box with the tube was both a receiving station and a transformer. It would receive the energy that the doctor and Löwenstein sent up to them from the laboratory down on the prairie and convert it into electric current, which would then be conducted via the cables to the converted gramophone and set the device in motion.

"Quick, Phil," cried Czito, waving his hand at him, "where is the record?"

Philemon pulled the shellac disc out of its protective cover and laid it reverently on the turntable. His parents also owned a gramophone and therefore he knew how to operate the device. Only this one would not be powered by an internal spring but by wirelessly received electricity. At least that's what they all hoped. Gently, Philemon lifted the curved arm with the needle and lowered it onto the disk. It remained still and the gramophone remained silent.

Nervously, he wiped his sweaty fingers on his pants. Now everything was ready. The experiment could begin. He looked over at Czito, who was staring at the watch in his hands. Philemon moved over to him and also watched the small clockface, spellbound. It was almost windless on the summit, and they could hear the clicking of the small gears in the clockwork. Tirelessly, the hand made its rounds.

Two minutes to twelve.

Philemon bit his lips with anxiety. Would the experiment succeed? Would what Dr. Tesla had predicted work?

One more minute.

He didn't take his eyes off the hand as it counted down the final seconds.

Fifteen.

Ten.

Five.

Without being aware of it, Philemon counted quietly . . . until both hands of the clock met on the twelve. Immediately, magical sounds floated through the crystal-clear mountain air. A melody so beautiful and sublime that Philemon was instantly brought to tears.

"Freude, schöner Götterfunken, Tochter aus Elysium, wir betreten feuertrunken, Himmlische, dein Heiligtum!."

The Ode to Joy from Beethoven's Ninth Symphony rang out like a promise of life, and the voices of the choir rose into the sky on invisible wings. They flew out over the landscape in the distant sunlight, out to the people who were doing their daily chores.

"Deine Zauber binden wieder, was die Mode streng geteilt. Alle Menschen werden Brüder, wo dein sanfter Flügel weilt . . ."

Philemon took his eyes from the breathtaking view and looked at Czito. "It works," he whispered with a smile. "It actually works."

The Serb gave an emotional nod and wiped his eyes. "Yes, my friend. Today is a great day. Today the future begins."

CHAPTER 62

June 3, 2011
in the mountain
time unknown

When Ondragon regained consciousness, he felt as if he had pulled all the muscles in his body. He was dizzy and could only move his cramped limbs with difficulty. He turned his head and saw that he was lying on sandy ground in a small cave. Surprisingly, he had not been tied up and the exit of the cave did not seem to be guarded. Groaning, he sat up and brushed the sand from his face. Then he lifted his shirt. The place where he had been knocked out by the strange weapon hurt and smelled slightly scorched, as if he had been electrocuted. He lowered the shirt again and felt around for his gear. Unfortunately, the bastards had been pretty thorough and had taken everything he had been carrying, even the knife in his boot.

He looked toward the open entrance of the small cave. Still no one to be seen. Outside, bare light bulbs hung from the ceiling of the hallway, shining in at him. Ondragon looked around the room. A stack of wooden crates stood in a dark corner. He crawled over and wiped the layer of dust from the side walls. Underneath, an emblem emerged that was more than familiar to him. An imperial eagle with outstretched wings, holding in its talons a swastika wreathed in oak leaves. Ondragon looked toward the cave exit, weighing things up. He could take this opportunity to escape. His gaze darted back to the crates. Or he could look at what was inside. Maybe it was the Junkers' cargo. Another glance at the exit and back to the crates. Exit, crates. Exit, crates. He felt the mystery reaching out to him, trying to hold him.

"Damn!" he whispered. "Fucking curiosity!" He turned to the crates and tried to open them. The lids were nailed tight, except for one, which was a little loose. Ondragon clawed his fingernails into the narrow gap, but quickly realized he was stuck without tools. He looked around, but there was nothing he could use for leverage. So he pulled his belt out of his pants and tried the buckle. He fiddled with the lid until he finally managed to pry the gap open enough to push the belt through at one corner. Then he pulled with all his might on both ends of the leather strap, and with a soft *crack* the nails finally gave way. The lid came off and Ondragon peered into the box. Hidden among the wood shavings and rags was something shiny. A device? He quickly pushed the packaging aside and looked at the contents, puzzled. The excitement he had just felt fizzled out.

Gold bars?

With his fingertips, he stroked the cold, rich yellow surface. They were handy 1000g bars, hallmarked DEGUSSA FINE GOLD 999.9.

No secret Tesla technology, sadly, just ordinary gold.

He sank back on his heels. Yes, okay, there was a whole lot of it. And if the other boxes were also full of it, there were millions of dollars' worth here, but somehow he had expected something more spectacular.

Disappointed, he was about to rise when a shadow suddenly fell on him from behind. Ondragon wheeled around and looked at the shadowy figure that had appeared in the brightly lit corridor. It groped along the wall, and a moment later the cavernous room was bathed in bright white light. Dazzled, Ondragon narrowed his eyes. How could such old-fashioned lamps be so bright!

When his retinas recovered from the shock, he realized that Clandestin LeNoire was standing in front of him. The little bastard gave an inscrutable smile, raised a hand, and gently tapped one of the light bulbs with his finger. It began to sway slightly, causing the room to involuntarily sway along with it.

"Tesla lamps," he said pensively. "Not those inefficient things made by Thomas Edison that give off more heat than light. Nikola Tesla redesigned them back in the day for the opening of the Chicago World's Fair, because Edison had forbidden him to use his patent after being edged out by Tesla in the contest to illuminate the exposition. It is a shame these light bulbs have been forgotten. If people used them today, they would be spared the hassle of those unspeakable energy-saving bulbs."

Ondragon looked at the guy in his traditional Arabian clothes in amazement. His appearance did not fit at all with what he was saying.

"Are you a scientist?" he asked.

Clandestin turned his gaze from the lamp to Ondragon and his features hardened. "No!"

"What then?"

The man stepped toward him and slapped him in the face so quickly that Ondragon could only stare at him in surprise. "But I'm not a murderer! Not like you!" he hissed angrily through his teeth.

Ondragon made to seize the opportunity and pounce on him, but more men appeared in the cave entrance. Their weapons were pointing at him.

Clandestin raised an admonitory finger. "No, no, Mr. O, the rules have changed. *You* are now my prisoner and *I* will show you how we deal with unwanted guests here!"

Without warning, he kicked him in the stomach. Ondragon doubled over and toppled forward into the sand. *The bastard is fast as hell*, he thought, and tried to get back up, but a series of well-aimed kicks kept him down. Ondragon gritted his teeth. He wouldn't scream. No way, no how. He'd sooner let himself be trampled to death!

When the kicks stopped for a moment, he raised his head. "You're angry about Achmed," he said, panting. "I understand that. But you brutally ran over a woman and shot my assistant!"

"All necessary measures. I'm even sorry about the agent. And your assistant would never have bled to death. I knew exactly where to shoot to impress you and keep you in check, Mr. O!"

Ondragon turned onto his side and dared to sit up. But this was immediately rewarded with a hard blow to the head. The pain shot down his injured neck and into his back. Protectively, he threw his arms over his head and let out a groan.

"What you, on the other hand, did to our brother Achmed," Clandestin hissed, "was cold-blooded murder! But first you tortured him, you sadistic pig!"

"Achmed had a choice," Ondragon countered coldly. "He wouldn't have had to die if he had told us what he knew!"

With a furious grimace, Clandestin snatched the pistol from the man next to him and pressed it to Ondragon's forehead. "You had a choice too! The choice to leave before you invaded this place."

Ondragon looked past the barrel at his adversary, who had managed to lead him around by the nose for so long. Would he actually have the guts to pull the trigger?

Clandestin bared his teeth, his breathing rapid. This Achmed seemed to have been closer to him than he had assumed.

"I have my principles," Ondragon explained calmly. "I couldn't just give up like that, because I have been given a mission. And I always fulfill my orders! No matter what."

"Well then, your principles will take you to the grave this time!" growled Clandestin contemptuously, and Ondragon saw his finger curl.

"Stop!" someone shouted suddenly from the entrance of the cave and everyone present turned around, startled. All except Clandestin, who continued to stare at Ondragon. The hand that held the weapon was trembling.

"I said stop!"

A man Ondragon had not seen before moved over to Clandestin, gently placed a hand on the weapon, and pushed it downward. He had snow-white hair, and his bearded face looked like the wise countenance of a prophet. He wore a traditional *derra'a* with an embroidered breast slit. Ondragon saw the tattoo on his neck. It was the Tenet cross with Roman numerals.

"Master Yaqub!" growled Clandestin with barely concealed anger. "It is my fault that this fellow is here, and it is therefore also my job to make sure he leaves!" He was about to raise his pistol again, but the old man stopped him and wrestled the weapon from him with a deft movement. Ondragon saw that he too was wearing one of those bangles. It appeared to be made of silver and had a polished surface with a tiny hole on it. A small green light glowed in it.

"Leave him!" the old man ordered. His French was clear and had no trace of an accent. "I want to talk to him."

Talk, Ondragon thought hopefully, *well, that sounds reasonable.* "Who are you?" he wanted to know.

The old man clasped his hands in front of his body and looked at him haughtily. "My name is Yaqub Kahn and I am the supreme leader of the Brotherhood."

"What brotherhood?"

"Now don't pretend you don't know who we are."

Ondragon rose and wiped the blood from his lip. He thought of the tattoo on each of the men. "The Creator preserves his creation?"

Yaqub's expression brightened. "There you go. You're not so stupid after all. *Sator opera tenet—tenet opera Sator.* That formula is our motto."

"Hence the tattoo."

"Yes, the Tenet cross with Roman numerals is our identifying mark. We are the Sator Brotherhood"

"The Sator Brotherhood," Ondragon repeated thoughtfully. "I've never heard of that before. How did you get here? I mean, where does your brotherhood come from? Rome, the Vatican? Are you an offshoot of the Illuminati or the Knights Templar?"

The old man shook his head in amusement. "You watch too many Hollywood movies, Monsieur Ondragon. No, we are not descended from the Illuminati, nor from the Knights Templar. And that we still exist is merely an accident of history, if you will. A twist of fate. The Sator Brotherhood is not as old as you might think. It was founded in 1941 by General Kammler—a gentleman you undoubtedly have heard of. At that time, the Brotherhood secretly pursued the goal of developing an all-destroying weapon with which the German people would win the war and thus conquer the entire world. Kammler sent out spies to obtain the necessary technology. The technology of Nikola Tesla."

"Then it was actually his spies who murdered Tesla. Were they also followers of the Sator Brotherhood?"

"Yes, they were," Yaqub replied, lowering his eyes in shame. "Not the most praiseworthy of our actions, I must admit. The spies were supposed to bring Tesla's technology to the general, but the apparatus was too big, so on the advice of an informant, they took only the notebook from Tesla's vault."

"What informant?"

"In the ranks of Tesla's confidants there was a man who, for money, told the Germans where they would find the book. As far as I know, his name was Georg Scherff. He was Tesla's accountant for many years. Fortunately, he was never a member of the Brotherhood."

"But in the end, the Nazis failed to complete this devil's machine before they had to surrender," Ondragon said.

"No, they did not, but they had been close when the Allies moved in. Kammler had to destroy the tower and the laboratories in Ludwigsdorf. He loaded all the important parts onto the Junkers and fled."

"But if the Brotherhood existed before the end of the war, where did the other members go? Surely there were some who stayed in Germany."

"Yes, but they scattered in all directions," Yaqub replied. "Have you ever heard of Operation Paperclip? At the time, many German scientists were promised immunity from prosecution by the US military if they emigrated to the United States and made their knowledge available to research there. One of the most prominent was Wernher von Braun, the inventor of the V2 rocket."

Ondragon nodded. "Everyone knows him."

"I think some of us went to America. After the war, we tried to contact our missing brothers," Yaqub continued. "Unfortunately, to no avail. Maybe they renounced the Brotherhood after the fall of the Third Reich Or they felt like failures and therefore did not reveal their identity. Therefore, we assume that we are the only survivors of the Brotherhood."

"And why are you here now in the middle of the desert?"

"This is that coincidence I was talking about. I told you my name, didn't I? Yaqub Kahn."

Ondragon frowned. Kahn? What was so special about this name, he wondered, but suddenly the scales fell from his eyes.

"Eschenberg, Schwarz, and Kahn!" he exclaimed. "The three scientists left here by General Kammler."

Yaqub nodded. "Werner Kahn is my father, and Albrecht Schwarz is the grandfather of this capable man here." He put a hand on Clandestin's shoulder.

Schwarz—Black in English, LeNoire in French. Of course! Ondragon would have liked to slap his forehead but tried to hide his annoyance at his lack of powers of deduction. "That sounds plausible so far," he said, "only unfortunately you don't look like the descendants of German scientists to me."

Yaqub looked down at himself and smiled. "I understand your skepticism. That's why I'll give you one more proof of our origin. *Bitte schön*," he said, switching effortlessly to German mid-sentence. "Although we may not look like it in your eyes, we are indeed descendants of the three scientists. These brave men made the best of their hopeless situation. They allied themselves with the nomadic inhabitants of the oasis and started families. So German as well as Sahrawi blood flows in our veins. But we were brought up entirely in the spirit of the Brotherhood."

"You mean in the sense of a Nazi brotherhood?"

"Something like that, yes."

Ondragon smiled involuntarily. It really was an irony of fate. There stood a group of dark-skinned people in front of him, claiming to be the offshoot of an old Nazi sect. Absolutely phenomenal!

"I can see that you find that funny, Monsieur Ondragon. And of course our fathers and grandfathers were supporters of National Socialist ideology, at least as long as Hitler was in power. But it was never to the fore. My father and his brothers in spirit revered science, and nothing but science. That was what they lived for. They quickly discarded the Nazi doctrine here in the desert."

"So you don't work for Groupe Hexagone at all?" asked Ondragon, cautious now.

"Groupe Hexagone has nothing to do with this. It was a false trail that Clandestin laid. With some success, I see."

Ondragon cast a baleful glance at Clandestin, whose chin was jutting proudly. He couldn't stand that dog, but he had to hand it to him, he was quite cunning! He turned back to the old man. "So that means you've been sitting here in the desert year in, year out, making sure no one gets too close to your treasure, and if there is any danger from the outside, you send out your mercenaries to eliminate it?" he summarized.

"Correct!" Yaqub looked at him with an expression that left no doubt about the truth of his statement.

"And where did that gold come from?" asked Ondragon, pointing to the boxes behind him.

"The gold," said Yaqub, unimpressed, "General Kammler wanted to take it with him to secure his prosperity. But the stuff, as we know, became too heavy for him. He had to discard ballast. And now it sits here. Every now and then we sell a bar to cover our expenses, but that's about it."

"So the boxes were in the Junkers. What else?"

Yaqub made a gesture. "Follow me and I'll show you!"

Ondragon hesitated. Why would the guy reveal all this to him so candidly? There was no reason for him to. The Brotherhood had to keep their treasure secret at all costs. It could only mean that sooner or later they would dispose of him. So he had better think of a way out while this Yaqub was still being so friendly. With a seemingly calm expression, Ondragon stepped out of the cave past the scowling Clandestin and joined Yaqub. Followed by the other men, they walked through the long corridors, from which countless other tunnels and caves branched off. Some of the rooms were filled with stacked crates and others were furnished like small apartments, with furniture, carpets, computers, and other modern technology. Ondragon noticed that red-painted metal barrels were everywhere.

"What's that?" he asked, pointing to one of the barrels as he passed.

"That's my precaution in case any stranger intrudes here," Yaqub replied without turning around. Ondragon thought it through and quickly followed the old man. Shortly afterward, as they passed some caves with elongated niches in their rock walls, Ondragon stopped abruptly. He could not help but take a curious look inside. On the floor were all kinds of clay pots with indefinable contents, and in the niches lay what looked like rag dolls. A thick layer of dust lay over everything, and a musty smell emanated from the cave.

"These are ancient burial sites," Yaqub explained. "But the mummies are not of the oasis dwellers; they come from a much older people, from the time when the Sahara was still fertile. We found vessels with wheat and millet. Certainly, an interesting site for archaeologists, but even the Sahrawis from the oasis keep it strictly secret. For them, this place is called 'The Mountain of the Dead' and it is taboo to enter it."

What a lovely ambience, Ondragon thought, and nodded.

Yaqub turned around and they continued their way through the catacombs. After several twists and turns, they finally reached the end of the corridor and entered a hall. Ondragon craned his neck in amazement. The cavern was the size of a cathedral and was crammed with strange technology: bizarrely shaped antennas, old-fashioned switch boxes made of black Bakelite, squat engine blocks, and coils of all sizes. The most fascinating, were the glass radio valves of various shapes, the size of a man, standing in rows on a brass base. From this protruded cables as thick as your arm wrapped in braided fabric, which connected with other strands of cable and snaked all over the floor. You had to watch where you put your feet. The cylinders gave off a phosphorescent glow, bathing the hall in a diffuse light. The whole place looked like the forgotten realm of a mad professor.

"And these devices were all already here?" asked Ondragon once his amazement had subsided.

"Indeed," Yaqub confirmed. "The station was built in 1943 and operated by a group of German scientists who lived and researched here before General Kammler arrived."

"But according to Dr. Schuch's report, the station was destroyed when he landed here with the Junkers," Ondragon interjected, "and all the scientists had left. It doesn't look like complete destruction to me here though, looking around. Who rebuilt it all?"

"That was the three who were left behind. After all, they had plenty of time to fix up the station."

"And where had the other scientists gone?" asked Ondragon.

Yaqub raised his shoulders. "There was no trace of them. Probably they destroyed the station and fled. Maybe they perished in the desert."

Ondragon looked at the tubes again. Above them hung a flicker, like hot air. Only now did he become aware of a high-pitched buzzing and notice that small indicator lights were flashing everywhere on the apparatus. Were they really live? Where was the power coming from? Was there a generator here in the mountain?

The old man caught his fascinated look. "These are special electron tubes," he explained. "Much of the Junkers' cargo consisted of them, and it borders on a miracle that the fragile glass cylinders all remained intact. But with their help, my father and his colleagues managed to get the station back in operation. The tubes are more valuable than all the gold in the world and a vastly underestimated but crucial aspect of Tesla's research. Just think of the radio he invented before Marconi. Tesla developed very special tubes for his world system during his creative period. They are coils of various sizes and designs. The glass tubes are vacuums or filled with gases and were built in Ludwigsdorf according to instructions from Nikola Tesla's notebook. The group of scientists also managed to re-create Tesla's Wardenclyffe Tower. That wonderful construction out there in the desert through which you entered our secret realm. Unfortunately, those tubes and the tower are the only samples that still exist, because Tesla's notebook and all other records inexplicably disappeared the same year they were stolen."

"And this is it?" Ondragon let his eyes travel over the myriad flashing devices. "Tesla's dream? His wireless world system!"

"Yes, it is." Yaqub nodded proudly.

"And what exactly can it do now? I mean, is it a weapon or a perpetual motion machine?"

Yaqub reflected. Then he answered. "Well, it has many functions. It is the perfect all-in-one device, to put it in today's terms. All the designers in the world can only dream of something like this. But Tesla already possessed the superior ability to think multifunctionally and on different levels. This was and remains unique to this day. Tesla's world system is as simple as it is ingenious, and has a number of potential applications. On the one hand, it is a construction that can wirelessly transmit energy and data from one place to another, of course only somewhere that has a receiving station. This doesn't sound very spectacular to we humans today, since we have long been able to transmit large data packages by radio, but this system alone, as you can see it here, is capable of producing enough energy to power all of Las Vegas!"

"Really?" asked Ondragon, skeptically letting his gaze travel around the cave. That sounded like an exaggeration.

"Believe me," Yaqub affirmed, "this invention can do even more! It would make all cables and overhead lines in the world superfluous. All devices, machines, buildings, and vehicles could be supplied with power wirelessly via a small component. Just as a cell phone is connected to the wireless network, devices and vehicles would be connected via a world-wide wireless power grid."

"That sounds great, at least if you hate all those tangled cables."

"You sound sarcastic, Mr. Ondragon, but this is significant. Imagine getting electricity just like that from the ether. Cars, trains, ships, and planes could all be converted to electric motors powered by the wireless system."

Amused by the fantasy, Ondragon shook his head and considered how he might escape from this madman. Surreptitiously, he let his gaze glide over the hall again.

"I see you still don't believe me," Yaqub said, abruptly pulling Ondragon's cell phone out of his tunic. "We took this from you earlier. Here, take it and remove the battery."

Ondragon did as he was told, and when he had the battery in his hand, Yaqub handed him a small brass box, barely larger than the battery, with a standard jack plug sticking out of it.

"This is a special receiver for wireless power. Plug it into your cell phone's headphone jack. And turn on the device!"

Ondragon did so, and raised his eyebrows in surprise. The cell phone display lit up and even showed full reception. And that in the middle of the desert!

"Okay, that's impressive," he said, and tapped Charlize's number. The phone began to dial. But before it could connect, Yaqub put a hand on it.

"Don't, Mr. Ondragon. That would be far too easy, wouldn't it?"

Ondragon grinned apologetically and turned off the cell phone. "That's great," he then said, "but where is the energy coming from now? Actually from the ether?"

"That's right!" Yaqub smiled. "With Tesla's world system, you would never need to charge your cell phone again. No one would have to pay for electricity anymore. We'd have energy for free. For all eternity!"

"Does it all work through that tower out there in the desert? Tesla's Wardenclyffe Tower? Does it suck the energy out of the ether?" Ondragon asked. Not just out of curiosity—he also needed to buy time.

Yaqub shook his head. "No, the tower is just the transmitter, a kind of intermediary between the ether and the material world, sort of like an antenna. The real miracle happens in those tubes there. How they work exactly, we don't know, but they are the core of this unique system. So it is indeed something like a perpetual motion machine, if you will. But not in the classical sense, where a wheel turns for all eternity; rather in the sense of a space energy converter. It captures space energy and converts it into electricity."

Ondragon couldn't help but think of Truthfinder, who would certainly have enjoyed this conversation. Unfortunately, the boy was sitting at his desk thousands of miles away, dreaming of great adventures.

"But call it what you like, Monsieur Ondragon," Yaqub continued. "Free energy, zero-point energy, neutrinos, or cosmic rays. In any case, it is an almost inexhaustible source of energy. Its origin is in space. Nikola Tesla discovered this type of high-energy particle quite by accident when he was doing research in his Colorado Springs laboratory in 1899. After publicizing the phenomenon, he was laughed at, but despite all the rejection and ridicule, he never gave up trying to find a way to capture and use cosmic radiation."

"That sounds great," Ondragon said. "But I'm still wondering how you can know this? Fine, you're a descendant of the men who built all this, but you're neither a scientist nor an engineer."

"That's right. We are only the guardians of this place. And the knowledge about it was transmitted to us by our fathers by word of mouth. That was and still is the safest way to pass on a secret. Unfortunately, a lot of knowledge has been lost as a result. For example, the functions of the system. Today, we are no longer aware of all of them. We know that it can also generate a so-called death ray, but we have no idea how to put it into operation."

"Most unfortunate. I would have been curious to see that demonstration!" He put his head back and looked up at the equipment pensively. "But if the system actually works now," he said, "doesn't it border on a crime not to make it available to mankind?"

Master Yaqub blinked and a thoughtful expression came over his face. Finally, he raised one hand and made an all-encompassing gesture. "These fantastic devices may be the 'Holy Grail of science,' but they also pose a great danger to the world. The heavenly, alluring light they radiate also harbors dark abysses. For man carries both light and shadow within him. Just like this fabulous machine. Evil and good are inseparably rooted in us. That is our nature. Do you know what would happen if we gave Tesla's dream to the people out there?"

"Well, I can think of one very important thing off the top of my head, which is that we would suddenly be free of the scourge of the energy companies—just my little suggestion," Ondragon countered.

Yaqub grimaced and Clandestin, still standing next to his master, exhaled contemptuously. "I'm afraid it's not as simple as you think," the old man began to explain. "For example, what would have happened if the Nazis had put the world system into operation? Right. They would not have seen the good in it, they would have used it for evil. For them, it was a weapon with which they would have done terrible things and extended their reign of terror over the whole world. And to pass that to today's governments . . ." He left a meaningful pause, during which no one dared speak. "That's right. No one could swear that the same thing wouldn't happen. That is the sad truth. And this is only one of the possible effects. Even without evil intent, the system would have incalculable consequences for our society."

"And which ones, pray tell?"

"Do you really not understand?" Yaqub looked at him, shaking his head like a teacher with a dull-witted student. But when he finally spoke again, every single word the old man said tightened like an oppressive band around Ondragon's stomach. At the end of the lecture, he felt as if he had been thrown in at the deep end. And now he stood there, shivering and freezing in the face of the scenario Yaqub had just laid out for him.

Yet it was as simple as it was logical. Of course, with the introduction of Tesla's world system, everyone would be free to consume as much energy as they wanted. They would have unlimited mobility, could build uninsulated houses, and not give a shit about emissions or energy loss. They could leave the lights on whenever they felt like it, and no one would ask them to pay. Energy would be infinite and environmentally friendly. A truly brave new world . . . which would also be doomed. Because every energy producer who relied on fossil fuels and nuclear energy would immediately be bankrupt, and whole countries with them!

Many countries held majority shares in these globally networked corporate giants or were propping up their ailing budgets with an energy tax. The consequence would be an immediate collapse of the established economic systems. The flow of money would come to a standstill, banks would go bankrupt, and stock markets would implode. Not to mention the effects on other industries and on the financial situation of every single citizen of the world.

Tesla's world system was a fucking Pandora's box!

"Do you understand now that Tesla's dream is a double-edged sword?" asked Yaqub.

Ondragon nodded. Oh yes, and how!

A sad smile appeared on the old man's features "Well, unfortunately, not everything that looks good at first glance is always good at second glance."

"Then why don't you destroy all this?" asked Ondragon. "That would be the easiest thing to do. Then you could be sure it would never fall into the wrong hands. And it would save you a lot of trouble."

"I have given that much thought," Yaqub replied. "A great responsibility has been placed in our hands, and every day I ask myself one and the same question: Is this the greatest invention of mankind or the beginning of the Last Judgment? Today, I am still not able to answer it. I am simply not able to make the decision to destroy the devices, or not. Maybe the generation of brothers that comes after me will succeed. I don't know and I am heartbroken about it. It is a dilemma. Tesla's works are a blessing and a curse at the same time. And perhaps man will never be wise enough to be able to use them properly."

"That may be. But I would now be very interested to know *why* you have showed me all of this."

Yaqub raised his head and looked at him. "That's easy: You are a man of mysteries, after all, Mr. Ondragon. Mysteries are your passion."

"Yeah, so?"

"I don't want you to die without solving this last great mystery!"

"Die?" asked Ondragon pretending naivety as his *centrifuge* raced. Now was the time. Now he urgently needed a way out! He looked around in search of help.

"Forget it," Yaqub said almost pityingly. "You won't get out. This mountain will be your grave! Didn't you know that? It was obvious I couldn't let you go."

"Well then, I'm just in time. What a nice chat between friends!"

Ondragon and Yaqub turned around, surprised, at the sound of the strange voice.

Behind them, a man in a black balaclava stepped out from the shelter of a machine and pointed his M16 at them. "Throw down your weapons, gentlemen, and raise your arms, please! If you would be so kind!"

That voice, Ondragon thought, *I know it!* Hope sprouted in him and he slowly raised his arms. Next to him, Yaqub followed his example. The intruder nodded and suddenly behind him, a whole unit of hooded men appeared. They wore sand-colored camouflage uniforms and were armed to the teeth. They waited patiently for their leader's command; he was standing with his legs planted wide. Everything about him bristled with confidence. Ondragon noticed that all color had drained from Yaqub's face and he had begun to tremble all over. The old man's worst nightmare had just come true. His secret had been revealed. The fate of the whole world was on a knife edge!

Suddenly, the leader of the storm troopers stepped forward and pulled the hood from his head. It was Agent Steiner. He had guessed right, Ondragon thought, and smiled at him in relief, but Steiner's expression remained hard. "Mr. Ondragon," he said coolly, "it's good to see you again. You can lower your arms and join us. Come."

Ondragon hesitated briefly. What did Yaqub think of him now? That he had betrayed his secret to the German secret service? But it wasn't like that. Even though he was happy about Steiner's appearance, he felt the need to make it clear to the old man that he had not planned it that way. Slowly, he walked toward Steiner and felt Clandestin's eyes burning into his back. At least it was clear what the latter now believed.

"Well now, you've done an excellent job," Steiner said, sounding more ironic than impressed as Ondragon arrived beside him. "Kubicki will be very pleased with the success of the operation."

"Where is Kubicki?" asked Ondragon.

"Out at base camp. With a dozen other men." Steiner turned to Yaqub and his followers. "So you see, it's no use resisting!"

Ondragon saw Clandestin tense involuntarily. The guy seemed to be up to something. Hopefully, nothing stupid.

"And what do you want to do now?" he inquired of Steiner.

"The first thing we're going to do is arrest those locals over there and take them to base camp. There they will be interrogated while we calmly survey the pretty machinery sitting around down here. It looks very promising." The BND agent's gaze slid greedily over the apparatus. "A delightful collection. Have they explained to you how the machines work?"

Does he want to test how much I know? Ondragon thought, but before he could answer, he saw Clandestin take to his heels and leap between the machines in one bound. From one moment to the next, he was gone.

"Run, Clandestin! *Sator opera tenet!*" Yaqub shouted after him, but one of the mercenaries abruptly silenced him by smashing his rifle butt against his temple. Groaning, the old man fell to the ground, while Steiner yelled to two of his bloodhounds to retrieve the fleeing Clandestin.

"I made a mistake, Mr. Ondragon!" said Yaqub in a quivering voice. "A big mistake!" With difficulty, he braced himself again, pressing a hand to his bleeding temple. "Clandestin should have killed you back in Brazil! It was stupid of me to let you come here. But I had hoped it would end more peacefully. Unfortunately, the Brotherhood failed."

Ondragon looked at the old man. A sudden jolt went through Yaqub. He straightened up and slowly broke away from the group of his followers.

"Stop! Where are you going? Freeze!" ordered Steiner, aiming the machine gun at Yaqub. Yaqub, however, was not impressed and continued on his way. He headed determinedly for one of the large switch boxes. Steiner fired once in the air as a warning, but the old man persisted.

Ondragon watched the spectacle and guessed what would come next, but Yaqub seemed unconcerned. He merely flinched a little when another shot from Steiner's gun shattered the silence. Instantly, a red spot appeared on Yaqub's tunic. It spread quickly, but the Brotherhood leader bravely kept on his feet and staggered to the control box. Breathing heavily, he propped himself against it. Some of his brothers shouted angrily and tried to rush to his aid, but Yaqub turned and held them back with a raised hand. His gaze traveled from his brothers to Ondragon. Blood ran from his mouth. The two men looked at each other for a long time.

"I have made my decision!" Yaqub finally whispered, and slumped lifelessly.

Ondragon stared at the control box. A red trail stretched from a frantically flashing light to the floor.

"What did that son of a bitch do?" shouted Steiner, glancing at the flashing button Yaqub must have surreptitiously pressed behind his back.

"I don't know," Ondragon replied, ducking down in anticipation of some kind of bang. But nothing happened. Everyone looked spellbound at the little light, which all at once stopped flashing. The silence that followed was almost palpable.

But nothing happened, and Ondragon heard Steiner breathe a sigh of relief.

"False alarm!" the BND agent said mockingly, turning around. "I guess the old idiot hit the wrong self-destruct button!"

Ondragon was still looking at the dead Yaqub, noticing his bracelet on which the small green dot suddenly glowed red.

Why the red barrels with the flashing boxes suddenly appeared in his mind, he was not sure later. The only thing he could be certain of was that his instinct reacted faster than his mind, and as the first red barrel exploded near them, he dove to the floor. Ondragon flew through the air and hit the ground hard, protected by a transformer. A wave of heat washed over him and an acrid smell hit his nose.

As the deafening bang faded, he could hear the shrill cries of pain from those less fortunate than he. With one hand pressed to his mouth, he peered around the transformer box. What he saw was worse than anything he had ever seen. It seemed as if they had landed directly in the front yard of hell. Flames blazed everywhere in the hall. Seemingly without effort, they ate into the metal of the apparatus and devices . . . but also into the human bodies. Ondragon looked with horror at the men, who were screaming and flailing about the room. It didn't matter whether they belonged to the Brotherhood or to the BND's Special Operations Command, each was struggling with the flames that had taken up residence in their clothes and hair. Some of the injured were missing limbs, others had only a bloody mask where their faces had been. There was a stench of burned flesh and chemicals. And everywhere among the hungry, lambent flames lay body parts and corpses mutilated beyond recognition. It was an unimaginable sight.

But then Ondragon caught sight of Steiner and he felt the blood freeze in his veins.

In the midst of the chaos, the BND agent was kneeling on the floor and, panicking, trying to beat out the flames on his cheeks. But they stuck to his hands and spread farther across his body with each attempt to extinguish them.

And only now did Ondragon realize what he was dealing with.

Phosphorus!

The bomb had been laced with phosphorus!

Aghast, he pressed his hand more firmly over his mouth and nose and watched the diabolical mixture of phosphorus and rubber spread unhindered over Steiner's face. The oxygen in the air caused it to ignite again and again and it could not be smothered with water or foam. It just kept burning. Mercilessly.

Ondragon saw blood oozing from Steiner's cheeks, but it seemed to coagulate again immediately and settle on his skin like a layer of congealed wax. The holes in his face grew larger and something bright flashed out. Steiner's teeth! But the phosphorus would not stop at that either! It would eat its way farther and farther into Steiner's skull until he died a miserable death!

And you will die too if you don't get your ass out of here!

Thanks to his inner voice, Ondragon managed to tear his gaze away from Steiner, who was screaming dementedly, and turn around. At the same time, several of the radio tubes exploded above him and a biting rain of glass shards pelted down on him. Protectively, he threw an arm over his head and ran. Away from the wailing wounded and away from the horribly disfigured Steiner.

He passed several more of the red barrels standing next to the endless row of machines, thinking that it was only a matter of minutes or even seconds before they too would ignite. One by one or all together, it didn't matter. There was certainly enough explosive stored in the corridors and caves to reduce the entire mountain to rubble.

As if these thoughts had triggered one of the invisible detonators, the next barrel exploded without warning—fortunately at the other end of the hall. With a loud *crack*, glowing phosphorus chunks shot through the air like lava bombs. Ondragon dove under a protective ledge and waited for the deadly rain to fall. White smoke spread out. Poisonous phosphorus fumes! Hastily, Ondragon took off his shirt and tied it over his mouth and nose. He had to get out of here as quickly as possible! His eyes burning, he looked around. Where was the route to the exit? It was impossible to tell in this maze. His only chance was to go out the same way he had come in. But where was that?

Who gives a shit! Run if you don't want to suffocate or get blown to pieces by one of the bombs! Ondragon gave himself a shake and ran. In doing so, he more or less deftly dodged the burning chunks on the ground. He heard more of the tubes bursting behind him, and the loud rain of splinters drowned out the desperate cries of the doomed. But he had no time for remorse or regret now; he had to see that he saved his own skin.

Stumbling, he reached a door and opened it. Behind it yawned a dark corridor. No fire. No light. The power of the wondrous ether power plant must have failed. Ondragon dove into the passage and followed it almost blindly until he bumped painfully against a wall. Groping, he identified it as a T-junction. He had to decide. Left or right?

He heard the thunder of further detonations behind him. The barrels were exploding one after the other. Were there any in the corridors here? It was likely. Yaqub had been very thorough, there was no doubt about that. Ondragon decided to take the left passage and felt his way along the wall. But at the next junction, he ended up in a room that turned out to be a dead end. Cursing, he searched for the exit. When he finally found it and made to return to the corridor, something suddenly shot past him. He could clearly feel the breeze and hear the rapid footsteps. It was a person. All at once, shouts rang out. They came from the other end of the corridor.

"Freeze! Or we shoot!"

Ondragon saw two lights dancing wildly toward him. It had to be Steiner's two mercenaries, he thought; they were still after Clandestin. So it might have been he who had just rushed past. Ondragon quickly retreated into the cave and heard the two mercenaries approaching. One of them fired a shot that rang loudly in Ondragon's ears. He bit back a curse and pressed deeper into the shadows. Again, an explosion shook the rock. There was a dangerous rumbling and small stones trickled down from the ceiling. Ondragon didn't look up, but he could clearly feel the weight of the mountain. He forced himself to wait a little longer and then moved toward the exit. Cautiously, he listened into the catacombs. Everything was quiet. Nothing more could be heard from the mercenaries. *If only I had at least one of their lamps*, he thought, and stretched out his arms again to feel his way, but abruptly he pulled them back again, because someone was coming running again.

Quite a lot of traffic down here! Ondragon took a step back and paused in the cave. The person walked past him in the dark without noticing him, and he wondered how the guy could manage so well without a lamp. He quickly stuck his head out of the cave and peered after him. In the darkness, a tiny red light swung up and down.

The bracelet! It could only be Clandestin! Ondragon quickly followed him. If anyone knew his way around down here, it was LeNoire!

While he tried to keep up with the small dancing dot of light, the thunder of explosions kept echoing through the catacombs. Ondragon increased his speed, but suddenly the red will-o'-the-wisp disappeared. Hastily, he ran to the spot and realized that the corridor bent around a corner there. But there was no trace of the light anymore.

Damn! Now he was screwed. Perplexed, he looked around. Darkness, everywhere. Without knowing which way to turn, he ran on and was painfully stopped by a wall a little later. Another dead end! Shit!

Furious, Ondragon gave the obstacle a kick. It sounded hollow. Hastily, he scanned the wall with his fingers and felt wood and a metal handle. A door! He opened it and stared in horror at the inferno beyond. One side of the large room that opened before him was ablaze, the other was enveloped in white smoke. An acrid stench assailed his nostrils, and Ondragon quickly closed the door again to protect himself from the poisonous smoke. But Clandestin must have run through there, he thought feverishly, there was no other way!

The shouts of the mercenaries echoed behind him. Those two idiots were all he needed! In their rush, they would likely mistake him for Clandestin and simply shoot him. *There is no other way. You have to go through the fire!*

Ondragon took a resolute breath, pressed his shirt tighter over his mouth and nose, and yanked open the door. Ducking down, he ran into the burning room and looked around frantically. He could feel the heat of the consuming fire on his naked torso. Where the hell had Clandestin gone? Where had he run off to? Several times Ondragon spun around on his own axis. The air in his lungs began to run out, and he pressed his lips together more tightly to avoid the temptation to simply inhale, for that would be outright suicide! Small bright spots blossomed before his eyes and his lungs began to protest. *Air!* they screamed. *Air! Do something!*

Then Ondragon's gaze caught on a place that looked vaguely familiar. He ran to the spot, realizing it was the entrance to the tunnel through which he had come with Clandestin. The door stood invitingly open, and without hesitation Ondragon ran into the passage. Just in time, for behind him the two mercenaries had entered the burning room. He could hear their voices, then their stifled screams as the corrosive phosphorus vapor entered their unprotected lungs. Ondragon closed his ears and fought the desire of his lips to open. His whole body was demanding only one thing: air! With all his might, he resisted the urge to simply give in and ran deeper into the tunnel. The bright dots in front of his eyes turned to shadow spots that spread like liquid ink farther and farther across his retinas. And soon he didn't know if it was the pitch-black darkness he was staggering through or just a vision of his brain screaming for oxygen.

You have to go farther. Much farther!

But then—all at once—his self-control failed.

His hand dropped from his mouth and nose, and while Ondragon's brain was still trying with all its might to regain control, his mouth gulped the air.

Once, twice, three times. He couldn't get enough of it into his lungs.

His hands resting on his knees, he stood there, breathing. But his mind continued to run amok.

I have breathed death!

How long will it be before I die?

But nothing happened. Until the little voice in his head spoke up again.

Even if you didn't drop dead on the spot, you still have to move on! You are far from being safe! There might be barrels with phosphorus here too!

Ondragon straightened up and stumbled through the dark tunnel. The route seemed much longer than the first time, and he gradually began to wonder if he wasn't dead after all and this was his own personal hell. Paul Eckbert Ondragon—doomed to eternal flight through dark corridors, spiced with a good old dose of fear of suffocation!

But then he finally reached the door and staggered into the tower. With burning eyes, he looked up at the gigantic coil and a crazy elation took hold of him. Without knowing why, he put his head back and laughed loudly up to the dome of the tower. A diffuse light reached him.

What are you waiting for, the voice in his head said. *Stop grinning like an idiot and get out of here before one of the barrels blows up!*

Quickly, Ondragon climbed the rusty stairs up into the dome. Once there, he realized that it was daylight that was falling through the entrance he had made. Unfortunately, the opening was several meters above his head. Ondragon took a run-up, jumped with both legs, and got a grip on the edge. Mustering the last of his strength, he pulled himself up. He almost didn't notice that he was cutting both hands on the sharp-edged copper. It was like a rebirth that could only take place in pain. A kind of purification. The way from darkness into the light.

On the other side, Ondragon fell out into the open like a dead fish, immediately scrambled to his feet, and ran out into the desert as fast as his battered body would allow.

Keep moving! You have to keep moving! Get farther away!

While his mind was giving him these orders, a tremendous dull bang sounded behind him. A hot jet of flame shot into the sky and threw Ondragon forward onto his knees. He could feel the force of more detonations in the ground beneath him and tried to get to his feet again.

The tower! It was flying through the air!

Ondragon managed to get to his feet and kept running, just kept running, until he could go no farther. Only then did he turn around and take a breathless look back at the dune where the tower had once been hidden. A large crater had opened up, and more and more sand was trickling into the smoking hole.

Bleeding and shaking, Ondragon dropped to the sand, and it was only when he looked up into the cool morning sky that he realized he had made it.

CHAPTER 63

June 3, 2011
in the desert
morning

Ondragon didn't know how long he had sat there, just staring at the sky. At some point he rose, felt his damaged bones, and finally looked out over the dunes into the distance. What he saw there in the morning light suddenly clouded his joy over his successful escape.

The whole ridge was smoking, emitting poisonous broth from all its holes. Black columns of smoke rose silently into the sky, where they coalesced into a threatening veil that was carried farther into the desert by the wind.

His lips pressed together, Ondragon turned away from the spectacle and let his gaze travel searchingly over the immediate surroundings. Somehow, he had to get away from here, if possible before it became scorchingly hot. Unfortunately, he could not see Achille anywhere. Had he fled or been captured? Or had he even followed him into the mountain and become a victim of the conflagration? If so, there was nothing he could do for his companion, Ondragon thought sadly. Then he noticed the fresh footprints leading out over the ridge of the dunes into the desert, and he felt a little hope. Were they Achille's? But they could also be Clandestin's. The guy had probably made it out into the open just as he had. Ondragon pondered, getting his flagging mind going with difficulty. Actually, he only had a few options left. He could follow the trail and find out who the footsteps belonged to. Or he could try to run back to the old camp, where the other half of their equipment still lay. The scooter was still there. He could drive to the oasis in it and ask for help. Maybe he could also look for Malin. He wondered what she was thinking right now, at the sight of the burning mountain. Whether she was already out there somewhere, searching for her white dromedary.

Ondragon turned around indecisively and suddenly saw a man standing behind him. He felt little surprise at this; perhaps his body was just too sluggish to react. Tiredly, he looked toward the man, who approached him slowly. He wore a sand-colored baseball cap, a uniform of the same color, and metal-rimmed glasses.

"Kubicki," Ondragon said moderately enthusiastically when he finally reached him.

The BND senior officer raised a hand in greeting and twisted his face into a pained smile. "There you are," he said. "What about Steiner and his troops?"

"Steiner? He's the one who really screwed things up for me! Until he came along, everything was going great." That wasn't entirely true, but Ondragon had little desire to tell Kubicki the truth. "I think he and the others are dead," he said indignantly, pointing over to the smoking mountain. "It would be a miracle if anyone survived in there. There was a large number of phosphorus bombs. If they even came close to all going off, the catacombs should be impassable for a long time. Not to mention the fire. Phosphorus burns at over thirteen hundred degrees and the mountain will be like an incandescent furnace. There'll be nothing in there but ashes."

Kubicki nodded. He looked disappointed. "What did you see in there?"

"Not much," Ondragon lied. "I only know the inside of the tower and the tunnel system in the mountain. The bastards intercepted me before I could find out anything and locked me in a cave. There were quite a few crates full of gold bars stored there though."

"Gold?" asked Kubicki brightly. "Did that burn too?"

Ondragon thought how fascinating it was that the idea of a huge amount of gold could throw people off their stroke.

"Yes," he stated matter-of-factly, "all burned. Apparently, General Kammler brought it here with the Junkers."

"I see." Now it was Kubicki who was looking at the columns of smoke. "And you didn't find anything else?"

"The cave where I was held captive must have been a bit out of the way," Ondragon explained. "The only thing I saw were ancient mummy graves. Where Tesla's machine was, whether it was even there at all, I don't know. I managed to escape when chaos broke loose."

"And you didn't even see anything during your escape through the tunnel system?"

"No, nothing. I didn't have a lamp and it was pitch black."

Kubicki scrutinized him. He didn't believe him, that was clear, but Ondragon didn't let on and looked back neutrally—poker face was one of his easiest exercises. Let Kubicki think what he wanted; he couldn't do anything to him. The whole thing was over! Even if in a most unpleasant way.

When the BND senior officer finally turned away, he sighed cautiously.

"I'm sorry about what happened to Steiner and the others," Ondragon replied with feigned dismay. "And I'm also sorry I couldn't be of more help to you and now everything is destroyed."

Kubicki raised his head and looked at him. A strange glint came into his eyes, but before Ondragon could get to the bottom of it, the BND man turned and said without any discernible emotion, "Come on, I'll take you to the camp! They're expecting you."

They drove to the guelta in a brand-new Land Rover. Ondragon noticed that the car was from a whole fleet of vehicles the BND mercenaries had used to cross the desert. They had to be similar to the DeForce Deliveries mailmen; a ragtag bunch that would do anything for money. Like him.

The men squatted in front of their tents, looking tired and dejected. No wonder, since their numbers had been suddenly cut in half overnight. Kubicki nodded to them as he passed and led Ondragon into the largest tent of the camp. Inside, it was dark and stuffy, but when he realized who was cowering on the ground there, guarded by three armed men, he pulled in his head as a precaution.

"Well, finally! There you are! Tell your people to release me, damn it. I'm a Swedish citizen, they can't just hold me like this. I haven't done anything. This wild horde of gorillas just stormed into our camp and arrested us, even though we have a residence permit for this area. It's a scandal! I will complain to the embassy. And my precious dromedary is getting away from me. Shit, now say something!" Malin glared at him furiously. Next to her squatted Pelle, looking no less angry. Only Achille was grinnning beatifically.

"*Mon ami*, you are still alive! God be praised!" the Frenchman shouted and went to get up and embrace Ondragon, who had the same thought as his companion, but one of the guards pushed him to the ground again.

"Hey! What are you doing?" protested Achille. "I already told you, that's my boss there."

Meanwhile, Malin was directing her torrent of angry insults at Kubicki: "I've already told you everything. What more do you want from me? How often do I have to repeat that I met this guy purely by chance? And we met again, purely by chance, here in the desert." She pointed at Ondragon.

"Okay, it sounds weird," he acknowledged wearily. "But it's like she says. The encounters were purely coincidental."

"You see," Malin continued, "this gentleman told me he was looking for a lost airplane, and I didn't think anything of it and helped him look a little, that's all. What, pray tell, is so forbidden about looking for a plane? And how was I supposed to know that the punk would run off here in the desert and that shitty mountain would blow up?!"

Kubicki wasn't looking at her. His mind seemed to be somewhere else completely. Meanwhile, Ondragon was delighted to have told Malin the story about the plane. Maybe that would get her out of this with only a black eye. Hopefully.

"Hello, you?" Malin raised a hand and waved to attract Kubicki's attention. "Do you understand? Me know nix. Me only hunter, I have order, *capito?*"

"That's right, we checked," Kubicki finally replied dryly. "You can go, and take your pilot with you. Go chase that camel or whatever, and when you have it, get out of there! But stay away from that mountain, or we'll meet again sooner than you'd like."

Malin jumped up and moved toward Kubicki until she was standing close to him. "You, Commander-in-Chief of whatever, have no command over me. *Fuck you!*" She thrust her middle finger almost in his face, and Ondragon couldn't help but admire her guts. She really wasn't afraid of anything! Not of dubious men with guns, not of intelligence organizations. He felt her gaze burning him and tried to withstand it. Malin wanted an explanation, he guessed, but apparently, she also realized that she would not get it. Ondragon looked silently at the ground and, disappointed, Malin turned away. That's how it always went with women. They always ended up hating him.

With a curt wave of her hand, Malin indicated to Pelle that he should stand up, and the young pilot rose. He threw Ondragon a winning, slightly mocking smile and followed his boss out of the tent. Resignedly, Ondragon looked toward the exit. *In the end, someone is always the loser*, he thought. Sadly, he had a strong feeling that this time it was him.

"And when can we get out of here?" he asked, addressing Kubicki. He had no desire to stay any longer in this unpleasant place.

"You can leave on the next plane," the BND senior officer replied. "Our pilot will fly you to Casablanca or Marrakesh, depending on where you want to go."

"And what about my payment?" Ondragon wanted to know.

"If you mean your file, it is ready for you in Berlin. You can inspect it at any time. And the money? Well, after all, you made every effort to complete the assignment. It will be in your account in a few days."

Ondragon nodded, then turned to Achille. "Come on, let's get out of here!"

A little later, as they sat in the BND plane and looked down at the smoking mountain, Ondragon felt an unusual emotional chaos raging inside him. On the one hand, he was glad to have gotten away once again, and even felt a little schadenfreude that Pandora had been destroyed and the BND had come out of it absolutely empty-handed. But on the other hand—and this brought him to the lower end of his emotional scale—it filled him with deep sadness to see Tesla's dream in flames and thus irretrievably lost. And all at once he understood even Master Yaqub's dilemma. Tesla's inventions were both a curse and a blessing. In this, the old man had been right. But Yaqub was no more, just as his secret treasure had been melted down into a single lump of metal. And in a fateful way, the purpose of the Sator Brotherhood had been fulfilled: It had saved mankind from a great stupidity. *Sator opera tenet*—the Creator preserves his creation.

When Ondragon emerged from these thoughts, they had already flown far out into the desert. Nothing but sand stretched out below them.

Exhausted, he leaned back and placed his bandaged hands in his lap. More than the vibration of the machine, he felt the fatigue threatening to overwhelm him now that he was leaving it all behind. But just before he closed his eyes and surrendered to his fatigue, his mind caught on something. A tiny disturbance in the pattern. The *centrifuge* in his head twitched, sending one last message. Something had been down there in the sand. Something that didn't fit there. A vehicle. A *very* strange vehicle.

The Snake?

Only who was driving it? Clandestin? Had he managed to find his way to their abandoned camp? Had he taken the Snake and driven it out into the desert? Unconsciously, Ondragon smiled. Of course it was him.

Clandestin. Good boy! Now at least some of the knowledge of the Sator Brotherhood would live on . . . and the treasure would live on too, in a sense.

With this comforting certainty, Ondragon's head tipped to one side and he fell asleep.

CHAPTER 64

June 8, 2011
Berlin
10:30 am

The traffic on this sunny Berlin morning was moderate. Ondragon turned the rental car off Viktoriastrasse onto the driveway of the BND headquarters and showed his ID at the checkpoint. The security guard opened the barrier, and Ondragon drove to the parking lot, where he left the car and walked over to the main building. He was gradually recovering. After dropping Achille off in Marrakech, he had flown on to Casablanca and had a thorough checkup at a hospital there. The toxic phosphorus gases had given him no peace. But when it had turned out that his lungs had only been slightly burned and that he would suffer no further damage, he had been relieved. He had been very lucky. Once again.

With a slight smile, Ondragon entered the foyer of the BND headquarters. He had to show his passport one more time there and state his request. After passing through the security gate, he was met by a man who had been waiting for him.

"Good afternoon. My name is Schröder. Mr. Kubicki has informed me of everything. Please follow me, Mr. Ondragon." He neither extended his hand nor smiled. Instead, he had pronounced his name correctly, which Ondragon acknowledged was in his favor. But there had been something in his eyes, a disparaging look that somehow irritated him. Kubicki had certainly told the man who he was and what he did, so a certain distrust was to be expected.

Ondragon followed the man, who walked the corridors with an almost military stride. They climbed a staircase to the second floor and marched through another desolate corridor until they stopped in front of an unprepossessing door.

Ondragon tightened his body. *So it's behind that*, he thought, and was seized by an abrupt excitement. The file, *his* file. What would he learn from it? Things about himself and his family? About his brother? He briefly thought about paying a visit to his parents while he was in Berlin, but quickly dismissed the idea. He had no desire to meet his father.

The man named Schröder raised a hand and looked at him enquiringly. Ondragon nodded. He grasped the handle, pushed it down, and opened the door. The room beyond was large. In the center was a table at which sat a gray-haired man. He had his back to him. On the table in front of him was a document.

"Let me know when you're done, Mr. Ondragon," Schröder said, closing the door.

Ondragon stood there indecisively. Who was that guy over there at the table? Just another minder? Suddenly, the man raised his hand, and Ondragon could see the ring on his little finger. It was a signet ring with a dragon's head engraved on it.

The realization hit him like a blow and literally hurled him backward. He stood there on shaky legs, propped himself up against the wall, and stared at the man's back. He still did not move.

I know who you are! I know who you are! But I don't want you here!

Finally, Ondragon managed to break free of his stupor and approached the man with careful steps. He could hear him breathing, it was so quiet.

"I'm glad you came . . . Paul," the man said quietly, turning around. He looked at him with watery blue eyes. Full of disdain and coldness.

Ondragon stared down at him. He felt seized by all emotions at once: hatred, anger, and the fact that he had been taken by surprise, but in addition there was something he could not place. Powerlessness? Or simply madness?

Without taking his eyes off his father, he stalked around the table and stopped behind the chair.

"Sit down, please," his father said, pointing to the chair across from him.

Ondragon complied reluctantly with this request. Everything in him rebelled, but finally he gained the upper hand over his seething emotions and sat down at the table. He pointed to the file, which was pink and looked completely unremarkable. *Ondragon/Gemini* was written on the cover.

"Are you here to read this to me?" asked Ondragon icily. "Or are you just trying to irritate me?" *And anyway, how do you know I'm here?* flashed through his brain.

Siegfried Ondragon's lips twisted into a thin smile. But it was anything but warm; it was the cold dragon smile that Ondragon remembered well from his childhood. Disgusted, he averted his eyes and pulled the file toward him.

I'm just going to ignore that son of a bitch and do nothing but read that file! Even if I can hardly stand being in the same room with him. At least it will be a good exercise for my self-control. He adopted a nonchalant expression and opened the file cover. His eyes widened in surprise.

Again, he was overcome by the feeling of being ambushed. It was not going at all as he had imagined!

"What the hell is this?" he snapped at his father. "What the hell does that mean? Why is the file empty?" He jumped up and almost smashed the folder into old Ondragon's face. But at the last moment he collected himself and hurled it across the room instead. Fluttering silently, the empty file drifted to the floor.

Ondragon glowered angrily at his father.

The smile on his face disappeared abruptly. Now there was only that hatred, that watery contempt. "It's quite simple," Siegfried Ondragon said with undisguised derision. "The BND was looking for a specialist in the procurement of a certain object, which will be known to you by the name Pandora. And I happened to know of someone who was qualified for such an assignment. Believe me, I didn't like the fact that it was you, but I knew you would not only find Pandora, but also the lost research station in the desert. That's why I recommended you to the BND. And since I now know you very well, I also immediately advised Mr. Kubicki to offer you a particularly tasty incentive. The file."

"Which doesn't even exist!"

"That's right, the file was just bait. And you swallowed it." Seemingly pityingly, Siegfried Ondragon shook his head.

A red mist rose before Ondragon's eyes. His own father had tricked him. Siegfried Ondragon had used him and risked his son's life for the mission!

A bomb of fire and anger exploded in Ondragon's stomach. And suddenly he knew what the feeling was that he had been unable to classify earlier. It had irresistible power and filled him with a powerful desire. The desire to kill!

What was the big deal? He could kill his father, here and now. Then he would be rid of him once and for all. Problem solved! The thought was tempting and his hands twitched. His gaze traveled to the scrawny neck. He could see the vein throbbing under the pale skin. It would be so easy.

But then the moment was over. Ondragon blinked and the red mist lifted. He had himself under control again. Nothing else mattered. Then he noticed his cramped hands and shook them.

"You're so pathetic, Paul! I can always tell what you're thinking," his father said snidely. "Right now, you think you've got yourself under control again, after you wanted to kill me a moment ago. Isn't that right?"

Ondragon gave him a look of hatred. *Yes, you enjoy your little victory, old man, but be careful that it doesn't backfire on you in the end!*

"Does Mother know you're here? Does she know what kind of a dirty game you play?" he asked with the bitter taste of bile on his tongue. It was time to expose all the lies of his family.

His father gave him a haughty look. "Why, yes, of course. Ava is waiting downstairs. You can see her if you like. She'd be delighted."

Ondragon's facial muscles froze and an icy coldness trickled down his spine, but he forced himself to ask one last question, "And how long has this been going on? With you and the BND?"

Siegfried Ondragon pursed his lips. Then he leaned forward in a leisurely manner and adopted a pitying expression. "Oh, Paul," he said softly, "if you only knew . . ."

CHAPTER 65

June 8, 2011
Berlin
1:20 pm

A few hours later, Ondragon was sitting in the Café Einstein on Kurfürstenstrasse with a triple espresso, mulling over the unpleasant encounter with his father. He could have done without seeing the old bastard again. Very happily! But on the other hand, it had given him something, and it was only now that he could really admit that to himself. Finally, he knew it: It was no longer a rumor but the unvarnished truth!

All the innuendos of that sleazy Swedish corporate heir back at Cedar Creek Lodge had actually been true! Of course, the guy and his blond crony had just wanted to provoke him then—and they had succeeded—but Ondragon had always assumed it was a well-judged lie they had told him. Now, however, he wondered where the two men had gotten this information, and it troubled him greatly that they had known more about it than he had at the time.

But it was true.

His family worked for the secret service. His father . . . *and* his mother!

Ava Birgitta Ondragon had lied to him.

And that hurt more than anything else.

But had he merely been mistaken about her, or had he been deceived?

Dejectedly, Ondragon propped his head in both hands and stared at the empty coffee cup in front of him. He desperately needed a vacation to think about it. He knew it would be hard to ever forgive his parents, if not impossible.

He thought about the conversation with his father. He had revealed almost nothing about his activities at the BND. That was typical of the old fart. He always gave mere hints and then shrouded himself in gloating silence, just to demonstrate his power. A pathetic little power game of "I know something you don't!" and unwavering arrogance. That deep-rooted contempt of the educated for the stupid. For a while, Ondragon had withstood the self-righteous grin, hoping his father would have mercy and at least throw him a little nugget of truth. But Siegfried Ondragon had remained mute. Silent as a dragon, guarding his unspoken secrets like a treasure.

Ondragon sighed. He would never get his old man to reveal his secrets. He would probably have to live with that. The only thing he could do was put the greatest possible distance between them. And the best time to do that was today.

He looked up and pulled out his cell phone. He used the Lufthansa hotline to book a flight from Berlin to Los Angeles for the following morning, and then beckoned to the waitress, ordering another espresso and a plate of tagliatelle in cream sauce. He hadn't eaten since breakfast and felt his appetite gradually returning.

After finishing his food, Ondragon dabbed his mouth with a napkin and looked around the wood-paneled room. The atmosphere in the café was quiet but dignified, and the tables near him were empty, which meant he could talk to Charlize on the phone without being disturbed. He quickly dialed the number of his office in LA. It was just eight o'clock in the morning there.

"Good morning, Boss! How is Berlin?"

"Shit!"

"Oh." Charlize was silent, obviously not knowing what to say to that.

"Never mind," Ondragon replied, "let's just say it went badly. The whole thing with the file was a fake. I'll tell you all about it when I get back. My plane lands at LAX tomorrow at noon. I'll come directly to the office."

"Okay." Silence again.

But Ondragon did not want silence now. He had had enough of that! "How's that hole in your stomach?" he inquired politely.

"It's as good as healed. I can hardly feel it anymore. The bastard had really good aim!"

"I'm sorry I couldn't kick his ass for that. But the BND beat me to it."

"I hope that fucking guy burns in hell!"

"Yeah, I hope so too, honey." Ondragon pursed his lips. He had not told her that Clandestin LeNoire was the only one besides himself who had survived the disaster in the mountain. That was why he had a guilty conscience; after all, he had promised her he would seek revenge. But he feared that Charlize would pull out all the stops to finish Clandestin off if she knew he was still alive, and Ondragon wanted to prevent that. For some unknown reason, he was glad *Monsieur Noire* was still out there somewhere, starting a new life. Or maybe he was just comforted by the knowledge that he didn't have to carry the secret of Tesla's miracle machine alone, that there was someone else out there to share it with him. That was indeed a comforting thought. Ondragon felt for the little brass box in his pocket, the miraculous adapter Yaqub had given him for his cell phone. Of course, it no longer worked, now that the world system had been destroyed, but it was still the link to those events in the mountain. And perhaps one day it would take on a new meaning. Until then, however, Ondragon would keep it in his safe at home.

"Oh, Charlize," he said with a sigh. "Somehow the whole thing was for nothing."

"Has the BND not paid its bill?"

"Yes, yes, the money has arrived, but I have a stale aftertaste."

"Because Pandora is lost?"

"Yes."

"I can well understand that. After all, I also gave my blood for it." She laughed.

Speaking of blood, Ondragon thought. He hadn't brought up the matter of her father since he left her hospital room in Fortaleza. Should he do it now? No, better not. That too was something better discussed in person. He felt his old curiosity stirring and smiled to himself. Suddenly, he felt better. There were still enough secrets in the world to uncover, enough problems to solve. He could safely leave his family's where it was. At least for quite some time. And he would soon forget the pain too. After all, from time to time a freezer had to be defrosted and freed from the crusting ice so that it would be nice and clean and functional again afterward. But first he had to get something off his chest.

"We did the best we could," he said. "Thank you for your help, Charlize. Without you—"

"Stop! Don't keep talking, Boss! Otherwise, I'll get emotional. And we don't want that, do we?"

"No, you're right. We definitely don't want that. I'll see you tomorrow in LA."

"Okay, see you tomorrow. Have a good flight."

"Thank you." Ondragon hung up. He was glad Charlize had restored some professional distance, and looked forward to his own return to "normalcy." Yes, he was actually looking forward to going home. That was very unusual, because in reality there was no such thing as home for him. Without having conjured it up, Malin's face suddenly appeared in his mind's eye. Her permanently suspicious expression and the inquiring gaze that had looked deeper into him than any had before. At least that's what he believed. But maybe he was just imagining it. Probably there had been no close connection between them at all. He pushed the absurd thought aside; after all, he had just decided to clean out his freezer.

Ondragon looked at his fingers, which were toying with the cell phone. He could dial her number. It would be easy. Then he could find out how she was doing and what she thought of him. His index finger stroked the display, brought up his contacts list, and scrolled to the letter *M*. He had her saved under her first name.

It would be so simple.

His index finger paused indecisively over the "call" button.

You're just afraid she might insult you again. Everything else is just a lame excuse!

Ondragon bit his lip. Was he really that cowardly?

No, that wasn't who he was! His finger lowered onto the icon with the green handset. At the same moment, the cell phone beeped. He had received a text message. With surprise, he realized that it was from Malin! He clenched a fist. She had beaten him to it again, his huntress. His hands almost trembling, he read the lines.

Hej hej, Paul. Am in Casablanca right now. Have caught the white dromedary and taken it to its new owner. I'm in the same hotel as before and I can't stop thinking about you, even though I swore I wouldn't! You're a fucking bastard, you know that? But part of me—probably the insane part—would like to see you again. Fancy going hunting together? Malin.

As Ondragon wrote his reply, he felt his heart beating faster than he would have liked. He hesitated before sending the text message, but finally did so and quickly put the phone away. Then he paid his bill and left the café.

EPILOGUE

January 1965
Colorado Springs
evening

Philemon looked up tiredly from his desk and out the window. It was getting dark outside, but he could still see the snow-covered summit of Pikes Peak shimmering in the distance. It was deepest winter here at the foot of the Rocky Mountains, but soon the days would grow longer and spring would come. Philemon shivered. His old bones froze quickly in this weather. He rose with difficulty, hunched over, shuffled to the fire-place, and threw two new logs on the fire. Then he went back to the desk and flicked on the little lamp above it. A small smile played around his lips, as it did every time he turned on the light and thought of the man they had to thank for all this. To him, it was a small miracle to this day. Unfortunately, such miracles had long since become so commonplace and self-evident that people no longer even noticed them.

As he settled back in the chair, he found himself humming a soft melody to himself. The Ode to Joy! Even today, Philemon could well remember the delighted face of Kolman Czito when they had listened to its magical sounds high up on Pikes Peak. The sounds of the future. But unfortunately, they had never seen that promising future dawn.

Sadly, he looked at what he had just put down on paper. His writing was shaky but legible. With the gout in his fingers, writing was difficult, but he did it anyway. A feeling inside him told him he didn't have much time left. Philemon picked up the pencil, examined it, and sharpened it afresh. He was almost ninety now, and this winter might be his last. That was why he had begun to write down his memories. The memory of that extraordinary man who had shaped not only his life, but that of many generations. Only most of them did not have the slightest clue about it. Nikola Tesla had been forgotten. No, that wasn't quite right, Philemon corrected himself in his mind; after all, he had witnessed it. Dr. Tesla had not simply been forgotten, he had been deliberately erased from the memory of humanity. Today, everybody knew the great names of Edison, Marconi, and Röntgen, but few people knew what Dr. Tesla had achieved. But for Philemon, the forgetting was not the worst thing; for him it was unbearable to have witnessed how Nikola Tesla, the great magician of electricity, had been turned into a crazy old fool in the end, squatting lonely in his room and only indulging in his confused fantasies.

Philemon wiped his eyes with the back of his hand. Then he pushed his thick glasses back up to the bridge of his nose and put pencil to paper. There was still so much he had to tell.

We had been so close then, in Colorado Springs. So close to changing the world. But in the end, the city would no longer tolerate us. The Pinkertons, who I later found out included a certain Joe Herkimer, had done a great job. They had not left at all, as the cunning telegraphist had told me, they had simply switched to another hotel, where they had blithely continued their perfidious game of inciting the inhabitants against us behind our backs. And after we had, to our great regret, failed in another experiment, unintentionally damaging the power station, we were finally chased out of town. But the perpetual Pinkertons did not leave us alone in New York either. We soon became better at recognizing them and avoided them as best we could. Today I know that it was not just the Olds Motor Car Company that was trying to stop Dr. Tesla's inventions. At the time, there were many other up-and-coming industries for whom his research was a thorn in the side. The copper works, for example, which produced cables for power lines, or the large automobile manufacturers, who had just equipped their models with combustion engines and feared Tesla's electric motors like the devil feared holy water! They were all blinded and only thought of their own short-term profit, not the welfare of the entire world.

"But let's get back to Dr. Tesla. He seemed to regret the failure in Colorado Springs, but he had no choice but to return to New York with the knowledge he had gained. After all, these notes, which became known as the 'Colorado Springs Notes" comprised over five hundred pages.

"To my great joy, I was allowed to remain in Tesla's service and continued to assist him in his New York laboratory, as did Fritz Löwenstein, who later became vice president of the Institute of Radio Engineers, and Kolman Czito, who unfortunately died in 1926 after a serious illness. In the end, I was Tesla's only confidant; myself and Georg Scherff, his accountant. It was not easy to see how the doctor, driven by his ideas, continued to go through ups and downs. How people on the streets sometimes celebrated him, sometimes mocked him behind his back. The doctor himself, however, was always above all that. He was only interested in his work. And if the world had been more open to his vision then, it would certainly be a different place now."

Philemon looked up briefly and chewed thoughtfully on his pencil. Tesla had been right about that too, he thought. His inventions had been so groundbreaking that people were downright afraid of them. And fearful people would never change the world.

He looked at the paper again and continued writing.

"After we continued the work from Colorado Springs in New York around 1900, Dr. Tesla succeeded in finding an investor for his planned world system. With the financial support of H. P. Morgan, hope returned that we might bring our work to a successful conclusion. As early as 1901, we began constructing the Wardenclyffe Tower on Long Island. The tower, whose drawing I had seen in Tesla's special notebook back then, was a magnificent structure of extraordinary elegance and functionality, and Dr. Tesla's passion. The doctor promised his investor a high-performance radio system to transmit sound and images, but only Tesla and I knew his real intention.

"But when Marconi won the race for the first transatlantic transmission and was the first to successfully transmit a signal from Cornwall to Newfoundland, Dr. Tesla came under pressure. Mr. Morgan demanded a return on his investments. The two men got into countless arguments about this, and I often heard their heated voices drifting out of the office while I was working next door in the lab. However, one day, when Mr. Morgan found out what the doctor really intended to do with the tower, namely to send energy all over the world for free, he broke with him and dropped out of the project. The construction of the tower came to a standstill. Dr. Tesla tried to raise money, but in the end failed because of people's stubbornness and had to give up his once so well-intentioned project with a heavy heart. He retreated to his laboratory and continued his research in silence. Despite the renewed setback, he achieved further groundbreaking inventions in the years that followed. For example, the bladeless turbine and radio remote control. He was also awarded the Edison Medal with great honor. The highest award besides the Nobel Prize, which he was also to receive; but he refused that because he would have had to share it with Thomas Edison! However, even this could not prevent the unfinished Wardenclyffe Tower from being torn down and scrapped by Tesla's creditors in July 1917. From that day on, the doctor was never the same, I could feel it. His wit, his fabulous powers of persuasion, had gone out, like the light of a star burning up. The magician of electricity had lost his magic. Electricity was now taken for granted and people were no longer so easily impressed. A new age had dawned. The age of disenchantment and the age of world wars. Dr. Tesla was very distressed about this. He kept telling me sadly that he detested war and was trying to work against it. But unfortunately, his efforts were unsuccessful, and his reputation changed from that of a once brilliant inventor to that of a scatterbrain whose whimsical ideas could at best be laughed at."

Philemon wiped away a tear that tried to steal from the corner of his eye. Even today, the memory of it made him infinitely sad, but also angry. Dr. Tesla had accomplished so much. So many miracles that people out there didn't want to know the first thing about. Damned bigotry!

As if of their own accord, his fingers groped in his pants pocket for the piece of paper. With a trembling hand, he pulled it out and unfolded it. The yellowed and tattered scrap was soft from all the carrying around and almost fell apart under his gaze. The writing, however, was still clearly visible. It almost seemed as if the ink was trying with all its might to outlast the paper.

For perhaps the thousandth time, Philemon skimmed over the calculations and drawings made many years ago by a man named Frederick Myers. He knew how valuable that little piece of paper was, yet he had not dared transfer it to a more permanent medium, nor to show it to anyone else. The note would die with him and be buried.

Gently, he put it back in his pocket and continued his report. His head was full of memories that had come to life.

"When Dr. Tesla was found dead in his hotel room on January 7, 1943, I was inconsolable. A great light of the world had gone out. Against all rationality, I had always hoped that this man so blessed by God would be with us forever. But even his death brought Tesla no peace. The authorities confiscated all his possessions and his descendants fought over the inheritance. For one thing was missing from Tesla's estate, and to this day I don't know where it disappeared to: his notebook. Toward the end, he had always kept it in the safe in his room, which he hardly ever left. After I had been interrogated a number of times and finally dismissed as a suspect, I could no longer endure the terrible struggle for Tesla's legacy. I packed all my things, bought a small house in Colorado Springs, and never returned to New York. From then on, I lived exclusively in my memories. They were what kept me alive. Until today. And if I had the opportunity to meet Dr. Tesla again, I would ask him only one question:

"If he could turn back time, with the knowledge of today, would he once again gift his inventions to the world?"

Philemon hesitated. Agitatedly, he moistened his brittle lips. His memory of the day when Dr. Tesla had let him in on his secrets in the laboratory on the prairie was clear before his eyes. He was just about to set the pencil in motion again and describe those events, when there was a cautious knock at the door.

Philemon raised his head. It was pitch dark outside now; another gloomy winter's night in the mountains. Who in the world would come to see him at this late hour? He hardly had any friends left who dared to join him up in the hills. Thoughtfully, Philemon scratched his head. Perhaps he had only imagined it. He was an old man and his senses were no longer quite clear.

But there was another knock. This time it was loud and emphatic.

Philemon rose, grumpily but much too quickly, and he had to pause for a moment, leaning on the table, until the pain in his joints subsided. Only then was he able to limp with small steps to the door. Halfway there, another knock sounded. It echoed hollowly throughout the house and made him feel suddenly lonely.

Who the hell was daring to remind him of it? He grabbed the handle and opened the door. A cold wind came sweeping in, chilling him to the bone. Shivering, Philemon drew his shirt collar together and squinted into the darkness outside the door.

There stood a figure.

"What do you want?" he asked gruffly, "Why are you disturbing an old man at this hour?"

Still there came no reply, only white clouds of breath rising from the figure's mouth. Then it stepped forward and the light fell on its face.

Philemon staggered back, shocked, and almost fell, but he managed to brace himself against the dresser just in time. Breathing heavily, he straightened up and stared in disbelief at the young man at his door. He had red hair and wore unusually old-fashioned clothes.

He looked like . . . no, it couldn't be. Or could it?

Philemon blinked.

And then he cried, "Frederick Myers! It's you! In the flesh!"

"Yes, Mr. Ailey. It's me."

"But why do you look so young?"

Myers shrugged his shoulders. "*Tempora permutas nec tu mutaris in illis*, I suppose."

"You change the times, but you do not change within them," Philemon translated the Latin phrase. "This is . . . this is . . ." He couldn't find the words. "But why on earth are you here? And what do you want from me?"

"I'm here to get my piece of paper," Myers said, extending a hand toward him. "The slip of paper with my notes . . ."

ABOUT THE AUTHOR

Anette Strohmeyer is a German crime writer. She began her career illustrating comic books but unfortunately never developed the skills to rival her role model, Jean Giraud aka Moebius, so she decided to focus on the speech bubbles instead.

Now, Strohmeyer is known for her fiction writing and meticulous, often immersive research work. She has participated in a voodoo ceremony in Haiti, eaten termites in the jungle, generated lightning in a high-voltage laboratory, and trekked through Japan's infamous Aokigahara Forest along the edge of Mount Fuji.

Since 2018, Strohmeyer has lived in Denmark, where she splits her time between Copenhagen and the island of Møn. She also writes as Anne Nørdby, author of the bestselling Tom Skagen thriller series.

Podium

DISCOVER MORE

STORIES
UNBOUND

PodiumEntertainment.com

www.ingramcontent.com/pod-product-compliance
Lightning Source LLC
Chambersburg PA
CBHW031055130726
47906CB00007B/53